I0760503

THEIR FAE GODDESS COMPLETE TRILOGY

CATHERINE BANKS

Their Fae Goddess Complete Trilogy by Catherine Banks.

Cover design by Ana Cruz Arts.

Published by Turbo Kitten Industries.

www.CatherineBanks.com

Turbo Kitten Industries™, P.O. Box 5012, Galt, CA 95632

ACKNOWLEDGMENTS

Thank you to the following people who helped make this book possible:

R.J. for answering all of my questions, telling me when I'm being ridiculous, and helping me keep sane amongst all the craziness that is involved with being an author.

C.R. for allowing me use her as a guinea pig and turn her into a RH fan. Also, for helping me with tasks that I would otherwise forget.

Lea for being my beta reader and allowing me to bounce ideas off of her constantly. And, to keep me straight on what is going on.

Jenica for being the bestest, helping me during my rough spots, and just existing.

As always, my amazing husband and best friend, Avery. Without you, this dream would not be possible. I can't wait until our joint dream comes true. The current dream I'm living in is pretty dang good as is, though.

Thank you also to my amazing Kickstarter supporters:

Alicia Rades
Andromeda Taylor-Wallace
Annette McElroy
Betheny Thompson
Brooke
Candace Wondrak
Christina
Christina Hunt

Claire Ellison
Daniel Tice Jr
Derek Murphy
Helen Scott
Jacqueline Hayley
Jathan McBride
Kaiya Kagon
Jennifer Laslie
Jessica Paige
Jessica Robbins
Karri Allen
Altheda Rutherford
Kathy
Kristal Melton
Lance McKee
Leslie Twitchell
Marie Andreas
Mettie A.M.
Winter Bruno
Michael Green
Michelle McFarlin
Nikki Jefford
Sunny Side Up
Cali Mann
Rachel Strehlow
Shannon
Sky A Fallows
Stephanie Meier
Stuart March
Tanya
Wanda
Jaycee DeLorenzo

QUEEN OF THE STARS

BOOK ONE

USA TODAY BESTSELLING AUTHOR

CATHERINE BANKS

QUEEN OF THE STARS

1

THEIR FAE GODDESS

Queen of the Stars by Catherine Banks.

Cover design by Ana Cruz Arts.

Published by Turbo Kitten Industries.

www.CatherineBanks.com

Turbo Kitten Industries™, P.O. Box 5012, Galt, CA 95632

ACKNOWLEDGMENTS

Thank you to the following people who helped make this book possible:

R.J. for answering all of my questions, telling me when I'm being ridiculous, and helping me keep sane amongst all the craziness that is involved with being an author.

C.R. for allowing me use her as a guinea pig and turn her into a RH fan. Also, for helping me with tasks that I would otherwise forget.

Lea for being my beta reader and allowing me to bounce ideas off of her constantly. And, to keep me straight on what is going on.

Jenica for being the bestest, helping me during my rough spots, and just existing.

As always, my amazing husband and best friend, Avery. Without you, this dream would not be possible. I can't wait until our joint dream comes true. The current dream I'm living in is pretty dang good as is, though.

Minloa

Linta

Silpo

Blustum

Crol

Menma

Klinsot

Dead Lands

Adlin

Treska

Eltare

Vlink

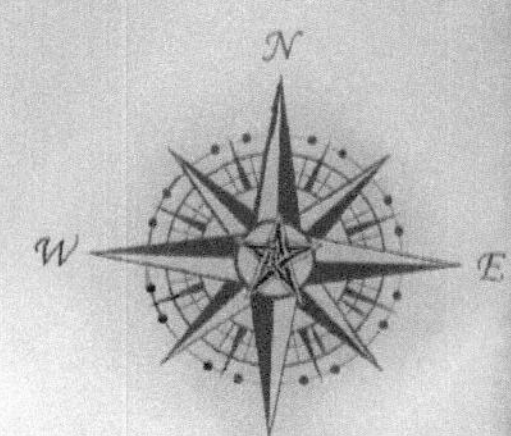

CHAPTER 1

ELARA

"Stay down, or I'll break your arm," Quin growled at me.

Already on my hands and knees, I didn't know when to give up. Quin had challenged me, which pissed me off on its own, but then he'd made the match magic-free because he knew I sucked at hand to hand combat.

Slowly, I got to my feet and stood. I spat out sand, and glared at him. "You hit like a pixie." Taunting him wasn't smart, but my mouth had a mind of its own most days.

He snarled, revealing slightly pointed canines.

Raising my fists to defend myself, I prepared for his attack.

He lunged and ran into a mass of muscled perfection with the name Kydrus.

Quin leapt backwards, eyes wide.

Kydrus hadn't even looked at Quin. His eyes were focused on me. "This fight is over. Elara, come with me."

Quin left in a hurry, probably trying to avoid Kydrus's wrath. Had I not been caught in his line of sight, I would have run away, too.

Kydrus spun on his heel and marched down the sidewalk towards his house.

With a sigh, I followed, hanging my head in shame.

Kydrus was one of the Four Warlords. Each warlord presided over a section of Minloa. Usually, with an iron fist. The warlords were the strongest Seelie fae in existence. They ensured the peace was kept, and kept the chaos many fae creatures craved at bay. They gained their titles after the Great War. Our world had been almost decimated, but the four stepped forward and brokered a treaty of peace. That was over one thousand years ago, which was the blink of an eye to the immortals.

Kydrus wore a simple pair of pants and a t-shirt. He had his sword strapped to his side, which ruined his otherwise normal-looking outfit. His dark hair flowed to the middle of his back, the top pulled back just to keep it from falling in his eyes.

His house was in the center of Linta, the main city of the Silpo sector. The three-story, wood and stone house looked as imposing as its owner.

He opened the door and motioned me inside.

Hesitation had me standing at the doorway, my hands gripping the hem of my shirt.

Immortals were patient, and Kydrus had the patience of a saint. He held still, allowing me to work through my issues and ask my question.

"Do you mean to cause me physical harm?" I asked softly.

"No," he answered, his voice as soft as mine had been.

Full-blooded fae could not lie. They could bend the truth and word things in a way that wasn't technically a lie, but his one-word answer gave no room for trickery. So, I entered his house. I had been there several times, and he had yet to harm me, but old wounds caused me to be wary.

Rich earth tones decorated the inside, lots of plush chairs and couches, and his office had a desk made from a dragon's skull. A dragon he had, in fact, killed with his own hands.

I stepped to the side to let him lead the way, keeping my eyes on the wooden floors.

He walked by, his black boots scuffed but clean as they passed.

I followed, my head down like a naughty puppy, and took a seat in one of the chairs situated in front of his desk.

He settled into his chair, his hands clasped in his lap. "What happened this time?"

"Nothing important," I whispered.

"This was the third fight this week."

"They challenged me."

He sighed.

"Kydrus, I—"

My throat closed up. I had been debating showing him my new powers for a week, but feared his reaction. Since he was the one who kept the peace, he would decide if I was too much of a risk, and if I should live or die.

"You can tell me anything, Elara." His voice was soft, coaxing.

My hands clenched into fists in my lap.

I raised my head, met his eyes, and said, "I'm sorry for causing you trouble." That was true. I would tell him about my power some other time.

He smiled, and my heart stuttered. Such a perfect man shouldn't exist. It ought to be against the law to be so handsome, strong, and powerful.

"You're not trouble, Elara. I just want you to stop getting into so many fights."

"I'll try not to get in any more," I said and swallowed past the sudden lump in my throat.

He walked around the desk, and I held still, trying to quell my shaking. Once he was at my side, he reached towards me, and despite my best attempt, I flinched. His hand stilled.

"I'd like to heal you," he whispered. "Unless you enjoy bleeding on everything?"

Taking a deep breath, I nodded.

He set his hand on my shoulder, and his magic flowed into me, speeding my healing.

"Someday, when you are up for it, I would like you to tell me what happened before you came here. Okay?"

"Someday," I agreed.

He removed his hand, and I felt better than normal.

"Thank you."

"You sure there's nothing else you would like to discuss?" he asked softly.

"Not today," I replied, avoiding eye contact.

He nodded and took two steps away from me. "My door is always open to you."

"Thank you."

Sensing my dismissal, I left his home, and walked across town to the small dwelling I called my own. But, as I stood before my empty home, I had no desire to enter. My house was nestled amongst the trees, giving me a break from the craziness of the town. There were two others who lived nearby, but they preferred solitude like me.

Only...I didn't really prefer solitude. I wanted a house full of warmth and love. Or, at least a house full of warmth and friendship. Most of my life I had lived alone. I feared I always would.

Instead of going inside, I headed towards the falls. Very few ventured so far, since it marked the edge of our sector, which was part of the reason I preferred the location. I had never been one to do as the others did.

I walked between the trees, trees that were thousands of years old, reveling in the power they contained. Life magic was very restricted, but we could all sense it. Every living thing contained magic. Using life magic was considered black magic, something the Unseelie used. I was sure to keep my magic tightly coiled when waking in this forest.

The roar of water grew louder as I approached the falls. I walked to the rock outcropping that served as my hide away, and sat with my legs folded beneath me.

From here, I could see the beautiful waterfall, the river it splashed into below, and watch animals come down the hill on the other side to drink water.

Just last week, I had seen a stag and his mate with a fawn. Their coats had been white and their antlers blue.

Most of the time, I was alone with the flowing water.

"I hoped I would find you here, alone," Quin said behind me.

I spun around, on my feet before I thought to do it. "What do you want?" I asked, all too aware that I was dangerously close to the edge.

He snarled, "Your death."

I prepared for his attack, but it didn't matter. He shoved me off the edge, and I screamed as I fell.

A moment before I hit the water, I had the sense to take a breath and hold it. Hitting the water hurt, as did the sting of the ice-cold temperature.

I kicked to the surface, and immediately slammed into a boulder. I cried out in pain.

"Elara!" Kydrus yelled from far away.

"Kyd—"

My word broke off as a tree branch slammed into me. The world went dark.

Someone pounded on my chest, waking me.

I rolled onto my side and vomited water.

Warm hands pressed against my back, keeping me steady.

I lay on the shore, but the landscape looked nothing like home. Golden fields stretched to each side, with flowers of a startling blue color.

"Good. You're alive," an unfamiliar male voice said beside me.

I sat up, and turned to see the speaker. My jaw dropped. A gorgeous man stood before me, shirtless. His silver hair complimented his tanned skin, and I could count every muscle on his ripped body if I had enough time. The muscles on his hips that formed a "V" looked especially delicious.

"Uh, thanks," I said once I got my brain under control and stopped ogling him, bringing my gaze to his.

"What happened to you?" he asked, his brow furrowed.

"Someone shoved me off a cliff," I muttered, rubbing my shoulder. I realized with a start that I didn't have any wounds. "You healed me?"

He nodded.

I looked around us again. "Where are we?"

"Memna," he answered.

Memna was in another sector, ruled by a different warlord than Kydrus. I couldn't remember his name, though.

My eyes widened. "Crap."

"Where are you from?" he asked.

"Silpo. Linta specifically." I ran my fingers through my hair, but it caught on several knots.

His eyes widened. "You're far from home."

Home. That word didn't really mean much to me.

"I can't believe I floated so far downriver," I whispered.

"Well, come on," he said and stood.

"Huh?"

He smirked. "You need some food and rest. I'll take you home with me, and when you're ready to leave, you can."

"Why help me?" I asked, standing and reaching for my sword, but it wasn't there.

He held out my sword. "I mean you no harm. I'm warlord here."

I had been reaching to snatch my sword out of his hands, but that statement stopped me cold in my tracks. "W-warlord?"

He nodded. "I'm Durlan."

Crap. He really was the warlord.

I stepped back and bowed. "I-I'm s-sorry."

"What is your name?"

"Elara."

"As long as you pose no threat to me or my sector, I will not harm you, Elara."

"How far is it to travel back to Linta?" I asked.

"A month's travel by foot," he answered. "Come, it's going to get hot soon, and I'd like to be inside before lunch."

I obeyed, walking behind him with my head bowed. I'd been unconscious through the night. How I hadn't drowned was a miracle.

"Your sword," he said softly, and held it out to me.

I took it, and strapped it to my hip. "Thank you."

"You were a slave?" he asked.

I flinched. Not even Kydrus had guessed.

"Kydrus does not know. If you speak to him, please do not mention it," I whispered.

"Why haven't you told him?" he asked, stopping to face me.

"I do not want him to pity me or view me differently," I answered.

"I will not tell him. It is your story, but I do not think he would pity you. He may view you differently, but not in the way you think. Kydrus is one of the kinder souls in the world."

"I'll think about it." I chewed on my lip.

He nodded and resumed walking. "How long have you been free?"

"Ten years."

He stopped again to face me. "How old are you?"

"Twenty-eight, I think." I didn't really remember the years before I was a slave.

"You escaped?"

I nodded, trying to push away the memories of that awful day.

"Elara, why did someone push you off the cliff?"

I exhaled. "I don't get along well with most of the people in Linta. They like to challenge me to fights, since they know I can't win. I still accept the challenges, though. Kydrus has started breaking them up, before they hurt me too much. It angers them. Quin had hoped to kill me, but his plan failed."

"Do you wish to return to Linta?" he asked, turning to walk backwards so he could look at me.

"What?"

"You do not have to return to Linta. You may stay here, if you wish," he offered.

"I have no home. No real skills. I would be a burden."

"What did you do in Linta?"

"Gathered herbs for one of the potion makers."

He lifted a brow. "What magic do you have?"

My lips pressed together in a tight line, fear worming its way into my blood. I couldn't tell him.

His head dropped forward, and he turned around. "Let's go. We can talk more later."

I followed him into the fields of golden grass, running my hands through it. Should I stay? It might be better than Linta. Though, I would miss some things about Linta, like its warlord.

CHAPTER 2
ELARA

DURLAN TOOK me down a small trail that led to a wide road, and then to a large city.

The city had at least twice as many people as Linta, and the buildings were made of concrete, which gave it a more modern feel.

People placed their hands in fists over their hearts in a sign of respect for Durlan as he passed. He smiled at them, and we walked down the street with no one stopping us.

Many looked at me, but none spoke.

Durlan stopped before an exact replica of Kydrus' house and opened the door.

"Do all the warlords have the same house?" I asked.

He chuckled. "Yes. We had them built at the same time."

Inside, his house was decorated differently than Kydrus's. Instead of earth tones, his house was decorated in bright tones, reminiscent of spring. He also had a dragon skull desk, but his was smaller.

"This way," he called to me, disappearing down the hallway.

I hurried after him, worried, because I had walked straight into his office on habit. "I'm sorry," I called after him. "Whenever I go to Kydrus's, it's to go in his office."

He chuckled. "So, you're a troublemaker."

"No," I said immediately.

He chuckled again.

I liked his laugh. Kydrus didn't laugh much.

"What do you like to eat?" he asked.

I followed his voice into the kitchen. "I'll eat whatever you offer me."

He was bent over the icebox, looking inside it. He glanced up at me. "Do you live alone in Linta?"

I nodded, my gaze dropping to the ground.

He mumbled something, that included Kydrus's name, but I couldn't make it out.

"Take a seat on a stool," he said. "I'll make us some lunch."

There were three stools in front of the kitchen island that I hadn't seen before. I obeyed, sitting on the stool on the right.

Durlan took out several items from the ice box, as well as from his pantry. I watched with growing confusion and interest as he cut items, put them in a pot or pan, and cooked them.

What was he making?

"Have you never seen someone cook before?" he asked as he stirred the items sizzling in the pan that rested on the stove above flames.

I shook my head.

"What do you usually eat?"

"Roasted rabbit or fruit."

"You don't eat during the festivals?"

I met his curious eyes and said, "I've never attended one."

His eyes widened. "How long have you lived with Kydrus?"

"I don't live—"

"In Linta," he amended.

"Almost seven years."

"Why haven't you gone to any?"

I lowered my eyes to the pan, my hands toying with the hem of my shirt. It was still a bit damp, but I didn't want to complain. "I don't like being around large crowds."

He dished out the food into two bowls and slid one to me.

It looked like soup, but there were more vegetables and meat than I was used to. Not soup...stew. I ate it, savoring the various flavors and the combined taste that was unlike anything I had eaten before. Once done, I took my bowl to the sink, cleaned it, and bowed to Durlan who had stayed standing on the opposite side of the island to eat. "Thank you for the meal."

"You don't need to bow to me, Elara."

I gnawed on my bottom lip and nodded.

"Do you bow to Kydrus?"

"Not anymore," I answered.

He chuckled. "Well, you don't need to bow to me either." He patted my stool, but then he scowled and looked at his hand. "Your clothes are still wet?"

"Sorry. I'll get a towel—"

He stood. "Come with me."

Fear consumed me. He seemed nice, but would he hurt me because I had gotten his stool wet? One would hope the warlords weren't so easily angered, but they were very old.

I obediently followed him, surprised when he led me to the bathroom.

"Why don't you take a shower or bath? I'll get you some clean clothes," he said and turned on the water.

He left before I could say anything.

Quickly, I stripped and stepped into the shower. The floor was recessed and there was a plug to turn it into a bathtub, but I preferred showers. It was much safer to be in showers.

"Here's your cloth—" Durlan said, then stopped.

I looked over my shoulder at him. "Thank you."

He walked to me, a scowl pulling his brows together, and a snarl pulling up his lips.

I froze. "D-did I do something wrong?"

He reached out and touched one of my many scars. "What are these from?"

"Whips," I answered, my heart beating faster than a hummingbird flapped their tiny wings.

He traced his fingertip along one, the puckered flesh still red despite it being over a decade old.

I shivered. No one had touched my scars before.

He raised his eyes to meet mine. "Where were you a slave?"

I couldn't tell him. If I did, I would be hunted.

"Who was your master?"

I shook my head as tears fell down my cheeks, mixing with the shower water.

"I won't hurt you. I must know what sector you were a slave in. Just tell me that."

"Tresca," I answered, my body began to shake despite the warm water falling down my body.

He rested his hand on my back a moment, closed his eyes, and before I could ask what he was doing, he shoved power into my scars.

I gasped and would have fallen had he not wrapped an arm around my waist and held me up.

Memories of my whippings and time as a slave flashed before me, as did memories of many of my fights in Linta. And then, it stopped.

I opened my eyes, surprised to find that I was sitting in Durlan's lap on the floor of the shower with the water falling on both of us.

My head lay against his chest, while he stroked my hair.

"Wh-what was that?" I asked with a hoarse voice.

Had I been screaming?

"I'm sorry. I won't do that again. But I had to see."

See?

My eyes widened. He had used magic to pull the memories from my scars. I had heard of a power like that but didn't realize it belonged to one of the warlords.

"Kydrus has never seen your back, has he?"

I shook my head. I should have probably stood and moved away from him, but he made me feel safe. It was nice to be held.

"Finish your shower and then meet me in my office," he ordered me as he stood, lifting me to my feet as he did.

Once he shut the door, I slumped back to the floor with my head in my hands. How could everything go so wrong in just two days?

I didn't want to keep Durlan waiting, so I quickly cleaned myself and dressed in the clothes he had provided. They were soft and smelled like him.

I stood in the doorway to his office, gnawing on my lip.

What would he do? I hadn't actually told him anything, so it wasn't my fault he had discovered who my owner had been.

"Come, sit by me, please," he said softly.

I looked up, and my brows immediately furrowed. He had placed a chair beside his, while three more sat in front of his desk. Who was he inviting over?

I sat in the chair he had indicated, and he smiled at me.

"They'll be here shortly."

"Who?" I asked.

"Elara!" Kydrus boomed as he entered the room.

I leapt to my feet. How had he gotten here so fast?

Kydrus strode forward, looking like he meant to touch me, but Durlan stepped into his path.

Kydrus scowled. "Durlan, step aside."

He shook his head. "You're scaring her."

He was, but how had Durlan known?

Kydrus's shoulders drooped, and he looked around Durlan at me. "I'm glad you're safe. I executed Quin, so you won't have to worry about him anymore."

Executed?

Kydrus smiled. "Did you think I would let him live after he tried to kill you?"

Yes.

"Sit," Durlan ordered him. He turned to me. "Kydrus won't hurt you. You're under my protection now, so no one will hurt you. Understand?"

No.

I nodded and sat back in my chair.

Kydrus sat as well. "What happened?" he asked me.

"Quin pushed me off the ledge, and I fell in the river. I woke up on the shore, here, with Durlan saving me," I answered.

"Why summon us all?" Kydrus asked.

"Patience," Durlan said with a smile and sat beside me again.

Two more males entered, and I knew they were the other two warlords without being told. Both were just as muscular as Kydrus and Durlan, but these two had short hair, cut close to their ears.

They stopped their whispering when they saw me.

The one on the right had magenta eyes, and three scars down his left cheek. He smiled. "Did you take a mate?"

I tensed. Mate? No, he wouldn't force me to be his mate, would he?

Kydrus scoffed. "She is *not* his mate."

The fourth male had massive shoulders, crystal blue eyes, and a scowl. "She looks familiar."

"Sit," Durlan said with a sigh.

They took the two remaining seats in front of the desk.

"I've brought you all here because one of us has broken the treaty," Durlan said.

Oh no!

"What?" the scarred man asked.

"Who?" Kydrus asked, his hand going to the hilt of his sword.

"How?" the warlord on the right demanded.

I flinched at their shouts, and Durlan set his hand on top of mine. His hand was warm and calloused. It also helped me relax.

"Venali, were you aware you have slaves in your sector?"

The man on the right turned towards the scarred man, while Kydrus looked at me with wide eyes.

Venali, the brute with the scars, asked, "What have you heard? I've no knowledge of slaves in my sector. I have no knowledge of slaves anywhere in Minloa."

They couldn't lie, and his statement let me relax. At least he wasn't involved.

"Elara," Durlan said softly and squeezed my hand.

I looked up at him, feeling like a child.

"Will you show them your scars?" he asked softly.

Kydrus tensed. "Scars?"

I swallowed, nodded, and stood, pulling off my shirt as I did, and turned my back to them. I clutched the shirt to my chest to hide my breasts.

Two of them, I wasn't certain which two, sucked in a breath between their teeth.

I turned, and dropped my hands, letting them see the scars on my chest and stomach as well.

Durlan's eyes widened. "You didn't show me those."

I shrugged. "You didn't ask to see the rest."

I started to pull off my pants, but Durlan stopped me. "That's alright. They've seen enough. You can put your shirt back on."

I obeyed, dressed, and sat, avoiding the gazes of the other men.

"You're certain it is my sector?" Venali asked.

Durlan picked up an orb from the shelf behind his desk, and then began replaying the memories he had taken from my scars.

I squeezed my eyes closed and tried to ignore the sounds of the whip, but flinched with each one. My teeth ground together, and tears threatened to fall.

"She was a child," the fourth warlord said. Since the other was Venali, that meant he was Amrynn, Warlord of the Blustum sector.

Venali hadn't spoken since viewing the memories.

Neither had Kydrus.

Durlan set his hand on mine again, squeezing gently.

I glanced up at him, and he slowly reached over to wipe my face. I hadn't realized that the tears had fallen.

"She never told me what happened before she came to Linta," Kydrus said softly. "I had my suspicions, but I didn't want to believe them. I also had no idea how badly the others were treating her."

Durlan nodded. "She told me."

I saw Kydrus's hands clenched into fists in his lap.

"I did not know about the slavery," Venali said finally. "I will end it once I return."

"Her owner?" Kydrus asked.

"He will be brought before us for punishment. To make an example of him," Venali said, his voice a growl. "Girl," he said softly.

"Elara," Kydrus and Durlan said at the same time.

"Elara," Venali said.

I looked at him. He looked pained. Why?

"Did they do more than beat you?" he asked softly.

Oh. That's why he looked pained.

"No."

All four males let out a breath.

"How did you escape?" Kydrus asked.

I stood and set my sword on the desk. "This belonged to his son. I took it. They didn't know I had been watching them and practicing with twigs."

"You killed them?" Durlan asked, shock coloring his tone.

I smirked. "No. I took an arm from each of them."

Venali reached for the sword, and I snatched it back.

"It's mine! I earned it," I growled.

Venali and Amrynn smiled at me, which was a strange reaction to a woman growling at them.

"I will not keep your battle treasure," Venali said gently. "I just want to touch it to identify the owners."

Now that I realized what I had done, I dropped it and sat down in my chair with my hands beneath my legs.

What was wrong with me? I had just snapped at a warlord.

Venali touched the hilt and closed his eyes. The sword began to glow blue, and then it returned to normal and he removed his hand. He nodded. "I know who they are."

"Were there other slaves?" Durlan asked me.

I nodded. "He sold most of them to another male. Only me and two others stayed with him."

Venali scowled. "Another?"

"At least two others, actually," I said as I thought back. "There might have been more."

"Would you like my assistance?" Amrynn asked Venali.

Venali nodded, his scowl still in place.

"Two weeks?" Durlan asked.

Venali nodded again. "That should be sufficient time for me to capture them."

"There's something else," Durlan said.

All eyes turned to him, including mine.

What else could there be?

Durlan turned to face me. "At sundown, you will show us your powers."

I gulped.

"What is the meaning of this?" Kydrus asked.

"She has hidden her powers from you," Durlan said, still looking at me.

How did he know? I hadn't told him what my powers were. Had he seen something when he'd touched my scars?

"Elara?" Kydrus questioned, his voice soft.

I swallowed again. "I was going to tell you...last night. But..."

"But what?" Kydrus prompted.

I met his eyes and said, "I was afraid you would kill me."

The tension in the room skyrocketed.

I resigned myself to my fate. I might be able to run from one warlord, but I didn't stand a chance with all four of them here. I lowered my eyes to my lap.

"Why not just tell us what the power is?" Venali asked.

"Because it must be witnessed," Durlan said. "She's quite glorious."

Glorious?

I looked at him, and he was smiling down at me.

"Am I allowed to hold my sword?" I asked.

He nodded. "It is yours."

I took it slowly and secured it to my side.

"Can I speak to her alone?" Kydrus asked.

"No," Durlan said immediately, before my fear could even register.

"I have no desire to harm her," Kydrus grumbled.

"You scare her," Durlan said. "She's been traumatized enough."

Fidgeting in my chair, I kept my eyes down to avoid meeting Kydrus's gaze, which I could feel piercing me.

"Elara will stay here until sundown. The rest of us will discuss other matters in the kitchen," Durlan ordered everyone.

I thought the warlords were equal, but he seemed to be ordering everyone around, and they were listening. Was there a pecking order even amongst the warlords?

Venali, Amrynn, and Kydrus left the room.

Durlan knelt by my chair. "Will you be alright in here alone?"

I nodded. "Yes, sir."

He set his hand on mine, and I looked up to find him smiling. "You can call me Durlan. I'll come bring you dinner when it's ready."

I nodded and watched him leave with a sense of foreboding. Either I died tonight, or my life was going to change. How? I didn't know, and that scared me almost as much as death.

CHAPTER 3
DURLAN

THE THINGS that Elara had dealt with in her short life appalled me.

For someone so young to have been beaten and enslaved, enraged me to the point of wanting to find the man myself and tear his head off. I wasn't normally one for violence first, but the ones who had hurt her deserved nothing less than death.

"What is special about her?" Amrynn asked, looking at me. "She feels..."

"You have to wait to see her magic," I answered with a smug smile. Their reactions were going to be priceless.

"You know?" Kydrus asked.

I met his eyes. "You don't?"

He scowled. "If I knew, I wouldn't be asking."

"This is turning out to be an amazing day," I chuckled. "I find a beautiful girl in the river, save her life, find out something none of you know, and get to watch your faces when she shows you who she really is."

"Just tell us," Venali growled.

I shook my head. "Not a chance. The last time I was able to surprise one of you was decades ago. I'm going to savor this."

"Are we going to have to kill her?" Venali asked softly.

I could hear the hesitancy in his voice, which surprised me.

She was magnetic, and her fear spoke to our animalistic urges to protect her. It helped that she was attractive, but I would have felt the same even if she hadn't been.

Venali was normally one to kill first and worry about the repercussions later. Was he hesitant because he felt partially responsible for her enslavement in his sector? Or was it her blood, which called to me, too? It appeared she didn't even know her bloodlines and the true power she possessed.

"No," I answered Venali. "In fact, you're going to want to be near her as often as possible."

"Why are you keeping me from her? I've been interacting with her for years before you were involved," Kydrus growled.

"You frighten her. She admitted she thought you were going to kill her when you discovered her magic. Plus, after seeing what she went through as a child, how can you not understand that she'd be hesitant for a man to touch her when he is upset?"

He grumbled under his breath in response.

"Let's make food, gentlemen. Then, when the sun sets, that terrified woman will forever change our lives."

And, I could not wait.

CHAPTER 4
ELARA

Durlan had delivered my dinner, and then he had left me to eat alone.

I was used to eating alone, but knowing they were together in the other room made me feel even more alone than usual. I felt like I was eating my final supper. The food tasted like dust, my heart pounding faster with each bite.

The sun set, and my heart pounded furiously in my chest while my hands sweated. The uncertainty of their responses to my magic was the worst. I rubbed my hands on my pants, trying to get them to stop sweating.

Durlan didn't seem worried or upset about my powers, but that didn't mean the others would share his opinion.

Durlan opened the door, smiling. "It's time."

I stood on shaky legs and walked to him.

"Do you need anything?" he asked.

"A bottle or jar with a lid?"

He smirked. "Are you asking or telling?"

"Both," I whispered, looking down at his boots.

He fetched me one, and then escorted me outside to the back of his house where a field of flowers swayed in the breeze.

Venali, Kydrus, and Amrynn stood side by side, waiting expectantly.

Durlan set the jar on the ground with the lid open, then walked to stand beside the other warlords, but I noticed he was turned so he could look at them at the same time as me.

This was it. The moment I would find out if they were going to kill me or not. I would use my magic, and then they would smite me or...I wasn't sure what they would do.

I met all of their gazes a moment, and then lifted my head to the stars. I stretched out my arms, let the light of the stars and planets fill me, making my body glow. I crouched, picked up the jar, and raised my hand to gently grab one of the stars. Carefully, I pulled it from the sky and put it in the jar. I closed the lid, secured the clasp, and held it out towards them. The light still illuminated my body, but it was a soft glow now, slowly fading.

None of them moved. It didn't even look like they were breathing.

I took a few tentative steps closer to them, set the jar on the ground just in front of their feet, and then hurried backwards, clutching the hilt of my sword.

Durlan squatted down and looked at the star and started to reach for the clasp.

"No!" I yelled.

He stilled, looking up at me.

"I can release it, but if you do that, it will just come out full sized, right here," I explained.

"She plucked a star from the sky," Venali whispered. Was that awe I heard in his voice?

"If it came out, could you shrink it again?" Durlan asked.

I nodded.

"It was you," Kydrus gasped. "The crater by the lake."

I flinched and nodded. I had tried to forget that day.

"She's her. It's her!" Amrynn moved towards me quickly, his mouth agape.

I drew my sword and backed up. The sword shook as I held it out in front of me, trying to keep him at bay.

He stopped walking and held out his hands. "Elara, do you remember your life before you were sold as a slave?"

I shook my head.

He smiled. "You're a princess. Well, queen now. You are *our* queen."

"We don't have a monarchy," I reminded him.

"We used to," he said and cocked his head to the side. "Was she frozen or something? She should be a lot older."

"We need to find Azael," Venali said.

Azael had been my owner. Why did he want to find him? Aside from him having been a slave owner, that is.

I lowered my sword. "So, you're not going to kill me?"

Amrynn walked forward slowly and dropped to one knee, his head bowed to me. "Quite the opposite. Queen Elara, I pledge myself as your guard and vow to give my life for yours, should the need arise."

This was a joke, right? He had to be joking.

"I'm not a queen. I am...I was a slave. I am nothing," I said, backing away from him.

"You are everything," Durlan said as he walked closer. He bowed on one knee beside Amrynn.

Venali broke from his stupor and came to a knee beside the other two.

This was insanity.

Kydrus still stood in the same place, staring at me.

"Kydrus, what do I do?" I asked him softly. "I don't understand what's going on. This is crazy."

He blinked a few times. Then, he walked to the others and

knelt beside them. "You let us help you. You let us protect you, my queen."

THE FOUR WARLORDS ESCORTED ME BACK INTO THE HOUSE.

Durlan took the jar with the star in it and set it on his desk. He promised to seal it so no one would accidentally unleash the star.

"First, we need to find the one who owned her, question him extensively, and try to find out what happened," Venali said.

The other three nodded.

"If I'm the queen, that means my parents were royalty as well."

My mind was still reeling from their proclamations and I felt that they had to be wrong.

All four turned to face me.

"They were murdered before the Great War," I continued. "I can't be that old."

"The only explanation would be that you were frozen or in a state of suspended animation," Amrynn said. "You went missing as a child, the night before your parents were killed, actually. Maybe they knew and sent you away."

"How could I have been frozen?" Or survived being frozen? People didn't just get frozen all the time. It wasn't a normal occurrence.

"There are a few who could have performed the spell," Kydrus said.

"This is insane," I whispered and walked to sit in front of the fireplace. I didn't want to be a queen. I just wanted to be free to do as I liked.

"We can't all stay in one place," Durlan said. "Our sectors will destabilize if we aren't there."

Kydrus sighed. "You're right, but what should we do?"

"What if we set up a rotation?" Amrynn suggested. "She could stay with each of us for one month at a time."

"One month?" Kydrus asked. "Why not two weeks?"

"It's not fair for us to make her move around that often. I'd rather it be once every three months," Durlan said.

"Once a month is a decent compromise," Venali commented.

I swiveled on my butt to face them. All four sat in chairs now, Durlan in his desk chair.

"Are you talking about me?" I asked.

Durlan nodded.

"We are discussing where you'll be staying and for how long," Kydrus explained.

"Why do I have to move around? Can't I just stay in one place?"

Moving always made me anxious. Being in a new place was always unnerving.

"Where would you stay?" Kydrus asked. He glanced sideways at Durlan before looking back to me. "You have a preferred place?"

"You need to be with one of us at all times," Amrynn said. "There are some who will not like the idea of having a monarch again."

"Maybe we shouldn't have a monarch," I said softly. "If they were so unhappy that they murdered my parents, they'll likely come for me, too."

"They will come for you. That's why you need to be protected," Kydrus said quickly, his brows furrowed.

"If we don't tell them who I am, and I return to a normal life, they won't know to come for me," I argued.

"They'll know," Kydrus replied.

"How? I lived in your city for almost a decade, saw you almost every single day, and you didn't know who I was," I snapped.

His expression tightened, and I immediately regretted my outburst.

"I sensed it as soon as I saw you," Durlan said. "I thought I was wrong, but the longer I was with you, the more I felt it."

"Felt what?" My brows furrowed, and I tried to sense anything different in myself.

"Cosmic power," Amrynn said with awe in his voice and admiration in his eyes. "We could tell you were different, we just weren't sure how."

"I don't want to be a queen. There's no reason to change our society. You four have been ruling and there have been no wars. Why change it?" I looked at each one in turn, trying to ensure they agreed.

All four were unconvinced.

"She will stay with me first," Durlan told them. "Amrynn next, then Venali, and then Kydrus. Then, we will repeat the cycle."

"This is ridiculous," I grumbled and left the office. I walked out to the grassy field and lay on my back, looking up at the stars.

Why wouldn't they listen to reason? I knew nothing of ruling. I could barely read!

Amyrnn lay on his back beside me, his hands beneath his head.

I waited for him to speak, but he didn't.

"Why don't you four have mates?" I asked while still staring up at the stars.

"I don't know about the others, but for me, none were ever the right one for me," he said. "Many were beautiful, but our personalities didn't mesh. Some had good personalities, but they just didn't feel right. I want a partner. I want someone who fits beside me and feels like my missing piece. Like their presence fills and completes me."

"That's a pretty tall order," I muttered.

He chuckled. "I suppose it is."

I turned my head to look at him. "What if you never find someone who meets those requirements?"

He smiled. "She's out there. I just haven't found her yet."

"I hope you find her," I whispered. He was so old already. Would he go his entire life being alone?

"What about you, Elara?" he asked.

"Me?" I asked, eyes widened.

He nodded. "You're beautiful. Why don't you have a mate?"

I wanted a mate. I wanted someone who would love me and only me for the rest of our lives.

"Because she hides from everyone," Kydrus answered.

I raised my head.

Kydrus walked towards us, scowling.

"I wondered when you would stop hiding in the shadows," Amyrnn whispered with a smirk.

"I don't have a mate because no man has approached me." I lay back down and looked at the stars. "I'm too different than them. My beauty pales next to my weirdness, I guess."

Both men chuckled.

I sat up to face them. "What?"

"I need to go," Kydrus said, ignoring my question. "I'll see you in a few months."

Amrynn stood and brushed himself off. "I should go as well." He held out his hand, and I set mine in it. With a quick pull, he had me on my feet and wrapped in a hug. He was warm and solid muscle. Being hugged by him was incredible. "I'll see you in a month," he whispered in my ear. "Stay safe, my queen."

He released me and disappeared.

"Can I walk you back to the house before I leave?" Kydrus asked.

"Sure," I replied, my cheeks warm from Amrynn's embrace.

Kydrus walked by my side until we got to the back door of Durlan's house. He leaned forward and hugged me quickly. Then he stepped back and disappeared. Had that been a pained expression on his face?

Was he upset that I was royalty? Did it pain him to know that I, the pathetic girl who caused so many problems for him, was a queen?

"There you are," Venali said, startling me out of my inner thoughts.

"You were looking for me?" I asked, looking up at him. I wanted to trace his scars with my fingertips but clenched my hands into fists to keep from doing so.

He stepped forward, closing the distance between us. "I have to leave. I'll see you in two months, okay?"

Of the four, he made me feel the safest. Like I knew he would kill anything that tried to hurt me. There was zero logical reasoning for this, and yet that was how I felt.

I nodded.

He bent a placed a kiss on my cheek. "Be safe."

"You, too," I whispered, my throat suddenly tight.

He smiled, and then he too disappeared.

"You look exhausted," Durlan said from the doorway.

"Does a pixie bite?" I scoffed. "I'm just in need of a long rest."

"Let me show you to your room," he said and held open the door.

"Durlan, why are you all so adamant that I become queen?" I asked as I followed him to one of the spare rooms.

He stepped into the room and leaned against the wall beside the door. "We prosper best when we have a strong matriarch."

"Are you four just tired of ruling?" I asked, leaning my hip against the dresser. Everything was in pristine condition, there wasn't even dust on the furniture. Was he a neat freak?

He smiled. "Even when you take over as queen, we will still be your warlords, and in charge of our sectors."

"Why do I have to be passed around every month? Why can't I find a place at the point all of the sectors meet and build a place there?"

"You don't want to stay with the others? Are you scared of them?"

"It has nothing to do with them," I said. And no, I wasn't scared of them. I probably should have been. "Why not just pick some guards for me and let me live in the middle?"

He scowled. "You want to find random men to guard you?"

"I would let you four pick them, so we knew they were trustworthy."

"Are we unappealing to you?" he asked.

"Your appeal has nothing to do with this," I grumbled.

He smirked. "So, you do find us appealing."

"Do I look blind?" I asked and scoffed.

He laughed and the sound made me smile.

"What does a queen even do?"

"That's part of why we will have you take turns staying with us. Each of us excels in different knowledge bases. For example, I'm the best strategist. Venalis is our best fighter, and so on."

"I didn't realize Venali was a better fighter. I thought you were all fairly equal."

He smirked again. "Do not misunderstand, we can all hold our own, but in a battle, Venali always gets the highest kill count."

"Did you bring the other two here when confronting Venali about my slavery in case he did know and attacked you?"

He nodded.

I exhaled and ran a hand through my hair. "I'm glad that wasn't the case."

"You and me both," Durlan said with a chuckle. "I didn't truly believe he knew, but I take whatever precautions I need to."

"Durlan, I..." I felt I should let him know my limitations. An illiterate queen would be laughed at.

He walked to me and set his hands on my upper arms with a smile. "You can tell me anything, Elara."

"I can't read," I blurted.

He nodded. “Kydrus told us.”

My mouth dropped open. “How did he know?’

He smiled. “He may not have consciously known who you were, but he always felt something with you. Didn’t you find it odd that he kept interrupting your fights?”

I had, but I figured it had been because of my obvious fear. And, because they kept picking on me.

“Do I have to stay in Linta for a month?” I asked softly, letting my head drop forward.

“You don’t want to be with Kydrus?”

My cheeks warmed. “It has nothing to do with him. I just don’t like Linta.”

“You should get to know each of us, the warlords, and our sectors.”

I looked up at him. “Get to know you? Why?”

He smiled again. “Because we are your warlords.”

The way he said it made it clear he was hiding something. The fluttering in my chest meant I wasn’t sure if it was good or bad.

He stepped back from me, dropping his hands from my arms. “You should sleep. Tomorrow, I begin your tutoring.” He closed my bedroom door after a quick, “Good night, my queen.”

CHAPTER 5
KYDRUS

ELARA WAS OUR LOST PRINCESS. How had I not seen that before? I'd felt a connection to her. I'd felt that there was something different about her, but I never would have imagined this.

The urge to protect her had been impossible to ignore the longer I was around her, which was why I had kept stopping her fights. But knowing who she was now, I wanted to resurrect Quin and kill him all over again.

She had suffered so much in her short life, and she should have never endured any of it. Had her parents not sent her away, she would have been protected, and none of this would have happened. None of those scars would mar her body. Not that it took away from her beauty. If anything, it made her even more beautiful, to have endured so much and still have so much love.

Or, had she stayed with her parents, she might have met the same fate as them. I wished to go back in time and take her to safety myself.

Her former owner would pay. I would kill him slowly.

And somehow, I would make her understand that I would never harm her.

CHAPTER 6
ELARA

TUTORING WAS CLEARLY a synonym for torture.

"Can we please take a break?" I begged Durlan.

We had spent the past three hours going over the history of Minloa, but hadn't made it to the Great War yet.

He chuckled. "Alright, we can break for lunch."

I doubted I had ever smiled wider in my life.

Durlan wore jeans and a t-shirt with dusty boots. He didn't carry a sword like Kydrus did, and when I had asked why, he said, "I don't have much need for it."

Durlan took out some ingredients, and then waved me over. I sat on a stool at the island, and folded my arms on the top.

"Do you want to learn to cook?" he asked.

"Yes," I said eagerly.

"First, we need to cut up these vegetables." He cut one of the vegetables with a large knife into small slices to show me, and then he slid the cutting board, knife, and other vegetables to me. "Now, you try."

I moved slowly, but my cuts were never the same size.

"Elara," Venali said loudly behind me.

I jumped, cut my finger with the knife, and hissed in pain. The wound immediately began bleeding.

Durlan reached across the table for my hand, but Venali beat him to it.

Venali cradled my bleeding hand in his giant palm and used his magic to heal me. "I'm sorry," he said softly. "I didn't mean to startle you."

"It's okay," I said. "It was just a small cut."

"I just came to let you know that I found Azael. And, he admitted everything," Venali continued.

"Did he say how he found her?" Durlan asked.

Venali finished healing me and took a damp cloth and cleaned the blood off my hand. For such a large and dangerous man, he was surprisingly gentle.

"He did. I'd like to show you something," he told Durlan.

Durlan glanced at me. "She'll have to come."

"I can just stay here, if you don't want me going."

Venali shook his head and met my eyes. "It's your past. You should come, too."

Staring into his eyes, I became very aware of how close he stood to me, the fact that he was still holding my hand, and that his leg was touching mine. His eyes swirled with emotions too fast for me to pinpoint one.

Durlan cleared his throat, and Venali moved away so fast that I thought I'd somehow hurt him.

"We were about to eat. Can it wait?" Durlan asked.

Venali nodded. "I actually haven't eaten yet. Do you have enough for me?"

"Yes," Durlan said.

I stood, grabbed a towel, got it wet, and then began cleaning the island, trying to get all of my blood off of it

Venali washed the knife and cutting board, threw away the pieces of vegetable my blood contaminated, and then with a speed and skill I doubted I would ever have, sliced the rest up in perfectly identical pieces.

He caught me staring, arched an eyebrow, and asked, "What?"

"Just impressed," I said softly.

He chuckled. "If that impresses you, I can't wait to see what you think when you see me fight."

Durlan whispered something into his ear that made the smile on Venali's face disappear.

"What?" I asked.

"You never ate meals with Kydrus?" Venali asked instead of answering me.

"No. Why would I?" I scowled. Who just ate meals with their warlord?

"Do you dislike Kydrus? Or are you scared of him?" Venali asked.

"I like Kydrus. At times, I was frightened of him. I was worried he would finally grow tired of me and kill me. Or, when he found out about my powers that he would kill me. Only an idiot isn't scared of the Four Warlords."

Both Durlan and Venali were smiling now. Clearly, they liked what I'd said.

"Your smiles worry me," I grumbled and averted my gaze, looking down at my hands.

"I'll finish up lunch. Why don't you go help her sharpen her sword?" Durlan suggested.

Venali said, "Sounds great. Come on, Elara. I'll teach you the proper way to sharpen knives and swords."

I cast a nervous glance at Durlan, but he was already cooking.

"I promise, I won't bite. Unless you bite me first," Venali whispered in my ear. His warm breath caressed my earlobe and made me shiver. I wouldn't mind a few bites from Venali.

I followed him outside to a wooden building I hadn't noticed before. He threw open the huge double doors with ease. When he headed in, I tried tugging on one of the doors. My suspicions were confirmed, each door was heavy, and he'd opened them like normal doors.

Inside were all the equipment and tools a blacksmith would have. Did Durlan make his own weapons?

"Sword," Venali requested.

I drew my sword, set it on my palms, and held it out to him.

He gently took it, raised it, and examined all of its angles. "Have you ever attacked someone with this?"

I nodded.

"Did you cut them?"

I shook my head.

He chuckled. "I didn't think so."

"Why do you say that?"

"It's incredibly blunt. If you'd had to defend yourself against us last night, and tried to stab one of us, we would have been really irritated at getting poked by this."

"I already know I don't stand a chance against you four," I mumbled, heat flooding my cheeks.

"What about one of us? You drew your weapon on Amrynn."

"If you were faced with opponents beyond your skill, but they were going to kill you, would you have drawn your weapon or just accepted your fate?" I asked with an arched brow and hands on my hips.

"We weren't going to kill you," he said softly.

"I didn't know that. And, you didn't answer me."

He smirked. "Yes, I would have drawn my weapon." He looked back at my sword. "It's going to take me a bit to sharpen this. I think our lesson will have to wait until you come see me. I'll sharpen your sword today while you observe."

I sat on a nearby stool so I could watch him. "Thank you."

"What has Durlan been teaching you today?" he asked while he worked.

"History," I said and tried to hide my displeasure.

He chuckled. "It is important to know your history."

"I don't want to be queen," I told him.

He looked up at me. "If I could prevent it, I would, but it is your birthright and destiny."

"Does that mean I'll be forced to mate some pompous man so he can be king?" I asked.

Venali set the sword down to look at me. "What?"

"I don't want to be forced to mate with someone I don't love," I told him.

"You don't have to worry about that," he promised me.

"I don't?"

He smiled. "I'll ensure it doesn't happen."

"How?" I asked skeptically.

"I'll kill anyone who tries to force you to mate with anyone against your will."

I believed him. The fire in his eyes, the power that flared around him, were all signs of his promise.

"Thank you."

He bowed. "I'll do almost anything you ask me to, my queen."

"Could you stop calling me that then?"

He chuckled. "I'll try."

"Will you do me one other favor?" I asked before I lost my nerve.

"What?"

"Teach me to fight."

He smiled so wide, I thought his face might get stuck that way. Not that it was bad. Actually, he was quite handsome when he smiled. "It would be my honor," he said.

We lapsed into silence while he sharpened my sword and then polished it.

When he was done, I could see my reflection in the blade.

He held it out, but before I could reach it, he drew it back.

"Why do you want to learn to fight? I will teach you, but I'd like to know why."

"I don't want to be helpless ever again. I want to be able to protect myself."

"We will protect you," he said adamantly, but his eyes were soft.

"You won't always be with me," I countered.

His head cocked to the side. "He hasn't told you?"

"Told me what?"

"We're your warlords. We are your guards and your assassins."

"You have sectors to keep in line. You can't leave them to guard me."

I remembered Amrynn vowing to be my guard, but I thought it had been metaphorical.

He smiled. "When you are queen, we won't have to rule our sectors. We will stay with you, and if something comes up, one of us will go."

"What if something happens in all four sectors at the same time?"

"Then you'll accompany me," he said.

"Why you?"

He smirked. "Because no one will touch you if I am by your side."

"Cocky much?" I teased.

"No, just honest." He shrugged nonchalantly.

"I suggested you find me guards, but Durlan didn't like that idea," I said softly.

"You would rather have random men guard you, then the Four Warlords?" His eyebrows rose, and he set my sword down on the anvil.

"I would rather find a place in the mountains where I could live in peace, than be queen. I would rather not be a burden. You are each over a thousand years old. I can't imagine you'd want to spend your time entertaining a child."

He scowled. "First, you aren't a burden or a child. Second, we would be protecting our queen. It is a very honorable job. Third, we may be old, but that just means we know what we want and what is fun."

"What do you want?" I asked, looking up at him.

He moved closer and stared down into my eyes. "The better question is, what do *you* want?"

He was so close, so warm, and so powerful. I knew without a doubt he could protect me. I hoped he would be loyal. I dreamed that he would kiss me. I wanted to be in his arms.

I swallowed and whispered, "To be l—"

"Lunch is ready," Durlan said from the doorway.

The spell was broken. I turned and smiled. "Great! I'm starving." I left the two men behind me, and hurried to the house. Instead of going to the kitchen, I went to the bathroom and sat on the floor with my head against the door. What was wrong with me? I had almost told Venali that I wanted to be loved.

I groaned and dropped my face into my hands.

I was a moron.

Hiding in the bathroom wouldn't accomplish anything. I had to face them.

With a deep breath for courage, I went to the kitchen and sat on the open stool between Venali and Durlan. I picked up the fork and ate the food on my plate. I didn't know what it was, but it was tasty.

Neither man said anything while we ate.

Once done, they stood and held out their hands to me.

I looked back and forth, not sure what to do. Was this a test? I didn't know either man well. I didn't have a favorite.

Durlan was nice and smart.

Venali was strong and dangerous.

I grabbed each of their hands, which earned me a smile from both of them.

Venali put my sword in my sheath, and then teleported us to a dark cave. I tensed once we arrived, fear clawing at me. The urge to escape, to run, was so intense that my legs were taut in preparation.

Venali pulled me into a hug, wrapping his strong arms around me. "Breathe, Elara. You are safe. We won't hurt you. And, I won't let anything else hurt you."

Slowly, my heart returned to a more normal rhythm. Or, as normal as it could be with Venali's arms around me.

He released me, but then grabbed my hand in his much larger one and tugged me after him.

This cave felt familiar. There was nothing out of the ordinary about the cave, and yet I felt like I'd been here.

Durlan followed silently behind.

We walked down a narrow tunnel, which was dark and probably filled with bugs. I was very glad I couldn't see them.

Light ahead drew my attention. It glowed like fey lanterns.

We entered the large cave, and my entire body went rigid.

Wooden furniture lay in broken pieces, scattered across the cave, a few books lay discarded on the ground, and what looked like a bed took up one side. What drew the most attention was the white wall with a child-sized hole.

I approached it, my hand raised, but Venali tugged me to a stop before I could.

"I'm not sure what would happen if you touched it," he whispered.

"They froze me here," I whispered. "Then, someone broke me out. They shattered the crystal with an ax," I told them as snippets of my memory returned. I'd been so scared when I'd woken up with unfamiliar men standing around me.

I sank to my knees, clutching my head as all of my memories returned, and I felt whole for the first time ever.

I stood and turned to Venali.

"Who froze you?" Venali asked softly.

"Take me to the castle," I ordered him.

"It was destroyed," Durlan said.

I shook my head. "No, it wasn't. Take me. I'll show you."

"We should bring the others," Durlan told Venali.

Venali nodded. "I'll wait at your house."

We teleported back to Durlan's front yard, and I sank to my knees on the grass.

It was true. I was the princess, now queen. My parents had sent me away.

Venali sat beside me, his brows furrowed. "Are you okay?"

"I remember," I whispered. "I remember that night. I remember my life before I was a slave."

His eyes widened.

Tears dripped down my cheeks. My parents, my loving and wonderful parents, were dead. Murdered. I was glad I hadn't witnessed it, but the stories about it had never affected me before. Now, now it hurt so much.

Venali repositioned himself so that his legs were on either side of me, then pulled me closer, so I sat with my back to his chest. He wrapped his arms around me.

I turned sideways so I basically sat in his lap and hid my face against his shirt.

"I'm sorry. I wasn't a guard back then. I can't imagine how scared you were when they broke you out of your crystal."

"So alone," I whispered, sniffling.

"You're not alone now," he whispered back and stroked my hair. "You'll never be alone again."

"When you find mates, I will be. Unless I've found a mate by then. Which, I doubt."

"We won't take mates," he whispered against my hair. "We want no mate besides—"

"We?"

"The four of us," he explained.

"What about you?" My tears had stopped. I wiped my eyes. "What do you want, Venali?"

"You to live a long and healthy life."

"You don't know me. Just because I have the same bloodlines as someone else doesn't mean you should care."

"You're young and haven't been taught," he said with a sigh.

I stood with a glare at him. "That's not my fault."

He stood, too. "I just meant that you need to learn what we really are to you. What it really means for us to be your warlords."

"Then tell me."

"We are your guards. Your advisors. And, your mates," he said softly.

I blinked. "Mates? I thought you said I wouldn't be forced to mate with someone I don't love?"

"You won't."

I rubbed my temples. "You are not making any sense."

"We are your mates, but you don't have to mate with us. If you choose to only mate with one of us, the other three will still be your warlords. So, really, we are your potential mates. Your mate options."

"What if I don't want any of you?" I asked, despite the thoughts already going through my mind about having them as my mates. They were the Four Warlords after all. Any woman would be lucky to have them.

He smirked. "Don't kill our relationship yet, Elara. We only met yesterday."

It didn't feel like it, though. I felt like I had known Venali my whole life.

"Sorry," Durlan said as he appeared beside us. "It took me a bit to find Kydrus."

Kydrus narrowed his eyes and walked up to me. I took a single step back out of nervousness. He stopped. "Why were you crying?"

"Let's go," I ordered them, turning to face Durlan. "I'll explain everything when we get there."

"Any dangers we should be prepared for?" Venali asked.

"Swords at the ready," I said with a nod.

All four widened their eyes and cast glances at each other.

I didn't really think there would be trouble, but I'd been gone a long time. I wasn't positive what we'd be walking into.

I set my hand in Durlan's. "To the castle courtyard, please."

Venali took my other hand, and I avoided eye contact and hoped my cheeks weren't as read as they felt.

WE TELEPORTED TO THE COURTYARD AND I SNICKERED AT how destroyed it appeared.

"You're laughing at the castle being destroyed?" Amrynn asked.

"Show yourself!" I yelled and moved away from the warlords. "I know you're here! Show yourself!"

Venali stayed close to me, his sword drawn.

"I sense no one," Amrynn said.

I turned to face Venali. "I need you to stay with them. I need space."

"If I'm too far, someone could—"

"Please," I interrupted him.

He scowled, but walked backwards until he was beside the others. They all stood in a large circle with their swords drawn.

I walked closer to where the front doors used to be.

"Elara," Venali growled.

"Stop hiding!" I snapped. "You know I hate it when you hide from me."

A deep male voice chuckled. "You kept me waiting a long time," the voice said.

"I was frozen, if you recall, and when I woke up, I had no memories. You said that wouldn't happen," I yelled back.

"Who is it?" Kydrus asked.

"How did you manage to gather the Four Warlords?" the invisible man asked.

I sighed. "Come on. Drop the glamour."

"But look at their confused faces. This is much more fun."

"Ryul!" I growled.

Large arms wrapped around me, and the illusion fell.

CHAPTER 7
ELARA

THE FOUR WARLORDS of Minloa were torn between disbelief at the pristine state of the castle, and fury at me being held by a man they didn't know.

To be fair, I had no idea how trustworthy Ryul was now. He could want to kill me for all I knew.

The instant that thought crossed my mind, my entire body tensed.

Ryul's large, muscled arms tightened a moment before he turned me to face him. The last time I had seen him, he'd been a gangly ten-year-old boy. Ryul had grown in the thousand years we had been apart into a well-muscled and handsome man. The glint in his eyes let me know the mischievous boy was still in there, though.

He frowned, his brows furrowed. "What's wrong?"

"Are you mad at me?" I asked softly.

His brows smoothed out, and he rested his calloused hand on my cheek with a smile. "I would wait ten thousand years for you, my queen."

His head lowered towards mine, and my heart beat faster. He was going to kiss me.

Kydrus pulled me back, while Venali slammed into Ryul's side, pushing him away from me.

Ryul spun around Venali with a speed that seemed impossible and punched him in the face. Ryul drew his sword and turned towards me and Kydrus. "Release Queen Elara!"

"Who are you?" Venali demanded, his grip on his sword so tight that his knuckles were white.

Ryul growled and advanced on Kydrus, his body glowing and blue flames slipping down his blade.

I had to stop this before they killed each other.

"Stop!" I ordered them.

Everyone froze.

I stepped out of Kydrus's hold and ignored his growl. I placed myself in the center of the five men. "You five will not fight each other," I told them. "You are my guards and need to learn to get along."

"What?" Amrynn asked.

"Sheathe your weapons and dispel your magic," I commanded them.

Everyone, but Venali complied.

"Venali," I said softly. "Ryul is not going to harm me."

"You don't know that. You haven't seen him since you were five years old. He's been away from you for a thousand years. Men change a lot in just one year. He could be your enemy now," Venali said, his lips pulled up in a snarl, showing off his fangs.

"You're right," I said and turned to my old friend.

"Elara," Ryul said with wide eyes.

"But, Ryul swore an oath. He would die within hours of hurting me," I said.

"What proof do you have of the oath?" Durlan asked.

Ryul raised his right sleeve, revealing the symbols magically etched into his skin that glowed a light blue. They were a reminder of his oath. "I am bound to serve and protect Elara, heir of Minloa. If I harm her or cause harm to befall her, my life is forfeit."

Venali's sword lowered. "How old were you when you made that oath?"

"Nine," Ryul said.

"Why didn't you search for her?" Kydrus asked.

"Our agreement was for her to return here. Apparently, someone broke the spell I placed on her, causing it to falter and block her memories." He met my eyes and bowed. "I'm sorry."

"How long would you have left her frozen?" Durlan asked.

Ryul straightened. "She was supposed to wake when the time was right. I had faith she would wake during my lifetime."

"Give him a break," I said to Durlan. "He was only ten years old when he used the spell. How proficient were all of you at ten?"

I walked to Ryul and set my hand on his right arm, over the symbols. They glowed and warmed under my touch.

"I've kept the castle secure. No one has been inside, except for me and the groundskeeper," Ryul whispered.

"We should go inside," I whispered. "We have a lot to discuss."

He took my hand in his, lacing our fingers together, and beamed, his white teeth sparkling and his canines white and sharp. "I've waited a long time to hear you say that."

I wasn't certain how Ryul felt, but it felt as if no time had passed since we were last together. Yet, I knew things were far different now that we were adults.

Ryul waved his hand and the front doors opened. He walked at my side, leading me into the entryway. "Welcome home, Queen Elara."

Everything was exactly as I remembered. The same chandeliers, paintings, and floors of my childhood.

I leaned my head against his shoulder and exhaled. "It's good to be home."

Ryul led the way to my father's war room and pulled out the king's chair.

I stared at it. The lion's head at the top of the chair looked smaller than I remembered it. I ran my fingers over the carved lion's paws, recalling sitting on my father's lap during his meetings.

I sat on the red, cushioned seat, and looked at the map, which had new markers since the last time I had been here. Ryul had added the new cities and indicated where the four sectors were.

Ryul sat on my right, and the others took seats as well.

"Who killed them?" I asked, looking at Ryul.

"Feno."

"You're sure?" I asked softly, trying to control my rage and pain.

"Yes."

Feno had been my father's guard. He had been like an uncle to me. Why had he betrayed them?

The table and bookshelves began to shake as angry tears slid down my face.

Kydrus pushed my chair back, ignored Ryul's growl, and picked me up into his arms, hugging me tightly. "Elara, we will find him and make him pay."

I sobbed, turned my head into his chest, and let the tears fall. Not at Feno for his betrayal, but for the loss of my parents. They had loved me more than anything. That's why they had snuck me out of the castle with Ryul when they learned of a plot against them.

The room stopped shaking.

Kydrus sat in my chair and cradled me in his lap while I cried. Once my tears were done, I wiped my eyes with my hand and stood. Kydrus stood and returned to his seat without another word.

"What happened after you were woken?" Ryul asked, his hands in fists in his lap.

I sat in my chair and let my head fall back. "Not many good

things," I admitted. "Some men broke the crystal you sealed me in. Then they sold me as a slave."

"What!" Ryul shouted, his fists coated in flames.

"Show him," Durlan said softly. "He needs to know the full extent of your trauma so he can guard you better."

Venali growled softly, but we all ignored him.

"Show me what?" Ryul asked.

I stood again, and removed my shirt, holding it just to cover my breasts, and turned so he could see my back.

"Who did this to you?" Ryul asked in a dangerously calm voice.

"We've captured him, and he is awaiting punishment," Venali said.

"There are more scars," I whispered as I put my shirt back on. "But, they are on my legs and I would have to remove my pants, which the warlords weren't comfortable with me doing."

Ryul arched a brow. "I find that hard to believe."

I rolled my eyes at him and sat down. "I escaped my owner and lived in Linta," I told Ryul. "Then, a man shoved me off a cliff in an attempt to kill me. Durlan pulled me from the water and saved me."

"She floated from Silpo to Menma?" Ryul asked.

Durlan nodded. "She had been knocked unconscious at some point, had two broken ribs, and a broken arm."

My mouth dropped open. "You didn't tell me that."

Durlan smiled. "You were in enough shock. Plus, I was more focused on getting you to stop fearing us."

"How did you know who she was?" Ryul asked.

"I pulled a star from the sky," I whispered while looking at my hands in my lap.

"Oh, boy," Ryul sighed. "I hoped you wouldn't figure out how to do that."

"What else can she do?" Amrynn asked.

"I need to test her, but she should be able to rearrange the stars, space travel, and harness the sun's power."

"The last person who tried to harness the sun's power burned alive," Durlan said with a frown.

That had me looking at Ryul.

Ryul nodded.

"Well, now that I have Ryul, you four won't have to worry about guarding me," I said, looking at them. My chest felt tight as I said it, but I ignored the feeling.

"Ryul being here changes nothing," Kydrus said, the hint of a growl on the edge of his words.

"We are still your warlords," Durlan said.

"You are her advisors, but she has no need for—" Ryul growled, but Venali interrupted him.

"The queen, when unmated, has always had, at a minimum, four guards. You can't truly believe you are strong enough to protect her on your own?" the malice in Venali's voice was unmistakable.

"I could have killed all four of you when you stepped into the courtyard," Ryul snarled.

"Are you so egotistical that you'd risk Elara's life just to keep up your appearance of superiority?" Durlan asked.

Ryul ground his teeth. "Of course not."

"Then it's settled," Amrynn said with a smile. "Our lovely queen now has five guards."

I glanced at Venali, but he wasn't looking at me. So, I turned to Durlan. "What now?"

"I still think you should spend time in each of the sectors," Durlan said. "You have a lot to learn."

"When do you plan to announce her as queen?" Ryul asked, crossing his arms over his chest.

"Once she is literate and is up to date on Minloa's affairs," Durlan answered.

"And, after she's learned to protect herself a bit," Venali added.

"And gotten her powers a bit more under control," Kydrus said.

"I think she should wait until she has chosen her mates before we announce her," Amrynn said.

"Oh, is that all?" I asked with a scoff. "So, when I'm fifty? Or should we wait until I'm one hundred?"

"You've been missing for one thousand years. What's another fifty?" Kydrus asked with a shrug, his face stone serious.

I stood quickly and left the room. "I need some air."

The men began arguing, their voices raising higher the farther I walked. Instead of going outside, I walked to my bedroom. I didn't know how safe the area was, despite Ryul's glamour. It was very unlikely, but Feno could come back.

My room looked exactly as I remembered it. Even my stuffed animals were there. I touched the silver comb Mother used to use each morning on my hair, and felt a deep sorrow, all the way to my bones. She would hum songs while she brushed my tangles, and then braided my hair.

I sat on the thick blanket at the foot of my bed, and closed my eyes.

The warlords were a lot to deal with. Not that I was surprised, but I hadn't expected them to stay once they saw Ryul was here and the type of magic he was capable of.

If Mother were here, what would she say to me?

Probably, "Let the men protect you. They are more experienced and have your best interests at heart."

Dad would tell me to work hard to prove them wrong.

Perhaps, I could do both.

"Elara?" Amrynn called through my door.

I sat up and rubbed my eyes. I had fallen asleep, but I wasn't sure for how long.

"Come in," I called around a yawn.

He opened the door, looked around my room, and then shut the door behind him. "Were you sleeping?"

I nodded. "It's okay. What did you need?"

He sat beside me on the bed and smoothed my sleep-ruffled hair down. "I just came to check on you."

"I'm sorry if I worried you," I said and stretched.

His eyes dropped to the strip of stomach exposed by my raised arms. "We've been treating you like a child, and I am sorry for that. We just want to keep you safe," he whispered and lifted his eyes to mine. "You are important. We tend to lose ourselves to protective instincts and impulses and forget about your feelings. I'll try to work on that."

"Was Venali being honest? About you four being my mates?"

He sighed. "He told you about that?"

I nodded.

"Yes, he was being serious. The four of us are your mates."

"Five," I said.

He frowned. "What?"

"Doesn't Ryul get added to the list, since he is my guard as well?"

Amrynn looked at the door, as if he could see the other man. "I suppose he would make it five."

"That's insane," I told him and stood. Then I began pacing. "Why would I need that many? Mom only had Dad."

"Our species has developed an odd issue. You see, a higher percentage of males are born than females. So, most females not only have their choice of mates, but also of how many mates they want to have. Queens, well queens tend to have a half a dozen or a dozen mates. Kings on the other hand, tend to have one mate. Though, some kings before your father had concubines as well."

I stopped and looked at him. "Really?"

He nodded. "Your grandfather had one mate, his queen, and five or six concubines. He treated them all very well, and from what I was told, loved them all."

"This is all insane," I whispered, resuming my pacing. "How am I supposed to pick between five men?"

"You don't have to pick," Amrynn said.

I turned and stared. I understood what he'd said, about women having the option for multiple mates, but I couldn't see the Four Warlords being able to share a woman. Such powerful men were used to getting their way and had their choice of mates. I knew a dozen women who would throw themselves at the warlords, given the chance.

Amrynn stood with a smile and set his hands on my arms. "You are queen. We are yours. Even if you did decide not to choose one of us as your mate, we'd still be your guards. But, we would all kill for the chance to be your mate."

"Because I'm queen?"

"It may start that way, but we are all incredibly attracted to you. I have no doubt that the longer I am with you, the more I will want you."

"You're warlords. You could get any woman you want," I reminded him, swallowing. He was so close. Just a lift of my toes and I could kiss him.

"We could." He rubbed his thumbs on my arms and whispered, "But, you call to us. Just like we call to you, no matter how much you try to ignore it."

"What is this calling?"

"Power," he whispered. "Those of similar power are drawn together. That's why we don't have mates. You're the first female to rival us in power in a very long time."

He stepped closer to me, his head angled down.

"A queen should never take advantage of her station or

power," I whispered, remembering my mother saying that to me on several occasions.

Amrynn smiled. "Do I look like I'm here against my will?"

"What do you want?" I asked.

"For you to give us a chance. To spend time with us and get to know us."

"And?" I asked, knowing there was something else.

He traced my lower lip with his thumb. "A kiss."

I placed my hands on his shoulders, stood on tip toe, and pressed my lips to his.

His lips were even softer than they looked.

When I pulled back, he smiled at me.

"We should find the others," he whispered. "Or, they'll come looking for us."

"One more," I whispered, shocking myself, and kissed him again.

He wrapped his arms around me, and kissed me deeply, supporting my weight easily.

I stepped back and ran a hand through my hair, biting my lower lip to keep from doing or saying something I shouldn't.

He kissed my cheek, opened my door, and bowed. "If you'll follow me, my queen?"

These men were going to be a handful. I wasn't certain I could handle it.

But I was damn well going to have fun trying.

"Lead the way, Warlord," I said, smiling wide.

We walked side by side down the empty hallways. The castle's emptiness bothered me the most.

"You are scowling," Amrynn said, eyeing me.

"It's just so quiet. I miss it being loud and busy."

He reached over and squeezed my hand. "It will be again, soon."

"In fifty years," I scoffed and pulled my hand back to smooth my hair down.

Voices ahead caught my attention. They were in the kitchen.

Amrynn pushed open the door for me, and the four men inside stopped talking to face us.

"What's for dinner?" I asked, hopped up onto the counter next to Durlan, and snagged a slice of cucumber to chew on.

"Stew," Durlan said, smiling at me.

I nodded, grabbed an apple, and then froze. "Where'd the food come from?"

Ryul rolled his eyes. "I've been living here, remember?"

I chuckled in embarrassment. "Right, sorry."

He stuck his lip out in a pout. "I can't believe you forgot about your best friend."

I hopped off the counter, walked to where he was chopping mushrooms, and hugged him from behind. "It wasn't my fault."

He set his knife down, turned in my arms, and lifted my chin with his finger. "I promise I'm not mad. There was a period of time when I was mad, but I had faith you would return to me."

"You have too much faith in me," I told him, staring into his familiar eyes. He had been my best friend. My confidante. The one I could go to about anything. Now, he was a man, a gorgeous man, and a candidate to be my mate.

Wait. Did he even want that?

"Can we talk...privately?" I asked him.

He nodded, took my hand, and led me out of the kitchen and to the dining room. He turned to face me, smiling. "What's up, El?"

"Do..." How was I supposed to ask this?

"Yes," he said.

I laughed. "You don't even know what I'm going to ask."

He shrugged. "It involves you, so the answer is yes."

"What if I was going to ask if you want to clean out my toenails?" I asked with an arched brow.

"Then, I'd take your shoes off and start to work," he said with a smirk. "Though, you used to have really smelly feet, so I'll need a mask."

I shoved his shoulder and laughed. "Punk."

He set his hands on my arms. "Ask."

"Do you have any interest in possibly being one of my mates?" I asked, my body tense with nerves.

He smiled. "Yes."

"You could wait to answer," I said. "Think about it."

"I've been waiting for you over a thousand years. There's no reason for me to hesitate. I would kill a million men for the chance to be considered." His eyes glowed slightly as he spoke, and the conviction in his statement shocked me.

"I'm sorry I kept you waiting," I whispered.

He tugged me closer, stroked a finger down my jaw, and said, "I'm sorry you endured such pain. If I could go back and change things, I would. I would take the pain for you."

I wasn't so sure I would. If I changed the past, would I still have met the warlords?

He lowered his head and kissed me lightly. "We should go back to the others."

One week ago, I was convinced I would be alone forever. Now, I had five men protecting me. Two of which I had kissed today. Life changed so quickly.

"El, are you planning to go to each of their sectors like they want?"

I sighed. "Yes. Part of me just wants to hide here, but I should learn more about Minloa."

"Then, I'm coming with you," he said.

"What?" I looked up at him, not sure I had heard him right.

"It's my job to protect you. I will go with you to their sectors."

"What about the castle?"

"I'll put the illusion up, and the groundskeeper is powerful enough to fend off the occasional trespasser," he said and smiled. "I just got you back. I'm not letting you out of my sight anytime soon. Plus, I want to get to know you. You're different now."

"You're different, too," I said. I wouldn't admit it to anyone, but having him with me would ease a lot of my anxiety.

"Come on," he said with a wide smile.

I followed him back to the kitchen.

The Four Warlords stood in a huddle in the kitchen, and I could smell the food cooking.

"Everything alright?" Durlan asked, his eyes catching mine.

The other three turned to face Ryul and me.

Ryul draped an arm around my shoulders. "Everything is great."

Despite the possessive gesture, I smiled. Everything was alright. At least, as alright as my insane life could be.

"How long until food is ready?" I asked Durlan, shrugged out of Ryul's hold, and jumped up to sit on the counter behind the Warlords.

"Twenty minutes," Amrynn answered.

I kicked my legs back and forth, remembering how I did the same thing as a child while the chef made me a snack.

"Tomorrow, we'll all return to our sectors," Venali informed me. "You'll go back with Durlan."

"Okay," I agreed.

Ryul looked at me, expectantly.

"There's a slight change to plans," I said.

Venali's lip twitched, and he glanced at Ryul.

"Ryul will be accompanying me," I informed them.

They all opened their mouths to argue.

I raised my hand. "This is non-negotiable."

"Why?" Kydrus asked.

"Because I am not going to leave him alone in the castle any longer than I already have. And, having him at my side will ensure I am safe."

"You'll be safe by our sides as well," Venali said with a frown.

I smiled at him. "This is not because I doubt your ability to protect me."

"Very well," Durlan said.

Venali and Kydrys spun to face him.

"But, you will need to follow some ground rules," Durlan added.

Ryul leaned his hip against the counter beside me. "Such as?"

"No killing, unless your life is legitimately in danger," Durlan said and held up one finger.

"Okay."

"You will leave punishment of anyone who attacks Elara to the assigned warlord," Durlan continued and held up a second finger.

"Fine," Ryul agreed, but the tick in his jaw let me know he didn't like that.

"And finally, you will give us five hours each day alone with Elara to train and teach her," Durlan said with a third finger raised.

Ryul's jaw clenched, as did his fists. "Five?"

"Should be ten," Venali grumbled.

"Five hours minimum. We have a lot to teach her, and your presence will be a distraction," Durlan said.

Durlan wasn't wrong about that.

"If I sense her life in danger, I will come to her aid, no matter the time," Ryul said.

"We're capable of—" Kydrus started with a growl.

"Agreed," Durlan said, raising his voice to be heard over Kydrus. "But, if you interrupt more than three times using that excuse, we will lock you up during our sessions."

Ryul's tense shoulders and locked jaw led me to believe he wasn't happy with this arrangement. However, he said, "I agree."

Durlan nodded once to finalize their agreement.

Looking at the other three men, it was obvious they didn't like the agreement either.

Amrynn had turned his back to us, and Kydrus's jaw was clenched so tight that his skin was white.

Venali kept gripping and releasing his sword's pommel like he was debating using it against Ryul.

"Venali," I whispered.

He released his pommel and looked at me. "Yes?"

"Walk with me?" I requested and hopped down. As I headed towards the hallway, I wondered how I would be able to handle these five. They were bound to fight at some point.

Venali walked beside me, his right hand resting on his sword's pommel, but at least he wasn't gripping it anymore.

"I understand this is not an ideal situation for you," I said softly to him once we were far enough away from the kitchen that the others wouldn't hear us. This hallway was one I had used the most as a child. I'd run from my room to the kitchen, or sometimes, I brought my father and his advisors snacks in his war room.

"I don't trust him. You have no idea what he has been up to for the last thousand years. And, I don't like how informal he is with you." Venali's hand tightened on his pommel.

"I've known you for an even shorter amount of time." I stopped and turned to face him, glad he was a bit back, so I didn't have to tilt my head so much. "I have no idea if I can trust you. The four of you, or even one of you, could be planning to murder me."

"I would ne—"

I raised my hand. "I am just pointing out that I am going on a lot of faith with all five of you. The least you could do is try to get along. I don't want you killing each other."

His right hand dropped to his side.

"In one day, my life was flipped upside down. I don't know what to do, so I've put my trust in you all. If I focus on the negative possibilities, I'll go insane. There are too many unknowns. Yes, he is informal with me. But, so are you four. I like it. I prefer it. I want you to be the real you. I want to get to know who you really are, not a courtly shell. How am I supposed to choose a mate if I don't know you? This whole mate or mates thing is really stressful, and it's only been a day! If I have to learn about each sector, learn all the life basics, date each of you, *and* worry about you killing each other, I'm going to die of insanity."

Venali pulled me against him, his arms wrapped around me like a cocoon. "I promise not to kill him unless he is trying to kill you or one of the other warlords. I'm sorry. I didn't mean to add to your stress. And, this is the real me. I'll never be anything else with you."

"Promise?" I mumbled into his shirt. He smelled so good. I wanted to roll in his scent, like a cat in catnip.

He tilted my chin up. "I promise."

I knew it was coming, and yet the kiss still made me gasp. His lips seared mine, and I wondered what it would feel like if his lips touched other places on my body.

Durlan cleared his throat down the hallway.

I stepped back from Venali, my cheeks burning.

"Food is ready," he informed us and went back into the kitchen.

Venali smoothed down my hair and pushed it out of my face. "I'm really looking forward to my month with you."

So was I.

"Come on. I'm hungry," I said with a coy smile.

He smiled back, and we returned to the others.

Our meal was a somber affair, and I returned to my room as soon as I finished eating.

I wanted to be loved. But I was being too forward with them. I barely knew these men. I shouldn't have let them kiss me until after at least a month of courting. Throwing myself at them was not a good idea.

A fun idea, but not good in the long term.

I fell onto my bed with a groan. How was I supposed to resist them when I'd be alone with each of them for a month at a time?

I was a horrible person. I'd remembered I was royalty, and now I had no issues courting five men at once, with the option of keeping them all.

My mother would have fainted if she'd seen me now.

I should enjoy life, but I needed to set boundaries.

Awful, horrible, boring, but necessary boundaries. The queen couldn't be seen making out with men in public. No matter how tempting the men were.

CHAPTER 8
VENALI

SHE WAS TOO TRUSTING, but for some reason I found myself agreeing with her judgment.

Elara was beautiful, smart, and I was falling fast for this young woman. Part of me thought I was thinking with my lower body instead of my brain.

Yet, I also couldn't discount the way she made me feel when I was with her. Or, even when just thinking about her.

No other woman had drawn my attention like her. Sure, I'd slept with other women, but Elara was the type that you wanted to show off and hide at the same time.

I wanted her by my side, to ensure no one ever hurt her again. I wanted others to see me with her. I wanted to hide her from every other man in the world.

She was a fighter and there was a connection between us that I could not deny. That I did not *want* to deny.

I would do everything in my power to keep her safe and happy. Even if that meant sacrificing myself. She would change the world. I could feel it.

I wanted to be by her side when she did, but watching her from the heavens would be good enough for me.

CHAPTER 9
ELARA

"YOU'RE GOING TO KILL ME," I gasped, sitting on the ground outside Durlan's house.

Ryul rolled his eyes. "Stop being dramatic."

Every night, Ryul spent an hour teaching me to control my magic. Apparently, my type of magic was hereditary, and he had done a lot of research on it during the thousand years I had kept him waiting.

"Can't I try planetary travel?" I asked. That would be way more fun than just channeling the stars' power.

"Absolutely not," Durlan said from the chair where he sat, reading a book. He set the book down. "What if you can't come back?"

I tugged on a blade of grass. "Minloa doesn't know I exist yet, so it wouldn't be that big of a deal or loss."

Ryul thumped me on the top of my head.

"Ouch," I hissed.

He scowled down at me. "You are not going to another planet. I'm not going to lose you again."

"I didn't say I was going to," I grumbled.

"Let's stop for the night," Durlan said and stood.

I lay on my back, looking up at the stars. "I'll stay here for a bit."

Durlan sat beside me and began massaging my temples.

I closed my eyes and sighed in pleasure. With so little physical contact most of my life, I craved it now. It was addictive.

"Shooting star," I said, raised my hand, and pointed while keeping my eyes closed.

"What else can you sense?" Ryul asked. "Can you sense the planets and whether there is life on them?"

"There's no life on the three planets closest to us. I can't feel beyond that."

"What type of planets are they?" Durlan asked, still massaging my head, but moving to my scalp.

"Only one of the three are a type we could inhabit. The other two have strange ecosystems. One is really hot."

"Could you draw a map of the system?" Durlan asked.

I nodded.

"Tomorrow, I would like you to do that," he whispered.

"I'm going to Amrynn's in a week, right?" I asked and opened my eyes to look up at Durlan.

"Yes," he answered.

The weeks had flown by. I wasn't sure where the time had gone. I had learned a lot, though. I could read well, and my writing was improving. Durlan had also given me a run-down of the current affairs. Which, to be honest, was boring. My slavery was the most talked about news in decades.

When the time came, Amrynn teleported near us, a smile on his face. "Good evening. Are you two ready to go?"

I hurried inside, grabbing the few items I had brought to Durlan's, and returned to the three men. "Ready."

Durlan pulled me into a hug, and I squeezed him back. "Stay safe and learn as much as you can."

"I will," I said with a salute.

Amrynn held out his hand, and I set mine in it, giving his a squeeze.

Ryul took my free hand, shouldering my bag for me, and saluted Durlan. "See you in a few months."

I smiled at Durlan, just before Amrynn teleported us to his house.

"Welcome to, Blustum," he announced, releasing my hand to gesture down the hallway. "Your rooms await you."

"Same room as at Durlan's?" I questioned, heading down the hallway towards the bedrooms.

"Yes. We thought it might make it easier for you to stay in the same room at each of our houses," Amrynn answered, following me slowly.

Amrynn's house was decorated in blues, reminding me of water and the sky during the day.

"Thank you. I think it will make it a bit easier." I pushed open the door and stared in silence at the room. It had the essentials: bed, dresser, side table. But it also had several clothing racks and over ten pairs of shoes on the far side. "What is this?"

"You don't have very many clothes," Amrynn said. "I thought you might like to pick some out. These should all be your size, but if they need altering, I can summon my tailor. The shoes should be your size as well, but if there is something specific that you want, please don't hesitate to ask."

I was in dire need of some new clothes. Living in Linta, I didn't make much money, and didn't want to spend what I had on frivolous things like clothes. Now that I had access to my wealth again, there was no reason for me not to upgrade my wardrobe.

I turned and hugged Amrynn, pressing a kiss to the side of his neck before I spun back around and started going through the clothes.

"Can I talk to you?" Ryul asked.

I turned, but he was speaking to Amrynn.

"Shout if you need me," Amrynn said, and shut the door with a smile.

I resumed my browsing and then started throwing clothing items I wanted to try on, and the ones I knew I wanted to keep. There had to be over one hundred outfits on the racks. Once I finished making my piles: yes, maybe, and hell-no, I turned to the shoes. I needed boots, sneakers, high heels, and flat sandals.

I looked at the pile of clothes and chose a pretty sundress I'd seen first. I tried it on, slipped on a pair of flat sandals, and stood before the full-length mirror in the bedroom. It made me look feminine and dainty. Old me wouldn't have worn it. But I wasn't that shy, timid girl anymore.

Someone knocked on the door. "Come in," I called while still admiring the dress.

"I was hoping you might pick that one," Amrynn said.

I twirled, letting the skirt flare around me as I turned to face him, a wide smile on my face. "It's beautiful."

He leaned against the doorjamb and smiled. "The woman makes the dress, my queen. And, you far outshine that scrap of cloth."

Amrynn, the wordsmith. He was by far the best with words and knew just how to use them to his advantage.

I'd gotten a bit of intel on him from Durlan before I'd come to prepare myself.

I curtsied and bowed my head. "Thank you."

He took my hand and twirled me around before pulling me against him in a dancer's hold. "Do you know how to dance, my queen?"

"Elara," I reprimanded him.

He smirked. "Elara. Do you know how to dance, Elara?"

"I remember a little from when I was a girl, but it has been a very long time."

"Then I shall be forced to teach you," he said with a dramatic sigh, spun me, and then dipped me.

When he brought me back up, I smiled wide, like a lovestruck idiot.

"Tonight, you should rest, though. Tomorrow will be a full day of learning." He bowed over my hand and kissed the back of it. "Good night, Elara."

I watched him leave, warmth blossoming on my cheeks long after he had left. I locked the door, and then flopped down onto the bed atop my piles of clothes. These men were so much older than me, so much more experienced. I was in over my head.

And, if I were being honest with myself, I loved every minute of it.

Quickly, I went through the clothes, tried on the ones I needed to, and then used the racks to separate the ones I was keeping and the ones I would be returning.

As I went to sleep, I pondered over the warlords. I felt no ill will from any of them and believed I could trust them, but could I really? Ryul was the only one I knew without a doubt wouldn't hurt me. The others were old, had much longer lives behind them, and were well-versed in deceit. They could play a long game of lies and subterfuge, stringing me along until they got what they wanted. I had to ensure that didn't happen. I had to ensure that they did not betray me like Feno had my parents.

Could I convince them to make an oath, like Ryul had?

It would definitely help me sleep better.

I would talk to them individually. I felt certain that Venali would make one as soon as I asked. Kydrus was the one I was most concerned with. He seemed like he cared for me, but he was always scowling when he looked at me. He was always the quickest to anger. Was it because he felt stupid for not realizing who I was? Or was it because of something else?

Politics made my brain hurt!

And, I had only begun to enter the political arena.

"Why couldn't I have been a farmer?" I muttered to myself.

"THIS IS TRE," AMRYNN INTRODUCED ME TO A MIDDLE-AGED man with golden hair. The man stood in the middle of the dining room, which had been emptied of furniture.

Tre held out his hand. "Nice to make your acquaintance," he said in a rich, honeyed voice.

I shook his hand and curtsied. "Nice to make your acquaintance as well, Tre. I'm Elara."

"Tre will be teaching you to dance," Amrynn explained.

I looked at him and he smirked. "Although I would love to teach you to dance, Tre is a much better teacher. I'll assist you with practicing, but Tre will be the one to teach you the steps and moves."

"Okay." I smiled and gave Tre a nod. "Ready when you are."

Tre waved his hand, and a white sphere floated out of a bag from the ground to his hand. He whispered something to the sphere, tossed it into the air, and then music began to play.

My eyes widened, and I stood, mesmerized by the sphere.

"It's my special brand of magic," Tre explained. "It will play the songs for us, and I can make it pause or go back to the beginning if need be."

"That is amazing," I whispered.

He chuckled and looked over my head at Amrynn. "She's adorable. I like her."

"Don't get attached," Amrynn said, smiling wide enough for his canines to show.

Tre rolled his eyes. "You know I don't shop in that store."

I tilted my head and scowled. "What?"

"I prefer men as sexual partners," Tre said, lifting his brow.

"Oh," I said and chuckled. "Shop at that store. That's a good one."

Tre held out his hand. "Shall we begin? Our dear warlord has informed me that you have some basic knowledge of dancing."

I nodded. "I can waltz. Or, at least when I was six I could."

"Six? The last time you danced was when you were a child?" Tre asked, scowling.

I nodded again.

He glared at Amrynn. "Whatever rock you found her under, blow it up. This beautiful woman should be gracing dance floors across Minloa. Don't worry, darling. I'm going to teach you all of our dances, so you can outshine every other woman in Minloa."

"She already does," Amrynn said.

I didn't need to look at him to know he was smiling.

Tre snickered. "Our warlord is besought with you. I don't think I've ever seen him flirt so openly with a woman before."

"He made one comment," I mumbled. "I hardly call that openly flirting."

"For him, it is," Tre said. The music started from the beginning, and Tre led me into the waltz. I followed him, surprised with how easy he was to dance with. He taught me a few other dances, some of which I remembered as well, and then waved behind me. "You dance with her. I may just be too good of a lead."

I expected Amrynn to come, but instead, Ryul took my hand and pulled me into starting position.

"You know how to dance?" I asked.

He smirked. "I was born and raised to become your guard. I've been trained to dance and continued to practice during your absence."

"Who did you practice with?" I asked, trying to hide my smirk and failing.

"I practiced alone," he said.

"Well, let's see if your solo dancing translates to dancing with me." I turned to Tre. "Ready."

Tre started the music, and Ryul led me into the dance smoothly. We spun around the room, and I became lost in Ryul's eyes. He spun me away, spun me back, and then dipped me as the song ended.

The world faded, only Ryul existed.

He leaned forward and placed a gentle kiss to my lips and then stood us both up.

"I don't think she needs anymore dance lessons," Tre said.

I looked up, shocked to see Amrynn standing inside the room, a scowl on his face.

"It appears not," Amrynn finally said.

Tre bowed to me and then left.

"What next then?" I asked Amrynn, smiling wide and trying to dispel the weird tension in the room.

"I'd like to take you out to the city," Amrynn said.

"We aren't announcing her yet." Ryul stepped between me and the warlord. "You showing up with her at your side will draw unwanted attention to her."

"It will be fine." Amrynn frowned at him and reached a hand out to me, crowding Ryul's space.

"I'm—" Ryul began and took a step to the side.

"This is my time with her. You will stay here. She will be safe with me," Amrynn snarled as he took my hand.

"Fine," Ryul huffed and then stomped from the room.

"Can I change first?" I asked.

"What's wrong with your current outfit?" Amrynn asked, looking over my pants and shirt.

"If I'm going to be in public with you, I'd like to at least look presentable," I said, rolling my eyes at him.

He strode towards me, a hunger in his eyes that excited me. "You are one of the most gorgeous women in Minloa. You could wear a burlap sack, and every man will be jealous of me being beside you." He bent and kissed my cheek. "But, if you'd like to change, I will not stop you."

I leaned into his warmth, tilted my chin up slightly and stood on tiptoe to brush my lips against his. "I'll be quick."

I hurried out of the room before I tried anything more with him. I wanted to touch him. I wanted him to touch me. I wanted to do so much, and yet I needed to hold myself back.

Once in my room, I stared at the clothing racks before me. What should I wear? The town would see me at Amrynn's side. Even if they didn't know that he was my guard and possible future mate, I wanted to look as good as I could.

I grabbed the sundress I'd tried on in front of Amrynn the previous night and slipped on the same sandals. After running a brush through my hair, I hurried out of the room, almost colliding with Amrynn who stood outside my door.

"Ready?" he asked, his eyes raking over me.

"One second," I said, walked to Ryul's room, and knocked on his door.

He opened it, a scowl on his face, but when he saw me, the scowl was replaced by wide eyes and a look I couldn't decipher.

"I just wanted to let you know that we are leaving," I said.

He looked over my head at Amrynn. "Okay. I'll see you when you get back."

"Okay." I gave him a quick hug, and then spun away before he could hug me back.

I walked by Amrynn and out the front door, waiting for him to catch up to me.

"This way," he said, hands clasped behind his back.

At his side, we walked away from his house, and towards the main city, Crol, down at the bottom of the hill. Unlike Linta, Amrynn's house was not in the middle of the city. He said he preferred to look over his city and to be able to see the entire area to know where he might be needed.

"Anything I should know? Is Crol different than Linta?" I asked.

"Not that I know of. People are used to me making random visits, but they do tend to come out in droves to see me and talk to me. Just stay by my side, okay? I doubt anyone will try anything, especially since they have no idea who you are, but I'd rather be safe than sorry."

"So, just avoid the glares of the women and stay by your side. Got it," I said with a nod.

He scoffed, but didn't deny it.

The town was comprised of mostly houses with a few lower level store fronts. There was also a healer's hut and a fruit and vegetable market.

A heavenly smell caught my attention, and I tried to discretely sniff it out, but Amrynn noticed.

He smiled. "That's our baker. I'll buy you a pastry when we get down there."

"I love pastries," I said with a wide smile.

"What else do you love?" he asked, turning away from me to smile and wave at a few people outside.

"Swimming, though I'm not very good at it. Listening to the sound of a waterfall, or the sound of rain. Running water, I guess would be a better general explanation. I love sweets but try to avoid them because I got really sick on chocolate one year. I loved dresses as a girl, but most of my life I couldn't afford dresses. I love hugs and hate—"

I snapped my mouth shut. Why was I rambling so much?

"Hate what?" Amrynn prompted, moving a bit closer to me.

"I hate being alone," I finished.

"Amrynn," a tall brunette woman with the most gorgeous figure I'd ever seen called out.

Amrynn stopped and smiled at her. A full, genuine smile. "Hello, Alicia."

She walked right up to him, gave him a hug, squishing her large breasts against his chest, and then kissed him on his cheek. "Where have you been? You don't usually go so long between visits."

He stepped back from her, his smile still in place. "I've been busy. Sorry if I worried you."

"Oh, who is your friend?" she asked, looking at me down her nose.

"This is Elara. Elara, this is Alicia." Amrynn's smile still didn't falter.

I held out my hand, smiling politely. "Nice to meet you."

"Did you take in another stray?" Alicia asked with a scowl at Amrynn, ignoring my hand.

I dropped it but kept my smile on. "Don't worry, I'm only here for a couple of weeks. Then, I'll be out of your hair."

"Oh? Are you a relative?" she asked, eyebrows raised.

"No," Amrynn and I said at the same time.

"I'm giving her a tour, so you'll have to excuse us. I'll come see you another day," he told her, placed his hand on my lower back, and gently pushed me forward.

We walked away from her, and I could feel her eyes like daggers in my back.

"So, why aren't you mated to her?" I asked. I'd wanted to be nonchalant but decided for blunt instead.

"She's too aggressive, as you found out. She thinks she is better than others, and that's not something I like. I've told her on several occasions that I'm not interested in mating with her, but she hasn't taken the hint."

Instead of responding, I walked up to the nearest vendor and perused their wares. The fact that he would turn down a woman as gorgeous as her, surprised me.

Then again, he hadn't said that he hadn't slept with her.

My guards were all over one thousand years old. I didn't want to know how many sexual partners they had had.

It was certainly far more than my number...two.

"See anything you like?" Amrynn asked over my shoulder.

"Everything is lovely." I smiled at the seller before walking back out to the main street.

"What's troubling you?" he asked softly, drawing closer to me.

"Just frustrated that I'm so inexperienced compared to you five," I whispered.

"We're at your service. Our experience will help us better assist you," he whispered back.

Naughty images filtered through my head of ways his experience could assist me. I coughed and lowered my head so my hair would cover my face and the blush that was there.

"So, what about those pastries?" I asked.

When we returned, Ryul sat on the front porch with his sword in his lap, polishing it. He didn't even look up before asking, "Did you have a nice time?"

"I did." I sat beside him. "But, sandals were not the right choice for so much walking."

Ryul sheathed his sword, snatched my legs, spun me sideways, and removed my sandals all before I could yelp. His warm hands began massaging my feet, and I moaned as I closed my eyes.

"Your feet are still stinky even after a thousand years." He huffed a laugh.

Eyes still closed, I smacked his shoulder playfully, a smile on my lips.

"Can I skip practicing tonight?" I asked Ryul, opening one of my eyes just a slit to be able to see him.

He chuckled. "No. You need to constantly work on your powers."

"Why? It's not like I use them for anything."

"Not yet, but you will. At some point, you will find the power almost too irresistible and will want to use it. I want to get you as prepared as I can, to keep you from destroying our planet or any nearby planets," Ryul said as he continued working on my feet.

"That would be very unfortunate," Amrynn said, leaning against the front of his house. "I rather like our planet."

"Are you ready for dinner?" Ryul asked.

"Yes, please." My stomach growled at his question, luckily it was too soft for him to hear.

"You cooked?" Amrynn asked, an eyebrow arched.

"I lived alone in the castle for a thousand years. I had to learn to cook," Ryul said with a shrug and put my sandals back on.

"I lived alone and only learned how to roast a rabbit," I muttered as I wiggled my toes, stood, entered the house, and headed for the dining room.

"You didn't have a kitchen like the one in the castle," Ryul said, catching up to me.

"True." I sniffed the air, not hiding the gesture this time.

The smell emanating from the kitchen told me that Ryul had learned to cook well, and I was really looking forward to tasting his food.

I sat at the dining table, knowing he wouldn't let me help him, and waited as he set a covered plate before me. He removed the cover, and I stared in disbelief at the roasted potatoes, chicken, and cooked carrots. It was plated just like our chef used to make them when I was a child.

"This looks amazing," I said with awe.

"Hopefully, it tastes at least as good as it looks." Ryul's eyes sparkled as he gave a bow. "Enjoy your meal."

He started to walk away and I called after him. "Wait. You're going to leave me to eat alone?"

Amrynn sat down beside me and smiled. "Of course not. I was just washing my hands."

I looked down at my dust covered hands and grimaced. "I should do that as well."

I hurried to the bathroom, washed my hands, and then returned to my seat and dug in. Amrynn and Ryul sat with me, but neither ate anything.

"Did you two already eat?" I asked between bites. "Amrynn, you were with me. You didn't have dinner yet."

"I'll eat in a bit," he said. "I like watching you enjoy your food."

"I ate earlier." Ryul shrugged. "I had to try the food and make sure it tasted good."

"It's amazing," I said and smiled at him. I resumed eating and felt a little warmth return to my normally cold heart. Having people to eat food with was a minor thing, but it meant the world to me.

"There have been reports of attacks on the ocean a few miles from shore," Ryul told Amrynn.

"How many?" Amrynn asked.

"Five in the past week," Ryul answered. "They're taking the supplies from the ships and then destroying them.

"Do their attacks seem to be making any patterns?" Amrynn asked, his brows furrowed.

"Not that I know of, but I don't know your area well," Ryul said.

"Wait. Why are you telling him about events in his own sector?" I asked.

"We found it was easiest if Ryul helped with requests for help while you are training with us," Amrynn said. "He can handle minor issues or bring up issues like this one to me. We don't want to leave you unguarded, so there will be times when one of us must leave to handle whatever is going on."

That made sense. Ryul was strong enough to be a warlord, and could handle whatever the other warlords could. But, it bothered me that they had to split up duties like this because of me.

"What do you want to do?" Ryul asked Amrynn.

"I'll go down and take a look at what's going on. I suspect pirates. If that's the case, I may need more than just the two of us to take them down. The last pirate crew I ran into had several strong members." Amrynn cringed as he recalled the memory. "I'd rather be over prepared than underprepared."

"Agreed." Ryul glanced at me. "Would you prefer Venali goes with you or stays with Elara?"

"Venali?" I asked.

Amrynn nodded. "He's our best fighter. I generally call him for backup when fighting tough enemies. In this case, I could have him stay to protect you instead, though."

"Oh, okay," I mumbled. I would rather go with them, but I knew that would never happen.

I took my plate to the kitchen and washed it.

When would I be useful? When would I be able to take the throne and work towards protecting Minloa? I wanted to do it now, but there was still so much to learn.

"I'll go talk to Venali," Amrynn said, walking into the kitchen. "Ryul will stay with you."

I turned and smiled. "Okay. See you when you get back."

He leaned down and kissed me. "I'll come back as soon as I can."

I watched him leave with my jaw barely staying closed. They were being so forward with me. Kissing me like it was something we just did now.

Was it? Was kissing just something we did now?

Not that I was complaining, but normally people waited a month, didn't they? I hadn't exactly been part of the courting ladies, so I didn't really know.

"El, what's going on in that head of yours? Your facial expressions are all over the place," Ryul asked as he entered the kitchen.

"There's just a lot for me to learn." I chewed my lip, half answering him.

"Come on, I want to give you something." Ryul gestured for me to follow and walked out of the kitchen.

I hurried to catch up, biting my tongue to keep from asking what it was. I hated surprises.

Ryul walked into his room, leaving the door open behind him. I hadn't been into his room, or any of the warlords' rooms. I hesitated at the door, looking in and watching him riffling through his bag.

He turned, a book in his hand, and smirked. "Afraid?"

I scowled. "No."

He held out the book, standing in the middle of his room.

It was just a room. Yet, it felt like so much more. It felt like this step meant something. It felt like this was a milestone in our relationship.

Ryul kept watching me, his smirk still in place, and hand raised with the book.

I wanted this. I wanted to move forward with Ryul. With all of them.

With a small step, I entered his room. Then a few more steps brought me to him and the book, which I took. There was no title on the outside.

"What is it?" I asked, opening the first page.

"History of Minloa," he answered. "I found it in your father's study."

"You totally snooped through the entire castle, didn't you?" I asked with a grin.

He shrugged. "What else was I supposed to do for a thousand years?"

Good point. I totally would have snooped, too.

"I haven't read much of it, but it dates back thousands of years before your father was crowned," Ryul said, looking between me and the book in my hands.

I closed the book, and took it to the living room so I could get comfortable and read.

"Do you want a snack?" he asked.

"We just ate." I said, a hand on my belly, but my eyes remained on the book. He didn't respond after a minute, so I answered, "Yes."

I heard his chuckle, but it was far away, likely in the kitchen already.

Stacking up pillows, I got comfortable, and started reading.

CHAPTER 10
ELARA

"How long has she been reading?" Amrynn asked when he returned with Venali sometime later.

I ignored him, engrossed in the history of Minloa. Of things I had never even dreamed of being possible. Our version of Minloa was drastically different. How had things changed so much?

"Four hours," Ryul answered around a yawn. "I was expecting her to fall asleep, but she hasn't put it down."

"Can't. Too interesting," I muttered, giving them my first response.

"She is alive!" Ryul exclaimed. "I thought she'd turned into a vegetable."

"Do you know what a shapeshifter is?" I asked, setting the book down to look at the men.

"Something that changes its shape?" Venali guessed.

"A person, who can turn into an animal and vice versa. They often exhibit animalistic behaviors as well. There are werewolves, werelions, werepanthers, and so much more!" I exclaimed.

"I've never heard of that before," Amrynn said and glanced at Venali.

"Me neither. What book is that?" Venali approached, a hand out towards my book.

I pulled it close to my chest. "You can't have it."

He smiled, sat down beside me on the couch, and said, "I just want to look. You can hold it out towards me if you don't want me to touch it."

I did just that, turning the book so he could see the passage I was reading.

"I recognize that handwriting from several of my scrolls. I believe this may be a legitimate historical document," Venali mumbled. "Durlan would be able to tell us once he touches it."

"Where did they all go?" I asked softly, resuming my reading.

"We're going to go to my study and discuss strategies for tomorrow," Amrynn said.

I waved. "Have fun."

Venali was the last to leave, lingering a bit. "You look well," he finally said.

I realized I hadn't even said hi to him. After setting the book down, I rose and hugged him. "Hi. I'm sorry. I wasn't trying to be rude. I'm just really interested in the book."

He hugged me tightly and bent to kiss my cheek. "It's alright. I know better than to come between someone and a good book. I still have a scar from the time I interrupted Kydrus." He kissed me again and said, "I'm looking forward to spending time with you tomorrow."

"Same," I breathed, hoping he couldn't hear how hard my heart was pounding.

He left me then, a smile on his face, and I returned to my book. I needed to find out what had happened to the shapeshifters.

"Alright, that's enough for tonight," Ryul growled and picked me up from the couch.

I clutched my book to my chest. "One more chapter," I begged.

"You're drooling on Amrynn's couch. You look undead. It is time for you to sleep. Just think, the sooner you get to sleep, the sooner you can wake up and read."

He had a point.

"Fine," I said and yawned, stretching my arms up over my head, and avoiding smacking him in the head as he carried me.

"You going to be alright without me tomorrow?" he asked.

"I'll have Venali to keep me company." I yawned again. "Just, be sure to come home tomorrow night. Unharmed. Okay?"

He set me down at my door and gave me a grand bow, complete with flourish. "As you wish, my queen."

I grabbed him for a quick hug and then shut my door.

I woke the next morning to Venali cooking in the kitchen. I sat at a stool, watching him.

"They left really early, and didn't want to wake you," he said.

"I figured they would sneak out early," I replied with a shrug. "It's okay."

"How do you like your eggs?" Venali asked.

"Uh, I don't know," I answered. "Cooked?"

He chuckled. "Okay. My choice, then."

He moved about the kitchen expertly, never dropping anything, or looking for something. He just grabbed what he needed and used it. Would I be like that some day?

When he finished cooking, he carried two plates to the dining room, and sat beside me as we ate. I'd expected him to sit across from me, but I actually preferred him sitting next to me.

"These eggs are really good," I said around a mouthful. They were mixed together instead of fried, like Ryul usually made them.

"I'm glad you like them. We call them scrambled eggs," he said. "They're my favorite. Especially, when put on a sandwich."

"Sandwich? That sounds good."

"Maybe I'll make you one for breakfast tomorrow."

"You don't think they'll be back tonight?" I asked, worry gnawing at me.

"They may spend most of today just searching for the pirates," he said, offering a reassuring smile. "Don't worry, Amrynn can handle himself. And, Ryul seems like he can as well."

"I hope so," I muttered. "Maybe it would be better if you went with them? I can just stay here? Or, you could take me to Kydrus."

"Are you trying to get rid of me?" he asked and stuck his lip out in a pout.

I scoffed. "That is not the case, at all." His lip looked so plump. I wanted to touch it, to see if it was as soft as it looked.

He stood, took my empty plate and his, and went to the kitchen.

I grabbed the history book from my room and sat on the couch in the living room, resuming my reading. There had been a war between the shapeshifters, Unseelie, and Seelie fae. I wanted to find out what the ending was.

Venali sat beside me, draping his arm around my shoulders, and began reading a book of his own. I tried to glance over at the book, but he had it angled in a way that I couldn't read it.

I closed my book and examined him. He looked well-rested and completely relaxed. Did he enjoy peace? He was their best fighter, and from the few Seelie fighters I knew, they preferred battle to peace.

My fingers reached towards his scar on impulse, but I froze and jerked my hand away.

He raised his eyes to mine. "You can touch the scars. They don't hurt me anymore."

"What happened?" I asked.

Scarring a fae was very difficult. It had to be a really deep cut that a healer was not nearby to heal, or done with a blood blade. Supposedly, all blood blades were destroyed now.

"During the Great War, I fought an Unseelie general named Lance. He was vicious, fast, and reveled in torturing his victims. He killed one of my friends before I could get there. We fought, and I realized one of the reasons he was able to defeat so many Seelie. Blood blades. He'd had blood blades attached to the tips of his fingernails. So, whenever he scratched you, the wounds bled profusely, and it cost you a lot of your strength and stamina."

Tucking my legs beneath me, I turned to face him, sitting up, engrossed in his story.

"I'd just sunk my blade into his stomach, when he tried to scratch out my eye."

I looked at the magenta eye, glad that such a beautiful eye hadn't been taken.

"I had to stab him again to kill him, but he left me with these mementos to remember him by."

I reached out and traced his scars with my fingertips. Had he scratched Venali earlier in the battle, Venali may not have lived to tell the story.

Venali closed his eyes as I traced the scars, his breath hitching a moment.

"I'm glad you killed him, and that you survived," I whispered, dropping my hand to his chest.

He rested his hand over mine and opened his eyes. "Me, too."

Our lips met, but I wasn't sure who had initiated the kiss. It didn't matter. I was just glad that we were kissing. He wrapped his hand around the back of my neck and deepened our kiss, his tongue sliding along mine.

I moaned into his mouth, and he growled in the back of his throat.

Normally, that would have frightened me, but I knew Venali wouldn't hurt me.

I slid onto his lap, slipped my fingers into his thick hair, and kissed him ferociously. He tasted like smoke and pines. It was intoxicating.

"Elara," he whispered, pulling back from the kiss. "I need to ask you something."

Warning bells rang in my head. I sat back beside him on the couch. "Okay?"

"Are you going to be okay with having multiple mates?"

I blinked. "Am I going to be okay? Shouldn't I be asking you that? Are you going to be okay sharing me?"

He smiled. "As long as I can claim a piece of your soul, I will be happy."

He already had it. Which was absurd, since I barely knew him. Yet, he did.

"I need to ask you something," I whispered, gnawing on my lower lip and avoiding his eyes.

He tilted my chin up with his forefinger. "Ask."

"Will you take an oath for me? The same one Ryul took?"

"Absolutely," he said with a nod.

I'd expected hesitation. A moment for him to debate his answer. But, he'd answered almost before I had finished my question.

"Really?"

He smiled and brushed his lips across mine. "I already plan to keep you safe. The oath will make you feel better, which will help our relationship. I have no plans to ever hurt you, so the oath will not hinder me in any way."

"What if you decide you don't want to be my warlord? Or don't want to be my mate?" I asked.

"If you decide you don't want me as a mate, the oath will still not hurt me. If I go insane and try to hurt you, I want the oath to kill me."

"I don't want you to die," I whispered, the thought bringing tears to my eyes.

He kissed each of my eyes, clearing away the tears. "We all die eventually, Elara. I will make the oath. Would you prefer Kydrus officiates it?"

"Kydrus?"

He nodded. "He is well versed in oaths."

"Okay." I hadn't really spoken to Kydrus much. I was certain he was mad at me.

"What is it?" Venali asked, staring into my eyes.

"Have you talked to Kydrus? Since you guys found me?"

He nodded. "Several times."

"Is he...mad at me?"

He smiled. "No, but I think Kydrus should answer your questions when it comes to how he feels. Come, let's go visit him. We can kill two birds with one stone."

He stood, picked me up as he did, and teleported us to Kydrus's house, right into his living room.

"Kydrus?" I called, climbing out of Venali's arms and walking into the hallway. "Are you home?"

"Elara?" he asked, coming out of his study with a deep scowl. "What's wrong? How did you get here?"

"I brought her," Venali said and stepped out into the hallway. "There's no emergency."

Kydrus's scowl lessened. "Oh. Did you need something?"

I looked down at my hands, which were tugging on the end of my shirt. I'd been able to interact with the others much more easily with my memories back. But, when it came to Kydrus, it just wasn't the same. We had a history. One where I had been a royal pain in his ass.

"Go on," Venali urged. "He's not going to hurt you. Are you, Kydrus?"

"I'll never harm you, Elara," Kydrus whispered. "You know you can ask me anything."

"I'll just wait in the living room," Venali said, abandoning me to the hallway, alone with Kydrus.

"Are you mad at me?" I asked Kydrus. "I know I lied. I know I hid my powers, but I really was scared." I looked up at him, tears shimmering on the edges of my vision. "I really believed you might kill me for my powers."

Kydrus took a slow step forward, and then another, approaching me cautiously since I often flinched or shied away from him. He reached out, took my hands, and squeezed them gently. "I'm not mad at you. I was never mad at you. I was hurt that you thought I might kill you, but when I looked at it from your perspective, I understood. You viewed the warlords as terrifying men with magic rivaled by few. You know our job is to keep the peace, and your magic is one that could cause a lot of issues. I was hurt that you didn't trust me, but I understand. I didn't at the time. Can we talk in my study a moment? I have something I want to tell you."

"Venali, we're going to talk in his study a moment," I called out.

"Okay. I'll just read while I wait," Venali called back.

Kydrus waved me to his study, and I walked into the familiar room, sitting in the chair I always sat in. Today, however, Kydrus chose to sit in the chair beside me instead of his chair behind his desk. "I'm sorry for not protecting you adequately when you lived here," he said. "Had I known how poorly the others were treating you, I would have done more."

"I didn't want you to know," I admitted to him. "I felt like a burden to you already."

He smiled, and it stole my breath. "You were never a burden or a bother. You were one of the few bright moments in my time here as warlord. When I saw you fall off the cliff, I feared you might be gone forever. I tried to find you, but you were swept away too quickly. I'm sorry that I wasn't there to protect you."

"You can't always be by my side," I reminded him. "Plus, I didn't think anyone would actually try to kill me."

"They're jealous of you," he said.

"How?" I asked, an eyebrow arched.

"You're beautiful, you catch the eye of anyone you pass by, and you draw people to you. Many people don't like that. They don't like being drawn to a person. Had they known you were royalty, they would have understood. Your bloodline draws us, makes us feel safe and happy, because you are destined to rule us."

"I think destiny is a dick," I mumbled.

Kydrus laughed, and I startled. I hadn't heard him laugh before.

"I should have recognized who you were, but I chalked my draw to you up to just who you were. You've always drawn me."

"You never said anything," I whispered around a gulp.

His smile wilted. "You were always scared of me. Worried I was going to hurt you. I didn't want to try to kiss you for fear it would be using my title to make you do something you didn't truly want to do."

"You...wanted to kiss me?" I asked.

He brushed his fingertips across my cheek. "Since I first saw you."

"I...I don't know what to say," I admitted.

"May I kiss you?" he whispered breathlessly, his eyebrows furrowing slightly as he focused on me.

I leaned forward and pressed my lips to his. He hesitated a moment, and then returned the kiss, gently and carefully, like he thought I might run away.

Scooting forward on the chair, I found his hands, pulled them around to my back, and kissed him again.

He hugged me against him, pulling me practically into his lap as he kissed me.

"I'm sorry that I hurt your feelings," I whispered when we separated. "I never intended to do so."

"Was this the reason you came to see me? Or was there something else?" Kydrus asked.

"I'd like you to perform an oath binding on Venali," I said. "He's agreed to it."

"Like Ryul's?"

I nodded. Good guess.

"Venali," Kydrus called and stood, going to his desk and taking something out.

Venali entered, looked over my face, focusing a bit on my lips, which were likely red from our kissing, and then smiled.

Smiled.

"You ready to perform the oath?" Venali asked, moving his gaze to Kydrus.

Kydrus set a stick on his desk, and a bowl. "Yes. Where are we putting the markings?"

"I figure the same place as Ryul's works," Venali said. "Someplace visible."

"It will glow when you're near her, which might blow her cover when she comes to your sector," Kydrus said.

Venali shrugged. "They'll assume I'm courting her, which I am, so I'm okay with that."

Courting. So strange to hear that word in regards to me.

"Alright," Kydrus agreed.

Venali stepped around the desk, standing beside Kydrus.

Kydrus touched the tip of the stick into the bowl which now had a weird ink in it. He spoke in the old tongue, most of which I didn't understand, and began to draw the symbols on Venali's arm. The symbols glowed once finished, and Venali's teeth clenched against the pain. Ryul told me that it felt like they were slicing his skin open with fire when he'd had it done.

I stepped forward, placed my hand over the symbols when the last one was drawn, and waited as Kydrus finished with a question.

Venali responded, "I make this oath of my own free will and agree to all terms."

Power zipped through me, making me gasp, and then the symbols glowed so brightly that I had to close my eyes.

The glow stopped, and I removed my hand.

"My turn," Kydrus said.

"What?" I asked, looking up at him.

He smiled. "Venali came to me because he can't perform the spell on himself. But he can perform it on me."

"You don't have to—"

"I know, but I want to," Kydrus said. "Hopefully, it will help you to relax around me a bit more once you know I won't and can't hurt you."

Venali took the stick from Kydrus, and we repeated the procedure.

Once done, I stared at their arms. They'd really done it. They'd really made an oath to never harm me. I couldn't believe it.

I threw my arms around Kydrus first, and then Venali. "Thank you," I whispered to them, tears leaking from the corners of my eyes.

"We would do almost anything you asked of us," Kydrus whispered and wiped one side of my eye.

Venali wiped the other side. "We will always be here for you."

I had no words to reply to them. How does one reply to such devotion?

"Would you like something to eat?" Kydrus asked.

"Actually, we should head back to Amrynn's. I don't know when they'll be back, and I don't want them to freak out if we aren't there," Venali said.

"He's right," I admitted with a sigh. I hugged Kydrus again and brushed my lips gently across his. "Thank you, again."

"I'll see you soon." He offered another smile that made my breath hitch.

I stepped back, took Venali's hand, and waved to Kydrus before Venali teleported us back to Amrynn's.

Venali sat in one of the giant reclining chairs, and without asking, I sat in his lap, angling my body a bit so that we were both comfortable and could read.

Venali gave me a peck on the cheek and opened his book.

I could definitely get used to this.

We cuddled in silence while we read until lunch. Then he made me lunch despite my protests that I wanted to make something. After we ate, we cuddled together more.

Touching. I loved touching and cuddling.

"I expected you to be more active," I said as I ate a snack he'd just brought.

"Active?" he asked, titling his head as he looked at me.

"You're the best fighter in Minloa. I figured you would be outside practicing or training, but you seem perfectly at ease just sitting and reading."

He smirked. "Even fighters need their downtime. It's good for your mind and soul to take breaks from training. Reading is good for you in general."

"We exiled the shapeshifters," I told him. "And banished the Unseelie to their island."

"What?" he asked.

I pointed at my book. "The Unseelie and shapeshifters fought us. They didn't like that the Seelie were always in control. It caused a war, one that the Seelie won, and we banished them from Minloa."

"There's no way that we used to live side by side with the Unseelie." He frowned. "They're evil."

I shrugged. "It says that we did. That the only reason we

banished them is because of the war and that they tried to usurp us."

"Why would our predecessors live with them?" His brow lifted as he peered at my book.

If they were evil, I wondered that too. But, perhaps the Unseelie weren't as evil as we thought. I knew very little about them, though, to make any determinations or judgments.

"I don't like that look on your face," he mumbled.

"Just pondering questions I don't have answers for," I said. "Don't worry, I'm not going on a journey to find them. I'm just thinking about them."

"If you do decide to run off, take me with you, okay?"

I smiled and kissed him. "Okay. You can be my adventure buddy."

He smirked. "I like the sound of that."

"Have you ever traveled out of Minloa? To one of the other continents?" I asked.

He shook his head. "No. I had heard some traveled out and never returned."

"I wonder what else is out there?" I asked. "What else this planet, Anderelle, has?"

"Can you sense other life forms outside of Minloa?" he asked.

I nodded. "Lots of them, but they're far enough away not to worry me."

"Can you tell what they are? Are they fae?"

I shook my head. "I can't sense what they are, just that they are humanoid. There are actually several other land masses like Minloa where these people live."

"Interesting," Venali whispered, his gaze going distant as his mind wandered.

My mind went to those other places. Did they have monarchies there? Did they also have magic? Where they fae? Or something else?

"It's late," Venali finally said.

"Will you wake me if they return?" I asked with a pout.

He nodded. "I will."

I stood, and headed towards my room but paused. "Promise?"

He smiled. "I promise."

I gave him a smile in return and went to bed, but my mind would not quiet. There was so much unknown out in the world. Out in the universe. It was terrifying and exciting at the same time.

CHAPTER 11
ELARA

Ryul and Amrynn did not return that night. Or the next night.

"Can we please go search for them?" I begged Venali for the hundredth time.

"I'm not putting you in danger. They brought me here to keep you safe." He frowned, but his eyes were sympathetic.

"They might need us! At least go look for them, please. Take me to Kydrus or Durlan."

He pulled me into a hug and stroked my hair. "It's going to be alright. Calm down, sweetheart."

I hadn't realized that I was so worked up until he hugged me. I clung to him and whispered, "Please, Venali."

"Alright. Let's go see Durlan," he said with a sigh.

When we teleported into Durlan's office, he immediately rushed over. "What's wrong?"

"She's fine," Venali assured him. "She's just worried about Amrynn and Ryul. They still haven't returned from their mission."

Durlan's brows furrowed. "They might be having a hard time finding the ship."

"Can you please check on them?" I asked, feeling like I was overreacting now that we stood with Durlan.

"I'll grab Kydrus and we'll go check out the situation." Durlan nodded, his hands clenched into fists. "You two head back to Amrynn's, in case we miss each other and they return."

I hugged him. "Thank you."

Venali grabbed me again and teleported us back. "Go sit on the couch and read. I'll make you something to drink to help soothe your nerves."

A drink wouldn't do anything, but I nodded and sat on the couch.

He returned with snacks as well as tea and set them on the table next to me. Then, he draped a blanket over my legs, and sat beside me.

"Tell me a story?" I asked as I closed my book.

"What type of story?"

I shrugged. "One about you, preferably. I'd like to learn more about you."

He silently contemplated a moment, and then started his story. "I went on a mission once, one I thought I could handle on my own. There had been a rash of thefts in a small village near my home. I went to the village, hid beneath a cloak, and stayed with a poor family. They said they never saw who the thieves were because they wore masks and dark clothes, attacking at night when there was very little light. I hid amongst the shadows, waiting for the thieves to show themselves."

I leaned forward, fully invested in this story, waiting to see what happened.

"I didn't see them," he continued. "But I heard screams coming from the house I had been staying at. I ran as fast as I could, but I was too late. They had killed the family, knowing somehow that I had been staying there. The thieves had also gotten away. Disappeared with no trace of their existence, except for the dead people. I staked the village out for two more nights. Finally, they returned. This time I saw them. There were ten of them. They moved with a stealth spell, which made it harder to see them. However, I'd been trained to see through those types of spells. I charged them, roaring my fury, and cut off two of their heads before they fought back. They'd never had someone able to see them before, so they were surprised, despite my war cry. Once they realized I was able to see them, they attacked. Mind you, I was only twenty or so at the time, so I didn't have the training I do now. I killed two more, but the others incapacitated me. They tied me up and took me back to their cave where they'd been hiding out and storing their loot. And, their other victims."

My hand raised to my mouth.

He exhaled. "They'd been taking women back to their cave. It took me half a day to recuperate. The next half of the day, I watched them and learned as much as I could. While they were sleeping, I managed to free myself from the bonds and freed the women. The men woke up after I'd freed the women, and I had to battle them again. I defeated them, but not without being heavily injured."

I couldn't help myself, I reached out and grabbed one of his hands.

He smiled and patted my hand with a smile. "I didn't know how to teleport yet, so I lay by their fire, their dead bodies around me, and waited for my body to heal itself. Two days later, people from the town came. The girls had returned and told them what had happened. When I didn't return, they feared the worst and came to check on me, prepared to bury my body if need be. I learned then that it wasn't always smart to take on things alone. It is better to be over prepared, than under prepared."

"Did you tell me this story to try to remind me not to run off on my own?" I asked, leaning back with a cocked brow.

He chuckled and kissed my cheek. "My story may have served two purposes. Will you tell me a story now?"

"What kind of story?" I asked nervously. I had more bad stories than good ones.

"Whichever one you are comfortable sharing with me," he said.

"Let me think a moment." I pondered over the stories I had.

He readjusted his sitting position so he could look at me easier.

"When I was a child, I'm not sure what age, my parents took me to the beach. It was my first time. I remember staring at the ocean from the beach, and thinking it never ended. I turned to my mother and asked if the water would swallow us up in the future."

Venali chuckled.

"She assured me that the water would not swallow us up. Once I was assured, I didn't want to leave the beach. I loved watching the waves and listening to them crashing on the sand. I actually fell asleep watching the waves, and my father had to carry me back home."

"They loved you, very much," Venali said softly. "I saw them with you once, and the pride and love for you shone brightly."

"I miss them," I whispered. "I can't believe they're dead. I mean, I know they are, but it's just hard knowing I won't see them again."

Venali hugged me tightly. "I'm sorry."

"You didn't kill him," I whispered, melting against him. "You weren't there to be able to stop it either."

What had happened that night? Where had the rest of the guards been?

"Do you want to learn some fighting moves today?" he asked as he stroked my hair.

I hadn't had a man stroke my hair before. It was very relaxing.

"Not today," I whispered.

He chuckled softly but continued stroking my hair.

"If you could do anything right now, what would you do?" he asked.

Dirty thoughts ran through my head, but I quickly pushed those away. "Visit the beach," I said and laughed. "Talking about it made me remember how much fun it was."

"When you come visit me, I'll take you," he promised.

"If you could do anything, what would you do?" I asked back.

His hand stilled on my hair. "I'm not sure," he admitted. "Right now, I'm pretty content to sit here and pet you."

"I'm pretty content to be pet," I whispered, my eyelids starting to droop.

"You're so beautiful," he whispered in my ear. "You smell amazing, too," he said and inhaled from the top of my head.

"What do I smell like?" I asked, my lower body tightening.

"A goddess," he whispered back, kissed my head, then my cheek, and worked his way down to my neck.

I gasped and arched into him.

"You're such a touchy person. How did you survive living alone all those years?" he asked, sliding his hands down my sides, and then around to the small of my back. He pulled me forward, until I sat in his lap.

"I don't know," I said breathlessly. "I think I may be addicted now. I don't think I'll be able to live alone again."

He slid his hands beneath my shirt, his warm, large palms sliding along my bare skin. "I promise, you won't have to." He kissed my collar bone, making me gasp softly, which then made him growl.

"I shouldn't be so forward with you," I whispered, not moving away from him even a hair. "Even as my guard, I shouldn't be like this."

"You can feel it," he whispered. "The pull. Our connection. I don't know what it is for certain, but it is definitely not just attraction."

"Is it because of the oath?" I asked, but I knew it wasn't. I'd felt it since I met them. I'd just been ignoring it.

"You know it's not," he said, pushing me back so he could look into my eyes. "There's something drawing us together. Part of me thinks that's a sign to run, but the rest of me thinks that part is a coward, and that you're perfect."

Heat rose to my cheeks. "I'm far from perfect."

"Perfect for me," he whispered.

"Venali, we hardly know each other," I reminded him.

"I saw your past. I've glimpsed more than what Durlan showed us. It's part of my powers. I can see your desires, and I know that you are a beautiful woman, inside and out. You want to be loved. You want to help people. You want the life you deserve to have. And I want to give it to you."

His lips crashed into mine, and there was nothing gentle about it this time. He lay me down on the couch, positioning himself above me, and slid up my shirt so he could rest his hand on my stomach. I kissed him back, need and want filling me in equal measures. He brushed his thumb along the bottom of my breast and I gasped as I arched up into him.

I hadn't been touched there before by a man.

He slid his hand up slowly, giving me ample time to stop him, but I didn't dare. He cupped my breast, and groaned into my mouth.

He broke the kiss, pushed my shirt up to expose my breasts, and moaned again. "You are gorgeous, Elara."

I tugged at his shirt. "Fair is fair."

He smirked, removed his shirt, and I let my hands wander over his chest and abdominal muscles. He was so ripped. So much more muscular than most of the men I'd seen in Linta with shirts off.

He cupped a breast in each hand, and slowly ran his thumb over my peaked nipples. They were so sensitive and just his touch made me moan in pleasure. He lowered his head, never breaking eye contact with me, and drew my nipple into his mouth. Once fully inside his mouth, he sucked and ran his tongue over it. I let out a cry and then slapped a hand over my mouth.

He smiled. "Don't be afraid to make noises, Elara. I want to hear you moan and scream my name."

"What if the others come back?" I asked.

"Would you prefer we move this to your room?"

This. What was this?

"I don't think I'm ready for-"

"I know," he said. "I'm not suggesting we have sex. Yet." He picked me up, pressing our chests together, and I wrapped my legs around his waist. My nipples ached as they rubbed against his chest. Then he carried me to my room.

He shut my door behind him, and then lay me down on my bed, immediately taking my other nipple into his mouth.

I arched up into him again, gasping. He slid a hand down between my legs and rubbed me through my pants. He drew his mouth away. "Is this too fast?"

I shook my head, trying to resist from rubbing myself against his hand.

He smiled, kissed me deeply, and continued rubbing me. He broke the kiss to flick his tongue over one of my nipples and then the other.

"Yes," I gasped, giving in and grinding myself against his hand.

"I want you to come for me, Elara. I want you to come, knowing that I was the one who did it."

"Yes, Venali," I answered, gasping in breaths.

His growl was one of satisfaction, and I realized that he enjoyed me saying his name.

I grabbed his hand, slid it into my pants, and moaned as soon as he touched my warm core.

"You're so wet," he growled, sliding one finger in slowly.

"Venali!" I gasped.

He growled, bit my neck, and began pumping his finger in and out of me, while rubbing my sensitive nub with his thumb.

My senses were on overload. I made sounds I had never made before, and then bit his shoulder to stop them.

He licked my neck, used his free hand to squeeze my breasts, and then whispered in my ear, "Elara."

I released his shoulder and screamed his name as stars danced before my eyes and the pleasure crashed over me. I thought it would be a single experience, but it came in waves, and the pleasure began building again as he continued to pump his finger in an out of me.

I thought there couldn't be anything better, and then he slid a second finger in with the first, and I gripped his back with my fingers, trying not to scratch him, but hardly paying attention.

"Say it again," he whispered as he pumped his fingers faster and faster.

The pleasure grew again, and another round of waves crashed over me. "Venali!"

This time, he removed his fingers, and gathered me up, cradling me against his chest, our bare skin touching, and he lay down with me draped across his chest.

We lay together in silence for a long time, my heart slowing and my body boneless in satisfaction.

"What do you think our connection is?" I asked Venali. "And, why didn't it show up all these years that I've been with Kydrus?"

He shrugged. "I don't know. Maybe the time just wasn't right. Maybe you weren't ready."

Ready? How could I have ever been ready for this?

I walked to the living room, put my shirt back on, and then stood with my mouth opening and closing but no sound coming out.

"Hi," Ryul said, while Amrynn smiled at me. Durlan snickered but kept healing Amrynn. Kydrus was nowhere to be seen.

"Uh, how long have you been here?" I asked, heat rising to my cheeks.

"We just got back," Amrynn answered. "Durlan was healing us, and Kydrus went to try to find you."

"Found them," Kydrus said behind me.

I yelped and spun around.

Everyone laughed.

Venali snagged his shirt from the couch and put it on. "So, what happened? Did you catch the pirates?"

Kydrus nudged my hip, pushing me towards the couch. I sat, and he sat beside me.

"It took us two days to find them. When we did, they were ready for us," Amrynn said. He snarled, his lips pulling back to reveal his sharp canines. "We defeated them, but it took a lot out of me."

"I couldn't use my illusion power, since it is still up over the castle," Ryul explained.

"We should hire guards for the castle," I said. "Then, you can take the illusion off."

"What do we tell people who see the castle?" Amrynn asked.

"That we've been rebuilding it because you've found the queen," I said.

"You want us to announce you? Why?" Durlan asked.

"Not me specifically, just that you've found the lost princess, queen, whatever," I said. "I don't think we should hide it. I think people should know that we are going to go back to a monarchy."

"That the warlords are off the market?" Venali asked with a smirk.

"I don't care about that," I said and meant it. I trusted that they wouldn't cheat on me. Not that they were my mates yet, anyway, but yeah. "It's going to take the people a bit to get used to the idea of a monarch coming back. There are going to be some who don't like it."

"Which is why we want to wait until you're ready," Kydrus said.

"Will I ever be ready?" I asked, looking at each of them. "Really? I don't think anyone is ever truly ready to be queen or king. They just take the position and listen to their advisers. And, I have five of the best advisers in all of Minloa."

They didn't look convinced.

"Let me finish my visit here, and then go with Venali, and once I've visited all of the sectors, we can make our final decision," I acquiesced.

"Skipping me?" Kydrus asked.

I looked at him out of the corner of my eye. "I know enough about Silpo for a lifetime."

He hooked his arm around my waist and pulled me close. "I apologized about that."

I kissed his cheek. "I know."

"What happened while we were gone?" Amrynn asked us.

Kydrus and Venali held out their arms, showing the other three the oath marks.

All three of the other men's eyes widened.

"It's not mandatory," I said quickly and dropped my eyes to the floor.

"Would you prefer us to make an oath as well?" Amrynn asked.

I didn't know how to respond to that. I would prefer it, yes, but I didn't want them to think they had to. I wanted it to be their decision. Yes, I had asked Venali, but that was different. Right?

"That's a yes," Amrynn whispered.

Ryul chuckled. "It's okay to tell them how you feel."

"I don't want anyone doing anything they don't want to do," I said, jerking my head up to meet their eyes. "I don't want to overstep my place. I don't want you to do things because I'm technically queen."

"You aren't 'technically queen'. You are queen," Kydrus said, squeezing me. "Even if we haven't told anyone else yet."

"Kydrus, will you perform the oath for us?" Amrynn asked.

"Durlan didn't say he wants to do it," I said quickly.

Durlan smiled and stopped healing Amrynn to face me. "I most certainly will take the oath."

"You don't—"

"We know it isn't required," Durlan said. "We already plan to keep you safe. The oath will help with your peace of mind, though."

Hadn't that been what Kydrus had said? Had they already discussed this without me knowing? Were they already prepared to do this?

"I'm very suspicious of you all," I mumbled, eyeing the five men.

The smiles they gave me were equaling disconcerting.

"Kydrus?" Amrynn asked again.

Kydrus kissed my cheek and stood. "I assume you have everything in your office?" he asked Amrynn.

Amrynn nodded. "I may not be able to perform it, but I have all the supplies."

"Good," Kydrus said and the three of them left.

I walked to Ryul and hugged him. "You were gone too long."

He hugged me back, pulling me into his lap. "I'm sorry. There was no way to avoid it."

"You came back, so I guess I'll forgive you. This time."

"How gracious, my queen." He chuckled.

"I am a gracious queen," I agreed.

"You and Kydrus seem to be better," he said.

I nodded. "We talked and got some things out in the open. Now we are good."

"Good," he said, pushing me back to look at me. "You look happier."

"I feel better. Happier." I glanced at Venali, but quickly looked away. "I'm finally accepting my destiny, I think."

"Elara," Kydrus called. "We need you."

"Oh, right!" I shouted and leapt up from Ryul's lap. "I forgot." I hurried to the office and rushed over to the three warlords.

I set my hand on Amrynn, who was the one making the oath currently, and then repeated for Durlan. Once done, we all made our way to the kitchen for drinks and snacks.

I stared at the five men before me, disbelief, warmth, and so many other emotions swirling within me. I wanted to thank them. I wanted to kiss them. I wanted to do so much, but I just stayed silent and watched them work side by side in the kitchen.

How had I become so lucky?

CHAPTER 12
RYUL

I'd waited over one thousand years for Elara. All those years, I'd worried that she had died, and that my magic had failed her.

When she'd walked into the courtyard and yelled out for me, I had been certain I was dreaming. Her mother's beauty paired with her father's confidence had turned Elara into a gorgeous woman.

I'd daydreamed about what she would look like, had pictured her when taking care of my needs. But my imagination could not compare to the real thing.

She was beauty personified.

During my time alone, training and intelligence recognizance had been my pastime. To be her guard, her mate, I had to be as perfect as possible. I had to ensure that I did not fail her, as her parents had been failed.

Had I known she would encounter and round up the four warlords, I might have gone to her first. They weren't bad men, but I had envisioned Elara and I being together, alone. Now, I had four other men to compete with for her time.

My protective instincts were gone when around the warlords

now that they had all taken their oaths. It helped me sleep easier knowing that they would not harm her.

I could see she already cared for them and them for her. I knew she cared for me, which was all I needed.

She didn't understand the connection she and I shared. Part of her was still buried, forgotten, and I was worried how she would react when it finally freed itself.

Her magic was powerful, more powerful than it should have been with her bloodline. Her mother had chosen her father to help dilute the magic, but Elara was even more powerful than her mother had been.

I would need to train her extensively, quickly, and ensure she did not destroy us.

Had she known when she was a child about her powers, she could have easily destroyed the men who had kept her as a slave.

My teeth ground together, and a snarl ripped from my throat at the thought of them. Enslaving someone was horrid, but enslaving a child was inexcusable. The warlords had jurisdiction over his punishment, which irked me. I wanted to destroy him, hurt him ten times for every time he had hurt her.

The fact he had scarred her, a Seelie fae, meant he had used a whip laced with magic, or he had whipped her so many times, that it permanently scarred her.

I wanted to kiss every inch of her, to praise her as a goddess, and to show her that her scars mattered not to me. I would worship her for the rest of my days. I would do anything for her.

Even putting up with the warlords.

CHAPTER 13
ELARA

"There are two people in an argument, and both are claiming the property belongs to them. What do you do?" Amrynn asked.

Amrynn had begun teaching me about solving disputes. It was boring, frustrating, but totally necessary.

"What is the property?" I asked.

Ryul was in his room, giving Amrynn and I our alone time. Ever since the warlords had taken their oaths, Ryul had been much more trusting of them and willing to give us free time. It was nice.

"A dog."

"Can we make them stand far apart and call to the dog? Whoever the dog goes to wins?" I asked.

He chuckled. "What about if the property was a necklace?"

"Threaten to smash it?"

"Is that a question or statement?" he asked with a chuckle.

"Statement," I said with a nod, though I really wasn't sure.

"What if they both say they don't care or if they both yell out?"

"If they both say they don't care, then I smash it and move on.

If they both yell out, I flip a coin," I said, exasperated. "Do queens really have to deal with this crap?"

"Yes. A lot."

"Maybe I'll make that a warlord duty," I muttered.

"Good luck," he scoffed.

"Shouldn't I learn more about our laws?" I asked.

"Oh, there's an entire book for you to read," he said and laughed maniacally.

"That's such a reassuring and inspiring laugh," I said and stood.

He stood as well, pushed some of my hair behind my ear, and rested his hand on my cheek. "Let's go for a run," he whispered.

"Run?" I asked.

He nodded. "Get changed. Then, meet me back here."

I didn't really want to run, but I changed into my training clothes and sneakers, suspecting there was more to it than what he had said.

I stood in front of my mirror, trying to tie my hair back, but kept missing pieces.

"Want help?" Ryul asked.

I dropped my arms and sighed. "Yes, please."

He took my tie, gathered my hair up, and quickly tied it up. "There you go."

I turned and kissed his cheek. "Thank you."

He pulled me into a hug. "Where are you going?"

"For a run with Amrynn," I answered, breathless from being wrapped up in his arms. He was so handsome. So safe. So...Ryul.

"Train hard," he said, kissed me, and pushed me out of the room with a slap on my butt.

I snarled. "You're going to pay for that."

He chuckled. "Sweet words, with no bite."

"Oh, there will be a bite for you." I growled.

"Temptress." He purred.

I stumbled as I walked away, surprised by his flirting.

"You're keeping him waiting," he called after me.

I growled but hurried outside because he was right.

Amrynn looked me over, heat in his eyes a moment, but when he met my gaze, he extinguished it. "Ready?"

"I guess," I mumbled.

He smiled. "Come on. We will start off slow."

We started off at a slow jog, and he led me into the forests near his place. The animals skittered out of our way but didn't hide. There were several animals I had never seen before. I wanted to stop and ask about them but continued following Amrynn.

There were so many vibrant colors from not only plants, but animals, too.

"It's beautiful here," I whispered.

He sped up a bit. "It gets better."

I picked up my speed, eager to see what else he was going to show me. We ran down the animal trail, dodging low tree limbs, and jumping over fallen logs.

Noise assaulted my ears suddenly, making me skid to a stop. "What? What is that?"

"Come on, you'll see," he said, running again. I ran after him but yelled out when he jumped off a cliff right in front of us.

I looked over and glared down at where he swam in a deep pool of water. It was crystal clear, and we could see all the way to the bottom. The loud noise had been a waterfall that fell into the pool of water.

"Jump in." He waved up at me.

I obeyed, yelling out as I fell, and then closed my eyes and mouth before I hit the pool. The cool water surrounded me, and dragged me down a bit, weighing down my clothes.

I kicked and surfaced, gasping in a breath of air and wiping the water from my eyes.

Amrynn wrapped his arm around my waist, and pulled me against him. "See? This was much better than just running, right?"

"Yes," I said and moved away from him, floated on my back, and closed my eyes. "I missed the water." Lazily, I moved my arms, propelling myself around the lake or pond, or whatever it was.

"This is my favorite place to go. Especially if I need to think about something," Amrynn told me, his voice near my head.

I looked over and found him floating beside me. "Did you need to think about something today?"

"No. I heard that you liked water, and wanted to bring you here. You haven't really had much opportunity for relaxing. Figured it was time for you to have a little bit of fun."

"I have fun with you guys," I said and meant it. They often made me laugh, even during boring lessons.

"What do you want for your birthday?" he asked.

"What?" I scowled. "It's not my birthday."

"Your birthday is in two weeks," he said, frowning.

I dropped my lower legs into the water and faced him. "It is?"

His frown deepened, and he reached for my forehead. "Did your memories not fully return?"

"They are all here. I just didn't realize how much time had passed," I explained. "I thought it was still a month away."

He still looked worried.

"There isn't anything I want," I told him. "I have my memories back and I have you guys."

"There has to be something you want," he prodded.

"I'll think about it," I promised and started floating again.

"If you're unhappy, you can tell us. If there are things you want changed, you can tell us. We want you to be happy. We want to do whatever it is that will make you smile and laugh."

I wrapped my arms around his shoulders and kissed him. "You guys make me happy. I really don't have anything else I want."

"How much greedier could one girl be?" an unfamiliar female voice asked. "She's stolen our most eligible bachelor, and she still wants more things?"

"Why are you here?" Amrynn asked the girl over my shoulder. I didn't want to turn around and look at her, but my body betrayed me.

"Is this not open land? I'm allowed to walk around here. Or have you passed a new law?" she asked, an eyebrow arched.

She was gorgeous, had large breasts that almost spilled out of the top of her red dress, and long legs that were mostly visible with a huge slit down each of the sides. Her hair was almost silver in color, hung to her waist, and looked silky. Her eyes were full of fire, and I wondered if I could defeat her in a fight. What type of magic did she have?

"You know nothing of our relationship," Amrynn told her. "Do not speak to people as if you know them or what they think or feel."

She walked down to the shore before us. "You visit us less. You were gone, disappeared, for several days without letting anyone else know," she snapped. "You didn't do that type of thing before she came."

Amrynn climbed out, glaring at her. I stayed in the water, not wanting to give up my time yet.

Amrynn's lips were pulled back in a snarl. "I was on a mission for several days. That mission did not involve her. I did not notify any of you, because I had Venali here, watching over our sector. I do not answer to you. I do not have to explain my actions to you," he growled.

She scoffed. "We need to be protected. If you are not able to protect us anymore, perhaps we need a new—"

Her words were cut off by Amrynn's hand around her throat.

"I am Warlord. Not you. If you think you can usurp me,

please, try me. If not, then fuck off and leave Elara alone." His teeth snapped next to her face, and she whimpered, eyes wide with fear. He released her, and she ran from the area.

"That was a bit harsh," I whispered.

He sighed. "She needed a strong reminder not to mess with me."

"Well, I think she got the message," I whispered. I got the message and his wrath wasn't directed at me. I was slightly scared. Warlords were frightening men, filled with power. So much power. It was also really sexy. I was a horrible person to be turned on by his anger, yet here we were.

"I'm sorry," he whispered and swam back out to me.

"For what?" I asked, looking down at the small fish swimming below us.

"Scaring you," he said softly. "I don't ever want you to be frightened of me."

I traced the oath symbols on his arm and said, "I know you won't hurt me."

"I wouldn't have even without the oath," he whispered and captured my lips with his.

I wrapped my legs around his waist and kissed him back. His skin was so much warmer than usual. Was it from the sun? Or because the water was cooler.

He drew back. "If I am moving too fast, just tell me. Okay?"

I nodded and bit my lip.

"We should head back," he whispered, but kissed me again.

"We should."

He groaned and pushed me away gently. "If I keep touching you, I won't leave."

I laughed and followed him out of the water and back to his house. I wanted to hold his hand. The thought of that woman, or someone else, catching us had me fisting my hands at my sides instead.

"You're learning really fast," Amrynn said with a smile.

"Thanks."

I didn't feel like I was learning fast. I felt like I had a hundred years of things to learn. Was I going to have the same lifespan, since I'd been frozen? Or, was I already one thousand years down?

"Soon enough, you'll be taking the throne, and you won't have time for us," he said.

I stopped and turned to face him. "What are you talking about? I'll be spending most of my time with you five."

He chuckled. "I'm sorry. You just looked so concerned. I wanted to see if you were listening."

"Of course, I was listening to you. And, I was just thinking about my lifespan," I said and resumed walking.

He fell into step beside me. "Your lifespan?"

I nodded. "Just wondering if being frozen altered it."

"I'll have to talk to Ryul and find out."

We walked in silence, both of us lost in our own minds.

Ryul waved as we approached. "Have a nice run?"

I nodded, kissed his cheek as I passed, and went to the bathroom for a nice, long shower.

Using up all the hot water wasn't my intention, but I dried off quickly, and dressed in new clothes as fast as I could. My fingers were pruned from being in the water so long, but it was so worth it.

"In the living room," Amrynn called to me.

Ryul and Amrynn sat on different couches, Ryul writing a letter or something, and Amrynn with a book.

"What are you two up to?" I asked, running my fingers through my still damp hair.

"Relaxing," Amrynn answered without looking up.

Who should I sit next to? I'd just been with Amrynn, so it should be fine to sit with Ryul, right?

I was about to find out.

Instead of sitting right next to him, like I wanted to, I sat at the other end of the couch, folding my feet up beneath me.

I grabbed my book from where I'd left it on the table and began reading.

Hours passed in silence, and I found that I enjoyed just being near them while I read.

Amrynn cornered me in my room the morning I was supposed to leave to head to Venali's. He slid his hands along my sides, up and down my arms, and then intertwined our fingers.

"Don't be afraid to tell Venali if he is working you too hard. Sometimes he forgets that others don't have the same stamina as he does." Amrynn's words were soft, but his eyes were full of fire.

"Just say it already," I said with a smirk.

His lip twitched as he tried to hold back his smile, but then he gave in and smiled. "I'm going to miss you."

I kissed him deeply. "I'm going to miss you, too."

"You know, you can write to us while you're in the other sectors," he whispered, sliding his hands along my waist.

"I can't write well," I whispered back, my cheeks heating in embarrassment.

"Practice makes perfect," he said, smiling wide.

"Okay," I said with a sigh. "I'll write while I'm with Venali."

"Time to go," Ryul called through the door.

Amrynn kissed me deeply, our tongues intertwining just like our arms.

When he pulled back, we were both breathless.

He stroked my cheek with his fingertips and then opened my door and shoved me out of it. "I'll see you soon, my queen."

Not soon enough.

"Bye," I called over my shoulder and hurried outside to where Ryul and Venali waited.

"Ready?" Venali asked.

I nodded. "Ready."

He held out his hand, and I set mine in it. He gave me a gentle smile, then Ryul intertwined his fingers with my free hand, and we teleported to Venali's house.

"I'll take your bag to your room," Ryul said, releasing my hand and heading towards the bedroom.

"Anything eventful happened while we were apart?" Venali asked, leading me to his study.

I shook my head. "Nope. All quiet on the home front. What about here?"

"Nothing out of the ordinary," he replied, which wasn't really an answer. He sat in his chair behind his desk, and I sat in one of the chairs in front of it.

Ryul entered and took the vacant chair beside me. "Update?" he asked.

"Not much. It's been rather quiet," Venali answered.

"Too quiet?" Ryul asked.

Venali smirked. "I always think it's too quiet, but no. I don't think there is anything brewing. But I could be wrong."

"Let's hope you're not wrong," I whispered.

"Had enough excitement this month?" he asked.

I nodded and yawned.

"She hasn't been sleeping well," Ryul told Venali while looking at me.

"Nightmares?" Venali asked.

"No," I said.

"Yes," Ryul said.

I looked at him. "What?"

"You've been waking Amrynn and I up at night with your cries. You're having nightmares. Amrynn started sleeping in your bed at night to ease your fears, and that seemed to work," Ryul explained.

"I don't remember having nightmares and I sure as hell don't remember Amrynn being in my bed," I said. Not that I would be upset to find him in my bed.

"He left before you woke up each morning. We worried you might order us not to help you, but it was negatively affecting your health," Ryul told me. He turned to Venali. "I recommend you share a bed until we figure out what is causing the nightmares."

"You're okay with me sharing his bed?" I asked, an eyebrow raised.

He smirked. "They're your guards. They're going to be sharing your bed sooner or later."

I was speechless. He'd started off so jealous, but now he didn't mind me sharing a bed with one of them. Such a drastic change.

"Are you opposed to me sharing your bed?" Venali asked. "I can wait until you're asleep, if it would make you feel better."

I looked down, my blush so hot I thought my skin might melt off. "I'm fine sharing a bed."

"Good," Ryul said.

"Would you like to run a perimeter sweep?" Venali asked Ryul.

Ryul yawned. "Not tonight. I prefer to do a sweep while there's light the first time."

Venali nodded. "Smart."

"Can you show me your map?" I asked, still unable to look up at either man, settling for looking at them from my periphery.

"It's behind you on the wall," Venali answered.

I stood, even more embarrassed because I should have actually looked at his office when we entered, but I'd been more enthralled by the owner than the room.

There were a few knickknacks on his desk, but I wasn't sure what any of them were. His walls were lined with swords instead of bookshelves, which seemed rather fitting. One sword had a greenish tint to it, and I moved towards it.

Venali grabbed my wrist, stopping me from reaching the blade. "That's coated in magical poison. If the blade cuts you, you'll die within a day."

I flinched. "Noted. Don't touch green blades."

Ryul snorted behind me, but I ignored him.

Venali kissed my knuckles. "That's a good idea."

I turned to the map, trying to memorize as much of it as I could. It surprised me how alike the sectors were all set up. Not identical, but it seemed like they tried to make them somewhat similar. Was it to make it easier on the people?

"We made the sectors similar so we wouldn't have to worry about having to memorize several maps. It makes visiting each other and looking for each other much easier," Venali said.

I turned and gaped at him. "Did you just hear my thoughts?"

He chuckled. "No. I just assumed that's what you were thinking by the look on your face."

I looked at him from the corner of my eye. I wasn't sure I should believe him or not.

Ryul has a small penis. I thought.

Neither man said anything.

I exhaled a breath and resumed looking at the map. My eye drifted to the map of Minloa, specifically to the barren land around Klinsot and the castle. Was there a way to heal the land? To make it fertile and have acres and acres of crops, like we had when I was a kid.

Something tickled my nose. "Do you have the fireplace on?"

Venali scowled. "What? No, I don't—" His eyes widened, he grabbed a sword as long as he was tall from the wall, and ran from the room.

I ran after him, Ryul at my side. For once, he didn't stop me from running outside when there might be danger.

We stepped outside, and Ryul and I both gasped.

Fire. The town was on fire.

A loud roar had Ryul pushing me back onto the porch, and both of us looked for the source.

Where was Venali? I couldn't see him.

Venali roared nearby, our heads turned, and I gaped in shock.

Venali stood on the ground, holding the giant sword, and facing a real, live dragon.

I hadn't seen a dragon before. The last I'd heard, the warlords had culled their numbers on Minloa, and the only ones left were on different continents.

The dragon was red, easily three times that of an average horse, had spikes all down the middle of its body, and had massive wings, which it had currently flared out to make itself look larger. Not that it needed to look larger.

I wanted to call out to Venali, fear clawing at my chest to see him standing before the huge beast, but if I did, it could distract him. I didn't want to be the reason he got hurt.

"I need to help the town. Stay here, please. Let Venali handle the dragon, okay? Just stay on the porch."

I met Ryul's eyes. "Okay. Hurry." I could hear people yelling for help. "Make sure there's a healer. If there isn't one, contact Durlan."

Ryul kissed my cheek and ran from the house, headed towards the town, which was billowing smoke into the sky from the various fires.

Venali charged the dragon with a focused expression on his face, the dragon opened its mouth, and I bit my knuckles to keep from yelling out. The dragon spewed flames, but Venali slid beneath the fire, and struck with his sword, cutting the dragon's leg.

The dragon roared in pain, swiped at Venali with his other leg, long talons aimed to slice him apart.

Venali rolled away. Then he stabbed the sword into the dragon's side, burying it almost to the hilt.

I could barely breathe. I was so focused on Venali, on this fight, that I didn't care about anything else.

The dragon swung its head to the side and clamped its mouth around Venali, who cried out in pain.

"Venali!" I screamed, running towards him.

Without thought, I drew the power from the stars and our sun and blasted the dragon's eye with the light.

The dragon roared, opening its mouth and dropping Venali. It pawed its injured eye, but I was certain I had permanently blinded him.

Venali hopped up, jerked the sword from the dragon's side, and used it to slice the dragon's head off.

I collapsed to my knees, breathing heavily from using so much magic that quickly, and from relief that he was alive and moving.

Venali walked over, blood dripping from the bite wounds the dragon had inflicted and glared down at me. "What were you thinking?"

I opened my mouth and closed it several times before I could finally speak. "What?"

"You should not have left the porch. Ryul told you to stay there. What were you thinking?" He was snarling at me, his sharp canines shining in the light.

I stood, stared right into his stupid eyes, and said, "I was thinking that you were in a dragon's mouth and I needed to help you, you ungrateful jerk!" I spun to turn away, but he grabbed my arm, spun me back around, and kissed me.

I shoved his chest, and he released me.

"No," I growled.

"I'm sorry," he called after me as I stormed away. "You put yourself in danger. The dragon could have hurt you."

"You were in danger," I said, but didn't turn around to look at him. "I couldn't just let the damn dragon eat you."

"I'm sorry," he called again.

"Go help your people," I ordered him, stomped into the house, and slammed the door behind me.

"Men!" I yelled and then screamed wordlessly.

CHAPTER 14
ELARA

LUCKILY, the dragon caused no fatalities and very few injuries. One house was destroyed, but the owners were assured the house would be repaired within the month.

Venali offered to make a desk for me from the dragon's skull, but I refused. I had no idea what he ended up doing with the skull, or the rest of the dragon, but it wasn't on his lawn anymore.

I was still upset that he'd yelled at me for helping him. Especially, when Ryul had gotten upset with me as well, lecturing me when he returned to the house.

I ignored them for almost a full day, but I was slowly losing my anger, trying to see it from their point of view.

A few days later, and I'd put the event behind us. We had all been amped up in the heat of battle and the thought of losing each other.

"We're going to work on your hand to hand combat today," Venali said after I finished breakfast.

"Okay. I'll get changed." I had decided not to change out of pajamas that morning, because I had been so hungry.

"Meet us in the training ring," he said, eyes intense.

I saluted him as I walked away.

"You need to work on your writing after you train with Venali," Ryul called after me.

"Yes, sir," I called back.

I had sent two letters to Amrynn, but my writing still sucked. I feared I just had poor handwriting. I knew some people who claimed they couldn't improve theirs. What if I was the same?

After changing, I went outside, around the side of the house, down the hill, and to the dirt training arena Venali had. Venali stood in the center, talking to Ryul, who sat on the fence that surrounded the arena.

"We're having an audience today?" I asked, hopping over the fence to join Venali.

"He's going to assist," Venali said, though I was still confused.

"You don't need any assistance tossing my ass to the ground." I huffed and folded my arms across my chest.

He and Ryul laughed.

"We'll be gentle," Ryul said with a wink.

"Such gentlemen," I grumbled, stretching my arms and then my legs.

Venali smiled. "When you're ready, Your Majesty, attack me."

Alright. I could do this. I could fight them and not make a fool of myself. Right? Right. Maybe. Sure. Possibly.

Not a chance.

Raising my fists up to protect my face, I advanced, moving cautiously. I tried to keep them both in my sight, but Venali was making it impossible for me to see him and Ryul at the same time. He kept angling me in the opposite direction than I wanted to move.

Lunging forward, I tried to punch Venali, but he easily dodged and almost knocked my legs out from under me. I rolled away, coming up right next to Ryul, who had hopped down to join the fight.

Ryul tried to hit me, but I rolled away.

Now, I had a man on either side, both focused on me.

"How am I supposed to fight when you're on both sides?" I asked, keeping an eye on them.

"It depends on your opponents. I usually try to focus on one, attack him relentlessly and put him in his friends' line of sight."

"Easier said than done," I mumbled.

And, I doubted they would let that work for me here.

So, I decided to alter it a bit, and try to mix things up.

I ran at Ryul, kicking and hitting him as fast as I could. I felt Venali move closer, so I spun around, kicking at his stomach as hard as I could.

He caught my foot and jerked me forward.

I pushed off the ground, propelling myself up and onto him, wrapping my arms around his shoulders.

I'd expected him to release my leg, but he tightened his grip, preventing me from spinning around him like I had planned.

"While I enjoy hugs, I don't think hugging our enemy will make them admit defeat," Venali said, a wide smile on his face.

I shrugged, slightly out of breath. "It could work. Have you ever tried it?"

"No..." His smile became wry and his magenta eyes sparkled.

"Then, you don't know," I said.

"Come on, you brat," Ryul growled. "You need to take this seriously."

"I was," I said and kissed Venali's cheek before hoping down from his waist. "I planned to spin around him and choke him, but he didn't let go of my leg."

Venali laughed. "I knew you were up to something, but I didn't realize it was that."

"Let's go again," I said with determination.

We reset and tried again. This time, I didn't end up hugging him, but I still lost. We practiced ten more times, and each time I lost. But I was learning what did and didn't work.

"Break," Venali said.

I looked up from where I gasped for air. "Good idea."

Ryul pulled me up to my feet, and wrapped an arm around my waist to keep me up. "You hurt anywhere?"

"Nope. Just sore and tired," I said, leaning into him as we walked.

"You were improving, though," Venali came up beside me.

"Not much," I grumbled.

"You're better than you were this morning. That's all that matters." Venali offered a huge grin when we got to the house.

I gave him a smile, and then made my way to the bathroom for a nice shower.

After my shower, I felt clean but still exhausted. I trudged to Venali's office, and started writing my letters with Ryul nearby, scrutinizing my work.

"Ryul," Venali called.

"I'll be right back. Keep practicing." Ryul kissed my cheek and left the office.

I obeyed despite really wanting to follow and eavesdrop.

What could they be talking about?

Ryul returned a few minutes later, pointed to one of my letters, and said, "Fix that one."

I grumbled beneath my breath, crossed it out, and wrote it again.

Ryul nodded, satisfied.

"What did Venali need you for?" I kept my eyes still on my paper.

"Nothing important," he said.

I looked at him out of the corner of my eye.

He was smirking.

"You're a pain."

"You hate being left in the dark," he said. "Which is sad, because I'm not telling you."

"Whatever," I said with a sigh and gave up. He wouldn't tell me, so there was no use in pestering him.

"That's it?" he asked.

I looked at him. "What?"

He scowled at me. "That's it?"

"What's it?"

"You're not going to pester me more?" he asked.

I shook my head and focused back on my writing. "Nope. You won't tell me, so there is no point in asking again and again. We'll both just get frustrated."

He leaned back in his chair, staring at me.

Finished with my writing, I stood and stretched. "Done. What's next?"

"Go see Venali," he said with a dismissive wave of his hand.

I shrugged, happy to stretch my legs and searched the house for Venali. He wasn't on the first floor, though.

"Venali?" I called as I climbed the stairs to the second floor. In all this time, I hadn't been in any of the warlords' upper floors. I had no idea what they had up here.

From the looks of it, it was a bunch of bedrooms. I climbed to the next floor but stopped to take in the sight before me. It was a huge dining room, large enough to seat fifty people at least.

Venali sat at the end of the table, looking at a piece of parchment.

"Hey," I called out, heading towards him.

He waved.

"What are you doing?" I asked as I came to stand beside him.

"Looking over last-minute decisions," he answered.

I peeked over his shoulder. "For what?"

He folded it up before I could read it. "Amrynn said you are proficient in dancing."

I nodded. "Yes."

"Do you remember proper dining etiquette?" he asked.

I nodded again.

"Prove it," he said with a smirk.

I looked at the empty table. "Now?"

He rolled his eyes. "Downstairs, silly."

"Why were you up here, anyway?" I asked, taking another look at the room. It was larger than I thought. In addition to the table, there was a dance floor, a drink station, and a spot for a band. There were silver curtains hanging along the walls that gave it an ethereal feeling.

"You've never seen this room in Kydrus's house, have you?" Venali asked.

I shook my head. "I've never been above the first floor of any of the Warlords' houses. Except yours, today."

"Why not?" he asked, walking beside me as I headed for the exit.

I shrugged. "No reason to, I guess. I didn't want to snoop around."

"We don't have anything to hide from you. You're welcome to explore our homes."

I looked at him. "Should you be talking for the others like that?"

He chuckled. "We discuss a lot of things. And, we have known each other for over a thousand years. I can say with the utmost certainty that they would agree with me."

"If you say so," I mumbled, not fully believing him. Not that I was going to start snooping around their houses now that he'd said that anyways.

We walked down to the first floor, and Ryul was nowhere to be seen.

I scowled. Where could he have gone?

"He's on his border run," Venali said.

"What?" I asked, looking up at him.

"Every night he goes and runs around the border. It's to ease his worry, and for a bit of exercise," he explained, pulled out a chair at the dining table, and smiled reassuringly.

I sat without a response. Did it bother Venali that Ryul didn't trust him to protect me?

The table was set like it would be during a royal banquet. I stared at the three forks and a scowl pulled my eyebrows together. I had hated etiquette lessons. My instructor had been a mean old woman who smacked my hand whenever I had reached for the wrong fork.

"Silverware offends you?" Venali asked.

I snarled. "My prior teacher offends me."

He sat, tucking his napkin in his lap, and poured us both a cup of water. "Understandable. I've heard that etiquette teachers were the most hated."

"I had bruises from her. I thought I was going to have a scar on this hand," I said, examining my right one to see if there were any.

He took the raised hand, kissed it, and said, "Your hands are perfect."

"Flatterer." I gave him a coy smile while my cheeks heated.

He smiled in response and then said, "I've asked a few people to help with tonight."

On cue, two men walked in with platters of food. They set them down and left the room.

I put my napkin in my lap, took a tiny sip of water from my glass, and then smiled at Venali. "What a lovely presentation! You must tell me your chef's name so I might use him for a banquet at the palace."

His smile dropped a moment, but he quickly recovered. "Well, you're talking to the chef right now."

My eyes widened as I pretended to be surprised. "Oh, how lovely. You are such a well-rounded man. How are you still single?

I know a few girls who are very lovely that I am more than happy to send your way."

His smile dropped again "Okay, stop that."

I let my smile fall. "What?"

"Stop with this act," he said, with a slight curling of his upper lip.

I frowned, unsure why he was upset. "I'm just getting into the part. This is what I was trained to do."

"No. You don't have to do that. Just, be yourself. I just want to make sure you know which silverware to use and the other etiquette. I don't like this fake woman you're projecting."

"You realize that I'm going to have to act this way when we have royal events, right?"

"Why?"

"Because that's what monarchs do. We have to be nice, smile, and swap pleasantries with everyone. We have to pretend that we aren't bored out of our minds during these ridiculously long balls, and that the food their chef made isn't subpar to our father's, despite the fact he's not supposed to cook at all. This is what a queen does."

"You don't have to. You can just be yourself. Just because that was what they taught you, doesn't mean you have to follow it. You're starting the monarchy over. Be yourself. Don't be fake. Be the real you."

"The real me? I don't even know who the real me is anymore! I don't want to be a monarch. I want to live a peaceful life, but you five refuse. You five want me to be queen and rule Minloa. Fine. I've been trained for this. I will be queen, and to do that, I have to be fake. I have to smile even when I'm sad. I have to smile even if I'm fighting with someone. If someone calls me a whore and I overhear it, but they didn't say it to me directly, I have to ignore it. I've watched my mother do just that. I've watched my mother smile the entire night at a party, walk to her room, and then collapse and cry herself to sleep, not even bothering to remove her dress."

His eyes widened slightly. "You're going to change a lot in Minloa. Change how the monarchs are seen. Show the realm that monarchs are Seelie just like the rest of us. That you cry, bleed, and have fears as well."

"We are a beacon of hope. We are supposed to show the realm that even in the darkest of times, there is something to smile about. If you can't handle that, maybe you shouldn't be a guard."

His eyes darkened, and I immediately regretted my words, but they were already out there.

I picked up one of the forks. "This is for cheese and appetizers." I set it down, grabbed the next one and said, "This is for salad." I set it down and grabbed the last fork. "This is for the main course."

Shoving my chair back from the table, I left him sitting there in stunned silence, went to my room and locked my door for the first time ever, and lay on the bed with a sigh.

Why was I so upset? Because he was right. I could change things, but that felt like slapping my mother in her beautiful face. Like saying everything she did and endured was because she was too weak and pathetic to try to change things. My mother had been a beacon of light for me and many others. I didn't want to desecrate her memory just to make one man happy.

Then again, it would make me happier, too.

Not being queen would make me even happier, though.

"Elara?" Venali called softly through the door.

I didn't respond.

What would I even say to him?

He tried the door, found it locked, and sighed.

"Locked herself in her room?" Ryul asked.

"Yeah," Venali said. "I upset her."

"How?"

"Come on, there's food wasting in the dining room. I'll tell you what happened while we eat," Venali said.

"Okay."

I waited at least half an hour before heading to Venali's room to talk to him, but he wasn't there. I climbed into his bed, curling up beneath his blanket and fell asleep.

Sometime later, Venali climbed in behind me, wrapping his strong arms around me, and spooning his large body around mine. "I'm sorry."

I turned and kissed him. "No, I'm sorry. You're right."

"No, you're right. You will have to do things that I may not agree with, but I will have to bite my tongue. I'm just your guard. You will be queen and I have to defer to you."

I shook my head. "No. Please, don't do that. I don't want you to just be my guard. I want you to be—"

"What?" he asked, stroking his fingertips along my face and through my hair.

"My equal," I whispered. I wrapped my arms around his back and squeezed. "I want you guys to be my equals. Not just my guards, but my friends and my warlords."

"I can do that," he whispered and kissed me. "For you, I will do anything."

"I'm sorry I snapped at you," I whispered and kissed him back.

"I'm sorry I snarled at you." He left a trail of kisses along my neck.

"Venali, I don't like fighting with you."

He lifted his head to look down at me. "I don't like fighting with you either."

"Are we good?"

He smiled and brushed his lips across mine. "We're great."

I snuggled into him and fell asleep wrapped in his arms.

CHAPTER 15
AMRYNN

She was changing already.

I was glad and yet I wasn't. The sweet, innocent young woman we had met was turning into a beautiful and strong woman.

I stood outside, looking up at the stars and planets that she could touch and manipulate at her will.

What must it be like to have that much power?

I was powerful, but her power was different, stranger. Seelie would bow to her as soon as she showed them that power. Some would fear her. Some would worship her. Some would want her.

A snarl lifted up my lip. I was already jealous at the thought of others touching her. Not my fellow warlords, though.

One of the stars moved. A shooting star?

No. It moved in multiple different ways. What was it?

CHAPTER 16
ELARA

"Stop teasing me," I growled at Ryul.

He stood before me in just a towel, a smirk on his lips. "I'm not teasing you. I just got out of the shower."

"Put clothes on then." I squeezed my hands into fists, turning away from the drool-worthy sight that he was.

I heard the towel hit the floor and bit my lip to try to infuse my body with the willpower not to turn around and look. I'd come here to talk to him about my training and whether he thought it would be better for me to keep training with the warlords before I took power or if I was ready now. I hadn't expected to find him in just a towel, muscles and skin on display.

Warm hands slid along my bare arms. Ryul placed soft kisses along my neck, upper shoulders, and my jaw. "You need to relax, El."

I turned, keeping my eyes on his, and said, "I have a lot on my mind."

He smirked, and I watched as a droplet of water slid from his hairline, down the side of his face, and dripped from his chin to land on his chest.

I licked my lips, the desire to lick the droplet from his chest was so strong.

Ryul dropped to his knees, slid his fingers into the hem of my pants, and dragged them down slowly.

I gulped, watching as he undressed me.

He leaned forward, flicked his tongue out, and I gasped when it hit its mark.

"You need some distraction," he growled, stood, and crushed our mouths together.

I wrapped my arms around him, falling into the kiss.

He laid me down on the bed and slid inside me in the same movement.

I gasped into his mouth, arching against him.

He drew back and moaned. "I didn't realize you were so wet already. When was the last time you had sex?"

"I, uh, it's been awhile," I admitted.

He rocked back and slowly entered me again.

I may not have had sex in a long time, and hadn't had orgasms during sex then, but I had had orgasms from other things. But they were nothing like orgasms from sex.

I screamed into our kiss, which urged him to move faster.

I lost track of the number of orgasms I had before he withdrew, finishing on his towel on the floor.

Heat rose to my cheeks. I hadn't even thought about that. My hormones had overpowered my brain, which should have reminded me that pregnancy was not something we wanted right now.

He collapsed on the bed beside me, and I rolled over to lay my head on his chest.

He lazily stroked my arm.

"Is it always like that with you?" I asked.

He looked down at me and smirked. "No, it's usually better."

My eyes widened. "Better?"

He nodded. "Once you learn what really turns the other on, and what buttons to push, sex gets even better."

I didn't want to ask it. I shouldn't have asked it, but I did.

"How many women have you slept with?"

"Two," he admitted.

"That's it?" I asked, looking at him in disbelief.

He nodded. "I regretted both."

"Why?" I asked, petting his chest.

"Because they weren't you," he said. "It was during the time that I was mad at you."

"I don't care that you had sex with other women while I was gone. You had no idea what I was doing or where I was. Plus, we weren't a couple when you froze me."

"No, but I knew I would be your guard and future mate. I shouldn't have done it."

"Ryul, should I wait to become queen?"

He exhaled. "That's really up to you. I agree that you are learning really fast, and while there is still a lot for you to learn, I think you've learned enough to start as queen."

"I'm scared," I admitted.

He hugged me. "You've got the five of us. Everything will be fine."

I SAT WITH DURLAN AND RYUL ON THE GRASS, TELLING THEM about the various planets and stars in our solar system. I'd made a full circle with the warlords and was back at Durlan's. I decided to give them all one more rotation, and then I'd take over as queen. All had agreed.

"That's a cold planet," I told them. "We wouldn't survive long there."

"The entire thing is cold?" Durlan asked.

I nodded. "Covered in ice."

"Could we go skiing there?" Ryul asked with a smirk.

Laughing, I shook my head. "We'd freeze to death."

Venali teleported in front of us, clutching his stomach, and coated in blood.

"Venali!" I yelped and rushed to him.

He dropped to a knee and lowered his head against my shoulder. "They've got Amrynn," he whispered.

"Who?" I asked.

Durlan placed his hands on Venali and began healing him.

"They came from the sky," he whispered.

"What?" Ryul asked, standing close by my side, his sword drawn.

"A huge machine came down from the sky. Beings came out, yelling in a language we didn't understand at first, but then they switched to our language. We tried to fight them, but their weapons are far more advanced. They took Amrynn and their leader said, 'Bring me the one who steals stars.'"

Me. They were after me.

"Take me to them," I said.

"No," Ryul and Venali said at the same time.

"We need to find out their intentions first," Durlan said. His brows were furrowed while he continued to heal Venali.

"They have Amrynn," I reminded him. "They could be torturing him right now! Take me to them."

"Not going to happen," Ryul growled.

I couldn't teleport, or I would have left on my own.

"Ryul, stay with Venali and Elara. If I don't come back, hide her," Durlan ordered him.

I grabbed his arm and stood as he did. "Don't go. Please."

Durlan bent and kissed my lips. "I'll return, my queen."

"Durlan," I yelled, but he disappeared.

"Let's get inside," Ryul said and helped Venali stand.

He seemed mostly healed, but he was still weak, judging by the way he leaned on Ryul.

I looked up at the night sky. If Durlan didn't return, I would just have to find a way to direct the intruders to me.

Ryul grabbed my wrist and dragged me into the house. "Get inside and behave, or I'll tie you up."

"You should tie her up as a precaution," Venali said.

"I find myself agreeing with you more and more," Ryul said to Venali. "It's disconcerting."

"Don't worry, I'm sure it won't happen very often," Venali offered with a weak smile.

"You need to shower," I told Venali.

"Will you be joining me?" he asked with a smirk.

Ryul growled.

My cheeks heated as I envisioned a wet and naked Venali.

Oh, I definitely wanted to see that, but...not tonight.

"Sit," Ryul ordered me as he walked Venali into the bathroom.

I sat on the floor of the hallway, my eyes glued to the front door as I waited for Durlan to return.

Ryul came out, alone, and shut the door behind him. "Let's go wait in the living room," he suggested.

"Will Venali be okay in there alone?" I asked as I stood.

"Interested in joining him?" Ryul asked, a small growl slipping out between words.

I looked up at him, my mouth agape. "No! I just don't want him to be hurt any more than he was."

Because of me.

"This isn't your fault," Ryul said, draped an arm around my shoulders, and he led me to the living room.

"How'd you know I was thinking that?" I whispered.

"Your expression, and the type of person you are." He squeezed me. "You have a good heart and will blame yourself for almost anything."

"Whatever," I mumbled since I didn't know what else to say. We sat on the couch, and Ryul kept his arm around me. Probably, because he was worried I would run off.

Venali came to the living room and sat beside me. His leg touched mine, and I tried really hard not to notice...and failed.

"Are you alright?" I asked as I turned to him.

He nodded, scowling at Ryul's hand between our shoulders.

My eyes started to droop.

No. I needed to stay awake.

"Did they have magic?" Ryul asked.

"No. Their weapons shot electrical charges and others shot fire, though."

Ryul pulled his arm from behind me and set his hand on mine. "You couldn't defeat them with your magic?"

My head fell forward, and I threw it back, opening my eyes wide. Why was I so tired?

Venali set a hand on my thigh, the heat from it was making me even sleepier.

"You're doing this," I slurred, realizing Venali was using magic on me. I looked into his eyes.

He smiled and rubbed his thumb over my leg. "Yes. I am."

"I don't want to sleep," I said, but my body fell to the side, leaning against Venali.

He tucked me under his arm and kissed the top of my head. "Good night, Elara."

"Jerk," I mumbled before his magic took hold and knocked me out.

I WOKE WITH A START, SHOOTING UP IN BED. SCANNING THE room to get my bearings, I realized two things. One, I was in my room in Durlan's house. Two, Ryul was asleep in a chair at the end of my bed.

Ryul's head was at an odd, extremely uncomfortable looking angle.

As quietly as possible, I slipped out of bed, only to get caught by my arm on something, and thump loudly to the floor with my arm still on the bed.

I glanced at my wrist to find a rope tied to it.

Ryul yawned and stretched. "I figured you would try to sneak out while I was sleeping."

"This is no way to treat your queen," I growled at him, and tried to untie my arm.

Ryul stood and untied it for me. "Protecting you is the most important thing. When we are back at the castle, and I know you're safe, I'll treat you like a queen."

"A queen is always in danger," I grumbled and rubbed at my now free wrist. "Did Durlan return?"

"I did," Durlan said from my doorway.

Before my brain registered my movements, I was throwing my arms around Durlan's neck and hugging him.

He squeezed me and chuckled. "I'll go on more missions if this is the type of welcome I'll receive upon my return."

"Did you get Amrynn?" I asked, stepping back from him. Strangely, I didn't feel embarrassed by the hug.

Durlan shook his head.

I marched to my dresser and took out a change of clothes.

"You're not handing yourself over to them," Ryul said.

"Yes, I am," I told him while changing. "I'm not leaving Amrynn in their hold."

"They will likely kill you," Durlan said.

I finished dressing and turned to face him. "I'm not abandoning him. I may have royal blood in my veins, but Amrynn is one of the warlords. He's done more for this realm than I have."

"He wouldn't want this," Durlan growled.

"I don't care. I'm doing this. You can't stop me."

"We stopped you last night," Venali said from behind Durlan.

"You'd rather keep me prisoner?" I asked.

All three males tensed.

I slipped on my shoes, and I wondered for a moment if it had been Ryul or Venali who had taken me to bed and removed my shoes.

I went to Durlan's office, grabbed the star from his desk, and turned to face Durlan. "Take me to them."

Durlan's brows were furrowed, but he held out his hand.

"No!" Ryul yelled and leapt towards us.

Durlan's hand closed around mine, and we teleported away before Ryul could touch us.

We teleported to an open field, where a monstrous silver thing sat. I had never seen anything like it. My mouth hung open as I stared. How could such a large thing even get off the ground?

"I'm against this," Durlan growled as we waited for some of the invaders to approach us.

Five guards, who appeared to be male, walked forward, holding strange devices.

"What do you want?" one of them asked Durlan.

"I've brought the one responsible for your missing star," Durlan explained.

"This way," the same guard ordered me.

I followed and wasn't surprised when they surrounded me.

"Elara!" Durlan yelled. "Let me go with her."

"Return to the others," I ordered him without looking back.

We approached the giant metal thing, and the ramp that led up into it.

"It won't eat me, will it?" I asked one of the guards softly.

They all chuckled.

"It is inanimate. It's just a bunch of metal," one said.

That helped me relax a bit.

Many more guards looked at me as I ascended the ramp. None said anything or did more than look, many of their eyes going to the star I carried in a jar.

Inside, the walls were white and seemed to be made from a different metal than the outside of the ship. They had lights illuminating the path, and I tried not to gawk at all the strange equipment.

We paused at a door, and one of the guards went inside.

I looked around and then bent closer to examine the suit of the guard beside me.

"You look like a kid in a candy store," he said with a laugh.

I bristled. "I may be younger than my companions, but I'm not a child."

"What are you? Twenty?" one of the guards on my left asked.

I nodded.

"That's basically a child to us, too," he said with another laugh.

"You age into the thousands, too?" I asked with wide eyes.

"Thousands? Did you say thousands?"

"Bring her in," the guard who had entered the room said, interrupting our discussion.

We filed into the room, which looked like a laboratory with really weird machines.

Amrynn sat in a cage, his face drawn and pale.

"Amrynn," I yelled and rushed to him. I slid on my knees next to his cage and reached through the bars to touch his face.

He opened his eyes and scowled. "Elara? What are you doing here?" The last words were said in a growl.

"Trying to save you," I whispered. "Are you injured? Did they torture you?"

"Most certainly not," a male voice said with undeniable indignity. "We aren't savages."

"Sedated me," Amrynn whispered.

That explained why he hadn't just teleported out of there.

I stood, blocking Amrynn from the newcomer's view. "What do you want?"

He was tall, somewhat muscular, but nothing like the warlords. His hair was dark brown, and his eyes were brown with caramel specks.

He held out his hand. "I'm Barry."

I stared at his hand a moment and then looked back up into his eyes. "I'm Elara."

His hand lowered to his side, but he didn't seem perturbed by my refusal to shake hands. "You're the one causing all this trouble?" he asked.

I held up the jar for him to see. "I didn't know my actions were causing trouble."

Amrynn discreetly placed his hand on the back of my leg. I fed him some of my power, so he could overcome their sedatives.

Barry leaned towards the jar. "Is that one of the stars?"

I nodded.

He tried to grab it, but I wrapped my arms around it. "Let him go, and I'll put your star back."

"You can't put it back from here. You'll misplace it." Barry frowned.

"What do you want me to do then?"

"Prepare for lift off," he yelled.

The other people on the ship began scrambling around.

"What are you doing?" I demanded.

Amrynn stood and tried to bend the metal of his cage apart.

"I'm going to take you to my universe, and you will put the star back in its proper place. Then, I'll return you to this planet."

"I can't just disappear! I have to tell the others," I yelled over the loud speakers shouting instructions. I didn't even know what they said, but it was loud and fast.

Barry scowled. "You're an important person?"

I nodded despite not feeling that way. "I'm royalty."

His eyes widened. "Well, how about if you write a note, and I'll send one of my people to deliver it?"

And tell him where the others were? Not a chance.

He noticed my scowl. "Or, we can leave your note below, so when they come searching for you here, they will find it."

I nodded. "Fine, but what about Amrynn?"

Barry frowned. "Who?"

I pointed behind me.

"I'm not leaving you alone on this ship," Amrynn growled. "I'm staying with you."

"He may stay. But, if he harms anyone, I'll cage him and sedate him. Understood?"

I nodded.

Barry handed me a strange parchment-like item and a writing utensil. I handed them to Amrynn.

"I'm not great at writing," I explained when Barry arched a brow.

Amrynn wrote a long letter, folded it up, and handed the writing items back. I transferred the items to Barry, who sent one of the guards away with it.

"How do we know you're—"

Barry interrupted me and pointed.

A screen appeared on the wall, and we could see the person securing the note on the ground before coming back in.

The ship shuddered and loud noises filled the air.

Amrynn gripped my arm through the cage, while I gripped the cage.

"Take off," Barry ordered them.

The ship moved, but despite not feeling it much, it still made me nauseous. My grip on Amrynn tightened.

"Elara?" Amrynn's brows were pinched with worry.

"Nauseous," I whispered back, turning away from him.

"That will pass in a moment," Barry said. "Once we are off planet."

Off planet. Something I had never in my life expected to hear. Being able to touch the stars and planets had made me long for the ability to travel through the solar system.

But not like this.

Not abandoning Ryul and the other three. They were going to be furious that I had left without them.

The ship slowed and the ride smoothed out.

I released my death grip and turned to Barry. "Let him out."

Barry tapped some keys on the front of the cage and Amrynn stepped out.

"Remember, no harming others," Barry said.

Amrynn stood between me and Barry. "I am here to protect Elara. Nothing else."

"If you'll follow me, I will take you to your rooms."

"We only need one," Amrynn said with a frown.

I looked up at him, trying to keep my mouth from gaping open.

Barry tilted his head to the side. "Oh? I didn't realize you two were—"

"We're not," I said a bit too quickly.

"Guards don't sleep in separate room when we're in hostile territories," Amrynn said.

Barry scowled. "Hostile? We aren't hostile."

"You were going to show us to our room?" I reminded Barry, not wanting them to fight.

Barry nodded and led the way.

Amrynn took my hand in his, threading our fingers together.

My hand looked so dainty in his.

"Are you alright?" Amrynn glanced down at me, but he was focused on our surroundings.

"Yes. No. I think so?"

He chuckled and squeezed my hand. "I feel the same."

I squeezed back. "I'm glad I have you here with me."

Barry stopped at a doorway. "This will be your room. You are free to explore the ship. We have surveillance that allows us to see everywhere, so please don't consider sabotaging the ship. I'll let you rest, but I would like to talk with you, Elara."

"What about?" Amrynn demanded.

"Your planet. Your abilities. I'm willing to trade information."

"I'll consider it," I said with a nod.

Amrynn entered the room and did a quick look. Then he tugged me in, and shut the door in Barry's face.

CHAPTER 17
ELARA

AMRYNN IMMEDIATELY PULLED me into a hug. "You stubborn, wonderful woman. Why did you come for me?"

I wrapped my arms around him, reveling in the fact that he was safe. "I couldn't let you get hurt because of my mistake. I thought they were torturing you."

"Careful, you might make me think you like me." He chuckled.

I looked up at him, scowling. After all this time I'd spent with him, how did he not know? "I do like you."

He smirked and traced my jaw with his fingertip. "I like you, too."

My stomach swirled in anticipation, but he just kept staring. I threw my arms around his neck, pulled him down, and kissed him.

Screw my boundaries. He had decided to stay with me while I traveled to a strange planet. He was handsome. And, he was my guard.

Without hesitation, he kissed me back, pushing me until my back hit the wall of the room, and then pressed himself into me.

I opened my mouth to him, letting him claim mine and then claiming his in return.

He drew back, stroked his fingertips down my cheek, and smiled. "That was an unexpected reaction."

"You should rest," I said and looked more closely at the room. There was a single bed, a door which I hoped led to the bathroom, a couch, and two chairs.

"We need to find food. We both lost some magic earlier."

He was right, but there didn't appear to be any food in the room.

"Stay here, and I'll go find us some food," Amrynn ordered me.

"No," I said immediately.

His brows pulled together.

"I don't want us separated. I don't trust those aliens. They could lock us apart in this huge ship and I don't know if I could find you." I shook my head and held his hand tighter.

He nodded and squeezed my hand. "Okay. Let's go together."

The hallway was relatively empty, save for a few guards, but they didn't stop us as we walked. This seemed to go on endlessly.

"Excuse me," I said to a passing human. "Where can we find food?"

"The replicator in your room makes food," she said.

"The what?" Amrynn asked.

She sighed. "There's a silver button on the wall next to your chairs. Push it. A table with a machine will slide out of the wall. You tell it what you want. It makes it."

"It makes anything?" I gaped at her. Where had they acquired these machines?

"Anything in our database that is edible," she nodded.

Amrynn took my hand and pulled me back to our room. I sat in one of the chairs and watched him use the machine.

First, he made rabbit stew, which I ate with relish. Then, he made sandwiches. An hour later, we were both full and satisfied.

"Sleep," I ordered him. "Venali knocked me out last night, so I'm well rested. You probably haven't slept since they captured you."

"Warlords are trained to function at full capacity with very little sleep. We could go—"

"Amrynn, go to sleep." I growled.

He sighed, but removed his boots, set his sword to lean against the wall beside the bed, and lay atop the sheets.

Within moments, he was snoring. He looked so peaceful when he slept. All of the warlords had such hectic lives. It was a wonder they ever got restful sleep.

What were the other three warlords doing now? Were they back to their normal courses of action? What about Ryul? Would he temporarily take Amrynn's place as warlord over Blustum?

Ryul was no doubt furious with me. Would he forgive me this time?

When I made it back, I would have to apologize profusely.

If we made it back.

If.

For all I knew, they would have me put the star back, and then keep me for experiments. Or execute me as an example to others.

No. Amrynn wouldn't let that happen.

But. They did overpower him before. It didn't seem too far-fetched that they could do it again.

I had to do everything within my power to keep Amrynn safe. This was all my fault anyway. I had to fix it.

A strange noise woke me. I opened my eyes, shocked that I had fallen asleep.

Amrynn still lay on the bed, his eyes closed.

Had I imagined it?

The noise came again.

Turning, I saw a red flashing light next to the door. There was a button near it, so I pushed it.

A screen turned on above the button, displaying the area outside our door.

Barry stood there, smiling. "Hello, Elara. I was hoping to speak to you."

"Let him in," Amrynn grumbled behind me.

I yelped, not having heard him get out of bed or put his shoes and weapon back on.

He smirked but made no apology.

"Okay," I told Barry and walked to sit in one of the chairs.

Amrynn opened the door and stepped back so Barry could enter.

Barry smiled at Amrynn as he passed and sat on the chair facing me. "Where do your powers come from?"

"We are all born with them," Amrynn answered from where he stood behind me.

"Most of your questions are better answered by Amrynn," I said. "He is much older than me."

Barry frowned. "He doesn't look much older? What? Ten or fifteen years at most."

"Try a thousand," I snickered.

Barry's eyes widened. "Thousand? You are over a thousand years old?"

Amrynn sat on the arm of my chair. "Technically Elara is, too, but she was frozen for about one thousand years."

"I'm not claiming those years," I grumbled. "I was a child when I came out of the crystal."

"You're technically still a child," Amrynn teased.

I flinched. Yes, I did know.

"What do you call yourselves?" Barry asked.

"We're fae. Specifically, Seelie," Amrynn answered.

"See...lee?"

"There are Seelie and Unseelie. The Unseelie are barbarians who use dark magic and revel in killing."

"They are your enemies?" Barry asked.

Amrynn nodded.

"Can Seelie become Unseelie?"

I perked up, curious of this answer as well. My parents had never explained the Unseelie to me. Just that they were evil, and I should run if one ever attacked. I had heard stories over the years, but no true explanation.

"There are some who are born Unseelie. There are some who are twisted and turn Unseelie. Turning is very rare. It has happened less than a dozen times."

"Can they become Seelie?" Barry asked.

"No," Amrynn said. "Once you touch black magic, there is no going back."

"What are your normal lifespans?"

"Four of five thousand years."

"Am I correct in assuming there are male and female?"

Amrynn nodded.

"Do you give live births?"

"Yes."

"What type of powers can Seelie possess?"

While Amrynn and Barry went back and forth, I sat there feeling uneasy. The Unseelie hadn't been seen in a long time. Why not? What were they doing?

"Elara!" Amrynn shouted.

I jerked away from him but had nowhere to go because I was in the chair still. "What?"

Barry frowned at me, and Amrynn looked concerned.

"Would you like our medical team to evaluate her?" Barry asked Amrynn, while staring at me.

Amrynn shook his head. "We don't get sick. She's just tired."

Had I done something? I had just been sitting there, hadn't I?

Amrynn scowled. "I'll be alright while you sleep. The nap I took helped."

I wasn't worried about that, but I stood and went to the bed. I cast a glance back at Amrynn, but he was deep in conversation with Barry again.

I tried to sleep. And the bed was incredibly comfortable, but my mind wouldn't shut off.

They wanted me to be queen, but did Minloa need a monarch? If they didn't want to be warlords anymore, I was certain we could think of something else. Why not find people that were respected and have the people of that sector vote?

Or, host a tournament and the top four victors would be the new warlords.

That idea had the most merit. Fae respected strength and power. A tournament provided entertainment and helped find the strongest among us.

Yes, once we got back, I would set into motion the tournament. After confirming with the warlords that they did want to give up their stations.

Once they were no longer warlords, I was no longer queen, they wouldn't need to guard me, so they could go find mates.

That thought hurt.

Thinking of them with other women really angered and upset me. I would have to get over it. I shouldn't keep the four of them...even if I wanted to, unless that was truly what they wanted. I didn't want them trying to stay with me out of obligation.

Barry left, and I rolled over to look at Amrynn.

"What's wrong?" he asked, coming to kneel beside the bed.

I sat up, crossed my legs, and looked at him. *Really* looked at him. His eyebrows were furrowed, eyes full of concern, his strong hands rested on the edge of the bed as he surveyed me.

"If you were free, what would you do?" I asked.

"Free?" He arched a brow. "I didn't realize I wasn't free."

"If you weren't a warlord. Or my guard," I added.

His eyes widened a second before returning to normal. "What?"

I sighed. "Come on, play along. If we were in Minloa, you weren't my guard or a warlord, what would you do?"

He looked at the wall behind me, silent, for several moments. I thought he wasn't going to respond at all.

"I suppose I would travel a bit, look for a mate, buy some land," he finally answered.

"I could make that happen for you," I whispered. "I could free you from all of this."

He stood and scowled down at me. "What are you talking about? What do you mean? You're going to fire me from being a warlord? You don't want me as a guard?"

The corner of his eyes were pinched.

Crap. I had hurt his feelings.

I stood and placed my hands on his chest. "Easy. I didn't say any of that."

He placed his hands over mine as he stared into my eyes. "I'm not leaving you. I will remain by your side until I die, or you force me away." He smirked. "I'll probably still stay close to you, even if you don't want me as a guard."

"I didn't say I don't want you as a guard."

"What did you say then?"

"That you have choices."

"Choices?" His left eyebrow rose.

I nodded.

"What if I don't like those choices?"

"What choices do you want?"

He raised a hand and rested it on my cheek. "The choice to touch you like this."

He kissed my lips. "The choice to kiss you."

He leaned forward again and nipped my nose. "The choice to tell you when you're being *ridiculous*."

I rubbed my nose with a scowl. "I just want you to be happy."

"I'd be a lot happier if we were on Minloa right now," he grumbled.

I leaned into him, and he wrapped his arms around me. "Me, too."

We stood like that for a while, and then I stepped back and went to the replicator to make more food.

"Did you find out anything from Barry?" I asked as I ordered food for us both.

"They are called humans. They live on a planet called Earth. Their average life span is eighty-five years. They tend to have a single mate, who they stay with for life. They do not have the same issues we do with male to female ratios. They use science to create their machines. They have weapons that shoot pieces of metal thousands of feet in a second."

My mouth dropped open. He had found out a lot. And, some of it was terrifying information.

"They're actually a very weak being. The only way they've survived so long is because of their weapons and science."

"Their weapons sound insane," I whispered.

His arms wrapped around me from behind. "We'll get through this."

I hoped so.

We ate in silence, both of our minds focused on other things.

Once he finished, Amrynn stood and said, "I'm going to continue training you while we are here."

"What type of training?" I asked as I stood as well.

"Everything I can possibly think of. We don't know how long we will be here. So, I want to give you a crash course on everything you didn't learn while on Minloa. If we have more time, I'll expand on certain areas."

I nodded. "Okay."

He frowned as he examined our room. "We need a different space. Come, we will go explore and find a place to train."

We walked for what felt like an hour and came to an intersection. There were signs, but I couldn't read them.

Amrynn turned right and pushed open a door, waiting for me to follow. Hopefully, he would remember how to get back to our room like he did earlier.

Inside the doors was another hallway, but it was thankfully shorter than the previous one and led to a large flat area with blue colored floors.

Amrynn knelt and touched the floor. "Mats," he said. "Perfect."

About a dozen people were in the room. Some were sparring, but most were lounging about, talking with each other.

Amrynn walked to an open spot and turned to face me. "Ready?"

"For wh—"

He charged me and knocked me on my back.

"I wasn't ready," I growled at him.

"Your enemies won't wait for you to be ready," he said and stood.

I stood quickly, put my hands up, and faced him.

He scowled and charged again.

I sidestepped and punched his stomach.

He grabbed my arm, twisted it up behind my back, and snarled.

I snarled back and spun out of his hold, kicking his chin.

He leaned back, so my kick only clipped him.

"You're better than I thought you would be," he said as he released me.

"I've been in my fair share of fights in Linta. And, I did train with Venali. Plus, you're holding back."

He was holding back *a lot*.

"I'm trying to avoid hurting you," he said, brows furrowed.

"I won't learn if you don't—"

He cut me off. "You won't learn if you're just constantly on the ground."

"You seem pretty sure you're the best fighter," one of the human men said, standing in a group, watching.

Amrynn didn't even bother turning to face him. "In this place, I am."

"Prove it," the man said, approaching us.

"Don't kill him," I ordered Amrynn.

The human took off his shirt, and I was temporarily put in a stupor as I looked at his muscular body. He looked as muscular as Ryul.

Amrynn growled at me, and I quickly averted my gaze.

Whoops. He'd caught me gawking.

Amrynn turned. "My queen?"

"Queen?" the man asked.

"Sparring with bare hands. Submission. No killing," I said.

Amrynn bowed. "Yes, my queen."

The man stared at me.

"Well?" Amrynn asked him with arms folded over his chest.

The man pulled his eyes away from me and nodded to Amrynn. "Agreed."

Amrynn unbuckled his sword and gave it to me. I backed up to the wall and leaned my upper back against it.

Barry walked in and stood beside me. "What's going on?"

"He challenged Amrynn to spar," I said. "Don't worry. I told Amrynn not to kill him and I have his sword."

Not that he couldn't kill the humans without his sword. It just made lesser beings feel better when they saw fae without weapons.

Barry perked up. "Wonderful. I was hoping to get footage of him fighting."

"It won't be a long match," I mumbled and bit my lip to hide my smile.

Amrynn and the human faced each other. The room was silent as everyone waited.

"Elara?" Amrynn called without taking his eyes from the man.

"Oh, right. Sorry. Fighters, ready?"

"Ready," the both called.

"Fight!" I yelled.

Before I had even drawn my breath back in, the man was on the ground, unconscious.

"What happened?" Barry asked.

"He punched him on the jaw," I said, hiding my smirk.

Amrynn knelt, pressed two fingers to the man's neck, and smiled at me. "He's alive."

"Did you use magic?" Barry asked.

Amrynn shook his head and walked towards me.

"Fascinating," Barry whispered.

Two people dragged the unconscious man off the mat.

"Would you be willing to fight more people?" Barry asked.

"I don't want him hurt," I said before Amrynn could answer.

"I swear it will only be sparring," Barry replied.

"Perhaps more than one at a time would be better?" Amrynn suggested with a smile.

Oh, he was enjoying this. Showoff.

Barry tapped on a metal rectangle in his hand. "Agreed."

A dozen more people entered, all wearing guards' uniforms.

"I'd like you to spar with our guest," Barry informed them.

"Four at a time, first," Amrynn said. He turned to me. "Pay attention to what I do. You need to learn to fight multiple opponents at once."

I nodded and sat cross-legged with his sword resting on my lap.

The newcomers removed their jackets and rolled up their shirt sleeves.

Four stood in a circle around Amrynn.

Amrynn bowed to me.

"Ready? Fight!" Barry yelled.

Two men fell as Amrynn darted between them and hit the back of their necks. The other two gaped, and then lunged sideways away from him as he ran at them.

"No magic!" I ordered him as he headed towards one.

Amrynn's leg shot out, and the man fell once it connected with his cheek.

The last man faced Amrynn with his hands raised, no fear showing.

Amrynn tilted his head as he examined him, and then he swept the man's legs out from under him and wrapped his arms around his neck.

The man tapped Amrynn's arm, and Amrynn released him.

"You're holding back," I said, my eyes wide.

Amrynn scowled. "You said not to kill them. If I move at full speed, I'll break their bones and probably kill them."

I dipped my head. Fair enough. He was most likely right.

"What about you?" Barry asked as he turned to face me. "Are females of your species as strong?"

"Most, yes. But, not me," I admitted.

"Would you be willing to spar?" Barry asked.

"No," Amrynn growled and marched towards us.

"He is my guard," I told Barry. "The moment he sees me in danger, the logical side of his brain shuts off, and he will attack anyone he views as a threat, or who has hurt me."

Amrynn stopped, folded his arms over his chest, and glared. "I am not controlled by my instincts. I'm not a young boy."

I smirked. Hook. Line. Sinker.

"Then, let me spar."

His lips twitched in a snarl. "No weapons."

I held out his sword and then gave him mine.

Once on the mat, the first guy Amrynn had knocked out stepped forward. "I'll spar with her."

Barry's wide smile was telling.

"You rank high in your military?" I asked.

The man smiled. "Yes."

I nodded. "Very well. No weapons, and submission or knock out."

"Agreed," the man said.

After stretching, I took a fighter's stance and said, "Ready."

The man looked at Barry, who nodded.

He moved quickly, but not as fast as my males could. I spun around his punch, ducked his back hand, kicked his legs out from under him, and sat on his hips, holding his arms down.

"Submit?" I asked with a smile.

Beneath my hips, his cock jumped.

My eyes widened, and I leapt away, heat rising to my cheeks.

He attacked, using my distracted state to get my arm behind my back, then tripped me.

I stumbled, spun to face him, and broke his hold before punching him in the stomach.

His abdominal muscles absorbed the punch, and before I knew what happened, I was in a headlock and unable to breathe.

I flailed as I tried to break free, but his hold was strong. Passing out wasn't an option. Amrynn would overreact. So, I tapped his arm in submission.

As soon as he let me go, I ran from the room and headed for our quarters.

Amrynn called after me, but I ignored him.

Once inside the bedroom, I quickly went to the bathroom, and shut and locked the door to keep Amrynn out.

I'd felt men's erections before. Sometimes they couldn't control them. I knew this.

What I hadn't expected was the lust I felt towards the human man. Or, my embarrassment.

"Are you injured?" Amrynn asked through the door.

"No," I whispered and slid to sit, leaning my back and head against the door.

"What happened? He didn't say anything, and I didn't see him do anything that should have upset you so much to lose."

"Just drop it. Please?"

"What happened?" he asked again.

That man wouldn't tell him. And, I didn't want to either. So, I stayed silent.

Amrynn sighed softly and then walked away.

Why had I reacted to that human? Was I so starved for attention that I would stoop to sleeping with a lesser being?

"I'm sorry," the man I had fought said from the other side of the door.

"Amrynn!"

"I'm here," he said outside the door. "He asked to come apologize.

Wonderful.

"You're beautiful, and normally I am better at controlling myself. I apologize for upsetting you."

Dammit. I didn't want them to think I was a child. I didn't want to be viewed as delicate.

"You've no reason to apologize," I told him, trying to sound nonchalant. "But I appreciate your apology."

Quickly, I turned on the water for a shower. I didn't want to see if they took the hint. I stripped and showered.

Being clean relaxed me a bit, but my hormones wouldn't quiet. There was one thing to do, and I was glad I was in the shower to be able to do it.

I reached down and touched myself, closing my eyes and

picturing my guards. I recalled the kisses I had shared with them and how sexy they all looked shirtless.

What would it feel like to have them lay atop me? To have their hands on my naked body? To have their tongues—

"Elara, we should—" Amrynn began as he entered the room. His eyes lowered to where my hand was, and they widened.

I was so close, and if I stopped now, I would be in a horrible mood the rest of the day.

"Amrynn," I growled.

"I, uh—"

"Are you going to just watch?" I asked, then bit my lip. That had come out more as an invitation than a scolding.

He dropped to his knees before me, the water of the shower soaking him and his clothes instantly, seared my lips with his, and slid his hand down the front of my body, not pausing until he pushed two fingers inside of me.

I gasped into his mouth, moving my fingers faster over my already sensitive nub.

He nipped my lip, then my neck. "What do you want me to do?" he asked. "How do you want me?"

Oh, sweet nectar! How could I answer that?

I wanted him in every way.

"What do *you* want?" I asked him back.

"All of you," he whispered in my ear in a husky voice. "But today, I'll just pleasure you."

"Why?"

"When I claim your body, it will be because you want me. Because you can't go a minute more without letting me spill my seed inside you," he growled softly as he pumped his fingers in and out of me.

I arched into his hand, my breaths coming in pants.

"I want you," I whispered. "I want all of my guards. It should feel wrong, but it doesn't. I want you all so much."

"We want you, too," he rumbled. "For now, I'll settle for making you scream and come on my fingers."

His head dipped, and he drew my nipple into his mouth.

I moaned, arched again, and then screamed as the wave of my orgasm, both from my clit and his fingers, crashed over me at the same time.

His fingers continued to move after my own stopped, bringing me three more orgasms before I finally felt sated. I fell back against the side of the shower.

He withdrew his fingers and licked them clean one by one. His eyes closed on the last one, as if he were savoring it.

Amrynn was a god compared to the humans. An immortal who could kill before they blinked. He was loyal to me, and I wanted him. I wanted all of him.

"You taste even better than I imagined," he whispered as he opened his eyes and looked at me.

"Why do you warlords have to be so perfect?" I breathed, my heart still thundering in my chest.

He smirked. "We are far from perfect."

"Can you help me stand?" I requested.

He picked me up, turned off the shower, and carried me to the towel rack. "He really was sorry."

"Who?" I asked as I dried off, out of his arms.

"The human you sparred with."

I sighed and dropped my head. "Can we just pretend that didn't happen?"

"For males, it is an involuntary reaction. Especially when seeing a creature as beautiful as you."

Clearly, we were not dropping the subject.

"I know it was involuntary," I mumbled as I dried my hair.

"Then why were you upset?"

I dropped the towel and glared at him. "I am supposed to

control my urges. I'm a royal. We are supposed to compartmentalize everything."

"Sexual urges can't be compartmentalized. Yes, you can control how you react, but not how your body does."

"Can we please drop this topic now?" I begged. I didn't have a change of clothes, so I put the ones I had worn earlier back on.

Amrynn didn't respond.

I turned, and my heart leapt into my throat.

Amrynn lay on his back, eyes closed, on the ground.

I rushed to his side, pressed my fingers to his neck, and checked for a pulse. It was there, strong as it should be, and he was breathing.

"Amrynn?" I whispered, gently setting my hands on his chest.

I looked around, trying to find something that could have hurt him, but found nothing.

Did they have devices in the wall? Could they inject us with sedatives without us knowing? Without needles?

"Amrynn, please don't leave. I need you," I whispered.

I didn't know what to do. There were no injuries to heal. His magic appeared fine. It was as though he'd fallen asleep.

Leaving him on the cold bathroom floor was not my wish, but I didn't want to move him, just in case something was wrong.

Gently, I lowered myself onto my side, rested my head on his chest to more easily monitor his breathing and heartbeat, and pressed myself as close to him as I could. Hopefully, my body heat would keep him a little warm.

I could summon Barry, but I wasn't convinced this wasn't his doing.

To keep from freaking out, I sang one of my mother's lullabies. I forgot a few words, so I hummed those parts. She used to sing to me all the time. Personally, I thought she just enjoyed singing, and I had given her a convenient excuse.

"That's a beautiful lullaby," Amrynn whispered.

I jerked upright to look down at him. "Are you alright?"

He nodded and sat up. "I'm sorry if I worried you."

I threw my arms around his neck. "What happened?"

He hugged me to him, stood with me in his arms, and carried me to the bed. "The others used a spell to communicate with me. It knocks the receiver unconscious to put them in a dream state." He climbed in beside me and covered us with the blanket.

"What did they say?" I asked, not wanting to let go of him yet. I lay on his chest again, his heart beat as strong as before.

"There was a lot of yelling and cursing. They found my note. They suggested we try teleporting, but I told them you were adamant about returning the star first."

Their anger was expected.

"How mad are they?" I asked in a whisper.

"They're not mad at you," he whispered back. "They're concerned for your wellbeing."

"Ryul is probably the angriest," I commented.

"He is very distraught. He made some impressive threats to me, should I fail in protecting you."

"Anything else?"

"Nothing important," he said as he began rubbing my arm.

"I'll get you back home," I swore, lifting my head to meet his eyes.

He smirked. "I'm certain that is my line."

"Minloa needs you," I said. "I'll get you home so you can live out your dream."

And, I would do whatever I had to, to get Amrynn back to Minloa.

CHAPTER 18
DURLAN

SITTING in the grass in front of my house, I stared up at the stars. Elara had been taken, and it was my fault. I'd teleported her to them. I had handed over my queen to those...people.

Ryul had attacked me, and I hadn't even bothered to try to defend myself. I'd deserved the beating.

Looking at the symbols on my arm, I drew in a stuttering breath. If she died, I would die as well. If she died, the magic would destroy me. And I would deserve it.

Failure.

I had never failed at anything in my life. Yet, one of the biggest moments, one of the most monumental times for me to succeed, and I had failed.

Venali had pulled Ryul off, but that hadn't done anything to calm his fury.

He viewed me as responsible for our queen's disappearance. I agreed.

I needed her to come back.

Rubbing the middle of my chest where pain had started as soon as she'd left the planet, I wondered what would happen if she and I did die. Would Ryul take over as warlord? Amrynn was gone with her, too. So, they would need to find a replacement for him as well.

Making a list of possible replacements for me seemed best. That way, Venali would be prepared.

Kydrus hadn't spoken to us since she had left. The pain etched in his face and eyes haunted me. He didn't share his emotions well, or speak much, but I knew he loved her. I knew he had loved her for several years. The moron just hadn't wanted to overstep his boundaries and risk her thinking she had to submit since he was warlord.

Our connection to her was pulled taut, separated by who knew how much space. She hadn't mentioned the connections, but they were there. If she didn't agree to be our mate, the connection would still be there. It would hurt to lose her as a mate, but we would still stay by her side as a guard, no matter what.

The connections worried me. Only one woman before had had connections like this, and if things were as they seemed, our world was going to change more than I liked.

I would endure. I would do anything for her. Just one more day with her was all I wanted.

"Come home," I whispered, looking up at the stars and planets above. "Come home, Elara."

CHAPTER 19
ELARA

"You're not taking her blood." Amrynn snarled at Barry and the woman Barry had brought with him.

"It will only hurt for a moment, and it's not very painful," Barry pressed.

Amrynn stood between me and the humans, his sword drawn, and his teeth bared.

I'd caught a glimpse of his bared fangs when I had tried to step around him.

"What do you want it for?" I asked.

"To compare it to ours. See if there are differences in your DNA. Perhaps an extra or different chain that gives you your magic," Barry said as matter-of-fact but his wide eyes remained on Amrynn.

"No. You'll use her blood for experiments. You might try cloning her," Amrynn snapped.

"The last thing we need is two of me," I grumbled.

"We wouldn't clone her. We outlawed that practice decades ago."

Barry was trying to sound convincing, but even I could tell he was hiding something from us.

"No," I said. "Final answer."

Barry let out a long sigh. "If you reconsider, do let me know."

Amrynn didn't relax until they had left the room and walked several feet down the hallway.

"He's hiding something," I whispered.

Amrynn sheathed his sword and turned to face me. "Immortality."

"Huh?" I sat in one of the chairs and he sat across from me.

"They are a short-lived species. He wants to tamper with your blood to see if he can use it to lengthen their lifespans. If he succeeds, he will hold us prisoner, keeping us alive just to take our blood."

"You sound sure of this," I said with an arched eyebrow.

"It is what we might do, if we were in his place."

My mouth dropped open. "What?"

"It doesn't matter. He's not getting our blood."

His entire body was tense, coiled and ready to attack. I looked into his eyes and saw a predator. A gorgeous and frightening predator.

His gaze softened as he reached to take my hand. "What is it that has you flustered suddenly? You've gone a bit pale, but your eyes don't show fear." He rubbed the back of my hand with his thumb.

"You," I admitted.

His thumb still and eyes widened. "Me? I've scared you?"

I shook my head. "No. Well, yes, but no."

He scowled. "You're not making sense."

"You do scare me. You're a warlord, one of the most powerful fae in existence. Yet, I trust you not to hurt me." Had that made sense? Did I explain well enough, or just confuse him more?

His lips pulled up into a smile. "I'm glad I've earned your

trust. And, you don't need to be scared. Never. I will never hurt you."

Not my body at least. My heart...I had no idea what would happen to it.

Someone knocked on the door.

Amrynn sprung up, sword drawn.

I hadn't seen him draw it.

"What?" he demanded without opening the door.

"We have reached our solar system. Barry would like you to come to the captain's deck," an unfamiliar guard said.

After ensuring we had everything, we followed the guard.

Amrynn stayed close to my side, his sword still drawn. The hallways were filled with people, moving quickly.

The guard pressed a square thing he'd had hanging at his hip to a weird device. The device turned green, and two doors next to the device opened.

My mouth dropped open.

A dozen people examined machines with colored lights. Barry sat in a chair facing a huge glass window. Outside of the windows, I saw planets. I could feel the energy thrumming through me. I could destroy the planets with a gesture. The most immense power came from their sun.

"Ah, there you are. Come in," Barry beckoned.

I walked passed him, pressing my hands against the glass. "So much power," I whispered.

Amrynn set a hand on the base of my neck. "Don't give in to it. Yes, the power is there, but it is not for you to use."

"Can you return the star now?" Barry asked.

I could create a new star. I could multiply their planets. "I need to be outside," I whispered.

Amrynn knelt before me. "My queen, stay with me. Seal your aura."

"I don't know how," I said, my eyes fixed to the planets before me. Besides the power coming from the planets and sun, I felt another power deep within me. It was sealed and barely visible, but it was there. I had no idea how to coax it out, though.

"Can you get us to a planet where we can breathe?" Amrynn asked.

"Yes," Barry said and barked orders at the other humans.

"Do it, quickly," Amrynn said. He took one of my hands. "I can help, but it won't feel good."

"I don't want to," I whispered.

"You could burn yourself up if you use the power. You're untrained. It will overwhelm you."

"You don't know that for sure." I growled, showing him my fangs. I was queen. I ruled these stars. I could create and destroy.

Amrynn sighed. "I'm sorry."

My brows furrowed in a scowl. What was he apologizing for?

In a single movement, he pinned me to the floor, his teeth around my throat.

I gasped and went limp, almost dropping the jar with the star in it.

"What are you doing?" Barry demanded.

"S-sorry," I whispered. Tears sprang to my eyes and slid down my cheeks. The power was there but muted now. He had forced me to submit, and on instinct, I had reverted back to my slave self, sealing my power back inside.

He released my neck and picked me up, cradling me like a child with his hand wrapped around the back of my neck.

"Get us to a planet. This won't last long," Amrynn ordered them.

His touch was reassuring and not at the same time. I hadn't been forced to submit for over a decade. I had forgotten how much I hated it. I hated feeling weak and helpless.

"I'm sorry," he whispered. "I'm sorry, Elara."

"Put me down, please." I hardly recognized my own voice. It

sounded so small and pathetic.

Reluctantly, he set me on my feet.

The guard I'd sparred with stood nearby, his hand on his weapon. Had he come to try to rescue me?

The chill I felt had nothing to do with the room. I wrapped my arms around myself and stared out the window, watching as we approached a planet with strange plants and animals. I carried the star in its jar and faced the guard. "Lead the way," I ordered him, barely keeping from adding a please to the end.

The effects would wear off soon, but for now I couldn't meet anyone's eyes.

Amrynn walked behind me, his presence reassuring and yet causing my shoulders to slump at the same time.

We boarded a strange ship and sat on seats with weird straps.

Amrynn reached a hand out towards me but lowered it when I flinched.

The smaller ship we were in flew out of the big one we'd taken to get here. we landed on the planet, and I tried to get the strap off, but couldn't figure it out.

I was about to use my sword, when the guard who always seemed to pop up, helped me.

The door opened, and I ran out. The dark night's sky greeted me.

"Do you know where it goes?" Barry asked.

I opened the jar, held the star in my fingers, and closed my eyes. Slowly, I turned, letting the star direct me.

There.

Raising my arm, I released the star.

"Brock?" Barry whispered.

"It's in the right place," an unfamiliar male voice said.

People cheered.

"Return us to our home," Amrynn ordered Barry.

"We have to refuel and restock first," Barry said, heading back towards the small ship.

"How long will that take?" Amrynn demanded.

"Are you alright?" the guard asked me.

I nodded. The magic beat through me, becoming stronger by the minute.

"You don't have to stay with him," the guard whispered.

I looked at him. "Who?"

"The male you came with. If he abuses you—"

"He doesn't."

"What he did on the deck—"

I stopped him. "He did it to save your home. There is a lot of power here. I could have destroyed this planet."

His frown was proof enough that he didn't believe me.

"He's saying it will take them a week to prepare for our return flight," Amrynn growled.

"A week? That's ridiculous," I shrieked. "I want to go home now."

"It takes time to refuel and restock. Plus, they will do a full inspection of the ship," the guard said.

My hair stood on end along my arms and the back of my neck tingled. Something wasn't right.

Barry beckoned us back to the small ship.

"Why are we getting back in that thing?" I asked, feet planted.

"To fly to our base. We landed far away, in case something went wrong when you tried to put the star back," he explained.

Amrynn and I reluctantly followed the guard and took our seats again.

The machine rose into the air with a roaring sound that made me grip the arms of my seat in fear.

Amrynn did the same.

They flew for quite a ways, and then landed at an area with dozens of buildings, lots of strange machines, and too many humans to keep count.

We followed the group, and I didn't care how stupid I looked as I gawked at everything.

What did they do with all of these machines? Were they all weapons?

"We all need to go through decontamination," Barry said as he came to my side. "You step into a room and are sprayed with a powder that cleanses you."

"We will go in together," Amrynn said.

Barry shook his head. "You can't. you can go in rooms that are next to each other, though. They have clear glass, so you'll be able to see each other."

I didn't like this. Not one bit.

"Fine," I said, but glanced at Amrynn to let him know I was wary, too.

"It'll be fine," the guard said with a smile. "They blast some air and dust on you, and then you're done."

The powder wasn't what worried me.

"I can go first, if it will make you feel better?" he offered.

I nodded.

We headed into an enormous building and stood in line for the decontamination.

The effects of Amrynn's forced submission hadn't worn off yet. I could use some of my powers, but a very limited amount.

The guard went into a glass room, lifted his arms, and white powder sprayed him from every direction, coating him. The powder stopped and then air blew most of the powder off. He stepped out the other side, and smiled at me.

"I don't like this," Amrynn whispered to me.

I let my hand find his and squeezed. "Me neither, but we have no choice."

He snarled and went into the room on the left, while I stepped into the one on the right. The door shut and cut off all sound with it.

I turned and Amrynn's eyes met mine.

"Raise your arms," a voice instructed us.

I looked for the source but only saw the guard outside the door in front of me. He raised his arms in demonstration.

I obeyed, looking at Amrynn to find him doing the same.

"Close your eyes and mouth, and hold your breath," the unknown voice said.

I obeyed.

The powder sprayed, and it took all my willpower not to freak out. It coated my exposed skin and stuck to me.

The air blew a lot of it off. I wiped at my eyes and turned to find Amrynn lying on the ground in his room.

I hit the glass between us. "Amrynn!"

He didn't move.

I drew all of the power I could from their sun and released it as an explosion of fire. The glass walls and doors exploded. People yelled, and I took two steps towards Amrynn, but two unfamiliar guards held weird weapons to his head.

He still wasn't moving. I focused and heard his heart beating.

Relief surged through me.

"Release him or I will destroy your planet," I threatened.

"If you come with us quietly, we will keep him alive," Barry told me in a cold tone that was very unlike him. "If you fight, they'll blow a hole in his head. Which, I'm fairly certain your species can't survive."

That bastard. I would kill him. I would kill them all.

But...

I looked at Amrynn's limp body and growled. "If you hurt him, I will destroy everything in your solar system. Do you understand?"

"Perfectly," Barry said, and I could hear the smug satisfaction in his voice.

Two guards came for me, and one stabbed a needle into

my arm.

The last thing I saw before I passed out was the guard shouting at Barry from the other room.

"You can't keep us here forever," I growled weakly at Barry.

My arms and legs were strapped down to a bed, a weird tube was inside my arm, pumping a clear liquid into my veins and another tube was inside my other arm, slowing draining my blood.

Amrynn lay in the room across from me, in the same predicament, but he was unconscious.

It had been a week since they'd captured us, and I didn't know how much more I could take.

They kept me heavily sedated, so I couldn't use my powers. Not that I would since they had weapons aimed at Amrynn constantly.

"Your DNA is amazing. It's similar to ours, but—"

I tuned him out. He liked to talk and wouldn't shut up for a long time, droning on about things I didn't understand.

He left a while later, carrying a bag of my blood with him, a gleeful smile on his face.

When we escaped, I would destroy this planet. I would crush them like the bugs they were, so they could never hurt us again.

Failure.

Pathetic.

Prisoner.

Slave.

I was all of those things.

Tears slipped down my cheeks, and I didn't bother to hold in my sobs.

I didn't want Amrynn to die because of me.

I didn't want to die.

Ryul, Venali, Kydrus, and Durlan would never know what happened to us. They would never get closure.

I would never see them again. They would keep me alive, to steal my blood, and I would never see my four guards.

These monsters could return to our world, capture the rest of my people, and strap them all to tables, stealing their blood, too. I had no idea if they would even stop at the adults. They might take the children, too. They could turn us into slaves.

I thought I had escaped being a slave.

Now, I had caused one of the warlords to become a helpless slave. A bag of blood.

"El...ar," Amrynn whispered.

"I'm sorry!" Tears dripped from my cheeks, to the bed, and then to the floor.

I couldn't be queen. I couldn't even protect one of my people.

Useless.

Powerless.

Pathetic.

If I could go back, take it all back, I would. I would have never touched the stars. I would have never met the warlords. I would have never gone to Linta. Ryul would have found out eventually that I was gone, and then he could have moved on.

I had caused nothing but pain and trouble for them.

If I made it out of here, I would do things differently. I would become queen, but rule differently than my father had. The warlords would be given a choice of leaving their stations or staying and becoming my mates.

I loved them. I loved each of them in their own way. I wanted to take them as mates, so that we could spend the rest of our lives together.

The lights went out, and then weird dim red lights came on, followed by loud sounds somewhere in the building.

The guard who'd sparred with me rushed in and began untying me and removing the tubes.

"What are you—"

"We don't have time. Just be quiet and I will help you escape," he snapped.

"They'll kill you. And, if I escape, I'll destroy your world."

He scoffed. "We deserve nothing less."

Finished unhooking all the things, he tossed me over his shoulder and moved to Amrynn.

"Why?" Amrynn asked softly.

"No one deserves to be treated this way. Especially not someone who returned our star," the guard said.

Free, Amrynn wavered on his feet, but stayed upright.

"Follow me," the guard ordered him.

Amrynn followed, his jaw set.

Was he really saving us or was this a ploy?

He pushed open a door and pointed, "Your swords."

Amrynn rushed forward, retrieving both of our swords.

We moved down a hallway but had to pause at an intersection when a group of guards rushed by. Luckily, they didn't spot us.

Once out of the building, he ran to the nearest machine, tossed me in the back, and ordered us to hide.

Amrynn covered me with a blanket and laid down next to me.

"Are you hurt?" he whispered.

"Sedated and drained of blood," I answered.

His lips pulled back in a snarl, but he didn't speak.

The machine made loud noises, and we headed away from the buildings.

Sometime later, he stopped the machine.

"All clear," he called out to us.

Amrynn tossed the blanket back and helped me out of the machine.

I looked around with a scowl. There was dirt and not much

else. I could see the buildings where we'd been, but they were far away.

"I don't have a ship for you, or anyway for you to return," the guard said. "But I couldn't let them keep you like that any longer."

"They'll kill you if you return," I said.

He shrugged.

"Come with us," I said quickly.

Amrynn's head fell back and he looked up at the sky with a soft groan.

"I can't," the guard said with a sputter.

"I'm going to destroy this planet. If you don't come, you will die."

"I don't belong in your world." He frowned and shook his head.

"What's your name?" I asked.

"Jensen."

I hugged him and kissed his cheek. "Thank you, Jensen. I won't forget this or your sacrifice." I laced my fingers with Amrynn's, and said, "Last chance to come."

"What are you doing?" Amrynn muttered.

The guard stepped back. "I appreciate the offer, but I'll stay."

"Thank you," Amrynn said to him.

The guard smiled. "Take care of her."

I opened myself, drew in as much power as I could, and teleported Amrynn and I to the furthest planet in the system.

The planet was hot from being so close to their sun. I teleported us again as quickly as possible.

Amrynn groaned, curling around me.

"Hold on," I begged him. "Almost home."

My next jump took us to a freezing cold planet. I inhaled, and instantly regretted it. The longer we stood, the more frozen I became.

Crap. I needed to get us out of here before we froze to death.

My energy was already waning. I wasn't sure how many more jumps I could make.

Closing my eyes, gritting my teeth, and summoning more energy from their sun, I jumped out of their solar system and into our system, on the planet furthest from our sun.

We landed in a pile, Amrynn's body atop mine. He weighed so much more than I thought he would. Or, perhaps that was the gravity of this planet making him weigh more.

"Amrynn," I groaned, pushing at his shoulder. "You're squishing me."

He moaned but rolled off me. "Sorry," he exhaled.

I hopped us to another planet, closer to ours, but the use of so much magic was taking its toll on me and I was unsure where we were. Amrynn clung to my hand, but groaned.

I looked around. This planet looked familiar, felt familiar.

Oh, it was Pinolt! We were just three planets from home.

"I've got this." I gasped. Slowly, I wedged my shoulder and arm beneath Amrynn's, and jumped again, aiming for Sulma, the planet closest to ours.

We landed on a hill, sliding straight towards a bunch of jagged rocks.

I tried to teleport again, but my vision kept going dark.

"Elara," Amrynn groaned. "Elara, you can do it." He stabbed his sword into the ground, slowing our descent, and then finally stopping us when it hit a thick tree root.

I gasped in several breaths. "I'm sorry. I just need to make one more jump."

He looked down at me. "You've used too much energy. We should just rest here."

I looked down at the jagged rocks below us. "This is not an ideal resting place."

He chuckled. "Beggars can't be choosers."

I snorted and then laughed hysterically.

"Just rest for a couple minutes," he whispered, hugging me tight.

"You've been in and out of consciousness this entire trip. You could drop me," I whispered.

He growled. "I will not drop you."

"You could."

"I won't."

"But, you could."

"Elara!" he snapped, growling loudly. "I will *not* drop you."

I smiled, kissed him, and said, "If I don't survive, just know that I died happy."

"Wh—"

I jumped one last time, and the world darkened around me.

My eyelids fluttered open a moment later, and I stared at the ground rushing up towards us. We were falling from the sky towards Durlan's house.

I had teleported us to our planet, to Durlan's home, but in the sky above it.

"Whoops," I whispered. I looked over and groaned. Amrynn was unconscious. I didn't have the power to teleport us again. But I also didn't think I could teleport such a short distance. It felt like I could only travel across planets. "Amrynn! Save me!" I yelled.

Amrynn's eyes flew open, he took in our situation, gripped me tightly, and then teleported us safely down to Durlan's grass.

Safe. We were safe.

We collapsed on the grass, separating as we took in our safety.

My breath came in short and raspy gasps, and I felt the darkness encroaching again.

Amrynn sat upright, looking around a moment, and then he bellowed, "Durlan!"

Durlan, Ryul, Kydrus, and Venali burst from the house, and then froze when they saw us.

Ryul was the first to recover, running to me and setting his hands on my chest to check and heal me.

"You're alive," he whispered.

"Barely," I groaned, watching as several Ryul's shimmered around me. "There's three of you, no four. Four of you. I don't think I can handle four Ryuls."

"What happened?" Kydrus asked Amrynn.

"It's a long story. She needs rest and healing," Amrynn said and picked me up, ignoring Ryul's protest.

I closed my eyes, a smile on my lips. "I did it."

Amrynn brushed his lips across mine. "Yes, you did. You're truly amazing."

He lay me down on one of the couches, and Durlan took over healing me. Ryul stood behind the couch, looking down at me with a frown.

"How did you get back?" Durlan asked.

"Planet hopping," I whispered and then groaned. My entire body was sore, like after my training sessions with Venali. "It was hot then cold and then we got close and then we were falling." I giggled. "Falling."

"Stop talking," Amrynn growled at me. "Let me answer their questions."

I mocked him silently, mouthing back his words without saying them, a smile on my face while Durlan's body blocked me from Amrynn's sight.

Durlan smiled, while Kydrus scowled at me.

"How long were we gone?" Amrynn asked.

"A month," Ryul growled.

My mouth dropped open. "What? No, we were not."

"I was afraid time might move differently when we left our planet," Amrynn mumbled.

"A month? We were gone a month?" I asked, looking at Durlan and then at Ryul.

Ryul's jaw clenched.

Kydrus said, "Yes. You were gone thirty-two days to be exact."

I held up my hand, and Ryul grabbed it without hesitation, bending so he could place my palm against his cheek.

"I'm so sorry," I whispered, and then before I could stop them, tears streamed down my face, and my body shook with heavy sobs.

Durlan pulled me into a sitting position and wrapped his arms around me. Kydrus sat at my feet and rested his hand on my shin. Ryul placed several light kisses to the palm he held.

"I'm so sorry," I gasped between sobs. My brain was finally functioning correctly, which sucked since all of my emotions came with it.

Amrynn shoved his way in, grabbed my face between his hands, and stared into my eyes. "You have nothing to apologize for, Elara."

"You almost died...because of me," I sobbed, clutching his wrists. I sucked in a stuttering breath. "I couldn't protect you. I don't deserve you, any of you. I—"

"You did what you could," he whispered. "If it weren't for you, they would have killed me. Or, kept me as a blood donor on some distant planet. You rescued me."

"Jensen saved us," I reminded him.

"Because of you," he said and wiped the tears from beneath my eyes.

I shook my head but couldn't find the right words to say to him. There was something I could do, though.

"I need...stones," I gulped. I extricated myself from Amrynn's hold and wiped my face on my shirt. It took several breaths to calm myself fully.

"Stones? What kind of stones? For what?" Ryul asked.

"In my study," Durlan said. "I have lots in the third drawer from the left."

I hurried to his study and grabbed a handful of beautiful gemstones. "Perfect," I whispered.

"What are you doing?" Ryul asked.

I handed him four of the stones, keeping one in my hand. "Protecting our planet," I said, pushed open the door and strode out onto the grass.

Kydrus followed me out, right on my heels. "Elara, don't do anything that could hurt you. You need to rest. You need—"

"I need to protect Minloa," I snapped. "I won't let them come here. I won't let them take any of you and drain your blood. I won't let them use us as blood bags!"

Everyone except Amrynn halted, eyes widened at my proclamation.

I looked up at the sky, closed my eyes, raised my hand, and focused. Barry was far away, but I could still sense the sun and the planets. Since I had used power from them, I was even more connected than before. I grabbed the planet Barry inhabited in my hand, pulled it down, and shoved it into the gemstone. I opened my eyes and beamed at the glowing stone, with a single planet swirling within it.

"Holy shit," Kydrus gasped.

"She...a planet...what?" Ryul sputtered. "I've never heard of that before."

"Next," I ordered Ryul and set the current gemstone I held on the ground. He held out another gemstone, and I took it, then repeated the process until all of the planets were in gemstones. The last thing was their sun. I picked up the first gemstone, the one with Barry's planet in it, and pulled their sun into the gemstone. Now, I would use their sun and their planet as my power source. Like they had wanted to use my blood to fuel their research.

I turned and smiled at my guards. "Now, they'll never be able to harm us again."

The world tilted, and my eyes rolled up in the back of my head. I fell into a warm body, and fainted.

CHAPTER 20
ELARA

"You're mad at me," I whispered.

I had woken up a few minutes earlier, found Venali sitting in a chair in my room in Durlan's house, and stared at him silently. He hadn't said a word to me yesterday. He hadn't even touched me.

"I thought you were dead," he whispered.

I tossed the blankets back and walked to stand before him, surprised I was no longer sore. Durlan and Ryul must have both taken turns healing me.

I dropped to my knees and bowed my head. "I'm sorry, Venali. I made a huge mistake. It almost cost Amrynn his life. I'm so sorry. I understand if you don't want to be my guard. I'm willing to free you from that obligation. You can go do what you want. Start a new life. Get a mate. Do whatever you would do while not being a warlord or tied to me."

He slid to his knees before me, lifted my chin, and said, "You bow to no one, least of all me. I don't want to stop being warlord, and definitely don't want to stop being your guard. I was not mad at you for leaving. I was mad at myself for not being able to protect you. For failing to defeat our enemies. I thought you were dead. I thought I would never see you again. And, when I finally saw you, I was so overcome with emotions, that I couldn't let you see me in that state. We were certain you were dead. With no connection to you, and you gone for a month, we had no way of knowing what had happened. That was the worst part. Not knowing. Every night I looked at the stars, wishing for you to come back, wishing I could see you. Every day I ached for you to return."

His eyes gleamed with unshed tears.

"I don't deserve you," I whispered and rested my hand on his cheek, tears brimming in my own eyes.

"Please, don't leave us again. It was torture," he whispered and leaned into my hand.

I threw my arms around him and pressed my lips to his.

His arms wrapped around me, and he turned my frenzied kiss into a slow and deep one. One that left no doubt in my mind what his feelings were.

I pushed his chest, and he lay on his back on the floor, never separating our mouths. I lay atop him, reveling in his warmth a moment, the feel of his tongue sliding along mine, and then reality struck.

Kydrus knocked on the door. "Wake her up already. We need to meet," he said gruffly.

"Alright," Venali called back.

Kydrus's booted footsteps could be heard headed towards Durlan's study.

Venali stood, bringing me with him, and kissed me deeply. "I'm not quitting being warlord. I'm not quitting being your guard. I will stay by your side for as long as you will have me. And, hopefully, one day you might consider taking me as a mate. Okay?"

I nodded. I understood that was how he felt currently, but... "It's okay if you change your mind."

He sighed and rested his forehead against mine. "My beautiful queen, you constantly underestimate and undervalue yourself."

"I missed you," I admitted, and tears began leaking down my face. "I thought I was never going to see you again."

He hugged me tightly. "I missed you more than you will ever know."

"We should go to the others," I said and kissed him. I wanted to sit in his arms for eternity, but I wanted to see the others. I had something I needed to do.

He kissed the tears from my face, linked our fingers together, and led the way.

My four other guards instantly turned to watch me when I entered, their eyes glued to me like I might disappear again.

I sat on Amrynn's lap, kissed his cheek, and asked, "What are we meeting about?"

"How are you feeling today?" Durlan asked.

"I feel back to normal," I answered.

"You look upset," Ryul said, his brows furrowed.

Now was as good of a time as any.

I stood from Amrynn's lap, walked to stand beside the desk, and faced the five of them. "I'm going to take over being queen, but I'm going to do things a bit differently."

All of their eyes were wide, and mouths shut as they waited for me to tell them what the plan was.

"I will be queen, I will have warlords, but slightly different than before. My warlords will be my equals. I understand that you five may not want to be my warlords any longer, which is totally understandable. If you'd like to give up your station, there will be no punishment. I plan to hold a tournament for your replacements, to find the strongest in Minloa. However, if you stay with me, you will not only be my warlords and my friends, but, if you'll have me, my mates as well."

"You want the five of us as mates?" Kydrus asked.

I nodded. "If you don't want to be my mate, or can't handle sharing, I fully understand and there will be no hard feelings. I will take my place as queen in two months. I'd like to meet with you all individually to discuss your answers to my offer of being mates and your continued place as warlords. So, you can discuss amongst yourselves what order you come out, or just come when you want. I'll be outside waiting."

I left before they could say anything, shutting the office door behind me, then made my way outside and sat down. I had no idea what the five would decide. I assumed Ryul and Venali would stay with me, but I wasn't certain of Amrynn's response. Or Durlan's. He was so much more reserved than the others. Even more reserved than Kydrus, which was something I hadn't thought possible before.

I wanted them all. I wanted to keep all five of them, but I didn't hold hope for that outcome.

I had expected Ryul to be the first one out, but Kydrus was. He sat down in front of me and said, "I would like to accept your offer to be mates."

He was always so serious.

I smiled. "You're sure?"

He nodded.

"Thank you. I was actually concerned with what you would think and what your response would be," I admitted to him.

He leaned forward and kissed me. "I will follow you through time itself, Elara."

Kydrus teleported away, and Amrynn came out next. He knocked me to the ground and peppered my face with kisses. "You already know my answer."

"I do?"

He leaned back and arched an eyebrow. "You think after all of that, I wouldn't want to be your mate?"

"You suffered because I was too weak to protect you," I said with a frown.

He shook his head and said, "You teleported us across several planets just to get me home. I will follow you until the end of time."

I kissed him and whispered, "I love you."

He kissed my cheek and whispered in my ear, "I love you, too."

"Stop hogging her," Ryul grumbled. "You had her all to yourself for a month."

Amrynn smirked, kissed me again, and then walked by Ryul with a slap to his shoulder, not bothering to explain that, to us, it had only been a few weeks.

Ryul pulled me up and hugged me. "Do I even need to answer you?"

"Yes," I mumbled, but knew already that he wanted to be my mate. That we wanted to be mates.

"I want to be your mate. I want to be yours and I have no problem sharing you. Having a sliver of you is more than enough for me."

"Thank you."

Venali came next, kissed me deeply, and whispered, "yes."

I hugged him, resting my cheek on his chest. "Thank you."

"Durlan's last?" he asked.

I nodded.

"He's always the gentleman," Venali said and chuckled as he left.

I stayed standing, waiting for Durlan to come.

Several minutes passed, but he still didn't appear.

My heart fell. Of all of the men, I hadn't expected Durlan to turn me down. We weren't as intimate together, but I thought that was just how he was. Had I read him wrong?

I heard the door open and looked up.

"You look so distraught," Durlan said. "Did one of the others refuse you?"

"No," I answered.

He smiled. "You thought I was planning to refuse you?"

I shrugged.

He stopped before me, dropped to one knee and held my hand in his. "You, my queen, are too perfect for us to pass up. Refusing you would be like refusing a goddess."

I blushed. "Were you drinking before you came out here?"

Durlan tossed his head back and bellowed with laughter. "No, my queen. I'm sorry if I made you wait. I assumed the others would take longer. If you'll have me, I'll gladly accept being your mate."

To answer, I threw my arms around him and kissed him.

"Tomorrow we celebrate!" Venali shouted.

I turned in Durlan's arms, facing my other four mates, all smiling.

"Celebrate what?" I asked.

"Your birthday," Durlan said with a light laugh.

"You five are more than I could have ever wished for," I said. "I don't need anything else."

"Well, too bad, because we are still celebrating your birthday," Ryul said.

"What birthday is this? Twenty-nine or one thousand and twenty-nine?" I asked.

"One thousand and twenty-nine," Venali answered.

"You've been alive that long, just a bit frozen for most of it," Amrynn said and chuckled.

"Just a bit frozen," I said and rolled my eyes.

"At least you aren't sour like pickled cucumbers after being sealed up," Venali said.

Kydrus pulled me from Durlan and into his arms. "I'm just glad we were finally able to thaw that cold heart of yours."

I wrapped my arms around his neck and kissed his cheek. "Me, too."

"Can't we give her our group present now?" Venali asked.

"Her birthday has already passed," Durlan said. "I don't see why we couldn't. We can still celebrate her birthday tomorrow and give her our individual presents then."

"Now that she knows we have something," Ryul said with a smirk. "I think we should make her wait."

"That's just because you enjoy tormenting me," I grumbled and folded my arms across my chest.

"I vote yes," Amrynn said.

"Alright," Ryul said with a sigh. "I guess I'm outvoted."

"Close your eyes," Durlan ordered me.

I obeyed, but then started trying to open one just a bit.

"No peeking," Kydrus growled in my ear and then nipped it lightly.

I bit my lip to keep from making an embarrassing noise.

Four pairs of hands touched me, running along my arms, sides, back, and through my hair.

My mouth parted in a gasp.

A finger traced my lower lip, and I flicked my tongue out over it.

Five groans followed.

"You're all teasing me on purpose," I growled. "Because I can't open my eyes to see who is touching me where."

"Who said we're teasing," Durlan purred in my ear.

"Can I open my eyes yet?" I asked, my legs were started to quiver as my panties disintegrated in a pool of lust.

All hands were removed, leaving me feeling cold and vulnerable. I bit back a whimper.

"Open your eyes," Amrynn instructed.

I obeyed, then gasped.

Before me rested a silver crown, made to look like branches, and along the branches set jewels. They were the same jewels I had put Barry's planets in.

"You had this made for me?" I asked.

"Durlan made it," Kydrus said.

I turned to him. "You made this for me last night?"

He rubbed the back of his neck and smiled. "Yes. I thought the jewels deserved to be shown off by you. They are a symbol of your protection of our planet. And, I know you needed a crown."

"Can I put it on?" I asked. "Or do I have to wait until the ceremony?"

"Ceremony," Ryul said.

"You can try it on," Durlan said with a chuckle. "Stop trying to antagonize her."

Ryul smiled. "It's just so easy."

"Come on, you need a mirror," Venali said. He hooked an arm around my waist and guided me inside.

I leaned into him, inhaling his scent as we walked. The others followed close behind, and I resisted the urge to look back, to make sure they were still there.

"This isn't a dream, right?" I asked, swallowing a ball of emotion that swirled within me.

Venali tightened his hold on me. "You aren't dreaming, Elara."

Ryul pinched my arm, which made me laugh.

"Okay, I'm not dreaming."

Everyone crowded into my room, all five of my guys stood behind me. Durlan placed the crown on my head, and stepped back.

With the crown on, I looked regal, like a queen.

When I turned around, all five men were down on one knee, bowing.

"We offer our swords, our bodies, and our hearts to you, Elara," Durlan said.

"We will serve you for eternity," Ryul said.

"We will guide you and protect you," Kydrus said.

"We will be your friend and a shoulder to cry on," Amrynn said.

"And, we will destroy anyone who threatens you or your happiness," Venali said.

I believed them. I believed they would do all of those things and more.

"As heir to Minloa, I accept your oaths. Rise as my warlords, guards, and mates," I said.

Power thrummed in the room, and something sizzled on the back of my neck. My body shimmered a moment, my clothes morphing into a beautiful leather warrior outfit. Then, it disappeared.

I reached back, rubbing at the spot. There was no blood, but it was tender.

"What was that?" I asked, turning to face the guys.

All of them looked as shocked as I was.

"Was that..." Ryul started to ask, but trailed off.

Durlan examined Venali's neck, eyes wide. "I thought it was just a fable."

"What? What is it? What happened?" I asked, my voice near a shriek, but part of me felt it. Felt the power thrumming within me, the truth simmering in the back of my mind.

The guys exchanged glances, some type of silent communication happening.

"Hey!" I snapped. "Did you learn telepathy or something?"

"*You did, too,*" Ryul said, in my head.

I gasped. "Wha—"

"She's got her walls up really thick," Ryul told them, clutching at his head. "Getting that tiny message through to her was really painful."

"She may not know how to take them down, or how to create a wall that only we can go through," Amrynn whispered.

"Talk to me," I begged. "Tell me what's going on?"

"There's a story," Durlan began. "About the Goddess Amara and her Consorts."

Amara.

"I know that name," I whispered, pain tearing through my chest and head at the same time. I clutched at them, trying to quell the pain and pressure now present.

"You recognize the name, because it's your true name, isn't it?" Kydrus asked.

I swallowed, trying to remember. Hadn't I regained my memories? I remembered being raised by the king and queen. I remembered growing up with Ryul, and then being a slave. I had the scars as proof.

"I'm fae," I whispered. "I was raised here."

"Your body is, but your soul isn't," Kydrus said. "You've been reincarnated. You need to stop fighting it and let your soul fully merge with your current self."

I shook my head. "No. You're wrong. No."

I couldn't be a goddess. I couldn't be. Right? No. That was insane. This was insane. Had we been drugged? We were all hallucinating, right?

"This changes nothing," I whispered, trying not to panic. "We're moving forward as planned. Nothing has changed."

"Everything has changed," Venali whispered, eyes wide as saucers. "You're not only the queen, but also the goddess. Everyone is going to want to see her. Everyone is going to want to touch her. The Unseelie will want to kill her."

"We can't let anyone find out that she's Amara," Kydrus growled. "We can reveal her as queen, but not as the goddess. Not yet, anyway. We need her to fully accept herself first."

Each time they said that name, it changed part of me. I didn't like it. I didn't like it one bit! I wasn't her. I wasn't a celestial. I was just Elara, heir to the throne, orphan, former slave, mate of the Four Warlords of Minloa. That's who I was.

"Stop saying that name," I growled, but they didn't hear me, their focus on each other.

"If we announce her now, some will notice and could expose her. They could expose us. They will see her for who she really is. There are many with the power to see into one's soul. They'll see how old her soul is. They'll know she's Amara," Amrynn said.

"How is she hiding Amara within her? She is her, but we didn't see it until the bond formed. How is it possible that she is Amara?" Ryul asked.

"Amara didn't die in the tales. She just disappeared. She and her consorts all disappeared," Durlan said.

"If she is Amara, then we've got to help her unite herself," Venali whispered.

"Stop saying that name!" I screamed, throwing my arms to my side in frustration.

Power flared out around me in the form of a strong wind, knocking the guys onto their backs.

I gasped, my hands flew to my mouth, and I fell to my knees, reaching out towards them. "I'm sorry. I didn't mean to do that. Please, just...stop saying that name. It's not me. I'm not her. Please."

They sat up and then surrounded me with hugs and touches. None of them were hurt.

"Okay," Durlan said, his warm breath sliding along my neck as he spoke. "We won't say it anymore."

I took a shuddering breath. "I can't...it's too much. Too much."

"What is?" Ryul asked.

"The truth," I whispered as bits of information filtered in despite my best attempts to keep it all out. "It's too much. There's too much." I stood, extricating myself from the men. "There's so much to do. So much change. I need to find them. I must find them."

"What is she talking about?" Amrynn asked.

"Who?" Durlan asked.

"I think she's freaking out," Kydrus whispered. "We should knock her out and let her sleep this off."

"Why have they been hiding? What have they been up to? Will they even remember? Will he give me an audience? What if they attack my guards? I can't let them hurt my guards. But I can't go alone either. I can't let them get me. I can't let anyone keep me hostage again," I muttered as I headed to the living room, where I began pacing.

"Elara, what are you talking about?" Durlan asked.

"Everything is going to change. It's all changing. Changing. Changing. Just like before. It's all changing. My fault. It's all my fault." I cried and bit my lip to stop it's trembling.

Venali gripped my arms gently, staring down into my eyes. "Talk to us. Your mind is so jumbled, your aura is flashing all over the place. Tell us what you're talking about. Who are you going to see? Who might hurt us?"

I shouldn't tell them. They'd overreact. Ryul would want to hide me. Amrynn would want to run far away. He might even suggest the planet we'd teleported to before here, since he knew it could sustain us. Venali would want to slaughter them all before they even had the chance to hurt us. Kydrus. I didn't know what Kydrus would think.

"Open up to us, Elara. We are yours. You are ours. We are partners, remember? Partners talk to each other. Partners share everything with each other," Venali whispered, stroking my arms with his thumbs. "Tell us."

"Who are you wanting to go and find? Who do you need an audience before?" Ryul asked.

I looked at them and decided I had to tell them. They were tied to me now, bound to me in a way that no one else would understand. I wanted them to be my mates, but I hadn't wanted them to be stuck with me for eternity. A lifetime, yes, but not eternity.

"You're stuck with me for eternity now," I whispered. "You realize that?"

"We're fine with that," Venali assured me. "But we need to know what enemies are ahead of us. We need to know what threats we will be faced with."

"Who do you need to see?" Kydrus asked, a bit of growl and order in his tone. He towered over me, not to intimidate me, but in anticipation of protecting me.

I stepped back and turned so that I could see all of them at the same time. They were all anxious, their bodies tense with frustration and worry, perhaps even a bit of fear. I knew I was afraid.

I licked my lips nervously, and said, "I need to see the Unseelie monarch. I need an audience with the Unseelie Court."

EMPRESS OF THE GALAXY

BOOK TWO

USA TODAY BESTSELLING AUTHOR

CATHERINE BANKS

EMPRESS OF THE GALAXY

2

THEIR FAE GODDESS

Empress of the Galaxy by Catherine Banks.

Cover design by Ana Cruz Arts.

Published by Turbo Kitten Industries.

www.CatherineBanks.com

Turbo Kitten Industries™, P.O. Box 5012, Galt, CA 95632

ACKNOWLEDGMENTS

Thank you to the following people who helped make this book possible:

C.R. for being such a fantastic person and helping me in ways she may never realize.

Lea for being awesome and helping me in so many ways.

Jenica for always being there. She means more to me than she knows.

As always, my amazing husband and best friend, Avery.

Anderelle

Zenlop

Minloa

Emortalia

S

CHAPTER 1
ELARA

"I NEED an audience with the Unseelie Court. I need to see the Unseelie King, or whoever their ruler is, specifically."

The five men in front of me wore varying shades of disbelief. The Four Warlords of Minloa were my guards and soon to be my mates. The fifth man was my guard and soon to be mate as well, Ryul. He'd been my friend when we were children, and had waited a thousand years for me to return to him.

"Absolutely not," Kydrus growled, his sharp canines showing.

"No," Ryul snapped.

"Why?" Durlan asked.

"There are some wrongs that need righted," I said and then grimaced. "I actually have a lot of travel I need to make."

"You're talking crazy," Amrynn said. "Where is this all coming from?"

Venali was the only one who hadn't spoken. Instead, he chose to glower at me, his eyes sparkling with an emotion I couldn't quite place.

"Have any of you been to Eltare before?" I asked.

The Unseelie had been forced out of Minloa, and lived on an

island near our continent. I wasn't sure how many Unseelie there were, but it had to be rather crowded for them to all fit on the island.

"No, none of us have been there," Venali answered when everyone else chose to stare at me silently. "And, I don't think it's wise for you to go there either."

"I guess we'll just have to travel the old-fashioned way," I said, ignoring his second comment. "By boat."

"You keep ignoring our questions," Ryul growled.

I sighed and ran a hand down my face. "It's complicated. I don't really want to get into it right now. The best thing we can do is sleep and then discuss our travel plans tomorrow."

"You said you have a lot of travel. Where else are you wanting to go?" Durlan asked.

He was the only one who seemed calm, though his frown led me to believe he didn't want me to go, like the other four.

I rubbed the back of my neck, turned away from them, and grimaced at the pain in my head.

"What's wrong?" Amrynn asked, coming to my side.

Of course he would know I was in pain without facing him. Our time alone had connected us a bit more than I liked to admit. And this new connection...I wasn't sure what to think about it yet. I knew what it was, but I wanted to stay in my land of denial, so I wouldn't even think of the name.

"Headache," I whispered, but that wasn't completely true. My head did hurt, but it was from holding back my power. I didn't want to be a goddess. I didn't want to be Amara. I was Elara, dammit.

I swayed on my feet, and Amrynn wrapped an arm around me to keep me upright.

"You're burning up," he growled, picked me up in his arms and carried me to my room. "What's wrong, Elara? Why are you ill?"

"She's being stubborn," Ryul growled. "Stop denying it and open yourself to the power. I can see it boiling within you."

Curse him and his stupid sight.

"What?" Venali asked him.

Ryul placed his hand on my forehead and stared into my eyes. "Elara, just admit it to yourself and let the power out."

"No," I growled. "I am Elara, heir to Minloa. That is all."

"You are Amara, Goddess and ruler of the universe," he corrected.

I growled at him. "Don't say that name. I already ordered you to not say that name."

He scowled at me. "Really?"

"Get out," I ordered him.

His hand dropped to his side. "What?"

"Get out of my room, Ryul," I snapped.

Venali set a hand on his shoulder. "Come talk to me outside." In a quieter voice, one he probably thought I couldn't hear, he said, "I need you to tell us more about what you know."

Ryul's eyes flashed, pain and anger both in his expression, but he finally lowered his gaze in submission and left.

All of my guards left, shutting my door as they did.

I relaxed on my bed and closed my eyes. I wasn't going to let her win. I wasn't her. I was Elara. I was Elara.

Elara.

Elara.

CHAPTER 2
AMRYNN

"SHE'S REFUSING to accept who she really is," Ryul said, glaring at the door as though he could still see Elara. "If she doesn't accept it, the power will make her more ill, and it could kill her."

"Why doesn't she want to admit it?" I asked.

My future mate was a stubborn and prideful woman, but I couldn't believe she would do something that could ultimately kill her. She was a goddess, reincarnated. Why wouldn't she want to admit that?

"I don't know. I wasn't alive the last time Amara was here, but we bear her marks on us. We are her consorts," Ryul answered. He ran a hand through his hair and exhaled loudly. "She kicked me out. I can't believe she kicked me out."

"You did say the name again, after she ordered us not to," Kydrus reminded him.

Ryul glared at him. "She has to accept it."

"Forcing her will do nothing but cause her to shut down more. She is stubborn and hates being ordered to do anything," Venali said. "She has to make the decision on her own."

"What if she doesn't?" Durlan asked, lifting his head to look at us. "What if she refuses to accept it and gets worse?"

None of us had an answer for that.

The thought of losing her made my heart twist and my gut drop. I'd almost lost her to Barry. I had been useless then, and I was useless now. I hated it. Oh, how I hated it.

"We should just give her the space she wants tonight," I said and swallowed the fear down.

"What are we going to do about her wanting to go to the Unseelie?" Durlan asked.

"We cannot let her go," Venali growled.

"She's going to go," I mumbled. "Whether we help her or not."

"She can't teleport on this planet. So, we should be fine," Kydrus said.

I scoffed. "She'll sneak out the first chance she gets. If she wants to go, she will. So, you all need to determine if you are willing to go with her or not."

"You're willing to let her go and face them? Those barbarians?" Kydrus asked, his eyes narrowed.

"I would rather she never leave Durlan's house again, but it is not up to me. She will go, and I will guard her. That is my job. Wherever she goes, I go," I answered.

Durlan sighed. "I'm afraid he's right. She will go, despite our opinions."

Venali growled and stalked out of the house and into the night. Knowing him, he was probably going to punch something until he destroyed it.

"I'll do some research," Durlan said, turning towards his study. "Everyone, just keep an eye on her, but don't go in her room or engage her."

"This is ridiculous," Ryul growled.

"We all agree," I said. "But there is little we can do."

CHAPTER 3
VENALI

Elara was finally mine. My mate. Yet, now more issues had arisen.

Amara.

Had I not been marked as well, I might not have believed it. She was our goddess. A fable, myth, that we told the children. How was it possible that Elara was her?

And, if I was her consort, did that mean I was a reincarnation of one of Amara's consorts, too?

I punched a tree, a hole forming in the wake of my fist.

If Elara didn't accept her power, she would die. I couldn't let her die. I'd thought she was lost before. I refused to watch her wither away now.

But she wanted to see the Unseelie. That also made no sense.

The Unseelie would steal her away or kill her, if given the chance.

I didn't want to take her to them, but if I didn't go, she would leave me behind and I would always wonder if I could have saved her.

This felt like a suicide mission. But, if I could save her, I would gladly forfeit my life.

No, we would all survive this. They would not kill us.

I would kill every last Unseelie if they hurt her. Or die trying.

CHAPTER 4
KYDRUS

My mind was still reeling from our revelations. Elara wanted me as a mate. She had accepted me, and then a symbol, one not seen for over two thousand years appeared on all of us.

Not only was she queen, but she was also the missing goddess.

Amrynn, Ryul, Durlan, and Venali sat around Durlan's study, all deep in their own thoughts. All were as worried as I was that our mate wanted to go speak to the ruler of the Unseelie.

Another thought occurred to me.

"Didn't Amara have seven consorts?" I voiced my thought.

Venali let loose a string of curses.

"Yes," Durlan answered. "I was thinking about that, too."

"Are you telling me two more guys are going to show up with the symbols on their necks?" Ryul asked, his jaw clenched and the words barely slipping out. His hands glowed and would likely become coated in flames if he didn't control his anger.

"Yes," Durlan said with a frown.

The blue flames erupted over Ryul's hands and up his forearms.

Venali growled loudly.

I tossed Venali a long log from beside the fireplace, which he promptly snapped in half.

I should have felt the same, but I was rather accepting for some reason.

"Who else could rival us in power?" Amrynn asked. "Not to brag, but I haven't run across anyone in Minloa who was nearly as powerful as us."

"She did mention that she has a lot of traveling to do. Maybe that's why. Maybe she needs to travel to another continent to find her last mates," Durlan said. His normally relaxed expression hardened. "I hate sailing."

Laughter burst out of me, uncontrollable and loud.

Durlan arched a brow.

"You're not worried about our mate finding more mates, ones we don't know. No, you're worried about sailing," I gasped.

He sighed. "I have accepted my fate. I am her guard and mate, I already share her with you four, so what's two more?"

"I don't like this," Ryul growled.

"It is what it is," I said and sat back, looking up at the ceiling. "Who knew such a timid creature would cause so much trouble in my life."

Venali leaned forward. "How are we going to travel to another continent? We can't leave our sectors unwatched for more than a week."

"I don't know," Durlan admitted. "I'm still trying to figure that out."

We lapsed back into silence, none of us coming up with an answer. We didn't want to leave our sectors, but Elara leaving without us was even more unacceptable. I'd been separated from her once, with no knowledge of whether she was alive or not. I would not do the same now. I would go insane wondering if she was alright, and if she did get injured, I would blame myself for not being there to protect her.

"Perhaps it is time we found new warlords," Amrynn said. "We could announce Elara, hold a tournament, and then we could all go with her."

I sighed but agreed. "I second this idea."

"You've changed," Venali said, lifting a brow. "Old Kydrus would have torn into Amrynn for suggesting such a thing."

"Old Kydrus wasn't a consort to a goddess, or mate to a queen. I have different priorities now. I won't stay here while she travels for months."

He growled and lowered his head, glaring at his hands. "Announcing her as queen and then disappearing for several months isn't exactly a great plan."

"She will be going on a diplomatic expedition," Durian said. "Royals used to do it all the time."

"Not immediately after taking the throne," Venali countered.

"Then we make her wait a month," I said.

Ryul rubbed at his chest, grimacing. "If she survives that long."

He had different magic than us, which apparently let him see her power. If he was right, we had to convince her to accept who she truly was as soon as possible.

"One thing at a time," Durlan said. "Amrynn, go tell Elara our plan."

"Why him?" Venali bristled.

"Because he can control his emotions and he spent the most time with her." Durlan sighed and rubbed the back of his neck, shoulders slumped.

Technically, I had spent the most time with her, but now was not the time to argue that point.

Amrynn stood and nodded. "I'll come back and let you know how it went."

CHAPTER 5
ELARA

My body burned and sweat poured down my face. I wanted to scream or punch someone. Maybe both.

"I am Elara, heir to Minloa," I growled for the thirtieth time since my mates had left me alone in my room. "I will not give in."

Maybe if I used just a bit of the magic, it would ease my suffering.

With a deep breath, I drew a tiny amount of my power out. It tried to escape in a tornado, but I held it at bay. The power came to me, and I used it to reach down the new bond with my mates. There should have only been five, but two additional bonds, not fully completed, glowed as well.

The two bonds tugged, trying to find me, to communicate. I slammed my barriers shut, using the power to wall myself off.

No. Not now. Now was not the time. Not yet.

Someone knocked on my door, so I quickly sealed my power again, bottling it up tight.

Surprisingly, I did feel better. I wiped my face and sat up.

"Come in," I called.

Amrynn entered, a scowl of worry marring his handsome face.

When he saw me sitting up, the scowl lessened. "How are you feeling?"

"Better," I answered truthfully.

He sat on the end of my bed, examining me. "We've decided on a course of action."

I glared. "Without me present."

He smiled. "Easy, Elara."

I sighed. "Go on."

"We're going to announce you. We are also going to hold a tournament to replace ourselves as warlords."

My mouth dropped open. "What? I don't understand. You all agreed to be my mates. We're bound magically, for eternity. And *now* you want to back out?" I stood, facing him with tears in my eyes. "I know you guys are upset that I haven't accepted this... development, but—"

He stood and gripped my upper arms, tightly, but not enough to hurt. "Elara, let me finish. We aren't backing out. We are your mates, now and forever."

Tears dripped down my cheek, and I sniffed loudly. "Okay."

He stroked his hands up and down my arms, while smiling softly. "We don't want to separate from you, especially not when you're going into enemy territory. However, we can't leave our sectors unattended either."

Okay, that made sense. My tears subsided, and I sniffed again, my fear and heartbreak gone.

"So, we're going to hold a tournament to find new warlords. That way we can leave Minloa in their hands," he continued.

"That's great," I said. "I'm totally on board with this."

He sat back on the bed, crossing one leg over the other. My eyes were drawn to his mouth as he resumed speaking. "After the tournament, you need to be here for at least a month, though."

"What? Why?" I asked, jerking my gaze up to his eyes.

"The new queen can't just disappear for months right after

taking up the mantle. You need to get things in motion and in order first," he explained.

I sighed and dropped my head forward. "You're just trying to keep me from going to the Unseelie."

"No. We all know you are going to go, and nothing we do will keep you from that. We are really just trying to get things set up correctly."

I looked up at him, scowling. "I need to see the Unseelie."

He scowled. "Is one of your other consorts Unseelie?"

My eyes widened and my mouth popped open. "You know about the others?"

He smirked. "She-who-shall-not-be-named had seven consorts. We assumed you would as well."

Crap.

"Is one of them Unseelie?" he asked.

"I don't know," I answered. "I can sense them, but I've blocked the bonds so they can't find me or contact me."

"Why?" he asked, titling his head slightly to the side.

I fidgeted with my shirt. "I'm not ready yet. We just confirmed our bonds. I don't want to add two more into the mix. I know it's going to be difficult for you guys to deal with."

"Only a couple of us are upset about it, but they'll come around," he assured me.

I sat on his lap and rested my head on his shoulder. "I don't want this," I whispered. "I just wanted us to become mates, and for me to take the throne with you five at my side."

Amrynn wrapped his arms around me, holding me tightly. "We are here for you. Always will be. We will get through this together. But you have to be honest with us. You have to trust us and give us as much information as you can."

"There are some things that are best left to discuss later," I mumbled, turning my face into his shirt. "Other things, I don't want to know."

"You're still feverish," he whispered. "Why won't you accept it? What is it that frightens you?"

"I don't want to be a celestial. I went from being a slave to being a Seelie queen. Isn't that enough of a jump for one lifetime?"

"You promise you won't let this kill you?" he whispered.

I nodded. "I'm not that stubborn."

He chuckled, but it was tense.

"When are you going to announce me?" I asked him, stroking my fingertips along his throat. I wanted to touch more of his skin, but since he was dressed, this was the best I could do at the moment.

"Tomorrow."

I tensed. Everything was going to change in the next few months. I wasn't sure if I was ready.

And my poor mates. They were going to give up their titles for me. It wasn't fair.

"Maybe you—"

"We are voluntarily giving up our titles as warlords," Amrynn said, interrupting me. "We are not being forced. We want to be with you much more than we want to stay warlords."

How did he know I was going to say that?

"Will you lie with me for a bit?" I asked and chewed on my lip nervously.

Without hesitation, he pulled off his boots, laid us down, and pulled a blanket up over us both. He spooned his body around mine and kissed the side of my neck. "Rest, my queen. I will keep you safe."

CHAPTER 6

RYUL

"She's sleeping now," Amrynn informed us as he stepped out of her bedroom. He shut her door and motioned at us to follow him to the living room.

"How did she take the news?" I asked.

"Surprisingly well," he said as he sat. "And, she admitted she does have two other mates, but she's blocked their bonds so they can't find her or communicate with her."

All of us grimaced.

I didn't want her to have more mates, but to have your mate block you and refuse to communicate with you would be torturous.

"Does she know who they are?" I asked. Not that it mattered. I had no say in any of this.

Amrynn shook his head and sighed. "She's overwhelmed. She had no idea this was going to happen, and wants to enjoy having us as mates first."

"Overwhelmed?" Kydrus asked. "I'm not surprised."

"She did go from being a slave to all of this rather quickly," Durlan said. "It's a huge change."

"So, she's fine with waiting for the tournament and a month after to go to the Unseelie?" Venali asked, folding his arms over his chest.

Amrynn nodded. "She understands our reasoning and said she is fine with it. She..." He looked down at his hands and sighed loudly. "When I told her we were finding new warlords, she thought we were abandoning her."

"What?" My anger skyrocketed, heat rushing to my face. After all we had been through? Could any of us even consider abandoning her?

"How could she think that?" Venali asked, his voice more growl than usual. "We're bound for eternity."

Amrynn looked up at me, and then Venali. "She's terrified of being abandoned. I can't say I blame her. Before she had her memories, she must have assumed her parents abandoned her to be a slave. She never fit in, and we've been pushing her to learn as much as possible. She needs reassuring. She's young."

"If she would accept her powers, she would regain her previous lives' memories. She would know that we won't ever abandon her," I snapped.

"Ryul, we understand your frustration, but snapping at her or being mad at her won't change anything. It will only make matters worse." Kydrus sighed.

I stood and glared at him. "She let out some of her powers. I felt it. She knows, yet she refuses to fully accept it. It's going to continue to weaken her and can kill her."

"She assured me she won't let it kill her," Amrynn said.

I scoffed. "She's more stubborn than any of you realize. You understand that our memories won't unlock until she accepts her powers as well, right? We'd have a lot more information at our disposal, and I am certain that is part of why she's holding back. She doesn't want us to remember. She doesn't want us to know the secrets she is keeping from us."

I turned and stormed out of the living room and out of the house. They were blinded by their love for her. Blinded by her childlike innocence. I loved her more than anything in all of the worlds, but my magic allowed me to see more than them. She was keeping secrets from us. Secrets I was certain were dangerous.

It bothered me most of all that she wouldn't confide in me. We were friends, weren't we? Why wasn't she confiding in me then? It hurt, but I would never admit that for fear of the others viewing me as weak.

"Want to spar?" Venali asked from behind me.

I stopped walking and turned to face him. "What?"

He smirked. "You look like you could use an outlet for some of that anger. I know I could."

I blew out a breath and nodded. Sparring would help me rein in my anger a bit. Hopefully enough to keep from blowing up at her. I knew Kydrus was right about my anger only making things worse, but it hurt to feel her dying.

"Let me know if her condition becomes serious," Venali said as we headed towards the fighting ring. "If she lets herself deteriorate too much, tell me."

"You think you can do something to change her mind?" I asked, jealousy rearing its head at the thought that he might be closer to her than I was. Part of that was my own fault. I should spend more time with her.

"I'm the brute of this group. She knows this. So, when I come to her and beg her for something, prostrating myself before her, she usually listens. I'm not going to do that until it's absolutely necessary, though," he said with a frown that stretched the scar on his face.

"She needs to wake up," I grumbled.

"You're being too hard on her. She's not as old as us, remember? She's still only in her twenties. Think about what you were like then. We were all naïve and stupid. She's scared and the only way to get her to open up to us is by showing her that she doesn't need to be scared. That we have her back no matter what."

For a brute, he was rather smart.

I sighed and rubbed a hand down my face. "You're right, but I'll stab you if you tell anyone I admitted that."

He laughed and clapped me on the shoulder. "Let's spar. I think there are a few tricks I can teach you that will improve your fighting. If we really are going to the Unseelie, we're going to need to be in the best shape possible."

CHAPTER 7
ELARA

THE ANNOUNCEMENT PROCEDURE was surprisingly simple. The warlords just gathered as many people as they could in their cities, and then spread the word by written decrees. These decrees also announced the tournament, which would happen in just under a week.

"You're sure that you want to give up your titles?" I asked for the fiftieth time.

All four of my warlord mates looked at me with the same expression. Blankness.

They had been reverting to courtly faces a lot around me lately, and it drove me insane.

"Fine, I get it," I grumbled. "You're going to give up your titles so you can travel with me because I'm more important than titles."

Amrynn's lip twitched, the only indication that they heard me.

"Venali, can you come with me?" I asked and stood.

Venali stood without question.

"We'll be back," I said, biting my lip as I headed out of the house.

Venali shut the door behind us, and walked at my side. His towering presence was reassuring.

I moved closer to him, and he threaded our fingers together. Relief surged through me, and I let out a sigh. Of them all, he would be the quietest, let me work things out in my head instead of discussing them, and would know what it was like to need some space.

"Just needed some air?" he asked, rubbing his thumb over the back of my hand.

I nodded.

"You should let me teach you some more fighting moves," he said softly. "So, you are fully prepared for our upcoming travel."

"I agree," I said with a nod. "Tomorrow we can start training."

He smiled down at me, and my heart tightened.

Mine. He was all mine.

I sat on the edge of the hill that overlooked the city below, and he sat behind me, sliding his legs along the outside of mine, and trapped me. I leaned back against his chest and closed my eyes. He wrapped his arms around my body and held me close.

"I love you," he whispered in my ear. "I will always love you. No matter what happens, I will always be by your side. You know that, right?"

I raised my hand and rested it against his cheek, and then turned in his embrace so I could look up into his eyes. "I do, but the reassurance is good."

He kissed my palm, and my heart sped. "You are the greatest gift I've ever been given. I didn't realize how much I was missing until I found you. You are beautiful, kind, and more stubborn than me."

I chuckled, and snuggled against him, resting my head on his shoulder. "I love you, Venali. I'm sorry for being stubborn."

"You wouldn't be you if you weren't stubborn," he said quietly, and I didn't need to look at him to know he was smiling.

"Can we sit here for a bit?" I snuggled in deeper.

"We can sit here as long as you like." His heartbeat quickened under my heads on his chest.

As long as I liked, ended up being a few hours, and then my stomach reminded me that it was past time to eat.

When we returned, I sat at the table with all of my mates around me, and smiled as we finished eating. As much as I hated that they were giving things up because of me, I preferred having them by my side constantly.

My smile wilted as one of my unclaimed mates tapped at the shield I had put up between us.

He tapped harder, and then slammed against it.

I cried out and doubled over, clutching at my head.

"Elara?" Ryul asked, grimacing as he squatted down beside me.

I reinforced the shield, and straightened. "I'm okay. Sorry."

"As much as I hate to say it, you really should let them in," he whispered.

I took a deep breath and said, "Not yet. It's not time yet."

"How do you know when it will be time?" he asked.

Ryul had been exceptionally snarky before, but he looked curious now, with no anger present.

"I just will," I said. I stood, had to put a hand on the back of my chair to keep my balance, and excused myself to my room.

CHAPTER 8
VENALI

"You're telegraphing your moves," I told Elara. "You don't need to wind up to throw a punch. Anyone who sees you is going to know what you're planning to do."

She sat on the ground, covered in sand and sweat, panting heavily.

I hadn't realized how out of shape she had become. Then again, she could be tired from holding back her powers.

She nodded in understanding and stood up, brushing her palms off. "Okay. How do I stop telegraphing?"

"Throw a punch at me," I ordered her.

She turned her right shoulder, and I held up my hand. "That. You turned your shoulder."

She froze and examined her stance. After a moment, her eyes widened and she whispered, "Oh."

"Let's go inside," I said. "You've done a lot today and learned some."

"I didn't learn much," she muttered, but followed me anyway. She walked with a slight limp, so I picked her up in my arms. She was so light, and soft.

"Hey," she gasped.

"You're limping. I don't want you damaging your muscles. I'll carry you to the shower."

"Will you be joining me?" she asked in a sultry voice and smirked at me.

My cock strained against my pants at the thought of showering with her and touching her naked body. "Yes," I replied immediately.

She relaxed in my arms, and whispered, "We better make it quick. I'm starving."

Inside, we passed by the others, all gathered to go over plans for the tournament. They watched us go, no doubt knowing what we were about to do, but I didn't care.

Inside the bathroom, I set her down on the counter, and then turned the water on to the temperature she preferred, scalding hot. I had no idea how she could stand such hot water, but we were all learning to handle it.

I turned around, and if I hadn't already been aroused, the sight of her naked before me, bruised, sweaty, and sandy would have done me in.

"What?" she asked and looked in the mirror, pushing her hair around. "Is there something on me?"

"Sand," I answered, turning away to undress.

She slid her hands along my back, around my ribs, and hugged me from behind. "I don't know if I can wash my hair. My arms hurt."

I ushered her into the shower. "I'll wash you."

She stepped under the water and sighed. The steam rose around her, and I wondered how long it would be before we could enjoy moments like this again, once she started her journey.

She swiped hair away from her face, and then dropped to her knees and took my erection in her mouth.

I groaned and leaned back against the wall of the shower. Her mouth was warm, wet, and she knew just the right amount of suction to make every logical thought in my head disappear.

I had to resist the urge to grab her head and pump my hips. It would be rude, and she probably wouldn't enjoy it.

Instead, I picked her up, spun her around, and thrust inside her while gripping her hips.

"Yes," she screamed, arching up. Her muscles tightened around me and I groaned loudly.

I was always conflicted. I wanted to finish quickly, but I also wanted to do this all day long and listen her to moans and screams as I made her orgasm again and again.

"Faster," she growled, resting her hand on the wall in front of her.

I obeyed, gripping her hips and thrusting faster and harder. With each orgasm, she grew slicker and slicker, and I grew closer to finishing.

I turned her around, looping one of her legs around my hip, pushed her up against the wall of the shower, claimed her mouth, and then thrust inside of her again.

She gasped into my mouth, which only made me hungrier for her to orgasm again.

She did, moments later, and then I couldn't hold it back anymore, and I finished as well.

I dropped my head to her shoulder, and drew in ragged breaths as my heart returned to a normal beating pattern.

CHAPTER 9
ELARA

THE DAY of the tournament dawned cool and clear. I had expected a large crowd, but it looked like all of Minloa had come.

I stood near the podium where I would be sitting to watch the fights, and surveyed the crowd.

Children ran between people, grabbing snacks from vendors and laughing. People chatted, most with smiles on their faces.

It was strange to see so many people who looked happy. It was even stranger to know they were happy and here to see me.

"Queen Elara," Venali whispered from beside me.

I jumped and reached for my sword, but stilled when I realized it was him. "Venali," I hissed.

He smirked, but quickly removed it. "You shouldn't be unescorted right now. Where are the others?"

"They were just nearby," I said with a scowl and looked around for my other mates.

He held out his arm, and I set my hand on his forearm. "Let me escort you to your seat."

"Do you think someone will try to hurt me here?" I asked with a frown.

He sighed softly. "I would hope not, but people will do many things to accomplish their goals."

He stopped at the throne they had built for me, and I sat on it. With a bow, he stepped to the side and took up his role as guard. His hand rested on his sword, and he looked especially menacing today. He'd worn his hair up, so his scars were more prominent.

Durlan walked up the podium and bowed to me. "Your Majesty."

"Durlan, is it about to start?" I asked.

He shook his head. "We have some time. Do you need anything?"

"Some food and drink would be nice," I said and then frowned when I realized there was only one seat on the podium, mine. "Where will you be sitting?"

"We will be standing behind you," Durlan explained.

I scowled. "You're supposed to be my equals, remember? You need chairs."

"Who will be on your right?" Durlan asked with an arched brow.

Dammit. I knew what he was getting at. Even if I said they were my equals, people would view whoever was on my right as the leader, as someone who had more authority and power than the others.

"What if you sat in a line behind me?" I asked.

"We wouldn't be your equals if we were behind you," Venali whispered.

"You're not my equals if you're standing behind me either," I muttered and then sighed. There didn't seem to be a way to win this. "Wouldn't you prefer to sit anyway? You'll be standing for hours."

"If we can't stand for a day, we have no business being your guards, let alone your mates," Venali scoffed.

"That means I won't be allowed to touch you guys all day?" I asked softly, my mood plummeting.

Durlan dropped to one knee before me. "I'm sorry, my queen."

"I understand," I whispered and leaned back on my throne.

Durlan stood and took a step back to stand behind me.

The stands filled up as people took their seats to prepare for the tournament. At the far end of the arena, a group of men gathered. They looked like warriors, which meant they had to be the contenders for warlord. I couldn't tell from this far away how much power they had, though.

"Venali," I called softly.

He stepped up next to me and knelt on one knee. "Yes, Your Majesty?"

"What are their power levels? Are there any on par with yours?"

"We've told you before that there are none in Minloa who are as powerful as us."

"Then are they really capable enough or strong enough to be warlords?" I asked.

He was quiet a moment, as though he were choosing his words carefully before answering. "They may not be as powerful as us, but that doesn't mean that they aren't capable of being warlord. I doubt they will ever have to fight enemies as strong as us, and if they do happen to find an enemy as strong as us, they can team up and defeat it together."

"Is that something you've done?" I asked and turned to face him.

He nodded. "A few times over the last several hundred years."

That surprised me. What type of beings had they fought that required them to team up?

"I'm going to get your refreshments," Durlan said. He paused beside me a moment and asked, "Do you want anything else?"

"A kiss?" I requested.

He smirked, bent on one knee, picked up my hand, and kissed the back of it. "As my queen wishes."

I glowered at him.

He laughed as he walked away.

"You're my mates. Why can't we kiss?" I grumbled to Venali.

"Soon, beautiful," he whispered and then stood back up and took his position behind me.

"Where is Ryul?" I asked. He'd been avoiding me the last few days, and I wasn't sure why.

"I'm not certain," Venali answered.

"Why is he avoiding me?" I asked softly.

"It is not my place to discuss what he is or is not doing," Venali said.

I turned and stared at him. "You're taking his side! You like him more than me."

He chuckled and shook his head. "I assure you, that I do not like any of the others as I like you."

"I hope not," I mumbled, and turned back around.

"Have you tried talking to him?" he asked.

"How can I talk to him when he avoids me?" I grumbled.

He didn't respond to that.

Another hour passed, and then all of my mates made their way to the platform and stood behind me.

As I'd expected, Ryul didn't meet my gaze when he came to stand with the others.

Amrynn set a small table beside me, and then Durlan set the food and drink he'd brought for me on it.

"Thank you," I said and smiled at the two of them.

They took their spots, and we let silence descend upon us for a couple of minutes.

Finally, Venali stepped forward, drew power, and then projected his voice over the whole area. "People of Minloa! The Tournament is about to begin."

People scurried to their seats, once there, they all stared at me and began whispering to each other.

"Who is she?"

"Is that the queen?"

"She does look like the paintings I've seen."

Venali waited until everyone was seated, stepped back, and motioned for Durlan.

Durlan stepped forward and projected his voice as well. "People of Minloa, it is my honor to present to you, Queen Elara."

I stood, and people cheered. Smiling, I waved to them. Durlan had taught me last night how to project my voice like they did. I used it now. "Fight well. I need the strongest in Minloa to take up the mantle of warlord. You will be protecting your sectors, and will be advisors to my mates."

"Fighters, prepare yourselves," Durlan announced.

I sat back down and got comfortable.

CHAPTER 10
ELARA

THE CONTENDERS WALKED to the front of the arena, standing before me in a row. There were at least thirty of them ranging in age.

As one, they bowed to me.

That was going to take some getting used to.

"Your first test will be hand to hand combat with no magic," Durlan announced.

Venali walked from the podium and hopped over the fence into the arena.

"What is he doing?" I hissed softly.

"He's going to fight them," Amrynn answered me.

"They can't defeat him," I grumbled. "He'll knock out all of them and we won't have any contenders left for warlord."

Amrynn chuckled softly. "He's going to go easy on them. The last ten standing will continue on to the next round."

I picked up a piece of fruit and chewed on it.

"This is a free for all," Durlan explained. "You will be fighting each other, as well as Venali. The last ten left standing will proceed to round two."

Venali turned to face me, bowed, and when he stood, gave me a wink.

"He'd better make this interesting and not knock them all out in the first minute," I mumbled.

Kydrus chuckled. "You underestimate how much Venali enjoys this type of thing."

The contenders had moved apart, giving themselves space to fight. One of them, a tall man with black hair and dark eyes, stared at me. His eyes were intrigued, but there was something else in his expression, too.

Pain?

"Anyone know him?" Ryul asked.

"Oh, you do speak," I whispered. "I thought you'd gone mute."

Ryul growled softly.

"And, he is not the only one staring at me," I added. "So, I don't think you need to be worried."

"I've never seen him before," Amrynn answered Ryul, completely ignoring my comments.

"He's masking his power," Kydrus said.

"I can't get a read on him at all," Ryul said. "Keep an eye on him."

The man in question turned from me to look at Ryul and the others behind me, his brows furrowing in anger, and eyes darkening, and then he turned to face the other contenders.

As much as I wanted to dismiss Ryul's worry, there was something different about that man. Something familiar.

Venali moved off to the side, surveying the group and looking excited. It was rare that I saw him this excited and my heart fluttered in response.

Durlan waited a moment while the crowd grew quiet, and then he said, "Begin!"

The man who'd been staring at me dodged an attack from a

man on his right, hit the man on the head, and the man fell to the ground and didn't get back up.

"Um, are they allowed to kill each other?" I asked, my heart beating faster.

"He's not dead, just knocked out," Ryul said.

"Well, that's good," I whispered.

I had expected the fight to be chaos, but there were a handful of men who were simply waiting on the outside, knocking out anyone who tried to fight them, and watching the fights inside.

The crowd roared and cheered. Some cheered for specific contenders, while others just cheered for the fighting.

Venali had yet to fight anyone, watching like the other men on the outside.

The men in the center, gathered in a small cluster, were engaged in pure chaos.

"Groups," Kydrus said.

"Interesting," Amrynn whispered.

"What?" I asked, having no idea what they were talking about.

"There are two groups of three in the middle. Each trio is working together to fight people off," Kydrus said, leaning closer to me.

Now that he pointed it out, I could see the groups as they stood back to back, fighting off attackers.

Venali finally joined the fight, leaping into the very center, knocking out one of the trios. I'd expected him to smile as he fought, but he looked stoic. The only excitement lay in his eyes.

The men who had been waiting on the outside joined the fray, knocking people out quickly, one after the next.

"Did they plan this?" I asked.

"Possibly," Kydrus said. "Or, they just know they're stronger and were biding their time so they didn't have to fight as many people."

The outliers made it to the middle where Venali and one of the trios were still fighting other contenders.

The numbers finally dwindled to ten, not counting Venali.

Durlan shouted, "Halt!"

Everyone froze, except the man who'd been staring at me. He took a step closer to Venali, who watched him calmly. The man said something to Venali.

Venali's face contorted in rage, and he lunged for the man.

"Venali!" I yelled.

Venali froze, but his eyes did not stray from the man.

The man teleported from the arena to stand before me.

Kydrus, Amrynn, and Ryul moved as one, their swords drawn and pressed to the man's throat.

The man looked extremely calm for someone who had three blades ready to cut his head off.

"State your business," Kydrus growled.

"You're hiding yourself still. Why do you pretend to be a weak shell? Have you fallen so far?" the man asked while staring at me.

"Who are you?" I asked, standing and drawing my own sword.

"You'd know if you hadn't put a wall up between us," he said and growled softly. "Was that your idea or one of theirs?" he asked, looking at Kydrus and Ryul who stood in front of him.

My eyes widened, and I lowered my sword. "No."

"What's the meaning of this ruse?" the man asked.

"Kydrus. Ryul. You two escort him to the house. Durlan and Amrynn, continue the tournament. We'll return shortly," I ordered.

"Your Majesty," Amrynn growled. "I don't think—"

I looked at him and said, "Do as I order."

Amrynn bowed. "Yes, Your Majesty."

"You three, let's go," I ordered, and headed down from the platform, towards the house.

Kydrus walked behind me, then the man, and then Ryul bringing up the rear to guard Kydrus's back as he protected me.

People murmured as we left.

"Are they going to punish him?"

"They're probably going to kill him," another person said.

I refrained from commenting. They didn't need to know what was going on.

Once inside the house, I led them to the living room, and stood in front of the fireplace, looking down at the logs. "Sit," I ordered them.

I heard shuffling and then silence.

I turned around and faced the man. "Drop your glamour."

He smirked. "I don't know what you're talking about."

"Drop your glamour," I ordered him.

Ryul and Kydrus tensed.

"Drop the wall between us," he replied, staring defiantly back at me.

I stepped forward, pressing my sword to his throat. "Drop your glamour!"

He didn't even flinch. His eyes never left mine. "You won't kill me. You can't kill me," he whispered.

My arm shook. He was right.

"She can't, but we can," Ryul said.

"Oh, brother. You've fallen so far as well," the man said. He looked at Ryul a moment, and then faced me again. "Come on, let me in. Why are you hiding? Why are you keeping me out?" He set his hands on my hips, and pulled me forward, onto his lap. "Let me in."

His touch made me gasp, and broke a bit of the wall I'd built up between us.

"It's too soon," I whispered. "You weren't supposed to be here. You were supposed to wait for me to come."

"You blocked me. I worried you were in danger," he whispered.

"Who is this guy?" Ryul growled.

He dropped his glamour, his appearance shifting slightly. He still looked basically the same, but his eyes were pitch black, and he had longer than normal canines, even for a fae.

"Unseelie!" Ryul barked, lunging forward.

Kydrus lunged towards me, but I held up my hands, stopping them.

"What is your name?" I asked softly.

"Myrin," he answered, pulling me closer, so I straddled his lap.

I dropped the wall between us, and our bond snapped into place, connecting us instantly. His feelings and the connection were so strong, that I couldn't believe I'd been able to keep him out for so long. I gasped, arching into him, and then leaned forward to kiss him.

My sixth mate.

"What is going on?" Ryul asked.

Myrin pulled back from our kiss, but held me against his chest. He turned, and pointed at his neck. "I'm Myrin, Amara's mate."

I growled. "Don't say that name. My name is Elara."

Myrin's brows furrowed as he searched my face. "I don't understand."

"An Unseelie is your mate," Kydrus whispered.

"No. This is unacceptable," Ryul snapped, drawing his sword.

Myrin stood, pushing me behind him. "Stand down," he ordered Ryul.

I stepped in front of Myrin, glaring at Ryul. "You will not hurt him. He is my mate. I understand that this is difficult for you to handle, but it is the truth."

Ryul turned his glare on me. "You knew? You knew you had an Unseelie as a mate?"

"I suspected," I said. "I blocked them as soon as I realized I had more mates. I did it so quickly that I didn't get much of a sense for them." I turned around to face Myrin. "How did you find me?"

He smirked and rested his hand on my cheek. "I will always find you. I am your consort. You are mine. Even with the wall you'd put up between us, I could find you."

"You remember our prior life?" I asked, my eyes wide.

"You don't?" he asked, eyebrows furrowed.

"She's refusing to accept who she is," Ryul explained. "We aren't allowed to even say her true name."

"That's why you're sick," Myrin realized.

I bristled. "I'm not sick."

"You are. I can smell it on you and sense it through our bond," he said. The hand on my cheek slid back behind my neck, and he tilted my head up to look at him. "Why won't you accept who you are?"

"I'm Elara, former slave and Queen of Minloa. I am not a goddess," I whispered.

"Former slave? What are you talking about?" Myrin asked, his fury sparking flames within his eyes.

"There's a lot you need to be told," Kydrus said, finally speaking for the first time.

"Clearly," Myrin mumbled. He bent forward, pressed his forehead to mine, and the coolness of his skin against mine made me exhale in joy. The heat continued to leave my body until the fog in my head cleared, and I felt almost normal again. Myrin leaned back and asked, "Better?"

I threw my arms around his neck, stood on tiptoe, and kissed him. "You're amazing," I whispered.

Ryul growled.

"You need to go back to the tournament," Kydrus told me. "And he can't go back out there looking like this."

"Like what? An Unseelie?" Myrin asked, snarling.

"Yes," Kydrus answered with zero hostility.

"You are so ignorant," Myrin said and sighed. "The Seelie have fallen so far."

"Watch it," Ryul threatened.

"Ryul," I snapped. "You will not fight Myrin. He is my mate, whether you like it or not."

Ryul snarled and stormed out of the house, slamming the door closed behind him.

"He'll come around," Kydrus assured me. "This is a lot to take in."

"Not for you," I noticed.

"Amrynn had a feeling one of the reasons you wanted to go to the Unseelie was because you had a mate there," he said.

"No. That's not the reason at all." I frowned and shook my head.

"You were planning to go see the Unseelie, to their den, without me?" Myrin asked, scowling.

I smiled and chuckled nervously. "Maybe."

He growled and lowered himself until his face was level with mine. "You never go to the Unseelie without me present. Do you understand?"

"Why were you in the tournament? Why not just come find me?" I asked instead of answering him.

"I wanted a chance to see you and your other consorts," he admitted.

"What did you say to Venali?" I asked. I'd been curious about it because Venali rarely lost his composure.

"That he was much weaker in this new body than he had been before," Myrin said, smiling.

That would do it.

"Put a different glamour on," I ordered him. "We need to go back to the tournament. You're going to have to sit in the crowd with the other people. Tonight, we can talk more."

Myrin bowed, and when he stood, he had on new glamour that

made him look like a different Seelie fae. "I am but here to serve my queen."

The idea of him serving me in other ways had me clenching my legs together. "Let's go," I ordered them. "I have warlords to pick."

CHAPTER 11
ELARA

VENALI STOOD on the platform with his sword drawn when we approached, his eyes locked on Myrin.

I walked straight up to Venali, and it took him a moment to remember where we were.

He dropped to one knee and bowed his head.

"You are not to hurt him," I whispered. "We will discuss this after the tournament. Do you understand?"

"Yes, my queen," Venali whispered.

"I love you," I whispered even softer.

Venali's lip twitched as he fought to hide his smile. "I love you, too."

"Do me a favor? Go find Ryul and make sure he doesn't kill anyone."

Venali's eyes widened, but he just bobbed his head and stood. "As you wish."

I sat in my chair, and my mates took their spots. I glanced at Durlan. "What is the status?"

"They are on a thirty minute break," Durlan answered. "When the break is over, we will move to the second round."

"How much more time on their break?" I asked. The nine remaining men looked rested. The people were talking and laughing and it seemed like some were even making bets.

"Two minutes," Durlan answered.

I nodded and grabbed my cup to drink from. I started to raise it to my lips, but smelled something foul coming from it.

Poison.

I wasn't sure how I knew or could smell it, but I had no doubt.

I tossed the drink out, being sure not to react in anyway. "Amrynn," I called.

He came to my side. "Here."

"Can you get me a different drink? The last one wasn't appetizing."

His eyes widened as he understood what I was trying to say.

Durlan growled softly, but his expression didn't change.

"I'll get you new refreshments, Your Majesty," Amrynn said, grabbed the cup from my hands, and picked up the tray of food as well. He took them to the house.

"I was here the entire time," Durlan whispered.

"Then we need to be especially careful," I whispered.

"Keep your drink in your lap," Kydrus ordered me.

"Very well," I said softly.

Knowing someone had tried to kill me should have upset me, but it only made me sad. Whoever this person, or persons, were, they wanted to kill me without even getting to know me. It hurt a bit.

Amrynn returned with new food and drink, and moved the table closer to me.

I kept the cup in my lap, and drank from it slowly.

"It is time for our next round," Durlan announced. "This round, we will test your magic."

This, I was anxious to see.

Amrynn jumped into the arena.

"You will be paired up and must use your magic against each other," Durlan explained. "No killing is allowed."

"There's an odd number," I whispered to myself.

"That's why Amrynn is there," Kydrus whispered to me.

"No one's going to be able to defeat him," I muttered.

"No, but he will know if the person's attacks are strong enough to pass the test and move forward," Kydrus replied.

I wasn't so sure I agreed with that, but I sat quietly as I waited for them to start the second round.

The contenders spread out across the arena, split into pairs.

I watched, curious which of them would continue on.

"Ready!" Durlan yelled and waited a moment before continuing, "Begin."

One of the contenders in the middle used a lightning spell that struck the man across from him.

The lightning struck the man, but the man did not react. He didn't even flinch. He just lifted his hand, and a bolt of blue light sped from his palm to the other man. The lightning user fell, his body twitching as he lay on the ground.

"One down," Kydrus said quietly, leaning toward me.

Only, that wasn't right. By the time I looked over at the other contenders, three more were down.

The man facing Amrynn used a spell I'd never seen before. It created a dark mist that moved into a humanoid shape.

I gripped the arms of my chair.

Amrynn raised his hand, and the man stopped, letting his spell dissolve. "Pass," Amrynn said, and walked back to us.

"What was that?" I hissed.

"You don't want to know," Kydrus whispered. "I haven't seen someone use that power in at least a decade."

Amrynn knelt by me. "He's going to be a warlord."

"You're sure?" I asked.

Amrynn nodded once and then stood. "I'm certain."

"Those remaining, prepare for the final test," Durlan called.

I looked at him. "More? But there are five."

"Trust me, Your Majesty," he replied, smiling.

I nodded once and tapped my finger on the arm of my chair. What could the final test be?

CHAPTER 12
VENALI

Ryul stood in the forest, gaze fixed on the canopy of leaves overhead. "She continues to withhold information from us," he said as I approached.

"She does what she thinks is right," I said. "We need to show her that we are truly her equals and deserving of her confidence."

He growled. "An Unseelie? Of all the circumstances to come up, that was not one I expected to have to accept."

"I don't like it either, but she is certain. If she is certain, then we must trust her."

He lowered his head to meet my gaze. "She is dying, still. It has slowed, but she is very weak."

"The more of her mates she has with her, the safer she will be," I offered.

"You've changed," he snarled.

"You haven't," I countered.

"She—"

"Has been trying to talk to you, but you are avoiding her. Tell me how that helps anyone?" I interrupted him.

"I can't temper my anger when I feel her dying. I just want to shake her and scream until she starts acting like the damn goddess she is."

"You should know by now that approach won't work with Elara," I said and shook my head.

"Since when did you become the reasonable one of the two of us?" he asked through clenched teeth.

"Since I got my memories back and remembered what it felt like not only to be parted from her while she was on another world, but also when she died," I said, rubbing my chest to ease the ache there. "I will not push her away. I will not do anything that will make her *want* to push me away."

"You're coddling her." Ryul growled. "I don't want to lose her either, but letting her kill herself and letting that Unseelie—"

"She is our queen, our goddess. She decides what we do. I cannot control her any more than I can control the future. And, that is how it should be. No one should control her. If you cannot accept that, if you cannot accept one of her mates, you will be left behind. I suggest you adapt. You don't have to like it, I know I don't, but we have to accept it and do what we can to keep her safe."

He snarled, showing me his canines, and then sighed and lowered his head. "I get it."

I nodded and turned. "Good. I'm going back to stand beside her. Hopefully, you'll do the same."

I understood Ryul's frustration. I did. But I refused to push Elara away.

Back at the tournament, I paused by her newest mate.

He glanced at me, but returned to watching the arena.

"Can you protect her in the Unseelie realm?" I asked softly, staring straight ahead.

"She's truly planning to go there?" he asked.

I nodded once.

"I can, but I will need your help. I'm not like Ryul, I can admit my faults, especially when it comes to her safety," he said softly.

"They don't have all of their memories back," I informed him.

He turned to look at me, smirking. "You do, though."

It wasn't a question, but I nodded anyway. "Most."

He chuckled softly.

"She is dying," I whispered. "Pushing her will not help."

"She's afraid," he said with a frown.

I nodded again. "This has been a rough life for her."

"Will you tell me what I've missed?" he asked, brow furrowed.

I let out a slow breath. "After this. Meet me in the house once we are finished."

He nodded, and I left to stand behind Elara on the podium.

"All is well?" she asked while staring at the remaining five men.

"Yes, Your Majesty," I answered, keeping my gaze fixed on her while I bowed slightly.

Her shoulders relaxed and she released an audible breath. "Good."

If Ryul didn't pull his head from his ass soon, I would beat him until it came out. She had enough to worry about. He didn't need to add to it.

Kydrus glanced at me before facing forward again. I could sense his anger from just that brief look.

It seemed I would have backup for beating Ryul.

CHAPTER 13
ELARA

DURLAN KNELT beside me and whispered, "You need to go into the arena."

"Why?" I asked without moving.

"The final test is them bowing to you," he explained.

I sighed, but did as he asked. When Venali tried to follow me, I raised my hand, stopping him and the others.

"Alone," I whispered.

Kydrus's lip twitched, but my mates stayed on the podium.

I hopped over the fence, and smoothed down my dress once on the ground. Hand on the hilt of my sword, I walked to the candidates.

They stood in a line, watching me, some with curiosity, but one with a darkness boiling in his eyes I did not like.

They'd bowed to me at the beginning, so this shouldn't be any different, right?

I stopped, drew my sword, and said, "To become my warlords, you must bow to me. Bow to me now, before all these witnesses."

The one Amrynn had faced with the strange power bowed immediately.

Another bowed.

And then the one glaring at me spit on the ground.

I cleared the distance between us in the blink of an eye, and pressed my sword to his throat.

His eyes widened, and his mouth dropped open.

"What is this?" I asked him.

"I...I will not bow to a slave," he said, though his conviction was not conveyed in his tone.

Oh. Well, that certainly made this easier.

"You owned slaves?" I asked.

"Your owner should have beaten you more," he hissed and raised his hand to hit me.

I grabbed his arm, twisted it up behind his back like Venali had taught me, kicked the back of his knees, and then rested my sword atop his shoulder, the blade touching the side of his throat.

"All witness his testimony of slavery? An act punishable by death?" I asked the crowd.

"Witnessed," hundreds of voices rang out.

My mates gripped their swords, but held their places.

"Your punishment is death," I told him, and then slid my sword across his throat, and stepped back to let his body fall.

His blood sprayed my face and arms.

Yuck.

One of the four behind me held out a handkerchief.

I took it with a smile. "Thank you."

After wiping off the blood, I turned to the crowd. "Behind me stand your new warlords. I expect them to be treated as well as the previous ones."

I started to walk from the arena, but someone in the audience asked, "How do we know you're really the queen?"

People stepped back from the man who had spoken.

I walked to stand before him, only the fence between us. Lifting my hand, I gripped the moon, and pulled it from the sky.

Thankfully, today was a clear day and one the moon could be seen even while the sun was out.

People screamed, some cheered, and the man teetered.

I held the moon in my hand, the size of a grapefruit, and asked, "Any other questions?"

The man shook his head from side to side.

I smiled and threw the moon back up to its rightful place. "Good." With a wide smile, I walked from the arena, through the crowd which parted for me, and to the house.

Once inside the living room, I fainted on the floor.

Worth it.

CHAPTER 14
ELARA

"You've always been dramatic, but that was over the top, even for you," Myrin said softly.

I opened my eyes, surprised to find us alone in the house. "I didn't want to waste time," I said.

"Beautiful one, why must you persist on causing me panic?" he asked and picked me up.

He carried me down the hallway.

"Where are you taking me?" I asked.

"To shower. You still have blood on you," he said and growled.

I knew he was my mate, but I only remembered snippets of him, and I did not know who he was in this life.

"I will not touch you or look at you, if that is your wish," he whispered.

"I..."

"Our bond has always been stronger than the others. It will take you some time to get used to. I will try not to pry into your feelings, if possible. I wish you would accept yourself, but this is your life and you must do what you think is right. I support you in whatever you do."

"So, Unseelie aren't evil creatures? I had suspected as much from the book I read, but it's difficult to release years of brainwashing so quickly."

He pushed open the bathroom with his foot and grumbled incoherently beneath his breath.

Once he set me down, I turned him to face me, and asked, "What of us?"

He scowled. "I don't understand."

"This is not my original body. Does it..." I bit my lip and looked at his chest. "Does it not entice you?"

"It doesn't matter what body you inhibit, Amara. You are my mate and I will worship you in whatever form you take. Though, I'd prefer if it were at least female forms."

For some reason, when he used that name, it didn't bother me.

He began unlacing my dress, his fingers moving expertly. "When I saw you today, it felt like I breathed for the first time. It was like I was sleep walking, and your presence woke me from my long slumber."

"I am not her," I whispered.

He helped me slide the dress off, and then looked me over, taking his eyes from my toes to my head. "Your body is not the same, but here..." he rested his hand on my breastbone. "...it is the same."

Heat stirred, and my core ached.

He stepped closer, dipped his head beside my ear and asked, "May I worship you, my queen?"

I didn't know what he meant, but nodded.

He placed a kiss on my neck, picked me up and lay me down on my back, and then began kissing every inch of me, including my fingertips and toes. He held himself over me, his body hovering over mine, but not touching. "You are gorgeous. You have forgotten that. My job is to remind you." He dropped his head and drew my nipple into his mouth.

I arched up with a gasp.

He released me only to take my other nipple into his mouth. Then, he peppered kisses down the center of my body until he got to my aching bundle of nerves. He paused, looked up at me, and said, "Let me show you what it means to be worshipped." His tongue swept over me, and he didn't stop until I was mush beneath his mouth.

His fingers massaged my inner legs, and then he plunged his tongue into my core.

"I will kill anyone who tries to take such sweet nectar from me," he whispered, licking me again and moaning.

"Please," I begged.

"Do not beg, Amara. You are the goddess. Order. I am your faithful consort. Tell me what you want."

"I want to be one with you," I said.

He removed his clothes, lay atop me so that our skin touched as much as possible, and then he slid inside of me, filling me up not only literally, but also emotionally.

He pumped into me, whispering praises the entire time.

Our bond solidified even more, and for a moment, there was only Myrin and I.

I screamed his name as I orgasmed, and he kissed me deeply.

I flipped us over, riding him and moaning loudly with each movement.

He rested his hands on my hips, stroking his thumbs on my hip bones. "I am your tool, Goddess. I will shape myself to your needs."

I peaked again, gripping his chest as the wave crashed over me.

He took over, pumping up into me to keep the orgasm going.

"No one can compare to you. You are perfect."

He moved faster, his eyes on me the entire time.

"Myrin," I moaned.

"Elara!" he yelled as he orgasmed, his body shuddering its final movements.

He leaned forward, placing kisses all across my chest.

"Now you need a shower, too," I chuckled.

He withdrew from me and said, "I suppose I do."

CHAPTER 15
KYDRUS

ELARA SPENT a lot of time with Myrin the few days following the tournament. We traveled to the castle, and she often opted to spend her evenings with him. Not that she refused to see us, or ignored us, but she definitely had a closer bond to Myrin, despite knowing him for the least amount of time.

I tried not to let it bother me, but seeing her so affectionate with an Unseelie unsettled me. He didn't appear to be evil, which further unnerved me. Everything we had been taught was wrong. Every prejudice we had against the Unseelie. Well, maybe not *every* prejudice.

"She's remembering more," Amrynn whispered to me as we watched her sparring with Venali.

I nodded, studying her movements. "It seems like Myrin broke her walls down a bit."

"Do you remember everything?" he asked, glancing at me before his eyes returned to our mate.

"No. Venali seems to remember the most, next to Myrin who knows everything."

"We should talk to him tonight," Amrynn said, crossing his

arms over his chest, his eyes never left Elara's form. "Learn what we can."

I nodded my agreement.

Then Elara stumbled, falling to her knees. When Venali reached out towards her, she held her hand up to ward him off. "I'm fine."

Only, she wasn't. Her goddess powers were eating at her. I clenched my jaw to push down my anxiety.

"What's going on?" Myrin asked as he came to our side.

"She's sparring," Amrynn answered.

"We'd like to talk to you tonight," I told him. "To learn as much as we can from you."

Myrin tilted his head and looked at me with an eyebrow raised. "You're calmer this lifetime."

"I don't know if that's a compliment or not," I muttered.

He smiled. "It's a compliment. You were rather rash last time." His smile disappeared. "It was part of what got you killed."

My eyes widened. "I thought Amara and her mates just disappeared."

He laughed bitterly and looked up at the sky. "If only that were true."

"We only remember snippets," Amrynn admitted to him. "How can you remember it all?"

Myrin shrugged. "I don't know. When she accepted you five as mates, the memories came back to me, and I felt her." He looked at Elara, scowling. "I felt her sickness, and started my journey to find her."

"You've been good for her," I said, as much as it hurt me to admit it. "She's accepting herself a bit more now that you're here."

"When she finds her final mate, she'll accept herself again," Myrin said, but the set of his jaw made me think that was just his hope.

"Who is her last mate?" Amrynn asked.

Myrin smirked and shook his head. "Nope. I am not ruining that surprise."

She cried out and fell again, and Myrin walked to her. She tried to push him away, but he squatted down and pressed his forehead to her. Her eyes fluttered closed, and then the painful twist to her features relaxed.

The knife's edge of pain I felt down our bond dulled. It was strange to feel another's pain or temperament. It was also strange to be able to communicate telepathically with the others. We'd closed down the bonds, since we didn't need to communicate currently, and most of us didn't want our thoughts shared with the others.

Myrin stood and walked back to us. "After she falls asleep, we'll meet. Make sure Ryul comes. He needs to hear what I have to say even if he doesn't like me."

I wanted to say Ryul would come around to Myrin, but I wasn't sure. Ryul's hatred towards Myrin was more than just him being an Unseelie, but I couldn't understand what it was.

Amrynn nodded, and Myrin left.

"What are we going to do about Ryul?" Amrynn asked.

I sighed and ran a hand through my hair. "No idea."

"We should talk to Durlan," I suggested.

After another long look at our mate, we turned and walked to Durlan's office on the far side of the castle. He sat behind the desk, reading something and scowling.

"You look like you're having fun," I said as I sat in a chair in front of his desk.

Amrynn shut the door and sat beside me.

Durlan sighed and tossed the paper on his desk. "Not in the slightest." He looked at us and scowled. "What's going on?"

"We came to talk about Ryul," I explained.

Durlan leaned back in his chair, rubbing his eyes before running his hand down his face. "He's the most stubborn of us.

Even more stubborn than Venali, which I didn't think was possible."

"He refuses to accept Myrin," Amrynn said. "If we aren't united, that jeopardizes Elara."

"Any idea what we can do?" I asked, leaning forward in my seat.

Durlan shook his head. "I think Ryul feels threatened by Myrin. He's only been here a week, yet she acts as close to him as she does Amrynn. Ryul was her best friend, or so he thought, and now his status is uncertain."

"He's her mate, that won't change." I frowned.

"No, but her attention has not been given to him," Durlan said.

"He keeps pushing her away and hiding. How is she supposed to give him attention?" I asked with a growl, hands fisting.

"He wants her to seek him out," Amrynn whispered and sighed. "I see."

"Why? To prove she still cares? He would know her feeling for him if he let his walls down a bit. He's causing her pain by ignoring her. I've seen the way she looks at him when he walks by without acknowledging her," I said and then took a deep breath and let it out slowly.

"He is acting childish," Durlan said with a nod. "But we can't call him on it or it will only exacerbate things."

"We've asked Myrin to speak to us tonight, to tell us what he can about our prior lives and Amara. He agreed to meet us after Elara falls asleep," I said.

Durlan smiled. "Good. I've been meaning to talk to him."

"We need to convince Ryul to come," Amrynn said.

Durlan shrugged. "We'll just tell him he has to come."

"We could tie him up, if he refuses," I said with a chuckle.

"He'll use his powers to deceive us," Amrynn said, raising a brow.

"True," I muttered.

"I'll talk to him," Durlan said and stood. "You two need to go work with the new warlords. They need a crash course on their duties. I think Elara is growing antsy to leave."

I'd sensed it as well.

Amrynn and I stood.

"See you tonight," I told Durlan and headed to find the new warlords. As much as I hated teaching, we needed to be sure we left the realm in good hands.

I just hoped we returned before anything happened.

CHAPTER 16
AMRYNN

"ELARA IS ASLEEP," Myrin announced as he closed her bedroom door.

"Magically or naturally?" I asked with a smirk.

He chuckled. "Naturally."

"We're meeting in the war room," I said to him, turning down the hallway.

Part of me rebelled at leaving Elara alone, unprotected, but we wouldn't be far from her, and she should, hopefully sleep the entire time we were gone.

"She'll be fine," Myrin said softly, smirking at me.

I let out an audible sigh. "I know."

He patted my shoulder while chuckling.

We entered the war room to find the four others gathered and sitting in chairs around the giant table in the center, where a map of the realm sat.

Myrin had a seat in Elara's chair so we could all see him.

I sat beside Ryul, in case I needed to restrain him.

"So, none of you have all of your memories?" Myrin asked.

We shook our heads.

"Venali has the most," Kydrus gestured towards him.

"Any of you remember our deaths?" Myrin asked, his voice dropping a bit.

We all shook our heads again.

"Let's start from the beginning," he said. "Amara chose to rule on this planet instead of from the stars. She said she couldn't understand the strife of her children if she wasn't here to see them. Being here weakened her, but since she could draw on the power of the stars, it didn't matter. We were her equals, able to make decisions even when she wasn't with us. Things were going well, until darkness came from another universe. It fell in Minloa, and Amara tried to stop it, but it was beyond her powers."

"Darkness from another universe? You mean a creature?" Kydrus asked.

Myrin shook his head. "No. It was a dark substance on a meteorite that landed here. A fae touched it, and it changed him. Amara didn't want to destroy the man, so she kept an eye on him. He did some things that were not quite moral, but nothing truly evil. She was conflicted. On one hand, he hadn't really done anything to deserve death, but on the other hand, he had spread the darkness to a few more."

"It spread through touch?" Durlan asked.

Myrin nodded. "Obviously, that's not the case anymore, but it was then."

"You touched it," Ryul guessed.

Myrin smirked. "Yes. I thought I was immune, but I was wrong."

"It changed you?" I asked.

He sighed and created a black flame. "Yes and no. I gained new powers, but my moral compass did not change. I was still the same. Amara could see that, but some of us couldn't." He looked pointedly at Ryul. "You tried to kill me."

Ryul's expression was carefully neutral.

"Amara made it a rule that we could not kill each other, unless our life was in danger. You became enraged, convinced I would kill Amara if given the chance," Myrin continued. "It took decades for you to realize that I wasn't a threat. Decades that prevented us from seeing the true danger building on Anderelle, our planet."

"True danger?" I asked.

"I don't want to ruin the surprise," he said, smirking, "but there are several reasons Elara wants to go on this journey. This true danger was the reason we all died. Amara sacrificed herself to try to save us, but her sacrifice was in vain. We all died, and she somehow saved our souls, so we could be reincarnated."

I crossed my arms over my chest. "I thought you were going to tell us everything?"

Myrin shrugged. "It's not my fault you can't access your memories."

"Why is Elara so drawn to you?" Ryul asked, his face still a courtly mask of nothing.

Kydrus and I leaned forward, anxious to hear this answer as well.

"I was her first mate. The last to die. And, the one who drew her back when she let the stars seduce her."

"I've done that," I whispered. "Though, the method I used won't work now."

"Tell me about her past in this life," Myrin ordered.

I glanced at Kydrus and Durlan.

Durlan sighed. "Fine, I'll tell him."

He told Myrin everything, and throughout it Myrin grew angrier and angrier.

Finished, Durlan sat back and watched Myrin.

Myrin closed his eyes, drew in a big breath, and let it out slowly. When he opened his eyes, the anger was gone. "That explains why she finds it so difficult to accept that she is a goddess."

"What's going on?" Elara asked, rubbing her eyes as she entered the room.

We froze, uncertain how to answer her.

"Mate meeting," Ryul said. "We didn't want to wake you, so we came here."

She sat on his lap, curling up her legs so she fit against his chest, and closed her eyes. "Okay. I'll just sleep while you talk."

Ryul's eyes widened, and then slowly he wrapped his arms around her. The mask fell, and we all saw the sadness there.

"How much time do you need to train the new warlords?" Myrin asked.

"A week," Kydrus answered. "They're pretty smart, and have been watching us, so they know most of our duties."

"We will set off as soon as they are ready," Myrin said.

"You're acting like you are in charge," Ryul said with a frown. "Who appointed you leader?"

Elara stirred, and then relaxed.

"She did," Myrin said, looking at Elara. "As first mate, I was dubbed leader."

Ryul growled softly.

Elara bolted upright, her head swiveling from side to side. "What?"

Ryul tugged her back against his chest. "Sorry. Nothing is wrong. Back to sleep."

She frowned, looked at each of us, and then slumped against him again.

Myrin sighed softly. "What do I have to do? Your distrust fractures us and puts Elara at risk."

Ryul looked down at Elara, scowling. "I don't know."

At least he was being honest.

"If you can't accept Myrin, you will put Elara at risk on our trip. If that's the case, it may be better for you to stay behind,"

Durlan said. His words were soft, but the conviction in his eyes wasn't.

Ryul glared at him. "I'm not staying behind."

"Then deal with the shit in your head, stop pushing Elara away, and accept Myrin," Kydrus growled and stood. "I tire of your childishness."

Had Ryul not been holding Elara, I was certain he would have taken a swing at Kydrus. As it was, he stood, cradling her, and left.

"That either fixed things or made it worse," I muttered.

Myrin shrugged. "When it comes to him, you never know."

CHAPTER 17
ELARA

Ryul woke me with kisses along my collar bone.

"This is one of my favorite ways to be woken," I said, opening my eyes to look at him.

His mouth crashed into mine, his need burning like a living flame, and engulfing me with it.

"I'm sorry I've been an idiot lately," he whispered as he removed my clothes and kissed my body. "I've been pouting and acting like a child because I felt like you were replacing me with Myrin."

I spread my legs, letting him dive into me, arching up and gripping his back as he buried himself in me. I was often wet enough for them to slide in without foreplay, and right now I was very happy for that.

"I'm sorry. I wasn't trying to ignore you or spend less time with you," I said.

He slid out of me and then slowly slid back in, moaning as he fully entered me. He stilled and looked down into my eyes. "I love you, Elara."

I smiled and pulled him down for a kiss. "I love you, too. Now, make me scream."

He sat up, smiling wide, and did as I ordered, making me scream several times.

When he had finished, we cuddled a moment before going to the shower, where he cleaned me.

"I'm sorry I was neglecting you," I whispered as I soaped up his body. "No one will ever replace you. I need you just as much as I need the others."

"You trust Myrin?" he asked softly.

"With my life," I said and nodded.

"Then I trust him, too."

We finished our shower, and the light was back in Ryul's eyes again.

I linked our fingers together and smiled up at him. "Let's get food. I'm hungry."

He raised our joined hands and kissed the back of mine. "Lead the way and I will follow. To the ends of the universe or farther."

"I'd rather stay in this galaxy," I said with a chuckle.

The four new warlords sat with my other mates, but quickly rose from their seats to bow.

"Please sit," I said, sitting between Amrynn and Durlan. "I'm hungry."

Durlan pushed a plate of food to me. "Here, my queen."

I kissed his cheek and dug in.

"Communication between the four of you is the most important thing," Kydrus told the warlords. "There will be times that you need one or more of the other's help. Don't be ashamed to ask for aid."

"Be sure to squash any challengers quickly," Venali said.

"And punish those who break the rules," Kydrus added.

"If they view you as weak, they won't listen to you," Venali told them.

"But that doesn't mean rule with an iron fist," I pipped up.

"Durlan was loved by his people for being kind and compassionate, but they also knew if needed, he would crush them."

Everyone turned to look at me.

"What?" I asked. "I learned things while in your sectors."

Most of my mates smirked at me, while the warlords looked curious.

"What's on my itinerary today?" I asked, stretching my arms above my head.

"You are free today," Durlan said.

I dropped my arms and gaped at him. "What?"

Venali chuckled.

Durlan smiled. "You have no itinerary today. You are free to do as you wish."

I frowned down at the table.

Do what I wished? What did I want to do?

I hadn't had free time since becoming their mate.

"We will continue our discussion elsewhere," Kydrus instructed the warlords. He dropped a kiss on my cheek before walking out with the warlords following him.

"You look upset," Myrin said, eyebrow raised.

"I don't know what I should do today."

"What did you do before you found out who you are?" Ryul asked.

I blushed and said, "Nothing."

"Would you like to have a picnic somewhere?" Ryul asked.

That did sound nice.

"What about a swim in the ocean, followed by a picnic?" Myrin asked.

I hadn't been to the ocean in a long time.

"The ocean sounds nice, as does a picnic," I said.

"Great, I'll get the picnic ready," Ryul said and left.

"I don't have a swimsuit," I mumbled.

"You could just swim naked," Amrynn whispered in my ear

and kissed my neck.

I shivered and arched my head to give him better access to my neck. "People will see us," I countered.

"Ryul can use a spell to hide us," Myrin said and then kissed the other side of my neck.

"If you don't stop, we aren't going to make it to the ocean," I groaned. Why was I saying this? Why was I stopping them?

Amrynn rested his hand against my forehead with a scowl. "I think she's sick."

"Clearly. I've never heard of her turning down sex before," Myrin said.

"Especially not with several of us at once," Durlan added.

"I just really want to go to the ocean," I said with a sigh.

"We've got plenty of time. It's still really early," Amrynn said, picked me up out of the chair, and crushed his mouth to mine.

I wrapped my arms and legs around him, holding on as he walked.

He walked without opening his eyes, and our kiss never stopped.

The door opened, and then he tossed me onto my bed.

I yelped, shocked at the sudden air time.

"How are we going to do this?" Myrin asked. "I've yet to participate in a group session."

"I think we should take turns," Durlan said. "That way it draws out her pleasure."

I licked my lips, watching as they stripped their shirts off. "I like that idea."

Amrynn grabbed his shirt from the floor where he'd just thrown it, tore a strip off, and then tied it around my eyes.

"What?" I gasped.

Hands touched me, removing my clothes, and then my body was repositioned so that I was on my back with my legs spread, and rump near the end of the bed.

The hands disappeared, and just as I was about to whine, a mouth covered my most sensitive part.

I gasped and grabbed the sheets.

"I think she likes that," Amrynn said off to my left.

The mouth sucked and then they used their tongue, driving me to the point of pleasure, and then stopping and moving away.

I cried out and reached for the person, but they were gone.

Hands slid up my legs, then I felt the head of a dick pressed against my entrance.

I tried to move, to get them to enter me, but they backed away.

I huffed and crossed my arms.

"No hiding those beautiful breasts," Myrin ordered me from my left.

Wait, hadn't Amrynn just been on my left?

"Stop teasing me then." I pouted.

The head was back, and then they pushed it inside.

"Yes," I moaned, arching up.

Whoever it was grabbed my hips, and began a fast rhythm that had me screaming in seconds.

Normally, they switched positions, but whoever was with me now just held the same position. Which was totally fine with me since they were hitting the right spot, and I had four orgasms before they found their release.

That person withdrew and then a new person replaced them.

This one flipped me onto my stomach, pulling me backwards until my feet touched the floor, while I still laid on the bed. I eagerly waited for them to enter me, but instead was greeted with a face between my legs. They licked and sucked and pleasured me until I peaked and cried out as I fell over the cliff of ecstasy.

Then, they pushed into me, and found a perfect rhythm of pleasure.

I was the luckiest woman in the world.

CHAPTER 18
ELARA

The beach was colder than I remembered, but I didn't let it bother me. We laid out a blanket, and ate lunch. We kept the food inside the basket unless we were eating it, so we wouldn't have to deal with the birds flying around the beach.

Leaning back against Venali, I closed my eyes and relaxed as the sun warmed me, yet the wind chilled me.

"This is nice," I whispered. "We should do this more often."

"We will try to set aside time for this," Durlan said with a smile. "Though, it will be difficult once we leave on our trip."

I cringed. There was so much to do on this trip. So much danger and so much that could go wrong.

"There are going to be some problems when we go to the Unseelie," Myrin said. "You're going to have to allow me to do most of the talking. Ryul, you're going to have to keep your mouth closed."

Ryul grumbled, but didn't argue.

"Could you teleport us to the Unseelie?" I asked Myrin. It hadn't been an option before, since the rest of us had never been there.

He shook his head. "I can't teleport. No Unseelie can."

Really? Why not?

"That sucks," Ryul said.

Myrin chuckled. "Yeah."

"So, two of us will have to double up anytime we teleport then," Durlan said.

Myrin frowned. "Two of you?"

"I can't teleport on this planet," I explained.

"She can teleport to other planets, but no small jumps," Amrynn added.

"Interesting," Myrin murmured, looking out over the ocean.

We lapsed into silence, and I enjoyed the calm, quiet time with my men. Soon, things would be hectic and dangerous, and I didn't know how we would fare.

As the sun dipped lower, I stood and brushed my clothes off. "We should head back."

They agreed and packed everything up. Then we walked to the castle and to our separate rooms. Ryul followed me to my room, and we showered together, but for once there were no other activities in the shower.

It was almost dinner time, so we headed to the dining room.

Kydrus pulled me into a deep kiss, making a smile spread across my face when he released me.

"What was that for?" I asked, brushing some of his hair back behind his ear.

"Do I need a reason to kiss the most beautiful woman in the galaxy?" he asked, arching a brow.

"Only the galaxy?" I asked, sticking my lip out in a pout.

He chuckled and kissed me again. "In all of the universes in all of the timelines that ever existed."

"Better," I whispered, smiling wide.

"I am here to serve, my queen," he whispered, and then nipped my earlobe.

I groaned and arched up into him. "No teasing me before dinner."

"Shall I wait until dinner or do I need to wait until after dinner?" he asked, his husky voice next to my ear and his words soft enough that only I heard them.

"He's just jealous that he didn't get to join in earlier," Amrynn said from the chair where he sat.

Kydrus released me and took his seat. "I'm not jealous."

"Disappointed," Amrynn amended.

"Broody," Ryul said.

"Pouting," Myrin said.

We all laughed and Kydrus smiled. "You all would feel the same."

Myrin nodded. "True."

I sat at the head of the table. "How was your training?"

Kydrus smiled. "They're doing well. I have no doubt they'll be ready."

"Good," I said.

"So, are you going to tell us everything?" Myrin asked.

"Did you know that a female red-toed lizard can run as fast as an owl can fly?" I asked, picked up my napkin and set it in my lap without looking at any of them.

"That was an amazing topic shift." Durlan applauded. "Any other Seelie would have no idea how to respond because they wouldn't be able to ignore your question, and yet you completely ignored theirs."

I beamed with pride.

"Yes, and now answer our question," Ryul said.

"No," I answered, folding my arms on top of the table. "Now, let's talk about supplies."

"We need to know what we're doing before we can determine what supplies we need," Kydrus said.

"Supplies for extreme heat, supplies for extreme cold, and

supplies for in between," I answered.

"How far and how long are we traveling?" Myrin asked.

"Far and at least a month," I answered.

"Farther than the Unseelie's island?" Ryul asked.

I nodded. "Much farther than Eltare."

All of the men turned to look at each other, and I was certain they were communicating telepathically with their new link. I wanted to peek into their conversation, but that would open me to my last mate, and I was trying very hard to keep him out.

They turned to look at me as one, which was rather creepy.

"Another continent?" Durlan asked.

I nodded.

Ryul cursed beneath his breath.

"So, we need a sturdy ship," Kydrus commented.

"I'll reach out to the harbor. I have contacts there," Amrynn said.

"I hate boats," Ryul whispered.

"Can you swim?" I asked him, tilting my head to the side. When we were kids, he hadn't been able to.

He didn't respond, just stared at the tabletop.

"We need to teach you to swim," Amrynn said. "The last thing we need is for you to drown during a sea storm."

"Sea storm?" he asked and gulped.

Amrynn nodded. "They're notoriously bad between continents in the open waters."

"Your food is served," a waiter said as he and three others brought out trays of food and set them on the table.

I still wasn't used to the fact that we had employees in the castle who did this type of thing. It was nice, and super convenient, but, recently, I had been cooking food on a campfire more than having others cook for me.

"She's brooding," Durlan said.

Kydrus looked at me. "You'll get used to it soon. If you hadn't been so scared of me before, you could have eaten with me and been a little more used to others preparing your food."

"It's not my fault you're scary," I mumbled, spooning some vegetables onto my plate.

"He's scary?" Myrin asked, eyebrows raised. "No offense, Kydrus."

"None taken," Kydrus said with a smirk.

"He was the most powerful being around me," I argued. "He could kill me with a snap of his fingers. Why wouldn't I have been scared of him as a poor little slave?"

"Former slave," Kydrus amended.

"You know what I mean," I mumbled around the food in my mouth.

"I still can't believe you were a slave as a child," Myrin whispered. "Your powers or your memories should have at least presented themselves enough to save you from such a fate."

"Tell them that," I muttered.

"At least you're not as skittish now," Amrynn whispered.

Kydrus scoffed. "You're telling me. Even when I was trying to heal her, she flinched or acted like I was about to hit her. I thought she'd had an abusive lover."

"None of my lovers were ever abusive," I whispered before taking another bite of food. I felt their eyes on me, so I looked up. "What?"

"Lovers? You had lovers before us?" Amrynn asked.

Whoops.

"Yes."

I focused on my food, ignoring the stares which were still focused on me.

"How many?"

I sighed and asked, "Do you really want to discuss this? Do you want to tell me your numbers?" I looked at Kydrus. "I saw the number of women who went in and out of your house." I turned to

Ryul. "You told me you slept with others." I looked at Amrynn. "Everyone talked about the revolving door into your house."

Each looked like they'd eaten something sour.

"Whoa," Myrin said, his eyes wide. "You cheated on her?"

"We didn't know she existed," Venali argued.

"Wait? You didn't sleep with anyone?" Ryul asked Myrin.

Myrin shook his head. "I never touched a woman until her."

"Liar," Venali whispered.

Myrin scowled. "I'm telling the truth."

"Did women ever touch you?" Venali asked.

This was so not a dinner conversation I wanted to have.

"Do we really need to discuss this?" I asked.

"No, I didn't let any other women touch me," Myrin answered. "I knew I had a mate, and I waited for her even if I didn't know who she was."

Now I was a little skeptical. "You're pretty good for someone who never had practice."

All eyes turned to me, most with anger.

I shrugged unapologetically. "Just being honest. He's good."

Myrin smirked, the smugness shining from him like a beacon. "I appreciate the compliment. No, I never slept with anyone or did anything with anyone else."

"Fine, no women, what about men?" Amrynn asked.

Myrin laughed loudly while shaking his head. "No. I don't swing that way."

I looked at everyone. "Do any of you?" Not that I had a problem if they were attracted to men as well. Though, I had no desire to share them.

"No," they all answered simultaneously.

"Can we change the subject?" I begged.

"Who did you sleep with?" Kydrus asked.

My eyes widened. "No. No way. Nope."

"What?" Amrynn asked.

"If I tell you, you'll probably go kill them or something," I said, shaking my head.

"No, we wouldn't," Amrynn said.

"You wouldn't," Venali whispered.

Ryul snarled and nodded.

I pointed at them. "See?"

"How many?" Durlan asked.

"More than one," I answered.

"More than five?" Kydrus asked.

"No," I answered.

"More than three?" Myrin asked.

"I'm done with this questioning," I told them. "It was before you guys. Before I remembered I was a princess. Well before I remembered I was...me."

"So, you admit you are more than a princess?" Ryul asked with a smirk.

I pushed my chair back and stood. "I admit that you're an ass." I left the room, snagging a roll on my way out, and went to the war room. "Pushy, assholes," I growled. I locked the door behind me, so the guys couldn't bust inside.

I reached beneath my dad's desk, hitting the secret button, and waited as the secret compartment opened. Inside lay a rolled-up piece of parchment. I spread it out on the desk, put a few items on the corners to hold it open, and looked at the map. It was the only map in existence, that I knew of, that showed the entire planet and the continents.

I took another piece of parchment, one I'd stowed in the same compartment, and resumed copying. I wanted to take my replica with me on the journey, so I could keep track of where we went. I added markers to a few places, and tried to figure out what course we would take. Which was the best way to visit the places I needed to visit.

"Elara," Ryul called through the door as he tried the locked handle. "Please let me in."

I rolled the parchment up, and put it back in the compartment, then walked and unlocked the door. I opened it and scowled up at him. "What?"

"I'm sorry," he whispered.

He did look apologetic.

"You're forgiven," I said and tried to close the door.

He looked over my head into the room. "Why are you hiding in here?"

"I'm busy," I said and pushed him. "Shoo."

He gawked at me. "Shoo? Did you just shoo me?"

"I did. Now, shoo," I said and pushed his chest.

He caught my hand, and his eyes glimmered with pain. "I wish you would trust us. We may argue with you, but we are your consorts. Your mates. We are here for you."

"Soon," I whispered. "Soon, I'll be able to fully trust you."

His eyes glimmered brighter, the pain sharper. "What can I do?"

"Leave me for now," I said. "And tell the others to leave me for the rest of the night."

He sighed and nodded. "Alright."

He released my hand, and it pained me to make him leave, but I needed to work this out on my own. Once I was sure he was gone, I locked the door behind me, and returned to the desk, pulling the parchment pieces out again.

"This is why you're hiding?" Myrin asked.

I yelped, and spun to push him in the chest.

He chuckled and caught my hands. "Didn't know I was here?"

"No," I gasped. "How did you get in? I thought you couldn't teleport?"

"I can't teleport, but I can faze through things, like the wall," he said. He walked to the desk and looked over the maps. "We're visiting all of the continents?"

"You're not supposed to see this," I mumbled.

"Elara, you may be able to keep them in the dark, but don't forget that I remember our prior lives. I remember you and everything about your personality. You're slightly different now, but the core of you is the same."

"Then you know that I need to rule over all of the continents, to unite them," I whispered.

"I wasn't sure if you were going to do that since you weren't accepting who you are," he said.

"I'm not going as...*her*. I'm going as Elara," I snapped.

He scowled, which made him no less handsome. Why was I so drawn to him? Of all my mates, I felt the strongest connection to him.

"I am most worried about the Unseelie," I whispered. "They've been demonized for centuries by these idiots."

"Bitterness runs rampant among the Unseelie." Myrin traced his finger from our current place to the island. "This will be our easiest journey." He traced from the island to the next continent, which had a lot of ocean between it. "This will be our most difficult."

"If I die..." I whispered, but couldn't finish my sentence.

Myrin closed the distance between us and stared down into my eyes. "You will not."

"If I do, please protect them. They are still unbalanced."

"They will be whole, when you are," he whispered. "Sweet, beautiful woman. You drive me crazy."

I smirked. "In a good way?"

I expected him to smile, but he did not. "Sometimes."

Scowling, I stepped away from him. "I'd like some time alone."

"Time to scheme," he whispered from right behind me.

"Call it what you will," I snapped. "But I'd like you to leave."

He kissed my cheek, and then disappeared.

I huffed and sat in the chair behind the desk. He irked me, but mostly because he was right.

Resuming my task, I added place markers, and mapped out our journey. The journey alone would take us a month, roundtrip. I wasn't sure how long each stop on our trip would take.

I was going to have to convince the leaders of the continents to let me lead them. To do that, I would need to use my powers. I wasn't ready for that yet. I needed to see the Unseelie first. I wasn't as nervous now that Myrin was here. I'd been scared what he might do to my other mates. Him coming with his full memory was not what I'd expected. I was grateful, though. At least I wouldn't have to worry about him when we visited the Unseelie. Now, he would be at my side.

I'd almost laughed when he had told Ryul he would have to keep his mouth shut. Myrin was right, though. Ryul had to learn to rein in his temper. And, when to be quiet and let others handle it.

Of them all, he was the most immature and unseasoned. He'd stayed in the castle most of the time, so he didn't have the experience that the others did when it came to battle. I hoped this trip would help him.

Finished with my work, I put the maps back in the secret compartment, and then returned to my room. Just a few more days before we left. A few more days of calm before the storm of my desire to unify our planet.

CHAPTER 19
DURLAN

ELARA WAS HIDING information from us. Some of it wasn't vital, she was allowed her secrets like we were allowed ours. But I had a feeling that some of it was very important and knowing it would help us.

"You're scowling," Myrin said as he entered my room. He shut the door behind him, and then sat in one of the chairs around the small dining table I'd had brought in.

"An expression I make often these past few months," I said and sat across from him. I folded my hands in my lap. "What can I do for you?"

"She's going much farther than I thought. This isn't just a trip to the Unseelie."

I nodded. "I know. She said we were going to other continents."

His eyes widened. "She did?"

"Yes."

He ran a hand through his hair. "Did she tell you anything else?"

"No, but it seems you may know more."

He smirked. "I know quite a bit more, but I'm not sure what I can tell you without getting in trouble with our queen."

"Enough that we won't be in danger?"

He tossed his head back and laughed. "Durlan, when it comes to our queen, our mate, you must know that everything she does will put us in danger."

I growled at him.

"I'm just saying, she likes to do things that are dangerous, and we, as her mates, go with her to protect her. She has a constant target on her back, and that has not changed in any of our lifetimes."

"You remember more than just our previous one?" I asked, leaning forward.

He waved his hand dismissively. "No, we've only had one before this."

Somehow, I didn't believe him, but I let that topic drop.

"You're worried, too," I said, seeing the tension in the corners of his eyes.

He sighed. "She's hurting every day that she doesn't accept who she is. She knows, but she won't accept it enough to release her powers. I don't know what to do to convince her to accept it. I am doing my best to keep her pain at bay, but soon it will overwhelm her."

"How soon will that happen?" I asked.

He shrugged. "A year. A month. Tomorrow. I have no idea. If she continues at the pace she is, most likely in a month."

"In a month, we should be on another continent," I whispered, looking off in the distance. What would that do? Would she be seen as weak, and whatever goal she has there be negated?

"Exactly."

"So, we need to convince her to accept herself within a month," I said, chuckled, and shook my head. "Easy."

Myrin laughed, too. "Yeah. Nothing is easy for us."

“Or for her,” I said. We might be hard on her, but it was only because we wanted her to be able to move on, beyond all the terrible shit she had had to endure.

“I think we should completely avoid the topic of Amara for the next two weeks at least,” Myrin said. “Especially while we are in the Unseelie realm.”

“Why? Wouldn’t it be better if the Unseelie knew she was a goddess?”

He scoffed. “No.”

“What should we expect when we go to the Unseelie?” I asked. I’d been wanting to discuss it with him for a while now.

“Anger. Resentment. Posturing. They’re bitter at the way the Seelie treat them. The ignorance has made them hostile. If Ryul can’t keep his mouth shut, and mouths off to one of them, he’ll likely have to fight an Unseelie.”

“And you don’t think he can win that battle?”

Myrin shrugged. “Each Unseelie has unique powers, just like the Seelie. I have no idea who he might go up against.”

“So, taping his mouth shut might help?” I asked with a smirk. I was joking, but if it came down to it, I would knock him out. I would not let him endanger Elara because he was green still. He might have been as old as us, but he did not have the experience that we had. He had never even been in a battle.

“Knowing him, he’ll still flex on someone and end up causing a fight. We can’t leave him behind, because we might need him if a fight does break out. There really is no good option.” Myrin looked up at the ceiling. “I’m worried, Durlan. This is a feeling I’m not used to.”

“Well, you better get used to it,” I said.

He lowered his head to look at me again. “I’d like to tell you something about yourself. From our previous life.”

I leaned forward expectantly. “Okay.”

“You’ve always been the one who worries the most.”

I sat back and rolled my eyes. "Really?"

He laughed. "Sorry. I do have something to tell you, though."

"Still waiting," I said and sighed.

"You were able to shield her. I don't know if you can do that now, but you were able to create magical barriers that prevented people from touching her or attacking her with magic. She has some magic that requires her to concentrate for a few moments before she can use it. You were able to shield her during those times, or when she was down and we weren't close to her. If you can't do that now, you should try. It was one of the only things that kept her alive as long as she was before."

A magical barrier? I'd heard of people doing that, but hadn't tried myself.

"I will work on that," I said.

He stood. "There's so much I wish I could tell you. Try to convince the others not to say anything to her about Amara, okay? It may help if we aren't pressuring her."

"You mean talk to Ryul," I said and smirked.

He nodded. "He and I won't ever get along, Durlan. No matter what I do, he is predisposed to hate me. I wish it were different, but that's where we are at. We should all take that into consideration and be prepared for him to try to screw me over, which could screw us all over."

"I'll try to break him down. You have to realize that he was in this castle for hundreds of years, just waiting for Elara. He doesn't have the experience the rest of us do."

He nodded. "I hope you're able to break him down a bit. I don't want to hurt him, but Elara is my top priority."

I nodded. "Agreed."

We smiled at each other, and for the first time, I felt a deeper connection with him.

CHAPTER 20
MYRIN

THEY HAD no idea of the possible scenarios when we went to the Unseelie. I'd kept mostly to myself, but my power level was easily visible, so they'd still noticed me. I had seen firsthand the darkness and hostility brewing there. Their hate for the Seelie was unrivaled.

The fact that my mate was Seelie would cause a stir. Me, bringing other Seelie back with me, especially prior warlords, would upset a lot of them.

I was likely going to have to kill someone. Elara was likely going to have to kill someone, too. She might have to kill several people to get them to acknowledge that she was powerful and deserving of their respect.

The current monarch was a handful. I had no idea how they would react to Elara.

"Hey," Kydrus called.

I stopped, turning in the hallway I had been walking down. I didn't have a destination in mind, so I'd started aimlessly wandering the castle.

"What's up?" I asked.

He stopped in front of me, his eyes gleaming with mischief. "You should come out to the arena with me."

I scowled at him. "If you think you're going to beat me or—"

He rolled his eyes. "I'm not Ryul. No, Ryul and Venali are fighting. I think you should watch."

Seeing Ryul's fighting ability would be good.

"Okay," I said. I turned and headed in the opposite direction, Kydrus at my side.

"Did you sneak into her room?" Kydrus asked.

I chuckled. "Yes, but she kicked me out."

"Not surprising," he muttered.

We didn't talk as we walked the rest of the way to the arena. Once there, we sat on the fence to watch them.

Venali glanced over. He smirked, which caused the scars over his eyes to crinkle a moment, and then he turned back to Ryul. "No holding back. Magic allowed."

"If I use magic, you'll lose instantly," Ryul said. He brushed invisible dust off his shoulder.

So cocky.

"Try me," Venali said.

Ryul held his hand out, and Venali froze.

What was he seeing? Ryul could manipulate reality, so it could be anything.

Venali shook himself, and then took a swing at Ryul, barely missing his nose.

Ryul backed up, scowling. "What?"

"I didn't break your spell," Venali said, advancing and swinging at Ryul. "But I have spent enough time with you to be able to sense you wherever you are, even with your tricks."

"Maybe you should actually fight him," I suggested.

Ryul gave me a glare, anger making his eyes flare bright. He dropped his spell and attacked Venali.

Venali easily dodged the attacks, and swept his feet out from under him.

I had to hand it to the brute, even in this life he was quick.

Ryul glanced at me, saw my smirk, and growled. He waved his hand at Venali, and something drastic changed.

Venali froze again, but this time agony twisted his face. "Stop," he growled, his voice sounding strained.

Ryul punched Venali, knocking the big man back a step.

Venali had tears in his eyes, and he didn't even try to fight back.

"It's not real!" I yelled.

Ryul continued attacking Venali, landing blow after blow.

What could he be showing Venali that would make him stop like this? He knew it was fake. He knew it because he had started this match.

"Stop!" Venali roared.

Ryul stepped back and released his magic.

Venali fell to his knees and dropped his head forward. "You're a fucking prick."

"You said use my magic," Ryul said, but he didn't sound quite so smug anymore.

"What did he show you?" I asked Venali.

"Why don't you come and find out?" Ryul taunted.

Venali had gathered himself again, and I could see the anger brewing. I leapt down and jogged to stand in front of him. "Venali," I whispered.

Venali turned away. "I'm fine."

"Try me," I said, facing Ryul.

Ryul tilted his head to the side as he looked at me. "You want the same as I gave Venali?"

I nodded.

"You sure?" he asked. "You saw how he reacted."

"Show me," I growled.

Ryul snapped his fingers, and all around me was a battlefield. Dead Seelie and Unseelie covered the ground, their blood painting everything red. A few were still fighting, Venali, Kydrus, and Durlan among them. The enemy was one I had not seen before. They looked similar to us, but their teeth were not sharp. I spun around, and the sight before me made my heart stop. In the middle of it stood a man with a spear, and before him, on her back, lay Elara. Elara held up her hands and begged the man to spare her.

I held still.

This wasn't real. This was just an illusion.

Tears streamed down Elara's cheeks, mixing with blood that seeped from several wounds on her face. She was covered in wounds.

"Remove your bonds with your consorts," the man said. "And I might spare you."

"Anything. I'll do anything but that," she wept.

The man raised the spear and aimed it at her heart. "Then, die."

She screamed as the spear plunged into her chest. Her blood burst out in an arc.

My body ached to run to her. To kill the man.

I knew it wasn't real. But the pain I felt was.

"What's going on?" Elara asked.

The image shattered, and I turned to find her.

She stood, wrapped in Venali's arms, her eyes wide as she surveyed us.

"That's a great magic for when you know the person and their worst fear. But what if you don't know them?" I asked.

Ryul chuckled. "I don't need to know them personally. Everyone has fears. Plus, I don't have to show them something they fear. I can just change the area so they don't know where I am."

"Venali, fight him again," I said. "This time, no horrors."

I switched Venali places, picked Elara up in my arms, and carried her to the sidelines. I placed several kisses on her cheeks.

She was here. She was safe. She was not dead.

"What's wrong with you two?" Elara asked, snuggling her face into the crook of my neck.

"Ryul showed us you dying," I said.

She tensed. "What?"

"We asked him to use his magic to fight us." I nuzzled her and kissed her forehead.

"I'm not dead," she said and hugged me around the neck.

Venali faced Ryul. His fists were clenched and a red aura swirled around him. "Show me what other tricks you have."

"Is this necessary?" Elara asked and then yawned.

"You should go to sleep." I adjusted my hold on her so that I was fully supporting her weight, and then hopped up on the fence beside Kydrus.

"What did he show you?" Kydrus asked.

"Elara being killed by a weird man with dull teeth," I said.

"Humans," Elara gasped. "That's even more cruel than showing my death."

"Humans? The things that took you in their spaceship?" Now I really wanted to punch Ryul in the face. I could understand why Venali was so angry now.

"Yes," Elara said. "Ryul is rude."

I chuckled. "He did what he was supposed to do."

Venali and Ryul began fighting. At first, they fought hand to hand, neither excelling over the other, but then Ryul used his magic.

Quickly, Ryul darted away from Venali, moving to his back, left side.

Venali froze for a second, the aura around his hands glowed, and then he flung a fireball at Ryul.

Ryul ducked, avoiding the fire, his eyes wide.

Venali ran after Ryul, catching him with one, two, three...seven punches.

Ryul fell onto his back and raised his hand. "I yield."

"You're barely trying," Elara said.

"I'm tired," Ryul said, sitting up. "This isn't an actual battle, so I don't *have* to fight. I need some sleep."

Or, he was embarrassed by how pathetic his stamina was, and didn't want Elara to see.

"It is time to go to bed," I said. "We should all get some sleep."

Elara hopped out of my arms, walked to each of the guys to give them hugs, and then returned to me and held out her arms.

I picked her up and kissed her. "You're pretty damn perfect. I hope you know that."

She scoffed. "I'm far from perfect."

"Perfect for us. And that's all that matters."

CHAPTER 21
ELARA

We left as soon as the sun rose, headed away from the castle with no fanfare or goodbyes. Just me and my mates headed to meet people who despised us.

Easy peasy.

Durlan had a contact at the pier, and there was a boat waiting for us with no crew.

"How are we going to get there?" I asked.

"We can sail," Kydrus said, smirking.

"You can?" I asked, blinking.

"Just because we've been on land most of our lives doesn't mean we didn't learn how to sail," Kydrus said. "I'm offended."

I chuckled. "Sorry. I just can't picture you guys sailing."

Now that I said that, I was totally fantasizing about them shirtless and sailing a pirate ship.

"Stop thinking naughty thoughts," Myrin whispered in my ear as he passed by.

I shrugged unapologetically. "Not going to happen. You guys are sexy and I enjoy thinking about naughty things with you all."

We boarded the ship, and the guys went into action to set sail.

I had no idea what was going on, so I just sat on the railing in front of the steering wheel, and watched.

They were all working well together, even Ryul and Myrin. I was glad. The sooner Ryul accepted Myrin, the better. And the safer we would be. I didn't want discord between them to cause anyone to be injured or killed.

Myrin took the steering wheel and turned it, guiding the ship away from the dock and out into the open waters.

"We're going to be alright, right?" I asked Myrin softly.

"Yes, my goddess. We will be fine. You will be in danger, but I will ensure nothing harms you," he said.

I turned to look at him. "I meant all of us. I don't want something bad happening to you guys either."

He smiled, but was focused on steering, so he wasn't looking at me. "We will survive the Unseelie."

This was the shortest part of our journey, since Eltare was so close to our continent. I hopped down and walked to the front of the ship, looking out over the clear water which teemed with sea life.

"Don't lean too far forward," Ryul said with a frown and shake of his head. "You might fall in."

"The water is too cold for a swim. I won't fall in," I said and smiled back at him. He stood almost next to the center mast, his body tense, and fists clenched.

"You sure about this?" he asked, looking past me, in the direction of the island.

"Yes," I said immediately, facing the ocean again. "One hundred percent."

The anticipation and unknown were starting to get to me. There was so much that could go wrong.

"You remember to keep quiet," I said.

Ryul scoffed. "I know."

"I mean it," I said and turned to face him fully. "I don't want everyone being put in danger because you couldn't control your rage and your mouth."

He glared at me. "I'm not a child, Elara."

"No, but you're green compared to the others. And, your stubbornness caused part of our demise last lifetime," I said, striding towards him. It was a low blow, but one he needed to hear and be reminded of.

He sighed. "I know."

"Then strive to be better. Be the man I know you can be," I said, resting my hand on his cheek. "I love you."

"I love you, too," he said. He leaned into my hand, and then turned and kissed my palm. "I'll do better this lifetime. I just really wish I remembered our last one."

"You will, eventually," I said.

We sailed for several hours, but no one spoke aside from necessary call outs for our sailing. Everyone was lost in their own thoughts and try as I might, I became lost in mine as well. In the various ways the Unseelie could hurt my mates. In the various ways that I could screw up this meeting and my plans. I had to ensure everything went as planned. I had to make them agree to join us. It was imperative.

"Island!" Myrin called out.

I turned in the direction we were headed and smiled. There it was, the Unseelie island, Eltare. I was ready for this. Or, at least as ready as I could be in my current state.

Surprisingly, there was a dock with a few ships, and several people walking around.

The guys went to work getting the ship docked, and then we disembarked. Myrin took the lead, followed by the rest of us in a circle with me at the center.

People watched us and murmured to each other as we passed.

There were Seelie, Unseelie, and a few other races I couldn't place. They had to have come from some other continent.

"Stop gawking," Kydrus whispered. "You're making us fall behind."

I snapped my head back straight, and saw he was right, Myrin was far ahead.

We walked faster to catch up, and Myrin glanced back at us. "Mouths shut from here on out," he said.

Everyone nodded.

He led us down a wooden path, into some trees, and then stood before what looked like a castle gate, but there was no castle.

I wanted to ask, but he'd said to be silent, so I held my tongue.

Myrin placed his hand against the gate, closed his eyes, and whispered something.

The gate groaned.

Myrin backed up.

Slowly, the gate lowered. Through the opening, we could see a busy courtyard, full of Unseelie. Myrin exhaled. Then I watched in almost horror as he put on a mask of unfeeling confidence. He looked like an assassin. His eyes were so cold and soulless.

"Follow me," he ordered, even his voice was different.

He led us inside, head held high, and ignored everyone as if they didn't exist. We made it to the castle steps before guards intercepted us, their swords drawn.

Thankfully, none of my guys drew their swords.

"What's this?" one asked Myrin.

"Our monarch is going to want to speak to them," Myrin said.

"Why? Who are they?" the guard who had spoken asked.

"I'm not going to announce that here, where everyone can hear," Myrin snapped. "Get the royal advisor if you won't let us pass to speak to the monarch."

The same guard turned and whistled to another guard. That one walked into the castle.

The guards before us were tensed, ready to fight. Yet, I could sense no darkness from them.

The Unseelie weren't evil after all. We had been lied to. All of the Seelie were being lied to.

Why? Why make the Unseelie into monsters?

The castle doors opened, the guard who had left returned, and an older man came at his side.

The older man stopped before Myrin. "What's the meaning of this, Myrin? Why have you brought these *Seelie* here?"

He said Seelie like it was a curse word.

Myrin leaned close to his ear, whispering so softly that we couldn't hear.

The man's eyes widened, and he focused his attention on me.

Myrin continued to speak, but the man's gaze never left mine.

Finally, Myrin pulled back, blocking the man's view of me.

"Bring them in," the man said.

"Sir?" the guard asked.

"Did I stutter?" the man said and growled.

The guard stepped to the side, letting us pass.

Myrin headed up the stairs, and we followed.

I held my head high, not meeting anyone's eyes, but still trying to look regal. I would not appear submissive here. I would not, for a moment, let them think that I was to be walked over.

I admired the paintings on the hallway walls. There were several decorative vases and other items as well. It was all very pretty.

"Not what you expected, is it?" the man asked me.

I looked at him, but did not respond.

He took the hint, turning and pushing open double doors.

Inside, over a dozen people sat in rows before a throne, where a beautiful woman rested. Her hair was long, blood red, and she had a gorgeous crown a top her head.

She had long fingernails, painted the same blood red as her hair. She was paler than me, but her eyes were filled with a curious light that gave me hope. "What have you brought me, Myrin?" she asked in a lilting voice.

Myrin stopped at the base of the steps that led to the throne, and dropped to one knee.

I had to pinch myself to keep from snarling. I did not like him kneeling to her.

"I've brought you the Seelie Queen," Myrin said. "She's requested an audience, and I thought she might entertain you."

The queen smirked. "The Seelie Queen. What brought you here, to this cursed island?"

I stepped forward, the guys parting to let me through, and dipped my head in acknowledgement. "I'm Elara, Queen of Minloa. What may I call you?" I asked.

"I am Aerith, Queen of the Unseelie."

"I've requested an audience because it's become clear to me that the Unseelie have been demonized by previous rulers, and I wanted to set the record straight. I wanted a chance to meet with you to find out what you and your people are truly like," I said.

She tilted her head sideways as she looked at me, evaluating. "You speak the truth. How interesting. Well, Elara, we are not the evil, blood thirsty creatures the Seelie make us out to be. But, how can I prove that to you? Your people would just say that we played nice for your visit."

"They would come to see the truth, once we united and some of you returned to Minloa," I said.

Her eyes widened. "You would allow us back?"

"We're getting ahead of ourselves," I said with a smile. "Are you willing to allow us to stay here for a couple of days? To learn more about you?"

"How do I know you and your guards aren't here to attack us, or attempt to overthrow me?" Aerith asked, sitting up straight.

"I have the power to overthrow you," I said nonchalantly, with a shrug of my shoulders. "But my goal is to unite the continents, not kill."

She arched a brow and her lip twitched as she fought a snarl. "You are so sure of your ability to overthrow me. Don't you think that's a bit presumptuous since you do not know much about the Unseelie?"

I held out my hand towards Durlan. Myrin glanced at us, scowling.

I'd worked this plan out with Durlan in secret. I hadn't wanted anyone to know what I planned to do, except our strategist. He'd agreed to it.

Durlan opened his pack, and pulled out my crown, the one with the human planets in it, and then set it atop my head.

I turned to face Aerith and smiled. "I am *most* certain of my ability to defeat you in battle."

"Queen Elara—" Myrin growled.

I gave him a glare, and he shut up and took a step back.

Aerith stood, her eyes glowing turquoise. "You threaten me in my home?"

I shook my head. "I threaten no one. You seem ready to fight me, though. If you wish a demonstration, I am more than willing to oblige."

She growled and yelled, "Kill the men!"

My eyes widened. "Defend yourselves!" I snapped.

The guys drew their swords as guards encircled them, separating me from them.

"You seem so worried about these men. If I destroy them, perhaps you'll be less cocky," Aerith said.

I narrowed my eyes at Aerith. "If you harm my men, I will obliterate you from this planet. If you kill one of them, I will find you in every lifetime from here to eternity to torture and kill you. Do *not* touch my men."

Her eyes widened, but she held her tongue.

Her men attacked mine, swords clanging.

Myrin stayed rooted to his spot.

I felt pain in my arm, and turned to find Ryul bleeding from a cut just above his elbow.

I turned back to face Aerith, and more than anything wanted to make her cower.

Screw it all.

I dropped my barriers, claiming and admitting that I was Amara, Goddess and protector.

Power greater than anything I'd experienced before coursed through me, making my body glow.

Aerith's eyes widened, and she backed up a step, hedging towards hiding behind her throne.

"I am the goddess Amara. You will not harm my consorts!" I yelled. With a sweep of my hand, I knocked everyone except my consorts to the ground.

"You can't be," Aerith gasped from where she lay.

I walked to her, sword drawn, and pointed it at her throat. "I came here seeking hospitality, to try to unify our people. Instead, you took offense because I was more powerful than you. Are you so pathetic as to attack someone's allies in an attempt to weaken them? Clearly, you are. I do not approve. You will be better, Aerith, or I will find a new queen for my dark children."

She rolled into a bow before me. "Forgive me, Amara. I will be better."

I turned towards my guys, and my jaw dropped open. They were all glowing, their hair flying in an unseen wind, and eyes glowing.

"I remember," Ryul whispered.

"We all do," Venali said. He walked closer to me, and dropped to one knee, bowing his head. "My goddess."

The rest of my consorts came to me and bowed as well.

"Stand," I ordered everyone.

Everyone stood.

I turned and said, “The time for hiding is over. The Seelie will learn the truth about the Unseelie. It is time for us all to unite.”

“Yes, Goddess,” everyone said.

I turned to Myrin. “Escort me to chambers. I would like to talk with you all.”

Myrin stood, and bowed at the waist. “Yes, my goddess.”

“I’ll talk with you more later,” I told Aerith. “For now, tell your people that I am here, and I am unhappy.”

I followed Myrin, head held high, and my crown thrumming with power.

Myrin led us to a large bedroom, and shut and locked the door behind him.

I glared at him. “If you ever bow to another person again, I will punish you.”

He swallowed hard. “Yes, Amara.”

“Now that we are here,” I said, my chest tightening. I felt my body beginning to shake, and gulped. “Someone, catch me.”

The power left my body as fast as it had come, and my strength went with it, causing my legs to give out, and I fell as my eyes rolled up into the back of my head.

CHAPTER 22
KYDRUS

AMARA'S EYES rolled up into the back of her head, her body stopped glowing, and she started to fall.

I leapt forward, catching her before she hit the ground, and cradled her in my lap. "Amara?" I asked, gently.

"What's wrong with her?" Venali asked.

"Her body isn't equipped to handle her goddess powers for too long," Ryul said. "She should wake in an hour or so."

I carried her to the bed and laid her down. Her hair fanned out around her like a halo, and she looked so peaceful as she slept.

She'd accepted who she was, unlocking our memories, but it seemed she would need to train her body to handle her powers.

I gently stroked her cheek.

"What was that back there, Durlan?" Myrin asked. "That was not what we had agreed to."

"Elara came to me last night and asked for me to keep her plan a secret. She said she was certain that the queen would not just accept her," Durlan said.

"She might have if she hadn't said she was stronger," Myrin growled.

"She wasn't wrong," I said softly. I spooned my body around Amara, or Elara, or whatever she wanted to be called. It was a bit cold in here, and I didn't want her to be uncomfortable.

"That's beside the point," Myrin said and threw his hands up in exasperation.

"Why are you upset? She accepted herself," Ryul said. "You should be happy."

Myrin looked at her sleeping beside me, and his face softened. "I am happy that she accepted herself, but she should not have kept such a plan a secret from me."

"You scared her when you prepared to come into the Unseelie court," I said.

Myrin's brows furrowed. "What?"

"When you closed off, became the aloof and cold blooded Unseelie you'd pretended to be all along, it scared her for a moment."

Myrin's brows furrowed more, but he said nothing.

"What's our plan?" Ryul asked. "Now that she's revealed who she is, it changes things."

"Not much," Durlan said.

She stirred beneath me, groaning, and her brows pinching.

I stroked her face from temple to jawline, and pressed a light kiss to the center of her forehead.

She relaxed, letting out an audible sigh, and stilled again.

I hadn't realized that the others had frozen during the moment until I turned towards them.

"This might make our trip easier," Durlan said. "They aren't likely to argue with a goddess about uniting."

"They will put up very little resistance," Venali said.

"I can't believe Aerith was going to have us killed," I whispered.

"She was close to killing everyone in the room," Durlan said.

We didn't need a name to know who he was talking about.

"For now, we stay together and protect her. I'm not sure what the others will think about her Seelie form," Durlan said. "She needs to be protected at all costs."

That was something everyone agreed on.

I would not fail my goddess, my love, again. I would not let her die.

CHAPTER 23
ELARA

I WOKE SWEATY AND THIRSTY.

"Water?" I requested weakly.

One of my consorts helped me sit up.

I opened my eyes, but it was pitch black in the room.

"Here," Kydrus said and a glass was pressed against my lips.

I grabbed the glass from him and gulped it down. Once I'd had my fill, I let the glass drop to my lap and asked, "Can we turn the light on?"

The lights came on, and I winced, covering my eyes with my hands.

"Sorry, there's no dimming ability," Ryul said.

I let my hands fall and looked at my guys. They weren't glowing anymore, but they still looked different. Godly somehow.

"What happened?" I asked.

"What do you remember?" Durlan asked.

"Fainting in the room," I said.

"You've been asleep since then," Kydrus said. "You slept for at least three hours."

I looked down at my arms. "I'm not a goddess still." I didn't want to say anything to them, but I wasn't sure I was fully Amara after all. There still felt like a separation between us.

"It seems your body can't handle you releasing your goddess powers for too long. You'll have to train to increase your stamina," Venali said.

I looked over at Myrin who hadn't spoken. "You're mad I withheld my plan from you."

"Irritated, but not mad," he said. He climbed out of the covers so he could sit in front of me. "But you accepted yourself, and that is well worth any irritation."

"I thought I would take on my goddess form permanently when I accepted it," I said. My brows furrowed in frustration. Why hadn't I become a full goddess?

"Is that why you wouldn't accept it before?" Myrin asked.

I nodded.

"What do you want us to call you?" Kydrus asked.

That was a tough question. I was Amara, but I was also Elara. Both parts existed within me.

"Elara when in this form," I said.

"How do you feel?" Durlan asked.

"Fine. I'm mostly baffled I still have this form."

"You're beautiful no matter what form you take," Ryul said.

I leaned around Kydrus, so I could see Ryul, and smiled wide. "Thank you."

"What's the plan?" Myrin asked.

I sighed and fell back on the bed, looking up at the ceiling. "I don't know. I was fairly certain I would end up having to kill the monarch here, but I've decided to be merciful."

"You were getting ready to kill everyone," Durlan said.

I scowled. "Ryul was injured. I warned her, and she didn't stop the attack."

Ryul chuckled. "It was just a flesh wound."

I rolled my eyes.

"The people are going to want to see you," Myrin said. "In your goddess form."

I nodded. "Let's hope I can summon it at will." And that I didn't have to hold it for long.

"We should get more sleep," Durlan said. "I have a feeling tomorrow is going to be a long day."

The guys climbed back into their positions, and I rolled on to my side, laying my head on Kydrus's chest. Venali wrapped himself along my back.

Despite knowing I should sleep, it would not come.

Something was wrong with me. I wasn't sure what it was, but I needed to fix it. Fast.

My last consort tugged on our bond.

Closing my eyes, I focused on our bond and sent a single thought to him, "Soon."

The tugging stopped, but I could sense his irritation.

He was too far for me to worry about right now. After we left the Unseelie, I would seek him out.

For now, I would focus on the tasks at hand.

AERITH BOWED TO ME AS WE ENTERED THE COURTYARD. She'd gathered as many of the Unseelie as she could.

I'd been able to take my goddess form, so I stood before them, glowing and looking badass with my crown atop my head.

"It is time for the Unseelie to come out of the shadows. It is time the Seelie learned the truth about you. We will not be divided. We will be united, and coexist together. It may take them time, but they will learn. After my journey, I will return to take volunteers back to the mainland to live there. You have a month to decide who among you is willing to go."

I turned and entered the castle, making long strides, but not long enough that it was obvious I was hurrying.

My consorts surrounded me, stern expressions on their faces to keep anyone who might want to talk to me away.

Fatigue pressed on me like a giant weight. My breathing became rougher, and I tripped.

Amrynn was right there with an arm out, somehow making it look like I just took his arm instead of tripping.

Myrin shut the door, and I collapsed in Amrynn's arms.

Durlan took my crown and placed it on the table. He inspected me with a scowl. "This doesn't make sense. You can command the cosmos, but you can't use your powers in this body?"

"No idea," I gasped. I lay limp in Amrynn's arms, my heart hammering like a caged bird.

"Drink some water." Kydrus held out a mug of water, and I gratefully accepted, gulping it down in two swallows.

"Do you need to do anything else before we head to our next destination?" Durlan asked.

Ringing started in my ears, and I felt hot and fuzzy. My mouth opened, but I couldn't make it speak.

"She's going to pass out," Amrynn said.

Durlan started using his healing magic on me, but this was beyond even him.

The world went dark, and I wondered if this was my punishment for holding back for too long.

CHAPTER 24
AMRYNN

"We should leave when it's dark," I said, still holding my sleeping queen. It had been two hours since she fainted, and while I could have put her on the bed, I preferred to have her in my arms where I could confirm she was breathing.

"That would look really suspect," Myrin said. "It may undermine what we're trying to accomplish."

"She needs to speak to Aerith once more before she leaves," Durlan said. "We'll have to wait until tomorrow. She'll speak to Aerith, we'll get on the ship, and then she'll likely faint and sleep for the first part of our journey."

Fainting so much couldn't be good for her health. Wasn't there anyway to help her body acclimate faster?

Someone knocked on the door, and all of our heads swiveled towards it.

Venali growled softly.

I carried Elara to the bed, laying with her so it looked like we were both asleep. Kydrus climbed on with us, laying on her other side.

Venali opened the door. "What?"

"Would Goddess Amara be willing to come eat with us?" a soft-spoken male asked.

"As you can see, she is taking a nap with two of her consorts," Venali said. "Perhaps another time."

"Queen Aerith was quite insistent." I could hear him fidgeting from here.

"I'll go," Elara said and sat up. She aimed a smile at the door. "I enjoy being in this form. It helps me learn more about my people."

Well, that was one way to handle the situation.

"I'll let her know you'll be joining us." The man hurried away with shuffling steps that meant an injured leg.

"Elara," Myrin growled.

"It's true. I wanted to be reincarnated in one of these forms so I could experience the pain and pleasure that my people faced. I hadn't planned to experience quite so much pain, but it was good. Besides, it will make me seem more empathetic and like a most understanding goddess," Elara said. She turned and looked down at me. "Why are you sleeping?"

I smirked. "We were pretending when the man came to speak to you. We weren't sure what they were going to want."

She returned my smirk, and then bent and pressed her soft, delectable lips to mine.

I wanted to devour her, taste every inch of her, but now was not the time.

She turned and kissed Kydrus as well, and then stood from the bed and stretched. "I don't think I have anything to wear."

"Just wear what you currently are," I said. "It will further the point that you wanted to live like them."

She smiled. "Okay."

"Well, I guess we're going to dinner," I said.

"Food!" Venali yelled.

CHAPTER 25
ELARA

My fatigue was gone, but having to be completely unconscious for several hours was not ideal. It put me at a disadvantage, and put my consorts in danger.

"What can I do to stop from fainting?" I asked Ryul.

"We need to have you use your powers for just a few moments and then release them. We'll have you increase the time little by little until you'll be able to hold it for long periods," he said.

His eyes glowed as he spoke, and I got distracted by them, stumbling a step.

"You're drooling," Myrin whispered in my ear.

"It's not fair," I said, turning to face him.

He arched a brow. "What isn't?"

"You guys are all..." I waved my hand, unsure how to explain it.

"All what?" Myrin asked, smirking.

"Hot!" I snapped. "You look all godly and gorgeous."

All of them laughed.

"I'm glad you're all amused," I mumbled. I folded my arms

across my chest and ignored them all as we continued down the hallway. Why did this place have such long hallways?

We finally made it to the dining hall, and two Unseelie guards stood in front of the doors.

The guards stared at me without moving.

"I was invited," I said. "Please, step aside."

"You were invited, but not your consorts," the guard on the left said.

I stepped forward, getting right up in the guard's face. "My consorts come with me. Now, move or I will have you moved."

His lip twitched in the beginning of a snarl.

Before he could move, Myrin was there, grabbing the guard and throwing him down the hallway.

Venali grabbed the other guard at the same time and tossed him to the side.

The guards leapt up, but realizing they were outnumbered, they held their place.

Venali and Myrin opened the doors for me, bowing as I passed.

"Such considerate consorts," I said. The smile on my face was smug and satisfied.

Hundreds of Unseelie filled the dining hall. At the front on a raised dais sat Aerith.

Everyone turned to look at me.

I felt my guys step up behind me, which gave me more confidence.

I slapped a smile on my face, and walked through the people to Aerith.

She arched a brow. "I did not expect Queen Elara."

"I took this form to learn about your lives," I said. "There's no reason for me to be in my goddess form all the time."

Her eyebrow lowered. "From what I'd heard, you were lost in this form for a long time, your parents killed."

I nodded.

"How can a goddess have parents?" an Unseelie behind me asked.

"Where do you think this body came from?" I asked, turning to face the crowd. "I did not create it. I just put my soul into it when it was born. My consorts were put into their bodies as well."

"That must have been rough," Aerith said.

"Worse for some of us," Ryul whispered.

"Where are we to sit?" I asked. I didn't want to answer anymore questions.

Aerith waved at a table just to the left of hers that had food on it, but no one sitting at it. "That table has been set up for you."

I sat at the table, and my consorts put food on a plate, and then set it before me.

I started eating, and they made their plates to eat as well.

The room was full of quiet murmurs, but I didn't try to listen in on any of them. I just wanted to eat and then leave for the next continent.

"You're missing a consort, are you not?" Aerith asked from her place.

I almost choked on my food. I took a long drink of water before answering.

"Yes, we're leaving in the morning to go get him," I said.

"You know where he is?" she asked. The way she said it, she sounded smug.

"Of course, I do," I said. "I have a bond with them."

"That's what the mark on your neck is, isn't it, Myrin?" Aerith asked.

Myrin nodded. "It is, but we also have a metaphysical bond that the mark is not necessary for."

"How interesting," she whispered.

"You have one Unseelie and five Seelie," an Unseelie near the back said. "Why is that?"

"I did not choose which body my consorts would take. I do

know that Myrin was the first Unseelie, so it makes sense for him to become Unseelie again," I said.

"The first Unseelie?" Aerith asked, eyes wide.

Myrin smirked. "Yes. I am the first."

The crowd gossiped loudly, and Myrin looked incredibly smug.

I finished eating and stood. "Thank you, Queen Aerith, for your hospitality. I will return and pick up those who are willing to return with me to the mainland."

"We will look forward to your return," she said, stood, and bowed to me.

We left the castle and were escorted by some guards to the docks.

I sat against the center mast and closed my eyes.

"You look exhausted," Ryul whispered.

I nodded.

"Is it because you're not with your last mate?" he asked.

"That's a big part," I said.

"Let's set out," Myrin said.

Ryul dropped a kiss on my head and went to help the others set sail.

I dozed on and off as we sailed away from the island.

Sometime during the night, the wind picked up, and the guys started yelling orders to each other.

The ship rocked wildly, and I slid across the deck.

I screeched, opening my eyes, and reaching for anything to grab as I slid towards the side of the ship.

Venali grabbed my forearm, jerking me to a stop. "Got you," he said.

I gripped his arm and smiled wide. "Hi."

He chuckled and pulled me up as he stood. "Napping on the deck isn't a good idea."

"I see that," I said. I held onto his side, hooking two of my fingers through his beltloop.

"Bring her up here," Myrin said.

Venali picked me up and carried me to Myrin and the ship's steering wheel.

I kissed Venali's cheek and then his lips when he turned his head. "Thank you."

"You're welcome." He set me down next to Myrin.

Myrin took a rope from his pack, tied it around my waist, and then tied me to the railing in front of the wheel. "This way, I can see you and I know you won't go flying off the ship," he said.

I glared at him, but decided it wasn't a terrible idea, so I let it happen.

For the first time, I looked out at the sea, and my mouth dropped open. The waves roiled and rose around us, some more than twice as high as the ship.

"We're going to die," I whispered.

"It's just a small storm," Myrin said. Then, the bastard laughed.

Lightning flashed and thunder boomed.

Amrynn dragged Ryul to stand beside me. "Stay with our queen," Amrynn ordered.

Ryul nodded and gripped the railing beside me with white knuckled intensity. His eyes were wide and full of terror as he watched the sea.

"Don't worry, Ryul. I've sailed in weather like this several times," Myrin said.

"Not reassuring," Ryul mumbled.

"What's wrong?" I asked Ryul.

"I can't swim," he whispered.

Oh, right. I'd forgotten.

I laid my hand on top of one of his and squeezed. "We'll be okay."

He wrapped his arm inside the ropes securing me to the railing, which helped me feel more secure as well.

The ship rocked to and fro, but the initial fear I had was gone now that I needed to reassure Ryul.

I set my hand on Ryul's atop the railing, and leaned my shoulder against his. It was cold, and my body trembled, but I tried to still as much as possible, not wanting him to think I shook from fear.

Myrin yelled orders to the others, and they ran about the ship, pulling ropes, and doing other things I had no idea about.

Hours passed, or what seemed like hours, and then the sea quieted and the sun came out from behind the clouds.

The waters stilled, and the ship sat in placid water.

Myrin sagged against the wheel and let out a tired groan.

Ryul quickly left, almost jerking away from me in his haste to be somewhere else.

I didn't let it bother me, though. Men like him didn't enjoy showing weakness.

After untying myself, I walked to Myrin and kissed his cheek. "You did well, Myrin."

He smiled, the movement slow and sleepy. "Thank you."

"Come on, let's get you to bed. I need you at full-strength should another storm show up," I said, and looped an arm around his waist and tugged his around my shoulders.

He picked me up, making me gasp, and carried me to the captain's cabin. "I'm not that tired, Elara."

"I am and I just stood there all night," I said and yawned.

He chuckled, shut the door behind us, and fell onto the bed with me on top of him.

I rolled off him, onto my side, and lay my head on his chest. "Storms have always interested me, but being in the middle of an ocean when there's one is not something I want to deal with again."

"We still have a long way to go," he mumbled.

"Go to sleep," I said. I jerked the blanket out from behind me, and tossed it over the both of us.

His snoring was almost immediate.

CHAPTER 26
RYUL

Fear was not something I was used to. Then again, being cooped up in a castle most of my life didn't leave room for much fear to enter.

My parents had tried to teach me to swim when I was a child, but I'd refused, saying there was no reason and I'd never need to swim.

Now, I wished I had listened.

As an adult, I hadn't been able to bring myself to ask anyone to teach me to swim.

Being in that storm, with nothing but water surrounding us, I had wished more than anything that I'd been taught to swim.

"You alright?" Durlan asked, setting a hand on my shoulder.

We all sat in the lower deck of the ship, around tables we'd rigged for eating our meals.

Elara and Myrin slept in the captain's quarters, Myrin's snores audible even down here.

I still didn't like him, but I respected him a bit more after watching how he captained the ship in the storm.

"Fine," I mumbled.

Amrynn sat across from me, a plate of food in each hand. He slid one towards me. "It's alright to be scared. Being scared once in a while is a good thing."

"I was scared at several points last night," Kydrus said. "Most notably when Elara started sliding down the deck."

That had terrified me. I'd wanted to grab her, but the fear of both of us falling into the water, with me unable to save her if that happened, had rooted me in place.

"I need you to teach me to swim," I said without looking at anyone of them in particular. At this point, I didn't care who it was, as long as it wasn't Myrin.

I shoveled food into my mouth, exhausted from my muscles being clenched so tight during the storm.

"When we get to land, we'll make some time for one of us to teach you," Durlan said.

I nodded.

"How can Elara sleep with Myrin snoring so loudly?" Venali asked and plopped down beside me at the table.

"She can't," Elara said, walking to join us.

She sat between Amrynn and Kydrus, leaning her head against Kydrus's shoulder.

The jealousy that had accompanied seeing her touching the others was gone now. With my memories back, I'd fully accepted my brothers being hers as well.

"Would you like to take a nap?" Kydrus asked.

She yawned, but shook her head. "No, I'll just sit here while you guys eat and maybe close my eyes."

All of us smirked.

She was a minute or less from falling asleep, and we all knew it.

Amrynn looped an arm around her waist, ensuring she wouldn't fall should the ship move suddenly while she napped.

"How many battles have you been in?" I asked Venali.

He smiled, but then frowned. "Too many to keep count, sadly."

"You?" I asked, turning and looking at Durlan.

"A dozen or so," he said.

"You've never been in one, have you?" Amrynn asked me.

I shook my head. "I stayed in the castle, protecting it from bandits."

"You regret that?" Kydrus asked.

I sighed and set my fork down. "I don't regret that I kept my word to Elara, to wait for her. I don't regret keeping the castle safe. But I do regret not learning more outside of books. I didn't understand how green I was until we went to the Unseelie. The situation was one I had no idea how to handle. And while I don't doubt my fighting abilities, I truly don't know what would happen if we were to fight in a large battle."

"Don't be too upset about not having to fight," Amrynn said. "Many of us wish we hadn't been in many of the battles we have. Yes, it gave us experience, but it also gave us nightmares, complexes, and we lost a lot of friends."

"Fighting isn't for everyone," Venali said. "It is important that you learn to defend yourself and our queen, but you don't have to experience battle to be ready for that."

Coming from Venali, that seemed like good advice. The brute loved battles.

"What is the plan when we reach this new continent?" I asked. Elara had kept close-lipped about it, so I had no idea what to expect.

"We aren't sure. We know she's going to find her final mate, and she wants to try to unite the continents, but we have no idea how," Durlan said. He scowled, and stabbed at his food.

He loved plans, and it seemed not having a plan bothered him a lot.

I agreed with him on that. Having plans made things so much easier.

"She needs to practice using her powers," I said. "Or she won't be able to prove she's really Amara."

"Have any of you felt *different* since you got your full memories back?" Amrynn asked.

We all nodded.

"I feel like I have another mode or set of powers I could be using," Kydrus said.

I nodded again. "Like she does when she turns into Amara. Like a god mode, right?"

Everyone nodded.

"But I haven't figured out how to unlock it," Amrynn said. "I tried right after Elara accepted herself, but despite feeling the powers and knowing they're there, I can't unlock them."

"Perhaps we have to wait until the final consort is here," Durlan said. "We aren't a complete unit yet. It could have something to do with that."

"Or, there's another barrier, something else she's holding back that we don't know about," Venali said, looking at Elara.

We all turned to look at her, peacefully sleeping on Kydrus's shoulder.

That was a possibility. She liked keeping secrets. And she hadn't figured out everything yet. Maybe we wouldn't be able to unlock our powers until she fully unlocked her ability to take her goddess form.

"She's awfully cute for such a damn handful," Venali whispered.

Durlan and I chuckled.

"You think we have the possibility of being reincarnated again?" I asked.

Durlan scowled and shook his head. "I don't think so. I think what happened last time was Amara's doing, but I am uncertain if she could do it again. Or, if she would want to do it again. If she can unite the continents, then there is no need for us to be reincarnated."

"I'd rather not go another thousand or so years without my mate again," Myrin said.

He sat on the other side of Durlan, looking spry and happy.

"Good nap?" I asked.

He nodded. His eyes fell to Elara. "My snoring kept her awake?" he asked.

We all nodded.

"Like it always did," Durlan said. "Even when she was a goddess, she couldn't handle your snoring."

"It's not like I can control it," Myrin said. He got up and grabbed some food from the crates.

"You'd think a goddess could fix something as simple as that," Kydrus said. His voice was soft, and not as deep as usual.

Was it to try to keep from waking Elara?

"She finds it endearing and doesn't want to fix it," Myrin said. "Or at least that is what she told me last lifetime."

"I think she just didn't want you to feel bad," I said, smirking.

Myrin chuckled and sat back down. "You might be right, brother. You might be right."

Part of me wanted to dislike him, distrust him still, but this new Myrin was improved. And, I was better this time. Or, I was trying to be at least. It was clear now that Myrin had no intention of harming Elara or Amara. And that his heart was exactly where mine was. To protect and love her for as long as we lived.

CHAPTER 27
ELARA

The moment land came into view, the connection with my last mate went taut and took my breath away for a moment.

Close. We were so close to him.

When we finally reached shore, I leapt from the ship and lay on the beach.

"Land!" I yelled, rolling on the warm sand. "We made it to Emortalia, finally."

The guys had to properly dock the boat, so they didn't join me for at least ten minutes.

Ryul was the first one to leave the ship, and he joined me, lying on the beach. "Land!"

I sat up and looked around, surprised that there were no other people around.

"I think we came to a port that's no longer used," Durlan said. "The ropes and everything are old."

"Should we sail elsewhere?" Venali asked.

"No," I snapped.

All eyes turned to me.

"He's close," I said, feeling my cheeks heat.

"Lead the way," Kydrus said and waved his arm inland.

I opened my bond and immediately felt a tug from the other end.

I turned slowly to the right until I faced the correct direction and then started walking.

Venali walked at my side, his hand on the sword at his hip.

"Excited?" he asked.

I glanced up at his face, finding him smiling at me. "Nervous," I said.

He frowned. "Why?"

"I don't know whether he's mad or not," I whispered.

"I'm sure he's not going to be mad at you," Myrin said behind me.

"It's not your fault he ended up on a different continent," Kydrus said.

"He may not know that," I said. "Just like Ryul didn't know that I had forgotten my memories and been taken as a slave."

All of them growled, which made me smirk.

"Well, even if he is mad, when we first see him, he will quickly get over it and forgive you," Venali said.

"I hope so," I whispered.

The sand was hard to walk up, and my progress was slow.

We finally made it out of the sand, and I released a happy sigh. "Let's not live near sand," I said.

Several chuckles followed my statement.

The bond tugged me to the left, so I altered our course towards it.

"You sure you know where you're going?" Amrynn asked.

I turned around to glare at him, walking backwards, opened my mouth to give a snappy retort, and tripped. My arms windmilling as I tried to keep from falling.

Venali grabbed my arm and pulled, helping me regain my balance.

"Thanks," I said, turned around, and resumed walking.

"I don't think I've seen her so flustered since before she remembered she was a royal," Kydrus commented.

We entered a heavily wooded area, and I had to dodge and weave around trees as we climbed up a hill. The connection felt stronger, and it felt like he was coming towards us.

"I think he's trying to find us, too," I said, picking up my speed.

We crested the hill. On this side, there were trees, but they weren't as dense, and there were several open areas, giving me a clear view.

And there, at the bottom was a man with golden hair, flowing in the wind. He raised his head, and our gazes locked.

Him.

Mate.

Mine.

His physical appearance was different, but there was no doubt who he was. The bond between us was undeniable.

Before I realized what I was doing, I ran down the hill, sliding and grabbing trees to keep my descent at a reasonable pace.

The others called out to me, but I paid them no mind. I had to get to him. I had to touch him.

He ran up the mountain towards me, his eyes glowing a soft amber, and his lips pulled up in a beautiful smile.

My hands were covered in sap and leaves, and the next time I tried to grab a tree, my grip slipped.

I yelped and started to fall, but warm, muscular arms wrapped around me, pulling me to a stop, and against an even warmer body.

"You," he whispered, "are just as crazy as the last lifetime, it seems."

"You're here. I'm here. We're here," I gasped out.

Lifting my head, I fell into his gaze and wasn't sure I wanted to ever be pulled out.

"My goddess, what are you doing in this body?" he asked and stroked my cheek.

"The same thing you are," I whispered, licking my lips.

He watched the movement like a starved wolf following prey.

"Are you mad?" I asked.

He arched a brow. "Mad?"

Loud crashing behind us drew his attention, though his eyes did not leave mine he tilted his head that direction.

"Brothers," he said without looking away from me.

"She's worried you're mad at her for putting us in these forms, and for being separated," Myrin said. "Though, she didn't choose our forms."

"I'm not mad. I've been dying to find you since you connected the bond, though," he said.

He had a strong jaw with light stubble. It was rather sexy. I wondered if I should have been bothered that he was human, but he didn't seem like a normal human.

"What are you?" Ryul asked.

"He looks human," Amrynn said.

"A shifter," my mate said. "I'll explain all about me later. First, I have something I need to do."

My brows furrowed and anger began to build within me. What could he have to do that was more important than me? I was his mate, separated for far too long, and he had more important things to do?

He tucked some hair behind my ear, smirked, and whispered into the now uncovered ear, "You may be in a different body, but your expressions are the same. You misunderstood what I meant."

"What did you mean then?" I asked.

He gripped my waist, pulled back enough to look into my eyes, and said, "That I needed to do this." His mouth crashed into mine, and he kissed me with a ferocity I felt equally.

I wrapped my arms around his neck and kissed him deeply.

Our bond solidified, and I gasped, pulling back from the kiss.

He smiled down at me and said, "That was much more important than showing them what a shifter is."

CHAPTER 28
ELARA

"What name do you go by?" I asked.

"Daniel," my golden-haired consort said.

"I go by Elara," I said. "In this form at least."

"Let's talk about these forms," he said and folded his arms across his chest.

He had biceps as large as Venali's. And a chest as wide.

"My eyes are up here," Daniel said, but I could hear the teasing in his tone.

"I wanted to experience life as my people do, so I could better understand their hardships," I said.

"Was this the plan should we die all along?" he asked.

I nodded.

"Did you know we were going to die?" he asked.

I shook my head. "I was concerned we might, but I don't see the future, never could."

"What is a shifter?" Durlan asked.

"It's a man who transforms into an animal," I answered, talking before Daniel could.

Daniel smiled. "How did you know that?"

"I read a book about Minloa history. It mentioned shifters," I said.

"You can transform into an animal? Like, any animal or a specific one?" Amrynn asked.

"A specific animal," Daniel said. His body glowed, and then before me stood a large golden-brown bear.

My hands and face were in his fur within seconds. "So warm," I whispered, rubbing my face in the thick and shaggy fur.

"That's intimidating," Venali said.

Daniel shifted back, which caused me to be cuddled up against his chest while he was squatted down. He picked me up, and I burrowed my face into his neck.

"I'll take you to my house," Daniel said. "Expect stares. People haven't seen Seelie or Unseelie in a very long time here."

"I can walk," I whispered.

"Nope," Daniel said. "I'm not letting you go the rest of the day. Maybe the rest of the week."

I was okay with that.

"She looks very disappointed," Amrynn said and laughed.

"We might have to pry them apart so she can do what she came here to do," Kydrus said.

"I'll tear your arms off if you try to separate us," Daniel said. The growl in his throat was deep, much deeper than a Seelie growl.

"Your growl is different than ours," I whispered to him.

He glanced down at me. "Well, I am an animal. Does it bother you?"

I shook my head and then rested it on his shoulder. "No, just commenting on it. I like it, actually."

"She says that until she has to hear him growling for an hour while we catch him up on what's happened," Myrin muttered.

"What's happened?" Daniel asked, slowing so he could walk beside Myrin.

"No," I snapped. "No serious talk until after I get some time with Daniel."

Myrin raised his hands in surrender. "As the queen wishes."

"Queen?" Daniel asked.

"Queen of the Seelie," Durlan said.

"Well, that's interesting," Daniel whispered. "I thought goddess was better, but queen does open other doors for you while in this form."

"How far is your house?" I asked.

I ran my fingertips over the stubble on his chin, loving the roughness. Seelie and Unseelie did not grow facial hair.

"Not far," Daniel said. He glanced down at me. "You seem fascinated by my hair."

"We don't grow beards," Myrin said. "You're the only of us who does."

Daniel smirked and for a moment I stopped breathing as I took him in. My other consorts were handsome, but Daniel was glorious. He oozed masculinity, even more than Venali.

"Stop drooling," Ryul grumbled.

Daniel licked the corners of my lips. "No evidence."

Sense left me, I grabbed his face, tilted it to the side, and kissed him, thrusting my tongue into his mouth and refusing to let him turn his head at all.

He kissed me back, his hands tightening on my body where he held me.

I pulled back, panting, and hid my face against his neck, closing my eyes. "Sorry."

"Don't apologize," he said, his voice rough. He cleared his throat. "I wasn't trying to tease you."

Exiting the forest, we entered a small village. Humans walked around, and many openly stared at us.

"Humans," I whispered and swallowed hard.

Amrynn stepped closer to me, his hand reaching out to rest on my forearm. "It's not the same ones," he whispered.

"What's wrong?" Daniel asked, looking from me to Amrynn.

"It's all part of our story," Amrynn said. "Lots to tell you."

"I didn't know we had humans on our world," I whispered.

"They're pretty harmless," Daniel said, but his hold on me tightened when he felt me shaking.

Amrynn and I growled at the same time.

"Okay," Daniel said, drawing the word out. He walked to a house along the outer edge of the village and pushed open the door. The guys walked in, and then Daniel walked past them, down a long hallway, and to a huge bedroom with a giant bed in it. He kicked the door shut behind him, slid his boots off, and set me on the edge of the bed. My legs hung over the edge, and he spread them so he could stand between my legs, and in front of me.

"While I would love to make love to you right now, I think we need to talk first," he whispered.

"They can help tell you what's happened better," I said, swallowing thickly.

Humans. Why did it have to be humans?

"You slept with men before them," he whispered. "Why?"

My head jerked up, and my mouth dropped. "I, uh, it isn't what you think. I didn't cheat on you. I didn't have my memories. I didn't know I was Amara until a couple months ago. If you let them explain, you'll understand."

"Who were these other men?" he asked.

How did he even know?

"They were no one. Just sex. Not even good sex. I didn't know. I didn't remember you. If I had, I wouldn't have slept with them. I swear." The words tumbled out of my mouth quickly, and tears began to build.

He exhaled and met my eyes. "Okay. I believe you."

"You said you didn't remember until the bond was formed with the others," I said. "So, you didn't—"

He shook his head. "I didn't."

"Most of them did," I said. "I can't fault them because they didn't know."

"I forgive you, Amara. It still hurts, but I can't hold it against you if you didn't have your memory."

The others hadn't made a big deal out of it. They were jealous, but hadn't been upset. I wasn't sure what to do.

Daniel wiped his thumb across my cheek, wiping away a few stray tears. "Come on, let's go talk to the others. I need to know what's happened to you."

I tried to slide off the bed, but he picked me up again. I frowned. "I can walk. You don't have to touch me if you don't want to."

"Amara, I—"

"Elara," I corrected. "I'm Elara in this form."

His brows furrowed, but he said, "Elara, I didn't mean to upset you. I just needed to know. I can smell them on you."

"That was over a decade ago," I said. "How can you still smell them?"

He said, "My nose is very sensitive. And when you share your body with another person, it leaves a mark."

"I'm sorry, Daniel. I—" I didn't know what else to say. I felt like I should beg him for forgiveness, but at the same time, it wasn't fair that he was putting this on me since I hadn't had my memory.

He walked to the living room where the others sat on the couches, talking quietly.

All eyes turned to me when we entered.

"Why is she crying?" Kydrus asked, his lip pulling up in a snarl.

"I smelled her previous sexual partners. I asked her about it," Daniel said.

"You can't fault her for that. She didn't remember even this form's life," Amrynn said.

Daniel sat, positioning me in his lap. "Tell me what's happened."

I stood off his lap and sat on Myrin's instead, burying my face against his chest.

Myrin rubbed my back and kissed the top of my head.

"She was born the daughter of the king and queen of the Seelie of Minloa," Durlan began.

It took an hour, all of them adding bits and pieces, but they finally finished the story of my life so far.

Daniel had sat quietly the whole time, not moving, growling, or making any noise.

"That's it," Durlan said.

"So far," Kydrus said and chuckled.

"Myrin, you and I need to talk later," Daniel said.

Myrin nodded. "Okay."

"My goddess," Daniel whispered.

I turned my head so I could see him, but looked at him from beneath my hair, using it as a veil between us. "Yes?"

"Come here, please?" he requested.

"No," I said.

His brows furrowed. "No?"

I stood, the anger that had been growing finally surged to the top. "No. I haven't reacted that way since Amrynn on that damn spaceship. I'm not that pathetic girl. I can't believe I let you make me feel that way. So, no. I'm not going to come to you. If you want to talk to me, you can wait. You can wait until I'm done being mad. Maybe you can wait a bit longer, too."

"Elara," Myrin whispered.

I spun and exited the room, searched until I found a back door, and then walked out into the forest.

"Elara," Ryul called.

"Leave me," I ordered him. "I don't want to see any of you for a bit. I just need some time."

"Did you stop to consider that you might be mad because you're mad at yourself for not remembering who you are sooner?" Ryul asked. "That you aren't really mad at Daniel?"

"You say one more word, and I'll take your voice," I threatened him, spinning around to glare at him. "I'm tired of you guys treating me like a broken doll. I can protect myself. I can be mad if I want to. I have feelings. I'm allowed to have them."

Ryul sighed. "I didn't say you weren't allowed to have feelings, I'm just—"

"Ryul! Leave me alone!" Power whipped around me, causing my hair and the leaves to float.

Ryul glared at me, but turned and left me alone.

I walked deeper into the forest. Humans. I had to deal with humans. Convincing them to unite with us might be more difficult than I thought.

Yes, I was mad at myself. But I was also mad at Daniel. If he'd just let us explain my past first, this could have been avoided. This unease inside of me would not be there.

I sat against a tree, leaning my head back and closing my eyes. Queen. Goddess. Slave. Seelie. They all fit me. Yet, I didn't feel like I fit any of them at the same time.

Did it count as cheating since I hadn't remembered them?

I knew the others had slept with women, and I hadn't been angry with them. Wasn't angry with them.

"I've upset you," Daniel whispered.

My eyes opened, and I stared at him crouched before me. He'd moved so silently. Was that part of being a shifter?

"Yes," I said.

"I should have let them tell me first. I shouldn't have isolated you to accuse you like that. I'm sorry. This was not how I wanted our reunion to go."

I stood and turned away from him. "Me neither, but here we are."

"You endured a lot. I only added to that. I'm a jerk."

"Yep." I headed deeper into the forest, farther away from his house.

"Elara," he called.

"Leave me alone to cool off," I said. "I just need space."

CHAPTER 29
MYRIN

Ryul stomped into the house, muttering to himself about stubborn women. Clearly, he was talking about our goddess.

"Didn't go like you planned?" I asked with a smirk.

He cut me a glare. "He's stalking her. Maybe he'll be able to calm her down."

"Or, she might just need some time to herself," I said and shrugged. "We've been at her side non-stop for a month. Everyone needs some alone time every now and then."

"Why's she so mad?" Ryul asked. "I told her she's really just mad at herself, which only made her madder."

Kydrus, Amrynn, Venali, Durlan, and I looked at each other, and then at him.

"You can't be that stupid," I said.

His fists clenched at his sides. "What?"

"Why would you say something so stupid to her?" Amrynn asked.

"What are you talking about? It's the truth," Ryul said.

"That's beside the point. Do you want her pointing out the stupid shit you did before and when you get mad, just remind you that you did it so you can only be mad at yourself? You'd still be upset with her, right?" Kydrus asked.

"She's mad at him. Yes, she's a little mad at herself, but right now she is mad at him. He accused her of cheating on him. She got upset because technically she did cheat on us, but she didn't remember. We cheated on her, too," Durlan said. "We didn't beg her for forgiveness. We didn't feel bad. Why? Because we recognized that it was before our memories were back. If we could go back in time and not do that, we would."

"There's a lot I would change if I could go back in time," I murmured.

"She's going to give you the cold shoulder again," Amrynn said and folded his arms across his chest. "I feel like I should punch you in the face, just because you deserve it."

"Same," Venali growled.

Ryul stared at us. "You're telling me I shouldn't point out her problems?"

"We're telling you that she's aware of the problems. When she's upset is not the time to pile them onto her," I said.

Ryul threw up his hands and walked out of the house.

Durlan looked at me. "Are you going to go after her?"

I shook my head. "Let's leave Daniel and her alone for a bit. The bear can protect her."

Durlan nodded and relaxed back against the couch.

Venali glared at the door Ryul left through. "That boy needs an attitude adjustment."

"He's young," I said. "He was young last lifetime. He'll learn."

"Before or after he hurts her more?" Amrynn asked.

I couldn't respond to that because that was exactly what I was worried about.

CHAPTER 30
ELARA

Daniel was following me. I could sense him, even if I couldn't hear him.

Why was it so hard for them to leave me alone? I was capable of protecting myself.

"Can't you just leave me alone?" I growled.

"Please, let me apologize properly," Daniel said.

I growled, clenched my fists, and spun around to face him. "Fine."

He stepped out from behind some trees to my right, nearly scaring me out of my skin.

He dropped to one knee and bowed his head. "I'm sorry. I'm a jerk. I messed up. I've been dying to find you and instead of focusing on the joy of being united, I overreacted and didn't give you a true chance to explain all that has happened. Please, forgive me, and let us go back to the beginning. Please?"

"I can't forget it happened," I whispered. No, that thought was now lodged in my brain. "But I can give you a chance to make it up to me."

He lifted his head. "Anything."

"Follow me," I ordered.

He obeyed, following right on my heels as I led him back to the house. I took him into the bedroom and spun around.

He shut the door to his room, and faced me, his eyes uncertain.

"I want to solidify our bond," I said.

He stripped his clothes off in seconds and then looked down at me.

I undressed slowly, well aware of his eyes on me the whole time.

He licked his lips.

"Are you going to be okay touching me when you can smell the others on me?" I asked. I hated that I sounded unsure, emotional, about it. I sounded like a self-conscious woman, which really irked me.

He wrapped me up in his arms, our bare skin touching, and his like an inferno against mine. "Yes. I will smother you in my scent, so it won't ever be brought up again."

I chuckled and rubbed my face against his chest. "I like the sound of that."

He picked me up and set me on the bed. Then he kissed me deeply. "You're so beautiful. So perfect." He kissed his way down my throat, to my breasts, and all the way down until he licked the spot that ached with need.

"Yes," I gasped and threw my head back.

With the skill of his tongue, I orgasmed faster than I ever had before. He licked his lips, and climbed up until he was positioned over me. He pressed his erection against my opening and stared down into my eyes. "You're the most perfect woman who has ever existed," he said. "I will worship you for the rest of our lives and beyond, through all of eternity." He slid inside of me slowly, closing his eyes and moaning when he was fully sheathed.

I moaned as well, the feel of him inside of me, finally, was orgasmic on its own.

His hips began moving, and I gripped his back, trying not to dig my nails into him.

He kissed my breasts and then sucked on one of my nipples as he continued his steady rhythm.

Our bond pulled tight, and when we shared our orgasm, it fully solidified.

We lay together, breathing heavily, and a smile on both of our faces.

Instead of dressing after cleaning up, we lay back down and took a nap.

Sometime later, Myrin woke me. "You need to eat, Elara. We can hear your stomach in the front room."

I stretched and squealed. Why did stretching feel so good?

Two pairs of hungry eyes stared at me.

"Food," I reminded Myrin.

He held out my clothes. "Dress first."

I sat up, leaning on my hands behind me, and giving them an unblocked view of my bare breasts. "Maybe I don't want to get dressed."

"Maybe I would rather make a meal of you," Myrin said.

I smiled and grabbed my clothes. "Food first."

Myrin tossed Daniel a pair of pants. "You, too."

Daniel chuckled. "Fine. I'll put pants on."

Someone knocked on the front door, and we all tensed.

Daniel finished slipping into his pants and walked down the hallway to a answer it. "Yes?" he asked the visitor.

"Can I borrow a cup of sugar?" a silky female voice asked.

My hackles instantly went up.

"One second," Daniel said. He left the door open, which gave the woman a perfect line of sight to the bedroom, and to me sitting naked on Daniel's bed.

Her cheeks flushed, and she dropped her eyes.

Daniel brought her a bag of sugar and held it out.

"I didn't realize you associated with Seelie," she said.

"They just arrived," Daniel said.

"Didn't waste time," she muttered.

"No, I didn't waste time bedding my mate," Daniel said, his tone harsh.

The woman's head jerked up, her eyes wide. "Mate? She's your mate?"

Daniel nodded.

The woman gave me a once over.

I kept my relaxed posture, meeting her stare with one of my own.

"Thanks for the sugar," she said and spun around.

Daniel shut the door and growled something too soft for me to make out.

"Someone has an admirer." I dressed to avoid looking at him or Myrin.

"You don't know the half of it," Daniel muttered. "Even telling her you're my mate won't stop her from trying."

Death would stop her.

"No killing," Myrin said.

I mocked him silently.

Once dressed, I walked out of the room and to the kitchen. Everyone else was already there, helping to make our meal.

"Her jealousy is so sexy, isn't it?" Venali asked Daniel.

Daniel smartly kept his mouth closed, though I did see his lips twitch.

"Tomorrow, I need you to take me to the leaders of Emortalia," I said.

"Are you going to be okay addressing humans?" Amrynn asked.

"Yes. I understand that these are not the same humans as the last," I said, slightly miffed that he asked me that, but at the same time I did understand.

"Are you going to go all goddess on them?" Ryul asked.

I didn't look at him, his comments from earlier were still upsetting. "I'm not going to reveal I am a goddess to anyone else. I will use my powers to persuade them to name me Empress, and fall into an alliance with Minloa. They can keep their rulers as is, but I will oversee everything."

"Why didn't you do the same with the Unseelie?" Myrin asked.

My cheek twitched. "Because she overstepped her boundaries."

"Because you lost your temper," Myrin said.

I growled, but couldn't refute his statement.

"They're likely to fight back," Daniel said.

I sighed. "Children always resist their parents. In the end, they'll see the light."

All of my consorts turned and looked at me with wide eyes.

"What?" I asked.

"Your personalities are blending more," Myrin said. "That's something Amara said before."

I shrugged. "It was bound to happen eventually. We are the same person."

"After food, you need to practice your magic," Durlan said.

I nodded. I'd already planned to work on the longevity of holding my goddess form.

The guys shared a look and then went back to making our meal.

"I'm going to go practice now," I said and stood. "Using my magic will make me hungry."

Durlan nodded. "Good point."

"I'll go with you," Daniel said.

Ryul opened his mouth to say something, but Venali elbowed him.

Daniel followed me to the living room.

I sat in the center of the floor and crossed my legs. "You can sit over there," I said and pointed at the couch.

He sat on the couch and watched silently.

Closing my eyes, I let everything fall away except for the magic in my core. With a slight tug, the powers released, and I took on my goddess form. Something felt different, my consciousness as Elara was dripping away until I was only Amara.

Daniel straightened as our connection sizzled between us. "Amara," he whispered.

I turned and smiled.

He slid off the couch and knelt before me.

With one hand, I pushed back his hair and kissed his cheek. "A bear is a rather fitting animal for you," I said.

"Your voice is different," he whispered.

"I have Amara's voice when I'm Amara and Elara's voice when I'm Elara," I said. "We aren't fully merged, and I'm not sure if we will ever fully merge. It will take you time to get used to the difference, but we have a lot of time left together."

He wrapped his arms around me and kissed my ear. "I've missed you, my goddess."

"I've missed you as well, my consort."

"How long can you hold this body without negatively affecting the fae body you're inhabiting?" he asked.

"Not very long, unfortunately, but her strength is improving. Soon, I should be able to come and go as necessary," I said.

"Go? Why would you need to go?" he asked, pulling back to look down into my eyes.

"This world needs Elara. She is a symbol of hope and peace. I am a goddess, yes, but the people need someone who has been through the trials and tribulations that she has," I said.

Something dark touched the corner of my mind.

I pushed Daniel away, stood, and turned towards it. I'd felt this darkness before. I *knew* this darkness.

It drew closer, curious, but hesitant.

My body shuddered and before I wanted to, I had to release the powers.

I collapsed onto the floor, gasping for breath. Fully Elara again.

"What happened?" Durlan asked as he rushed to my side.

"What was that feeling?" Ryul asked.

"Evil," Myrin said. "That was what evil feels like."

"Not evil really," I gasped. "Just...darkness."

"What was it?" Daniel asked. "I've never felt anything like it before."

"You have, you just don't remember," Myrin said. He squatted down beside my head and rested his hand on my cheek. "It was him, wasn't it?"

"I don't know," I whispered. "I had to release my powers before I could figure out what it was."

"What are you talking about?" Amrynn asked Myrin.

"Do you remember how we died?" Myrin asked.

"I do," Kydrus said softly, his eyes haunted.

"No, we don't," Durlan said.

"We were killed by a god," Myrin said and stood. "In the universe there must be balance. Good and evil. Light and dark. Amara is the light. The good. He is the dark. The evil."

"What's his name?" Ryul asked.

I slapped my hand over Myrin's mouth out of instinct. My cheeks heated as he looked at me. "I don't think we should say or even think the name."

He moved my hand away and nodded. "I agree."

My vision began to swim, and I slumped into Durlan. "Dizzy," I whispered.

Durlan began to heal me, to give me some of his power, but I pushed away. "No, let me be. I need to get used to this fatigue. I need to work through this and figure out how to function even while it weighs heavily on my limbs."

"Well, you're awake this time, which is an improvement," Ryul said.

I laughed. "True."

Carefully, I pushed myself up to my feet, swaying slightly.

Several pairs of hands reached out towards me, but I held my hands out and they all pulled away.

"See, I've got this," I said with a wide smile.

The guys looked unconvinced.

"I'm goo—"

Before I could finish my sentence, my eyes rolled up into the back of my head and I fainted.

CHAPTER 31
DANIEL

Venali, Ryul, and I caught Elara before she hit the floor.

My little goddess always liked to overextend herself.

"She's sleeping," Durlan said, waving his hand over her body to check her vitals.

I let Venali take her and lay her on the couch. Then I sat on the other end, so I could run my fingers through her hair.

"She hasn't changed," I said with a laugh.

"Nope," Myrin agreed. "She's still the same, reckless woman as before."

"What was she talking about?" Ryul asked. "The darkness?"

"You said we were killed by a god," I said to Myrin.

He sighed and ran a hand through his hair with a growl. "We were basically gods, once Amara took us as consorts. We weren't easily killed. How else do you think we would have died?"

"A god killed us. Why?" Ryul asked.

"Because he was jealous," Myrin said. "He wanted Amara, but she told him she could not be his consort. He could not understand why she refused him. He was powerful, the most powerful being in the universe, next to Amara. To prove his power, he started taking us out. Amara fought him, trying to save us. We caused her death in the end."

"You think he still wants her? That he will try to claim her for himself again?" I asked. Had I been in bear form, my claws would have dug into the arm of the couch. She was mine, ours, and we would not let some pompous god take her just because he was jealous.

"Most likely," Myrin said.

"Why didn't you tell us this before?" Ryul asked, snarling.

"I had hoped he was hibernating or had moved on. I hoped he would not bother us again. Amara proved that she would rather die than be with him. We'll have to be wary from now on," Myrin said.

"What did she mean about leaving? That this world needed Elara, but not her?" I asked. "She can't mean that she'll cease to exist, can she?" That thought sent a shiver of dread through me. It wouldn't be the first time that she came up with a crazy-ass plan.

No one responded, which was response enough.

What would that mean for us? What would that do to Elara to have Amara separated from her?

There were too many unknowns in our future that I did not like at all.

Elara sat up, looked around, and asked, "How long was I asleep?"

"Just a few minutes," Durlan said.

She smiled and lay back down. "I'm getting better."

"Yes, you are," I said and stroked her hair.

And, I would do everything in my power to keep her from dying this time. Even it if meant dying again myself.

CHAPTER 32
ELARA

The humans gathered were very unlike the ones Amrynn and I had met during our kidnapping. These ones were relatively docile and much more fearful.

Was it because they didn't have the advanced technology and knew I was more powerful as a Seelie?

Daniel had advised us that this continent, Emortalia, was broken up into three sections. Carnel, where humans and shapeshifters lived together. Plunce, where shapeshifters lived. And Distra, where humans lived. They were separated by the peoples' prejudices, but Daniel said it helped keep the peace to have a place for like-minded people to go. I thought it was stupid.

Daniel led us to a large building with a giant metal bell atop it. A few men were stationed out front, guards by the look of the swords on their hips. Daniel spoke to the guards for a moment, and then one went inside while the other gave me a glare.

"I don't think he likes me," I whispered to Myrin, who stood on my right.

Myrin snickered. "Or, he's wondering why I'm with you when you're Seelie and they know our kind hate each other."

"That will be fixed soon enough," I said.

The guard who'd left returned and waved us in.

I walked by the guard who was still glaring with my head held high.

I followed behind Daniel with Myrin at my back. The others had wanted to come, but I'd convinced them that bringing so many Seelie into one room would make the humans way too uncomfortable.

We were led to an open room with seating around the edges and a platform where three humans sat. The middle seat was the tallest, obviously meant to be a throne despite being made of wood, and had a fat, balding man sitting in it. Beside him was a woman in a pretty dress and his other side was a young adult boy.

Daniel stopped before the humans. "Greetings, Your Majesties. I bring before you Elara, Queen of the Seelie."

Several humans in the audience murmured to each other. The royals didn't even move.

"What can I do for you, Queen of the Seelie?" the king asked.

"I've come here on a mission of peace," I said, taking a step forward. "I've come to request that we unite our continents and kingdoms and foster better relations."

"Why should we unite with your kingdom?" the boy asked.

The king gave him a glare, but didn't say anything else, so I assumed they wanted me to answer.

"We have many things worth trading. We are powerful and have healers who could heal your people better than medicine alone," I said.

"And what do you want from us?" the king asked.

"Peace and unity," I said.

"You wish to open trade with us and barter for becoming allies?" the queen asked.

I nodded. "Yes."

"I find this very suspect," the king said.

I smiled. "We can sign a written trade agreement to ensure there is no miscommunication about our partnership."

"Very well," the king said. "I will review the trade agreement and if it is to my liking, I will sign it."

I glanced at Myrin who stepped forward with the rolled-up agreement in his hand.

The guards stepped forward, their spears aimed at him.

Myrin held out the agreement. "For your review," he said.

One of the guards pulled back his spear, took the agreement, and then handed it to the king.

The king opened it, and we stood in silence while he read it. He took quite a long time, and I began to wonder if he couldn't read. Several moments later, he raised his head and looked at me. "You're naming yourself Empress?"

I smiled. "More like advising you of my title."

"You think you can rule over us?" he asked.

"I have no intention of disrupting your rule of Carnel or taking anything away from you," I said. "I'm simply advising you of my true title. I will be going to the other rulers of the other continent to obtain their alliance as well."

"What of your own fighting between the Seelie and Unseelie?" the queen asked.

"That has ended," I said and waved towards Myrin. "As you can see, one of my consorts is Unseelie."

"And they have united under you, the Empress of the Galaxy?" the king asked.

I smiled. "Yes."

"May I read the agreement?" the queen asked.

The king handed it to her, and we waited while she read it. She sighed and said, "There is nothing in here giving her any powers over us. It is just giving her a title. Let the Seelie Queen have her title and let us open up peaceful trade between our peoples. The plagues have been bad this summer, and I would rather our people be healed with their assistance than die by our hesitation."

I really liked this queen.

"You are a wise and beautiful queen," I said. "I am glad we are able to make this agreement."

"Do you have any healers with you?" the queen asked.

The king signed the agreement and then motioned at me to come forward to sign. I did and then stepped back.

"I do have a healer," I said. "Do you have many who are sick?"

"About a handful," she said.

I turned to Myrin. "Will that be too many for Durlan?"

He shook his head. "No, but even if it was, many of us can heal also."

"How many consorts do you have?" the king asked, an eyebrow arched.

"Seven," I said.

The queen's eyes widened.

"Where are your sick?" I asked. "I'll fetch my consort right away."

"I'll show you," she said and stood.

Two women with swords came around from behind the queen's chair. I hadn't seen them standing back there, and that impressed me more than I liked to admit.

"This way," she said and walked out of the room with her two female guards behind her.

"I like her," I whispered to Daniel.

Daniel smiled. "I thought you might."

"When we get back to Daniel's home, we are going to talk, Empress," Myrin whispered in my ear.

I chuckled and continued walking without responding.

The queen waited for us outside of the building, her guards eyeing Myrin with suspicion and, if I wasn't mistaken, lust.

The urge to snarl at them was almost uncontrollable.

"This way," the queen said.

I caught up to her and walked at her side, though several feet apart. "Your land is beautiful," I said. "Are there more than humans here?"

She smiled. "We have shifters, as I'm sure you're aware with Daniel at your side. We also have some humans with a bit of magic, but sadly none of their magic includes healing."

Humans with magic?

"What type of magic do these humans have?" I asked, my voice a little too high for my liking.

"They can conjure fire, move water, and other elemental things," Daniel said.

"Like a toddler fae?" Myrin asked.

Daniel nodded. "Yes, but they don't progress beyond that."

"Are there fae creatures here?" I asked the queen.

"I'm not sure what you consider fae creatures or just creatures," she said. She looked at Daniel. "Do you know?"

He nodded. "We have a few fae creatures, but none of the truly dangerous ones."

I exhaled. "Thank goodness." There were some seriously dangerous creatures that I couldn't imagine the humans being able to protect themselves from without magic.

The queen led us to a large building with a giant "T" on it. "What does the 'T' stand for?" I asked.

"That's a cross, a symbol of the god of healing," she said.

"God of healing? Who do you pray to?" I asked, trying to keep the disgust from my voice. They definitely weren't praying to me.

"The god of healing," the queen said with furrowed brows. "Surely you have heard of him."

"Perhaps if you told me his name?" I requested.

"Dakath," she said.

I stopped walking and stared up at the symbol. Dakath was the name Durlan had gone by in our last lifetime. They prayed to

Durlan. The one I was going to bring to them to heal their people.

"Breathe," Myrin whispered in my ear.

"If I could bring Dakath here, would that seal my claim as Empress?" I asked the queen.

She spun around, her eyes wide. "You could bring him here? You speak to the gods?"

"If I could, would that seal my claim with you? Would you agree to refer to me as Empress?" I asked again.

"Yes," she said, her voice breathy.

I turned to Myrin. "Bring me my consort."

Myrin bowed and ran off, his stride so long that it took him out of the town before the queen had time to gasp.

I closed my eyes and acted like I was praying or summoning Durlan. I let a bit of my magic out, to let my body glow as I felt them approaching.

Several humans nearby gasped.

"She's glowing," one human woman said, though I wasn't sure who she was.

I opened my eyes and said, "Dakath, God of Healing, please assist these humans in their time of need."

The queen looked at me with uncertainty, and then Durlan teleported to stand beside me. "My Empress," he said and then bowed to me. "I am at your service."

"He's...it's him," the queen gasped.

"He bowed to her. He called her Empress," one of the queen's guards said to the queen.

Durlan straightened and faced the queen. "Show me to your sick so I may heal them."

She bowed to him and then quickly pushed open the doors and waved him in.

I started to follow, but Durlan turned to me and said, "Stay here, Empress. I will cure the sick and return to you, but I do not want their sickness to touch or taint you."

I dipped my head. "Very well."

Durlan shut the door behind him and Myrin jogged back to me. "You remembered that was his name after she said it, didn't you?" he asked.

I nodded. "I don't remember your names, but after she said it, it came to me. I remember our lives, events that happened, but not your names for some reason."

Myrin smiled. "Names are changeable and unimportant. Only the soul is what truly matters."

Daniel nudged me and guided me across the street to sit on the porch of a building there. We sat, watching the building that housed their sick. I couldn't tell what happened inside the building, but didn't really care. Depending on how sick the people were and how many there were, we could be there awhile.

"Thirsty?" Daniel asked.

I nodded. "And hungry."

"I'll get us food," he said and walked off.

Myrin sat beside me. "You look better today than you have since I found you."

"Probably since I used my powers recently," I said. I leaned back on my hands and watched the humans going about their lives.

Would they learn to make weapons like Barry's people did? Or something worse?

"You're scowling," Myrin whispered.

"The humans we encountered had advanced weaponry," I whispered. "I'm wondering if these humans will develop the same in their future."

"Humans are intelligent and inquisitive creatures by nature. They're also easily scared, and I don't doubt they'll come up with some type of creation to help protect themselves. Especially, since they'll be in contact with our kind more. We're terrifying to them," Myrin said.

"Is it our pointy teeth and ears?" I asked and bared my teeth at him.

He bared his teeth back at me.

Both of us laughed, and I leaned my shoulder against his. I didn't have favorites amongst my guys, but my connection with Myrin was definitely the strongest. He was my first consort however many thousands of years ago we'd met, so I supposed it made sense.

A few female humans slowed as they passed us, their eyes firmly locked on Myrin. Their cheeks heated, and they hurried by.

I looked over at him and saw the smile he'd given them. "You're going to make the men jealous if you flirt with the humans like that."

"Not you?" he asked.

I rolled my eyes. "You're not going to leave me. Not after this long."

He leaned over and kissed my cheek. "Never," he whispered in my ear.

Daniel returned with a basket of food and three mugs of water held in one of his hands.

Myrin took the mugs from him and handed me one.

I guzzled from it, not realizing how thirsty I actually was.

Daniel sat on the porch beside me and removed the cloth that had been covering the food.

"What is this stuff?" I asked. "It smells good, but I've never seen many of these things."

"Just eat," he said and chuckled. "I promise it's all safe."

I picked up one of the purplish round items. It was soft like a fruit. I sniffed it. It smelled sweet, too. I took a bite and my eyes widened. The inside was very sweet, but the skin was a little bitter, which combined made it delicious.

I grabbed another item and tried it. It was yellow and inside and outside was bitter.

Daniel laughed at me. "Your face."

"You put that in there on purpose, didn't you?" I asked, putting the yellow thing back in the basket.

He shrugged while smirking.

We ate in silence, the humans giving us a wide berth, and waited for Durlan.

Something dark moved at the edge of my mind. I jerked my head in the direction, the woods beyond the town, and squinted my eyes.

"Something's out there," I said and stood, brushing my hands off.

Myrin and Daniel stood with me, their eyes focused in the same direction.

"That's a fae creature," Myrin whispered. "I can't tell what type, but that dark aura is unmistakable."

"We don't usually have something that evil here," Daniel whispered. "Did you bring it over on the ship on accident?"

I looked up at Myrin who shook his head. "We searched the ship well before leaving the port to make sure no Unseelie tried to stow away."

Birds flew up into the sky and away from the front middle of the forest where I sensed the creature. Then, the trees fell to the side as it shoved them aside to step out.

Ten feet tall, mud covered skin, and a red cap upon its head, the creature chittered loudly, a sound that made my skin crawl.

"A redcap," I gasped. It had been over a hundred years since a redcap had been seen in Minloa. How had one made it here?

"Get the others," Daniel yelled to Myrin as he shifted into his bear form and charged the redcap.

The humans near us screamed and scrambled to seek shelter in one of the buildings.

"Don't fight it," Myrin ordered me. "Get the weak humans to shelter and stand guard, but do not go out there and fight it."

I glared at him, but nodded.

He gave me a final, hard look, and then ran in the opposite direction to go get the others.

A pregnant mother with two toddlers hobbled towards a building, but she moved slowly. I gathered up her toddlers and urged her on faster. "Stay inside," I ordered them.

She nodded and the trio huddled together inside the building with several other humans.

Durlan stepped out of the building. "What's going on?"

"Redcap," I said. "Finish healing the humans. The others are coming to help."

His eyes widened. "A redcap? They have redcaps here?"

I shrugged. "Apparently."

Daniel made it to the redcap, and I froze as I watched the redcap swing his giant club at him. The bear dodged the club and bit the redcap's leg, tearing into the muscle and causing blood to spray before he leapt away, back towards the forest.

He was trying to lead the redcap back into the forest and away from the humans.

Some human men had come out with swords and spears, including some of the king's guards.

"Go back inside," I ordered them. "We'll handle this."

"What is that thing?" one of the guards asked.

"A redcap. It thrives on murdering things," I said. "Stay with your women and children. If we fail, you're their last line of defense."

"Will you fail?" a wiry man with wide eyes asked.

I smiled and turned to watch as the rest of my consorts ran into town. "No, they will not fail."

Venali's magenta eyes were focused on the redcap, the smile on his face evidence of his excitement for a fight.

Ryul stopped by me. "I'll stay with you, my queen."

I nodded. "Okay."

Venali stopped a dozen or so feet away from the redcap and roared. The sound was unmistakably a challenge.

The redcap turned, ignoring Daniel, and roared back.

Venali laughed and ran forward.

"Why isn't his sword drawn?" a human asked beside me.

"Because he doesn't want the battle to end too quickly," Ryul said. "He loves fighting."

"You're insane," the wiry man said.

I chuckled. "They are a bit unhinged."

Venali leapt up and punched the redcap in the jaw, the sound as loud as a thunderclap, and the redcap dropped to one knee.

"Get inside," Ryul ordered the humans.

"Check on Durlan," I said to Ryul. "Make sure he's not using too much magic."

He looked at me.

"I'm staying right here. Promise," I said.

He scowled, but jogged into the building where Durlan was.

Kydrus and Myrin stood off to the side, arms folded, and watched Venali and Daniel fighting the redcap.

Obviously, they didn't think their brothers needed help.

That quickly changed when five more redcaps ran out of the forest and roared their challenge.

CHAPTER 33
ELARA

My legs tensed, ready to help, but Ryul ran out of the building and pointed at me. "Stay."

I folded my arms across my chest and held my spot. "Fine."

He nodded and ran to help the others, his sword drawn.

Venali dodged one of the redcap's wild club swings, ran up the arm holding the club, and embedded a dagger into the redcap's eye.

The redcap bellowed and roared back, slapping at his face to try to hit Venali.

Venali bellowed with laughter and leapt off the redcap, landing lightly on his feet.

I wanted to tell at him to stop showing off, but he deserved to have some fun after the past few months I'd put him through. Plus, this was probably the first battle he had been in for over a hundred years at least.

One of the queen's guards poked her head out. "Is it safe for us to take the queen to her castle?"

"Ask Dakath to teleport you," I said.

Her eyes widened. "We could never ask a god—"

"Tell him it was my request," I said.

Durlan stepped out, the guard pointed at the castle, and he teleported them to it.

I sat on the porch and resumed eating my food while the guys fought with the redcaps.

While I'd been distracted, two of the redcaps had been killed, leaving four left for the guys to defeat.

The same feeling prickled along my neck, this time from the other side of the town.

A woman screamed in that direction.

I took off at a full sprint, my arms pumping as I raced to save the human.

I skidded around a building, bumped my shoulder into the building across from it, and slid around the other side.

Three recaps surrounded a woman and her daughter, both cowering on the ground and crying.

"Hey," I yelled at the redcaps.

They turned and snarled at me.

I reached for my sword, but hadn't brought it with me for the meeting. I sighed. "Hey, why don't you pick on someone a bit tastier," I said and strutted towards them like their evil aura didn't make my stomach turn.

The redcaps chortled.

"Your magic will be tastier than this human," the largest of the trio said.

I stopped, spread my arms to my sides, and said, "Come get some."

They roared and charged at me, clubs raised over their heads.

I drew on the sun's power and blasted the largest redcap through the middle of his chest with sun fire.

He fell to the ground, the hole sizzling and oozing.

His friends stopped, looking at their fallen comrade with wide eyes.

I examined my fingernails. "What's wrong? You boys scared of one little fae woman?"

They roared louder than before and descended upon me with clubs and claws swinging.

I leapt, dodged, ducked, and slid out of the way of their swings.

"I'm going to gnaw on your bones," one of the redcaps snarled.

Durlan teleported between the redcaps and me, his lips pulled back in a snarl, and said, "I don't think so." He punched the redcap who had threatened me in the jaw so hard that it came unhinged and dangled crookedly.

I opened my mouth to tell him I had everything under control, but watching my normally calm and logical mate beat the snot out of the redcaps was a huge turn on.

Plus, he looked like he needed to vent some rage.

He pummeled the two redcaps with his bare hands, broke their arms and legs, and then cracked their skulls open.

When the redcaps lay still, Durlan turned to me, eyes glowing and fangs bared, and said, "You are in so much trouble when we get home."

I smiled and asked, "Promise?"

His lips lowered, his rage receded, and he laughed while shaking his head. "Incorrigible."

I skipped over to him, stepping on top of the dead redcap on his left to get up to his height and kissed his lips. "A lovable, incorrigible, handful that you couldn't live without."

He wrapped me up in his arms and kissed me back. "Yes."

"He killed them with his bare hands," the little girl yelled.

We both turned and I smiled. "Did you expect less from the god, Dakath?"

The mother and girl's eyes widened and before they could say anything, I took Durlan and led him back towards the other fight.

My other mates turned from where they stood over the bodies of the redcaps, their scowls almost identical.

"I'm alive," I called out and waved.

Only Daniel, still in bear form, and Ryul continued scowling while the others smiled.

I released Durlan's hand and skipped over to Venali, throwing my arms around his neck. "Did you have fun? You looked like you were having fun."

He swooped me up into his arms and kissed me deeply. "Lots of fun," he said when he pulled back.

"Where did they come from?" Ryul asked. He walked into the trees in the direction the first group had come from.

I hopped out of Venali's arms, hopped onto Daniel's furry bear back, and said, "Follow the broody one."

Daniel shook beneath me in what I assumed was a laugh as he loped after Ryul. The others followed.

I dug my hand into his fur and held on with my legs, like he was a horse.

"The humans are staring at us like we are insane," Amrynn whispered as he ran beside me and Daniel.

I shrugged. "We are to them." I looked around and realized Durlan wasn't with us.

"He went to finish healing," Myrin said.

I nodded and then gasped as we ran into a patch of forest that was black and looked burned.

Ryul grabbed Daniel and me, jerking us back out of the black area.

I clawed at my throat, the darkness blocking my airway.

"Shit," Kydrus hissed and dropped to his knees beside me, panting.

Ryul wrapped his hand around my throat, using his power to heal me.

Black tendrils of smoke floated from my mouth and dissipated in the air a moment later.

I fell into Ryul and gasped in air.

No. No. Not yet. He couldn't be here yet.

Myrin put his hands on either side of my face and forced me to meet his eyes. "He isn't here."

"It was a warning," I whispered hoarsely.

He nodded. "Yes."

Tears leaked down my face. "He's going to kill you again."

Myrin pulled me into his arms, and I sobbed against his shoulder.

I wanted to protect them. To keep my mates safe.

I wasn't strong enough yet. I needed to get stronger.

"Cleanse this area," Myrin snapped.

"Where are you going?" Ryul asked.

Myrin stood with me in his arms and walked towards the sound of roaring water. "To cleanse her. Daniel and Kydrus, come with us so you can be cleansed, too."

I let one hand drop and brushed my fingers through Daniel's fur. He licked my hand.

This had been a test. There was no doubt there would be more.

But why?

Why not just attack us now, when I was weak? What was he waiting for?

"We're all alive," Myrin whispered in my ear. "All of your consorts are alive. We need to be cleansed, but that won't take long. We are alive, Elara."

Yes, but for how long?

CHAPTER 34
DURLAN

"She was fighting three redcaps by herself," I said to Kydrus. "She wasn't even in her goddess form."

Kydrus sighed and pinched the bridge of his nose. "I'd say I'm surprised, but I'm not."

I bent over the human before me and resumed healing him. All of these humans had a strange disease that, left untreated, would kill them. "I almost lost it, Kydrus. I haven't been so furious in a century. The one said he was going to suck on her bones and my vision tinted red. I can't remember the last time that's happened."

He patted my shoulder. "It happens to us all. Especially, when our lovely little goddess is involved."

"You know what her reaction was?" I asked, growling.

"What?" Kydrus asked, leaning his shoulder against the wall. He could have helped me heal these people, but they thought I was a god, so we were keeping up the ruse for now. Plus, I had plenty of power to heal them.

"She got turned on," I said and sighed.

He threw his head back and laughed.

"The woman will be the death of me," I grumbled.

"Can you blame her?" Venali asked as he stepped into the room.

I had no idea how long he'd been standing just outside, but long enough to hear my previous statement.

"What is that supposed to mean?" I asked.

"You're usually so reserved and logical. This was most likely the first time she's seen you go all protective mate mode," Venali said. He leaned against the wall beside Kydrus, giving him a pat on the shoulder.

"He's right," Kydrus said. "The only thing she's seen from you is calm and collected Durlan."

"I'm not always logical," I mumbled.

"More than most of us," Venali said.

"Says the man who laughed as a redcap tried to crush him," I said and shook my head.

"She really faced off against three redcaps by herself?" Venali asked.

I nodded. "There was a human woman and her child in danger. You know she can't ever leave the innocent in danger."

"You should have called me over," Venali said.

I grumbled, but made no coherent words.

"What he meant to say is that he let his anger get the better of him, so he didn't want to share his kills," Kydrus said, smirking smugly.

I flipped him off, finished healing the human, and stood.

The human sat up and asked, "Am I really healed?"

I nodded. "You should rest another hour or so and then you'll be fine."

"I won't die?" he asked.

I shook my head. "Not from this disease."

He got to his knees and bowed. "Thank you, Dakath. Thank you."

Dakath. It had been so long since I'd heard that name. I preferred Durlan now, but hearing it had brought back memories I had long forgotten and hadn't come back when the other memories did.

Most notably, the night before we'd died. That night, I'd been with Amara, trying to persuade her to go into hiding. She wouldn't have it. She'd wanted to fight alongside us and nothing I said would sway her.

"The past is in the past," Kydrus whispered. "Leave it there."

I stood and wiped my hands on my pants. "Let's go find Elara. I don't like leaving her with less than four of us at any given moment."

"Especially, since he made his first move," Venali said and snarled.

Yes. He was already moving against her, which made me uneasy. Everything about this attack made me uneasy.

It had been too simple.

There had been too few enemies.

It had obviously been a test, but a test of what?

I hated the unknown. I hated things that had no obvious reasoning, even flawed reasoning was better than none.

What would he do next? And how could I protect Elara from it?

CHAPTER 35
RYUL

CLEANSING the infected forest had been easy enough, but the lingering fear it left in me was the hardest to deal with.

Why set this up? Why teleport those redcaps to us?

Had he wanted to test Elara? To see if she would turn into Amara?

Or, was he trying to sully her before the humans? Had he hoped the humans would have been killed first and then she would have been blamed?

Amrynn walked at my side, silent and brooding like me.

"Do the humans make you uncomfortable?" I asked him.

He sighed. "Sadly, yes. I know they aren't the same ones. I know they don't have the same technology, but I still can't help feeling on edge around them."

"She feels the same," I said. "Myrin said he could sense her unease when we went before their monarchs."

He nodded. "Daniel said he could as well."

"What do you think about this trap?" I asked softly.

I wasn't certain where Elara was and I didn't want to discuss this with her nearby.

He looked up at the sky and exhaled audibly. "I'm afraid to voice my concerns. I hope, pray, that I'm wrong."

"Who do you pray to?" I asked with a chuckle. "We're the gods of this world."

He chuckled as well. "To whoever else might be out there. Someone who might listen and help us."

I scowled. "Do you think there are others?"

He shook his head. "There is only *him* and her. We're unique in that we were ascended because of her."

"Do you think he could have similar companions?" I asked.

Amrynn laughed. "I doubt it, but who am I to say? I would have sworn on everything in the universe that no human could have ever taken me captive and yet that is exactly what happened."

I felt for him, it was an awful feeling to be defenseless, helpless, or useless. Especially, when you had been undefeated for a millennium.

"It would have happened to any of us," I assured him and truly believed that.

"History is doomed to repeat itself, and I'm terrified of what that means for her," he said.

He wasn't terrified of what would happen to us, though. No, we were all willing to die again. So long as she lived.

"Things will be different this time," Amrynn said, his shoulders drawing back and determination setting his jaw.

I nodded. This time, I would not let my inexperience cause our downfall. I would bite my damn tongue and listen to Myrin.

He might be Unseelie, but he loved Elara and Amara. I could see it every time he was near her or when he talked about her.

"Do you think the Seelie will accept the Unseelie?" I asked.

Amrynn smiled. "I don't think Elara will give them a choice."

"I thought Anderelle was bigger, but she's said there are only three continents. Is that right?" I asked.

Amrynn nodded. "She showed me a map of the planet before.

Anderelle only has three continents, but several islands interspersed around those continents. The continents are large and take up a lot of the planet's space, but there is also a lot of ocean. I'd say the ocean makes up two thirds of the planet."

"Andrelle really has that much ocean?" I asked, eyes wide.

He wrapped an arm around my shoulders and squeezed. "Don't worry, I'll give you swimming lessons soon, so you won't have to fear the water anymore."

Had it been anyone else, I would have thought they were teasing me, but not Amrynn. He meant it.

"Thanks," I said softly.

"I've got your back, brother. Don't you worry your pretty head about it."

I scoffed. "You're the pretty one."

He laughed and drew away. "I am rather pretty, aren't I?"

"The prettiest there ever was," Elara said as she, Myrin, and Daniel walked out to the edge of the town where we were.

"I thought you were the prettiest there ever was?" I asked with a teasing smirk.

She blushed and my cock twitched in my pants. The fact that I could still make her blush turned me on and made me want to do very naughty things with her.

"Flatterer," she whispered.

"We should check on Durlan," I said.

She smiled. "You mean Dakath."

Amrynn smiled. "Yes, Dakath. It's been so long since I've heard that name."

She nodded. "Yes, but it helped. Now, I'm officially Empress."

"Empress of the Galaxy," I said.

Her eyes widened, and she hopped up to kiss my cheek. "Yes," she shouted. "Empress of the Galaxy. It's perfect."

Perfect was right in front of me.

I grabbed her, spun her around, and kissed her deeply. "You're perfect."

Her breath caught, and she clutched my arms. "If we weren't in public, I'd ask you to show me how perfect you think I am."

If I hadn't already had a hard on, I would now.

"Tease," I said with a smile.

She laughed, kissed my cheek, and extricated herself from my hold. "Sorry."

Oh, I didn't mind. She could tease me all she wanted. Every day for the rest of my life. As long as I could touch her, kiss her, and look at her like this, I was perfectly fine.

CHAPTER 36
ELARA

THE GUYS WERE in good spirits the next day, which I contributed not only to the fight, but also our marathon group session the previous night.

I lay in Amrynn's arms, naked, and content.

"Aren't you hungry yet?" he asked and kissed my temple.

"A little," I admitted. "But I'm so comfortable."

"You're meeting with the shapeshifters today, right?" Amrynn asked.

I rolled over and lay my head on his bare chest. "Yes."

"Then, you need to get up and eat. Daniel can't teleport, since he isn't fae, which means we have to walk there. He said it will take about half a day."

"Amrynn, stop being logical and just cuddle with me," I muttered.

He chuckled softly and pulled me as close as I could get. "Five more minutes."

I placed a kiss on his chest and smiled. It was moments like these that made all of the other bull crap worth it. To be able to lay in my mate's arms and just be together.

Our five minutes came and went, and with it another five minutes.

Then, Durlan peeked his head in and ordered us to get up for breakfast.

Reluctantly, I got dressed and went to the living room where the others already sat. Daniel didn't have a dining room, so we sat on the floor in the living room instead.

Myrin kissed my cheek and handed me a plate of food. "Sleep well?"

I nodded. "You?"

He smiled. "Yes."

Daniel patted the floor beside him, and I accepted the spot. As I sat, I leaned my shoulder against his. He was so much warmer than the rest of my mates.

"Anything we should know before meeting the shapeshifters?" I asked.

"They like fighting and are probably going to challenge at least one of them to a hand to hand fight," Daniel said. He looked around at the guys. "Probably Ryul."

"Why me?" Ryul asked.

Daniel smirked. "Because it is obvious that you're the youngest. And, you give off a vibe that just begs someone to punch you."

I choked on my food, and Myrin patted my back.

"Just be prepared for anything and don't kill anyone," Daniel said. "I'll do most of the talking, but they're going to want to ask you questions. Shapeshifters are inquisitive by nature."

"I want to speak to your historians, if there are such a thing," I said.

Daniel nodded. "The elders are the oldest and wisest of us and know all about our history. I'm sure there are some books, too."

"Uh oh, don't tell her about the books. We'll never convince her to leave if she finds books," Venali said.

I stuck my tongue out at him.

"Let's pack some food for the trip and be on our way," Daniel said and stood.

I put on boots and lay on the couch as I waited.

How had my life gone from slave to goddess? It felt like an eternity ago that I was learning about being a princess and here I was trying to figure out how to unite the continents as their empress. Life was incredibly strange and unpredictable.

"You seem deep in thought," Durlan said. "What are you thinking about, beautiful?"

"How drastically my life changed," I said. "It's still unbelievable and yet...here I am."

"You've come a long way," Durlan said with a nod.

"Things are going to change even more in the next month," I whispered.

He set his hand on top of mine. "And we will be here, at your side, every step of the way."

I smiled and stood. "I love you."

He kissed my brow. "And I you."

"Ready?" Daniel asked.

I nodded. "Yep."

From the maps and research I had done, the continent was broken up into three sections, but ruled by two monarchies. The first section was where humans and shapeshifters coexisted together, ruled by the monarchs I'd met with the previous day. The second was the human only section, which those monarchs also ruled. Then, the shapeshifter section, which was ruled by a different monarch.

"How come you weren't monarch of the shapeshifters?" I asked Daniel as we walked out of his house.

"No matter how hard I tried, the majority of them wouldn't give up on their desire to live separate from the humans. They view the humans as beneath them, since they're weaker. I didn't want to rule people like that," Daniel said.

I tilted my head back to look up at him. "That's pretty moral of you."

He laughed. "Also, they have laws that the ruler must be mated. Since I wasn't going to mate with someone who wasn't you, that limited my chances of ruling."

I dropped my head and looked at the forest before us. If he hadn't had his memory, like the warlords, I could have come to find him mated to another. That thought hurt and infuriated me at the same time.

It also raised the question of why he and Myrin had their memories the entire time. They were the only non-Seelie members of my consorts. Did that have something to do with it?

Daniel draped an arm around my shoulders and tucked me against him as we walked. I rested my head against his side and drew in his scent. It was so much muskier than the others.

"What's your plan?" Durlan asked me.

"Talk to the shapeshifters," I said.

He sighed loudly.

"You should know by now that she prefers to figure things out as she goes," Venali said. "She'll get there and what needs to be done will just come to her. She doesn't work well with solid plans."

I turned and smiled at Venali over my shoulder. "Exactly."

Venali winked at me.

"Couldn't you form at least a broad plan?" Durlan asked.

"Talk to the shapeshifters. Convince them to name me Empress. Don't kill anyone," I said.

"Well, that is as broad as you could get, but definitely lays out your plan," Durlan said.

"Beautiful? When are you going to use your powers again? You need to practice," Kydrus said.

I tensed and pulled away from Daniel. I hadn't admitted it to any of the guys, but I was scared to use my powers again. *He* would sense me and likely set a trap or test for us again. I didn't want to use them unless necessary to limit our exposure to him.

"I'll practice more later," I said and picked up my speed.

Kydrus kept pace with me, his long legs easily matching my shorter ones. "We're going to be here to protect you, Elara. And, it might be good to have Amara speak to him."

"What?" Ryul, Myrin, and Daniel asked at the same time.

"If we could figure out a weakness that could help us defeat him, it might mean the difference between winning and losing," Kydrus said.

"He has a point," Durlan said. "Not that I want *him* to be anywhere near Amara or Elara, but if we could find a weakness it would help ensure our victory."

"Or, he could kill her before she's ready to face him," Ryul said.

"You're always so negative," Kydrus said to Ryul.

"No, I'm just practical. She isn't ready to face him," Ryul snapped.

"We have no idea how he will react to her. Plus, she can't hold her form for long. He might find her current state of existence upsetting and attack," Myrin said.

"Or, he might try to steal her," Venali said.

"Or, kill us," Daniel said.

They exploded into a yelling match and started getting into each other's faces.

"That's enough," I said.

No one listened.

I snapped my fingers and all of them froze. Eyes wide, I looked at my fingers and then at the guys.

Holy stars! I hadn't known I could do that.

Raising my head, I looked at them. "We will not discuss this anymore today. Do you understand? We have a lot of decisions to make and not very much time to make them. I don't want us fighting over something we have no clear answer for. No more fighting. Okay?"

They couldn't move, so I didn't wait for their responses.

I spun on my heel, marched away a dozen or so feet, and then snapped my fingers.

There were several groans, which told me they were moving again.

I smiled and swung my arms as I walked. I could freeze my consorts. That was so convenient. I could use this for so many things and in so many circumstances.

"Sorry," Kydrus said.

The others chorused his apology.

"You are forgiven," I said, trying to hide how chipper I felt.

"You're so proud of yourself for using that power," Myrin said with a chuckle. "I bet you didn't know you could do that."

"Nope, but I know how to now," I said in a sing-song voice.

"We're in so much trouble," Venali whispered.

I hummed a happy tune as I skipped through the forest, the guys chuckling behind me, and our argument, thankfully over. I had no doubt it was not forgotten, but hopefully it would not be brought up anytime soon.

CHAPTER 37
AMRYNN

ELARA WAS scared and that worried me.

She wasn't as fearless as Amara had been, which was a good thing, considering she didn't have all of her powers. Yet, she still found ways to drive us crazy by acting careless.

I wasn't sure how to react when Durlan told us about finding her fighting the redcaps. It was fitting to her character, but we were nearby and all she had to do was call. I would have teleported to her and protected her and the humans she wanted to help.

Watching her skip through the forest with a smug smile on her face helped lessen my worry. I loved seeing her smile.

Kydrus glanced at me, and we shared a grin. The frightened girl we had met was gone, transformed into a queen. I couldn't wait to see her change in the next few months, too.

"What's it feel like to shift?" Elara asked.

We all looked at Daniel, our curiosity probably as bad as Elara's.

Daniel hummed a moment before answering. "It's like a good stretch. One second I'm this size and then I'm in my bear form."

"So, it doesn't hurt?" she asked.

Daniel shook his head.

"Do you feel stronger in bear form?" she asked.

"In a sense. As a bear, if I hug you, I can crush your body. Or, I could bite you with my much stronger teeth as a bear. In this form I don't have the thick canines that my bear form does."

I smiled at him, showing him my pointed teeth.

"Your teeth are weak," Daniel teased. "I could probably snap off that little fang with my human hand."

"You could try," I said, smiling broader.

Elara rolled her eyes.

Daniel laughed.

"Did you not know there were humans on this planet before you came to my town?" Daniel asked.

Elara's face closed down. "I did not. I can sense sentient beings and animals, but not what race. I assumed everyone on the planet was fey and thought humans were only in the solar system that I took."

"Took?" Daniel asked, his face screwing up. "What do you mean took?"

Had we forgotten to tell him about that part? We must have.

"Durlan?" Elara asked.

Durlan pulled his bag off, rummaged around in it, and then pulled out her crown.

All of our eyes were drawn to the sun and planets swirling within the crystals on her crown.

Fury filled me as I thought back to the humans of that system and the way they had treated us. To Elara having her blood stolen while they kept her sedated.

"Amrynn?" Daniel whispered.

I looked away from the crown and realized everyone was staring at me.

Then, I realized that my lip was pulled up in a snarl. I lowered my lip and turned away.

Kydrus came to my side, a silent offer of support.

"So, these are their planets and their sun?" Daniel asked as he held the crown.

I kept my eyes away from it.

Had it been up to me, Elara would have crushed their planets in her fist and we would have been done with them forever.

Using them as an energy source was cosmic justice, but I wanted them dead. Especially, Barry.

Maybe I could convince her to pull Barry out and I could beat him to a bloody pulp.

Kydrus set his hand on my shoulder. "Breathe, Amrynn."

I exhaled.

"Will you have an issue working with the humans and shapeshifters, who are basically human?" Daniel asked.

I wasn't sure if he was asking me or Elara, so I didn't answer.

"There won't be a problem. I know these aren't the same humans. The humans who hurt me are trapped on the planets in the crown that you're holding," Elara said.

"Amrynn?" Daniel asked.

"Same," I said.

CHAPTER 38
ELARA

SEEING Amrynn react so strongly to the crown shocked me. I knew he still hated the humans of that world for what they had done to us, but I hadn't expected him to snarl at the crown.

He had seemed indifferent to the humans here, but I would have to keep an eye on him. And, I would need to talk to him.

"Can a human be turned into a shapeshifter?" I asked Daniel.

He shook his head. "No, you can only be born a shapeshifter if one of your parents is either a shapeshifter or a carrier of the gene."

"Carrier?" I asked.

He nodded. "Sometimes, the shapeshifting gene skips a generation."

Interesting.

"Are there any shapeshifters who have wings?" I asked. I would love to have a pair of wings.

Daniel chuckled. "No. There are only predatory mammal shapeshifters. Well, at least that we know of. I suppose there could be others on a different continent that I've not seen. Here, though, there are no shapeshifters with wings."

Pity.

"If someone hurts you..." I began, but stopped.

He pulled me against his side and kissed the top of my head. "I can handle any of the shapeshifters we're going to see. I've fought most of them already. If I do get in a fight, you must not intervene. Do you understand? They aren't allowed to kill me, and couldn't, so even if you're worried you must not intervene."

"I don't like this. If I'm challenged, though, you must abide by the same rule," I whispered. I feared the only way I would get them to join me was to defeat them.

"We'll keep her back," Venali said.

If someone tried to kill any of my mates, it would take every living being on this planet to keep me from protecting them.

"She's got that look on her face that means trouble," Kydrus said.

"Isn't that just her face?" Myrin asked.

I turned to give a snappy retort but found him smirking. He was teasing me.

"Yes, I am always causing trouble," I said. "It keeps you guys on your toes."

"That's definitely true," Ryul mumbled.

I stuck my tongue out at him, and he dashed forward, trying to catch my tongue with his fingers, but I sucked it back into my mouth before he could.

"Too slow," I said in a teasing tone.

He smiled.

I stepped away from Daniel and Ryul took my hand, linking our fingers together.

All of this traveling and strategizing made for little alone time with each of them. It was something I needed to fix. None of them had complained, but I knew they wanted to spend some time alone with me. I wanted some time alone with each of them as well.

Sadly, it wasn't in the cards just yet.

We only stopped to relieve ourselves. Food was eaten as we walked, even.

We entered incredibly dense woods and the hair on the nape of my neck stood up.

We were being watched.

Daniel's shoulders tensed. "You don't want to mess with my companions," he said, though he didn't turn to look at whoever it was he spoke to. He continued walking, so we followed him.

I smelled smoke, but kept the observation to myself.

Several minutes later, we entered a clearing with several log cabins. We were definitely in Plunce now. There were hundreds of people walking around in various states of dress, or undress as the case may be. The variety of people genuinely surprised me, but if they were all shapeshifters, then their ease at being together made sense. Like was drawn to like, and though they differed in other ways, the thing that tied them together was strong enough to overlook the rest. Or, so it seemed.

I saw a few children, but it was mostly adults.

All eyes turned to watch our party as we headed towards the largest cabin, where the smoke I had smelled was coming from.

Daniel opened the door to the cabin and bowed his head to me as I entered.

Inside, the cabin was unfurnished. Only chandeliers and wall sconces were present, both furnished with candles. There were six people, two women and four men, standing together at the other end of the cabin, talking quietly to each other.

"Alpha and council members," Daniel said. "I bring to you today the Queen of the Seelie."

All six turned to face us, and I could instantly feel their hostility.

"You've changed, Daniel," one of the men said. I'd forgotten that once our mate bond was solidified, he had started looking like the others, whose power never seemed to disappear, whereas mine had to be used sparingly.

"Seelie Queen?" one of the women asked.

I smiled. "Yes. I am Elara. It's nice to meet you."

"She doesn't look strong," the other woman said.

I smirked. "Neither do you, but I'm sure we both know that looks can be deceiving."

She returned my smirk with one of her own and then smiled broadly. "I like her."

Relief surged through me, but it was short lived.

"Who are all these men?" one of the men asked. He had a scar across his left eye, eerily similar to Venali's.

"Her warlords," Durlan said and stepped forward. "We are her advisors and—"

"Lovers," the second woman said, though there was no judgment or malice in the statement.

I tilted my head to the side. "How did you know?"

"You're covered in their scents. More so than just from being around them," she said. "And, your scent is on each of them." She turned her head and looked at Daniel. "Even you."

Daniel smiled. "Yes, she is my mate."

The woman who liked me gaped at him. "Mate? You took a mate? And a non-shapeshifter at that?"

Daniel looked at me, and I could see the love in his eyes as clear as the moon on a cloudless night. "Yes."

"Why are you here?" one of the men asked. He had a scowl that seemed never to waver. At least, it hadn't since we'd walked in. He looked older than the others, and the air of aggression surrounding him made me worry he would choose anything he could as an excuse to fight us.

"I am unifying our world," I said and took a step forward. "I ask for you to join us, to accept your place as equals amongst us."

They all laughed.

"Equals? You think you're equal to us?" the old man asked as he laughed.

Well, he wasn't scowling anymore.

"Let's take this meeting outside," I said and spun on my heel.

I sensed the old man move, gave my men a glare to hold, and as he came up to me, wrapped my hand around his throat and stared straight into his eyes, which were glowing amber.

"If you wish to test me, council member, outside is preferred so that I can trounce you in front of all of your people," I said sweetly.

I released him, and he snarled.

"You did not protect your mate," the first woman said to Daniel.

Daniel was snarling as he stared at the old man. "She ordered me to stay back. Trust me, if he tries to attack her from behind again, like a fucking coward, I will tear his head off before he touches a strand of her glorious hair."

The old man paled a bit.

Interesting. He was scared of Daniel.

"Daniel," I said softly. "I will accept their challenges in public. You will only be allowed to participate if I agree. Do you understand?"

"Yes, Elara," he said.

I turned back around and walked out of the building.

While we had been inside, most of the people had gathered before the building. Had they been expecting us to come out to fight?

Most likely from what Daniel had said.

"Shapeshifters," I called loudly. "My name is Elara. I am Queen of the Seelie of Minloa. I come to you today to ask you to join us as equals. To unify all of our continents in forming an open means of trade and communication. Together, we can accomplish much. Apart, we only suffer. Your council member has challenged me. I will accept his challenge. When I win, should another wish to challenge me, they may. You may also challenge any of my mates. However, these challenges will be to submission. If any tries to kill me or my mates, you will be obliterated without mercy. Understood?"

Everyone's eyes widened, including my consorts. Oh, right. I probably should have warned them I was going to do this.

I turned and faced the old council member. "Well, while I have all the time in the world, I know your kind don't live for very long. So, we should get this fight over with."

He snarled, stalked to stand in front of me, and then he exploded into a large grey wolf.

He was so beautiful, I almost reached out to stroke his fur.

"You are beautiful," I whispered, letting my awe show.

His wolf eyes widened, and then he snarled, remembering why he was here.

I took a fighting stance, smiled, and said, "Begin."

He launched himself at me, trying to tackle me to the ground.

I spun around him and punched him in the side just below the ribs.

He flew to the side, landing against the other council members.

Whoops. I hadn't meant to hit him so hard.

He hopped up and began circling me while snarling.

I watched him with a loose stance, yawned, and asked, "Are you going to attack today? Or are you only good at attacking unsuspecting victims from behind?"

Several people snickered at my insult.

The old wolf barked loudly and lunged, his mouth wide and claws extended.

He moved so slowly. Daniel was much faster than him. Was it because of his connection to me?

It seemed I really had been worried for no reason about him fighting any battles.

I smacked the wolf on the back of his head, being sure to rein in my strength, and he immediately fell to the ground, unconscious.

I turned. "Who's next?"

The female who had spoken second stepped forward. "I am alpha of this pack. I will accept your challenge."

I bowed. "I am honored."

She smiled and turned to Daniel. "You want to take her place?"

Daniel smiled at me. "Elara, now would be a good time to show them who you really are."

"You don't think I can defeat her as I am?" I asked.

"I have zero doubt you could, but I think it will make our day go much faster," he said.

"But I'm having fun," I complained and stuck my lip out in a pout.

"I'll make you a deal," the alpha said. "If you show me who you truly are, and can defeat me in under a minute, we will join you without question. If I defeat you, or you take longer than a minute, you accept your defeat and leave us to be as we are, separate from the rest of the races."

"That's not much of a challenge," I mumbled.

Her eyes narrowed. "You underestimate me."

I shook my head. "No, you just have no clue who I am."

"Fine, I'll up the ante. If you defeat the entire council in a four on one battle, then we will join you. Five minutes will be your time limit," she said.

I smiled and turned to her people. "Will you abide by her decision?"

"We obey the alpha," they all said in unison, which was *super* creepy.

I faced her. "I agree to your terms."

Durlan held out my crown and I set it on my head.

"You may not want to wear that," the other male council

member said. "It would be a pity if something so pretty was destroyed."

"Oh, it'll be fine," I said.

One of the other shapeshifters had dragged the old man off to the side, giving me plenty of room to move. Not that I needed it. For the trick up my sleeve, I only needed a moment and the shapeshifters would be bowing to me.

"Elara," Daniel called.

I turned to face him.

"Do not go easy on them. Full force without killing. Do you understand? You must make them understand how powerful you are," he said.

I blew him a kiss. "Yes, dear."

The remaining council members shifted, but instead of animal forms, they shifted into half-man and half-animal forms. It was a beautiful and terrifying meld at the same time.

There were two wolves and two leopards between them.

"So beautiful," I whispered in admiration.

"Show us and try your hardest to defeat us," the alpha said. "We will not hold back."

I raised my arms above my head, drew on the power of my sun as well as the one in my crown and released my hold.

My body glowed, I rose up until my toes floated above the ground, and I heard several shocked gasps behind me.

The council members' eyes widened.

"Who are you?" the alpha asked.

"I am Amara, Goddess of this Universe, but for now you may refer to my proxy as Empress of the Galaxy. Let me end this, my precious children, so that you may become united, as you should have been this entire time," I said.

They charged forward, claws poised to attack.

I had to give them credit, they were still attacking despite being faced with a goddess and that took some guts.

"Kneel," I ordered them, pulling on all of the power I had at my disposal as I hit them with my command.

They struggled a moment, trying to fight the order, but all four dropped to their knees and bowed their heads.

My feet landed on the ground and I stepped forward to set my hand upon the alpha's head. "You are amazing and beautiful. The world needs your kind and deserves to know of your existence."

At the edge of my mind, I felt *him*. He reared up, his presence growing stronger and closer.

I had to end this now, before he reached me.

"Submit?" I asked.

"We submit," they all said at once.

He flew towards me, his dark power like a hurricane as he approached.

I released my powers and was glad that I had my hand on the alpha's head, or I might have fallen.

The darkness vanished, but I could still feel his eyes on me. This was not good.

Someone roared behind me and I turned, eyes wide, as the old wolf charged at me with claws barred and eyes glowing with a strange blackish tint.

I didn't have the energy to dodge fast enough. He was going to cut my face.

Daniel stepped between us, shifting into the half-man and half-animal form, his head completely a bear's, and roared at the wolf.

The wolf continued forward, crazed, and foaming at the mouth.

Daniel swung his pawed hand, slammed into the wolf, and sent him flying to the side, into one of the cabins.

The wolf created a hole as he flew through the wall and into the cabin, and then another hole as he exited out the other side.

"He's possessed," I whispered to Daniel. "Don't kill him."

Daniel growled.

"Ryul," I called. "Excise him."

Ryul stalked over to the wolf, who lay motionless on the other side of the cabin. He put his hands on the man's head, whispered something, and then leapt back as the darkness streamed out of the man and coalesced into *his* form.

"Amara, my love, stop this needless hiding and come to me. I do not wish to kill you again," he said.

"I am Elara," I said. "Leave me and my mates alone."

His eyes darted to my consorts.

"These men always get into our way. If I allow you to keep them for your amusement, will you come to me? Join me as you should?" he asked.

"You and I will never be joined," I said. "It is the natural order of the world for us to be separated. You know this. Stop trying to defy nature."

"Soon, my love, you will come to me. I hope it is before I break your spirit," he said and then the darkness disappeared.

Myrin wrapped an arm around my waist, without it I wouldn't have been standing.

"What was that?" the alpha asked.

"Evil," Daniel said. "He is the darkness to Amara's light." Daniel walked to me, his body back to human. He stood before me, his eyes fierce, but his touch gentle. "He will not win this time. I will not allow him to hurt you again."

"Is that what you're fighting?" the alpha asked.

I turned to face her. "It's why I'm trying to unite you all. Once all of my children are united, I can face him and not worry if I die."

"She's talking like Amara again," Ryul whispered loudly.

"We are the same, but separate, mostly," I mumbled.

"We lost and we will join you and this unified world you seek," the alpha said. "I do not wish to be ruled by that...evilness."

Yes, he had exuded evil and malice. I found it odd that she wouldn't want that, since they'd been so bloodthirsty.

"I think we should stay here tonight. Just in case he sends another trial," I said.

Durlan nodded. "I agree."

"Follow me," Daniel said. "I have a house nearby."

Myrin basically carried me as we walked behind Daniel while making it look like I was walking on my own.

"He's not going to stop," I whispered.

"We will win," Myrin whispered. "I'm sure of it."

"He will only stop once he has me," I said, tears filling my eyes. "Is this inevitable? Is this fate?"

Daniel held open a door to a log cabin that looked like every other cabin there. Inside was a giant bed, large enough to hold his bear form.

Myrin helped me inside, and then spun me to face him. "The only fate that exists is our fate of being together. Our love is fate. His terror is not."

I wished I could believe him. I did believe we were fated lovers, but I also knew *he* would never give up. He had said I could keep my consorts. Had he been honest? Would it be better to accept his proposal?

Myrin set me on the bed, and I immediately rolled onto my side and closed my eyes.

I needed a plan. I needed a plan that ended with my consorts alive and well. My life did not matter.

They had to survive.

CHAPTER 39
RYUL

His evil aura had grown since the last time we'd fought him. Was he stronger? Was our fight impossible?

Elara had looked terrified when he'd spoken to her. Afterwards, she'd looked defeated.

That did not bode well for us. It made me incredibly nervous and worried.

If she didn't think we could survive, why should we? He was a god, while we were technically lesser gods, or half-gods.

As it was, Elara couldn't become Amara for more than a single magic use. He was already testing her and had come to see her in person. Would he increase these attacks and try to kill her while she was weak? Would she have time to learn to harness her powers more?

All of these unanswered questions, and that defeated expression on her face, made me antsy and ready to kill someone. But there was no one to kill.

"Breathe," Venali whispered in my ear.

I exhaled and loosened my hands which had clenched into fists in my lap.

"She's scared, but that's to be expected when she sees him for the first time. This will help her strategize for defeating him," Venali said.

"How can you be so sure? She looked utterly defeated," I whispered.

Venali looked over at Elara, sleeping peacefully on Daniel's bed. "Because I know her and I know that seemingly impossible tasks motivate her to overcome them."

"Does it not bother anyone else that people are agreeing so quickly to her becoming Empress?" I asked. "People who are supposed to be against mixing with other races just rolled over and joined."

Daniel turned to face me, his arms folded across his chest. He'd almost killed that wolf when he'd charged at Elara's back. It made me respect him a little bit more. "They faced a goddess and then met the dark god. They aren't stupid. They may be prideful, but they also want to continue living and know picking her side is the right decision."

"What if it's not?" I asked softly.

Daniel's eyes glowed as he glared at me. "I didn't realize you were such a coward now, Ryul."

I returned his glare. "I'm not a coward. I'm being practical. What if we lose again?"

"Then we all die," Myrin said, his eyes locked on Elara as they had been since she'd faced off against the dark god. "And this time, we won't come back."

"How do you know?" Durlan asked.

He'd been rather quiet this whole time, actually, all of them had been.

"I can't explain it," Myrin said. "I can just feel it. If we die this time, there will be no coming back."

"I don't think she plans on living past the battle," Kydrus said softly. "I think Amara plans to die and separate herself from Elara."

I'd gotten that sense as well.

Myrin's face fell. "Knowing her, that's extremely likely."

"What then?" I asked. "We go back to being the Queen of the Seelie's consorts?"

Venali turned to look at me, his eyes wide. "You have a problem with that? You didn't seem to have a problem being in that position before."

"That was before my memories were fully returned and I understood she was Amara, not Elara," I said.

"She's both," Amrynn snapped. "She is equally Amara and Elara. If we lose Amara, I'll be devastated, but will continue my life with Elara."

"I'm not saying I won't," I snapped back.

"I think everyone needs to take a breath," Durlan said and stood. "We don't know anything yet. *He* is likely to send one of his dark creations after her today or tomorrow. We need to be prepared. Bickering over what might happen won't solve anything."

"He's right," Venali said. "Let's set up rotations so we can properly protect her and the shapeshifters."

"I'll go out and do a perimeter check first," Daniel said and turned towards the door.

"We go as pairs," Durlan said.

"I'll go with him," Venali said and stood. "I need to stretch my legs."

Daniel nodded at Venali and the two left.

I sighed and leaned back against the couch with my eyes closed. They weren't taking my worries the right way. I wasn't going to leave Elara or Amara. That didn't mean I had to be okay with her plan. That didn't mean I couldn't be upset.

I had to think of the worst possible outcomes so I could

prepare for them. That was how I worked. Talking about the "what-ifs" was my perimeter check.

"It'll work out," Kydrus said. "I do think we should look at every possible outcome, like the ones Ryul was discussing. It will help us develop plans ahead of time."

Durlan sighed. "You're right. I'm sorry, Ryul. I've not been myself since that redcap fight."

"Alright," Myrin said with a sigh. "Let's talk it all out. Hit me with your worst case scenarios, Ryul."

I sat up, eyes wide and looked at each of them. "Really?"

Myrin pinched the bridge of his nose. "Yeah. We're all on edge. I shouldn't take your strengths and the way you view things for granted. I'm sorry."

I never thought I'd ever hear Myrin apologize to me.

"Alright," I said and leaned forward. "Find some paper."

CHAPTER 40
ELARA

I STOOD BEFORE A MIRROR, looking at Amara instead of my own reflection.

"They must be protected this time," she said.

I didn't need to ask who she meant. "Yes," I answered.

"They won't like it," she whispered. "My plan."

"What plan?" I asked. Although we were the same, there were still thoughts and memories she had that I could not access.

"We will fight *him* first. Or try. If we fail, I will give myself to him. Not in your body, though. I will separate us. You will take our consorts and you will continue living Elara's life. You will rule over Anderelle as Empress."

I blinked. "You can do that?"

She chuckled. "I am a goddess, remember?"

"Why does *he* want you?"

She looked through me, likely viewing memories. "When we came into existence, there were more of us. Light and dark, water and fire, earth and wind. We were the gods of this universe. Together we represented balance. Fire and dark craved to possess everything. It is in their nature. We fought a long battle that nearly destroyed the universe. Dark absorbed fire and earth. Water and wind asked me to absorb them before they died, to help strengthen me. It wasn't enough. His desire to rule supreme and possess more power overruled everything else. I didn't know at the time, but the other elements had created the boys for me. They created my consorts. He had captured me and was going to force me to merge with him, when they came. They rescued me and our bond made it so that *he* could never absorb me. It infuriated him. He killed them for their insolence, as he called it. My loves, my consorts lay dead or dying on the battlefield and I had to do something. So, I took our souls and sent them through the stars, hidden from *his* sight. Then, when the time was right, our souls merged with newborns. My soul took a little longer to find you, but that is because you were the only one fit for me."

"Why me?" I asked.

"You harness the power of the stars. You were ideal."

"What about my mother?" I asked.

She shook her head. "Too meek. Her soul was not strong enough for the merger. Yours shone like a beacon in the night."

"Can we kill him?"

Amara's eyes pinched and she dropped her gaze. "I'm not certain. I do not think it wise to destroy him."

"So, we need to contain him?" I asked.

Her head whipped up, eyes wide. "What?"

"We need to find a way to contain him. So that we keep balance, but he cannot hurt us?"

She smiled wide and screeched like a young girl. "Yes. I knew you were the perfect soul for me. Yes, we must figure out how to contain him. That will keep the balance but also keep us and our consorts safe."

"If we do that, what will you do? They love you. You are their mate. If you separate from me, they may go with you?"

And leave me behind.

Her gaze softened. "They love us, Elara. If we can contain him, I will figure out a plan for us and our consorts."

"Wait, does that mean their souls can be separated from their bodies?" I asked.

She shook her head. "I'm not sure why, but their souls fully merged with their host body. I could not separate them and give you your warlords while I keep my consorts."

Well, there went that idea.

"I will find a way that makes us all happy and try to figure out how to contain *him*. We must not merge more than is necessary to prepare your body for our attack. Twice a week. Do you understand? Any more than that and *he* will attack us. He may still, but I think that should keep him away," she whispered.

If only we had the technology that Barry and his planet had. I was certain they could figure out a way to contain the god. Or, would be better equipped anyway.

"That is a possibility," Amara whispered. "You would have to free their solar system to do so and run the risk of them capturing us again."

I scowled at her. "I didn't say anything out loud."

She laughed. "We are one. Don't forget that. Consider all of your options. I'd like to avoid freeing Barry. There must be a container on this planet. I had one, but it was lost. I will search for it. In the meantime, consult our consorts. We must figure this out, Elara. I won't lose them again. I will sacrifice myself long before I let them die."

I nodded. "That much we are in agreement on." I thought a moment. "Weren't there seven gods in the beginning?" I asked. I thought I'd read that somewhere.

She nodded. "Yes, I told you all of them."

I shook my head. "You only named six."

She counted on her fingers and her eyes widened. "I'm missing one. I can't remember. Who is it? Why can't I remember who the seventh is?" Her brows furrowed and she glared over my head. "Go to the men, they're probably worried because you're sleeping so much. I'll do some more research."

"I'll ask if they remember all the gods, too, but will keep from telling them you forgot one," I said.

"Okay," she said. "We will figure this out, Elara. It will work out for all of us."

CHAPTER 41
DANIEL

"You sure you don't want to go opposite me and meet in the middle?" I asked Venali.

He smiled. "Trying to get rid of me?"

"You want to talk to me, I take it," I said.

"Your powers started to show when you protected her from the possessed shifter," he said.

I sighed and dropped my head. "I overreacted. I sensed his bloodlust and the darkness when he neared."

"I wouldn't call that overreacting," he said.

"I threw him through a house," I reminded him.

He smiled wide. "That was very entertaining. It also made me really want to spar with you."

"That can be arranged," I said.

"You've been on edge," he said. "I thought you might need someone to talk to."

"I wouldn't say I want to talk," I muttered.

"You may not want to, but you should," he said.

"Aren't you supposed to be our brute?" I asked, snarling.

He beamed.

We continued walking, and after several minutes of his silent presence, I sighed and gave in.

"She's hiding something. I know you fae can't outright lie, but you can withhold information. She's withholding a lot. What I'm most worried about are the hints that Amara keeps dropping."

"What hints?" Venali asked.

"That she and Elara will separate at some point," I said.

He nodded. "I've been wondering about those as well."

"We cannot separate from these bodies. So, we would either be leaving Elara alone, or Amara. The thought of doing either is too much to bear. I don't know Elara that well, I know she is only the bearer of Amara's soul, yet just the brief time I've spent with her, having her by my side, I cannot imagine life without her. I'm sure it is even stronger for you guys," I said and glanced at him.

His eyes were pinched, and he nodded. "I love her—Elara. I also love Amara. I cannot imagine being without them at all. Yet, if she does separate, I would either have to choose, or they would choose for us, which makes my chest hurt, and pain unlike any I've known before course through me. I thought it would be easy to choose between them once I realized who she was and that she only had Amara within her, but I cannot. Elara is amazing and beautiful, and I love everything about her. I would not want to live away from her. Plus, I would not want to abandon her or leave her alone to be queen without us at her side. She would be devastated if we left her."

"So, somehow, we have to convince Amara to either fully merge with Elara, or at least stay within her," I said. "The question is, how?"

Venali nodded. "That is the question, but I have no answer."

Neither did I.

We finished our patrol and found nothing. I didn't think he would send us a test today. If my suspicions about him were right, he would send it tomorrow or the next day. He would try to let us fall into a false sense of safety, and then send monsters after us. Would it be more redcaps? Or something worse? I only knew about the fey monsters from my memories of our other lifetime. These people on Emortalia had never seen the evil fey creatures. I feared they were about to.

Just outside of the house, we could hear Elara arguing with someone, it sounded like Ryul.

"Does he always argue with her?" I asked Venali softly.

"He's trying to do what is right, but he never seems to go about it the correct way. He was like that with Amara, too. He has one goal, protect her. When she has plans that put her in danger, he doesn't want to hear it and wants to tell her how stupid she is being. Elara, much like Amara, does not answer well to that type of aggression. She digs her heels in and bares her teeth instead of backing down," he said. "He's better, but he is still learning how to convey his feelings to her. Some of us were born better at speaking to women. Also, while we were warlords, without our memories, we had over a thousand years of practice speaking to people and working out problems. He was in a castle, alone, waiting for her to return."

"So, he's not socialized properly," I said. Like a shapeshifter when we introduced them to humans, they had to be introduced slowly and learn how to react and interact with the humans.

Venali laughed softly. "Yes, I suppose you could word it like that."

"He loves her. I can see that. Maybe I'll try to give him some tips," I said. Not that I was an expert, but I had a lot of experience talking with volatile people and keeping them from exploding.

"Good luck," Venali said and pushed open the door.

We entered, and Myrin looked at us expectantly.

"Clear," I said.

He nodded and turned back to watch Ryul and Elara. Ryul

and Elara were the only ones standing, the others were lounging on couches in my living room, watching the argument.

"You're being ridiculous," Ryul said. "You always want to put yourself in danger."

"I'm trying to save us, you buffoon," she snapped. "Why can't you see that?"

I leaned my shoulder against the doorway and smiled. She was really worked up, her tiny fists were clenched at her sides, the tips of her pointed ears were pink, and her teeth were bared, showing off her sharp canines. She was gorgeous and I wanted to throw her over my shoulder and take her to the bedroom.

I took a single step to the side to adjust my pants which had gotten tighter as I reacted to her.

Ryul had said something, but I'd missed it.

She yelled and threw her hands up in the air. "Impossible."

Myrin looked over at me and smirked. He was enjoying the show as well.

"What is your plan?" Durlan asked.

Elara tensed and pivoted so she wasn't looking at any of us. "It's complicated."

No, she just didn't want to tell us, which meant it was dangerous.

"You're not sacrificing yourself," Kydrus said.

She spun around with a deathly glare. "I didn't say I was."

He smiled. "You didn't have to. Most of your plans involve you trying to sacrifice yourself."

"I'm not saying I'm going to sacrifice myself," she said. "I just need to find something and it is hidden in a rather dangerous place."

"Which is where you being put in danger comes in," I said.

She lifted her head and met my eyes. The fire that burned within her, the strength that such a small body held, made my erection grow stiffer.

"What is it?" I asked her. "Or where is it?"

"Zenlop," she said.

The air rushed out of my lungs, and I saw everyone else in the room tense.

Zenlop was not a place anyone went anymore. It had been taken over by ruthless humans who murdered anyone who got close to their land.

Myrin stood, his fists clenched and said, "No."

She looked up at him, towering over her, and said, "You can't tell me no. I am going to Zenlop. You're either coming or staying here and pouting."

Well, that was a new stance from her I hadn't seen before.

"No ships have been able to dock there," Durlan said. "They're all blown up before they make land. How do you expect to get there?"

"I didn't say I had all the answers," she grumbled and looked away from Myrin to stare at the floor. "I have to go there. I have to. Somehow. I'll swim if I have to."

Ryul paled.

Right, he couldn't swim. We would need to fix that soon.

"Are you sure you can't find the item you need here or on Minloa?" I asked.

She nodded. "Positive. Amara said so."

I narrowed my eyes. She hadn't referred to Amara as a separate being before. Was that a bad sign? Did it have to do with the hints at them separating?

"Maybe we need to talk to Amara then," Ryul said.

Elara shook her head. "She said we couldn't merge except for twice a week. She doesn't want to risk darkness coming after us when we're still unprepared."

Venali looked at me, his scowl a mirror of my own.

"Why don't you and Amara fully merge?" I asked.

She looked back at the ground. "We can't."

I walked to her, took her tiny hands in mine, and said, "If you two separate, there's a chance that we won't stay with you."

She jerked her hands away from me and shoved around me. "I'm aware of the possible consequences. Far more than you seven." She shoved open the front door and said, "I'm going for a walk. Don't try to talk to me."

The door slammed closed behind her, and it felt like my heart had cracked with it. She was preparing for losing us.

"Amara is going to sacrifice herself, isn't she?" I asked softly.

"Seems that way," Amrynn whispered.

"She wouldn't make us choose if she didn't sacrifice herself, would she?" Ryul asked, his eyes on the door Elara had walked through.

"It's possible," Myrin whispered through clenched teeth. "That damn goddess never thinks about herself. If she's sacrificing herself, then she'll leave us with Elara. But, judging by Elara's reaction to your statement, there's another option they're preparing for, which would leave Elara without us." He growled and black flames licked up his arms from his clenched fists.

"Don't burn my house down," I ordered him.

He met my eyes, a challenge in them for just a brief moment, and then he closed them and shook out his hands, the fire disappearing. "Sorry."

I set my hand on his shoulder. "This isn't easy on any of us."

"She'd really make us choose?" Ryul whispered, horror etched across his wide-eyed expression. He sat on the couch and dropped his head into his hands.

"Or, leave Elara alone," Kydrus whispered.

"I can't let that happen," Amrynn said. "I won't leave her alone."

"Calm down," Durlan said. "We're not choosing. We'll convince them to merge. We need to figure out how to get to Zenlop."

"You're going to take her?" Kydrus asked.

"She's going," Durlan said softly. "Just like she was going to see the Unseelie and come here. We have two choices: follow her or wait and pray she returns. I'm not waiting behind ever again. I'm not being separated from her for weeks or months like last time, never knowing if she was alive or not."

"You're talking about when she was taken on the spaceship, right?" I asked. I felt so out of the loop. They'd been with her months longer than me, which irked me more than I would ever admit.

Durlan nodded. "It was torture."

"It wasn't a picnic for me either," Amrynn mumbled. "Damned humans."

"You know I'm mostly human, right?" I asked with an arched brow.

He looked over at me. "You're a demigod, not a human. And, I know not all humans are bad. Just like not all Seelie are good."

"What are we going to do about her?" Ryul asked.

"First of all, we're not going to tell her she's being ridiculous," I said and folded my arms across my chest. "Talking to her like that won't get you anywhere."

"She *is* being ridiculous," he said and stood.

"Yes, but if you actually want her to consider your side of the argument you can't call her names or say things like that," I said.

"You all baby her," Ryul said.

"No, we just know how to talk like adults," I said.

He snarled at me, but stayed in place.

"He's right," Durlan said. "You suck at talking to her. I think we need to teach you how to properly talk to people."

"I know how to talk to people," Ryul said.

"It's not your fault you were isolated," I said. "But it is your fault that you won't learn and change your ways. She's dealing with a lot of heavy crap and you're not helping the situation."

Ryul plopped down onto the couch. “Yeah, you’re right. I’m sorry.”

All of us stared at him in disbelief.

He glared back. “I’m not stupid. I can learn and accept when I’m wrong.”

Well, there might be hope for him after all.

CHAPTER 42
ELARA

THEY WERE TOO DAMN PERCEPTIVE.

I walked through the forest around the house, not straying too far, just in case *he* decided to send a test while I was separated from the guys. Not that he could know that, but I wanted to play it safe.

Amara had said that the item to contain *him* was on Zenlop. It was in a museum, on display for everyone to see. The item would be able to hold him and seal him inside for eternity.

But Zenlop was inhabited by humans, millions of humans. And not humans like here on Emortalia. No, these humans were like Barry, minus the scientific advancements, at least from what I'd been able to find out from the humans on Emortalia. The ones on Zenlop were more likely to kill someone than greet them. Especially, if they had pointed ears and teeth.

I still couldn't believe there were humans on my planet. I could sense lifeforms, but not what type they were. Were the humans here from Barry's system? Or were they always here?

There had to be a way for me to get to Zenlop and get the item I needed. It was our only hope of saving the universe.

Daniel's statement had hit too close to home. It had felt like he'd punched me in the stomach, despite only holding my hands.

I didn't want to lose them. I loved them. I didn't want to be the Seelie Queen without my warlords at my side. Just thinking about it brought tears to my eyes.

But…I didn't want to separate Amara from her consorts. They loved her. They were created *for* her. How could I come between a goddess and her consorts? I couldn't. I didn't want to force them to choose between us either.

That only left a couple of options, two of which ended with either Amara or I dying. I didn't want to die. I had so much life ahead of me, but what could I really offer? I wanted to unite the planet, but what good would it do if Amara was dead and *he* won? Or, if Amara disappeared and we no longer had her to protect the universe?

No, I couldn't be selfish. If I needed to die, then that was what I would do, or I would give them up and separate myself from them. If things started to look like it would end up that way, I would need to distance myself from them to try to ease the pain. No matter what I did, it would hurt. Losing them would be like losing half of me.

Even the thought of losing Daniel, who I didn't know that well, hurt immensely.

"You're crying," Myrin whispered beside me.

I looked up, realizing I had stopped beside the house, next to the bedroom. He must have seen me through the window and opened it.

"It's nothing," I said and wiped my face. "Just a lot to deal with and I'm not sure how to handle it all."

"Can I come out with you?" he asked.

He had been Amara's first consort, and we had the strongest connection. I could not deny it, even when I tried to remind myself that it was truly Amara he was connected to.

I nodded.

He climbed out of the window and held out his hand.

I bit my lip, debating. Should I start distancing myself now?

"Please?" he whispered.

Immediately, I set my hand in his, and he linked our fingers together.

Warmth radiated up my arm and into my chest.

Yes, this was right. Distancing myself could wait until I was sure I needed to.

"Thank you," he said.

We started walking, and I leaned my shoulder into his, and then my head against his shoulder.

"You aren't alone, Elara. We are here. We want to help you, to share your burden. You don't have to keep secrets from us. I really wish you wouldn't keep secrets from us."

"You'll be angry," I whispered.

"Possibly, but I'd rather be angry than scared and unsure, which is what we are all feeling currently," he said.

Putting myself in their shoes, I could understand what he meant.

"I don't want to make you choose," I whispered. "If it comes down to that, I won't make you choose."

"We don't want to choose," he said and his hand squeezed mine. "We love you and Amara. I don't want to be away from either of you."

"There might be a way to save the universe, but it requires me getting an item from Zenlop. I don't know how we're going to get there. Or how I'm going to get the item, but I have to. We have to. I think it is our only option," I said.

"What is the item?" he asked.

"A pot," I said.

He looked down at me with an arched brow. "A pot?"

"It's a special pot. The humans there don't know that it is

anything other than a very old pot. It was actually Amara's, but it had been stolen at some point and now it is in a museum there."

"Humans? Did you say humans are on Zenlop?" he asked, stopping and turning to face me.

I nodded.

"Amrynn is not going to like that at all," he whispered.

I sighed. "I know. He's still not over what happened with Barry." Not that I was either.

"If we get the pot, then what?" he asked, nudging me back to walk again.

"I don't want to say it out loud, in case *he* is listening," I whispered.

Myrin sighed. "That does make sense, but it infuriates me."

I laughed and hopped up to kiss his cheek. "I'm sorry."

He spun me sideways, his arms wrapping around me, and pushed my back against a tree. "Your life has value, Elara. Even if Amara separates from you, you are a person who deserves to live a long and happy life. I will do everything in my power to ensure you survive this and go on to live a happy life as Queen of Minloa."

I swallowed thickly. "Sometimes sacrifices are necessary."

He trailed his fingertips down my cheek. "Yes, but your life is not one of them. I will sacrifice myself to save you. I failed Amara, but I will not fail you."

"I'm just a Seelie girl. I may be of noble blood, but I'm nothing in the grand scheme of the universe. Just a speck that will disappear before long. Your life is worth more."

He shook his head. "That's where you're wrong, my love. You will change the world. I will not. I was created as a tool. To fight and protect." He smirked. "And for pleasure and companionship."

His companionship was definitely pleasurable.

"Now that you know I'm not Amara, that we are separate, shouldn't it feel wrong to be my mate?" I asked.

He kissed me lightly. "Does this feel wrong?"

I shook my head, my heart pounding in my chest.

"No. You are my mate just the same as I am Amara's consort. I will do this until I am forced to stop, or you tell me no." He pressed his body against mine, pinning me to the tree and kissed me deeply.

I moaned into the kiss, wrapped my arms around his back, and gripped his shirt. He was my rock, my ever present and steady mate. He grounded me in a way that I didn't really understand, but wasn't going to try too hard to.

He pulled back, unbuttoned my pants, while staring at me, waiting for me to stop him.

We were in the middle of the woods outside of Daniel's house in the shapeshifter town. At any point, someone could walk by and see us.

That made me want to do it even more.

I reached out and undid his pants, gripping him once free.

He groaned, and his eyes rolled up into the back of his head.

"This will be quick," he said in a way that sounded like an apology.

I turned around, and he wasted no time slipping inside of me. I gasped in pleasure and arched into him.

He gripped my hip with one hand and reached up to fondle one of my breasts with the other hand. "You're my mate, Elara. I won't give you up without a fight. I want to be doing this with you for centuries to come."

I leaned forward to give him better access, gripping the trunk of the tree.

He growled softly and slammed fast and hard into me.

I screamed as I orgasmed and almost immediately orgasmed again.

Our session was short, but we both found the release we

needed, and for some reason, it felt like our bond was a little bit stronger.

After redressing, I leaned against him, hugging him tightly. "We can do this, right?"

"Go back to the house?" he asked.

I looked up at him with a frown. "You know what I mean."

"Let us work with you. Talk with us. We can do anything if we work together," he whispered.

I nodded and stepped around him.

We returned to the house and my mind was made up. I would go to Zenlop, I would get the container to seal the dark god inside, and I would spend every last second I could with these men, until they were taken from me.

Then, I would learn to live without them.

GODDESS OF THE UNIVERSE

BOOK THREE

USA TODAY BESTSELLING AUTHOR

CATHERINE BANKS

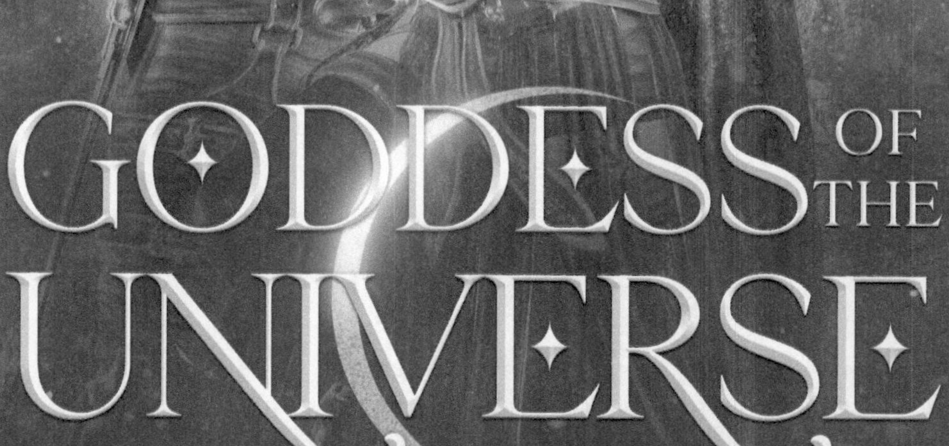

3

THEIR FAE GODDESS

Goddess of the Universe by Catherine Banks.

Cover design by Ana Cruz Arts.

Published by Turbo Kitten Industries.

www.CatherineBanks.com

Turbo Kitten Industries™, P.O. Box 5012, Galt, CA 95632

To those fans who have supported and continue to support me, thank you.

Thank you to the following people for being incredibly awesome and helping me with this book. You each made a difference and I value you more than you will ever know:

Jenica

Courtney

Ericka

Lea

Pauline

Michelle

Thank you Avery for your support and love. My life would be severely lacking if you weren't in it.

Anderelle

Zenlop

Minloa

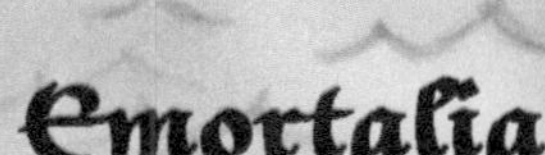

Emortalia

CHAPTER 1
ELARA

Four redcaps stood outside Daniel's house in Emortalia, hitting their clubs against their empty hands. It seemed they were trying to intimidate us with the display, but it wasn't working.

"Sit and watch," Durlan said and kissed my cheek. His long silver hair was pulled back and tied with a piece of leather. I preferred his hair free, but I also enjoyed the unblocked view of his handsome face.

I sat on Daniel's porch and tore into the dried meat Ryul had given me. "Okay," I said around the food.

Ryul sat beside me and chewed his meat.

Durlan, Amrynn, Venali, and Myrin walked away from the house, swords in hand.

Daniel leaned against the side of his house near me, his arms folded across his chest, and wore a bored expression.

"You could just let me have them all," Venali said, his magenta eyes glowing brightly with excitement.

"Not a chance," Durlan said, his hair whipping from side to side as he shook his head. "I need some exercise."

"There are other ways we can exercise," I called out loudly.

Durlan turned. "I plan on that after I've got you worked up from watching us kill these redcaps. Once we are done, I will take care of you."

He had been more aggressive lately, which I was pretty certain was due to the fact that he didn't have anything to strategize and was bored.

I was *not* complaining.

"Tease," I called back and took another bite.

He winked at me, and his sword began to glow.

Well, that was new.

"You underestimate us," the middle redcap growled. "It will be your downfall."

"We've killed at least twelve of your kind the past week," Venali said, still smiling, the three scars of his left eye slightly scrunched. "You underestimate us."

A few of the shapeshifters came out of their houses and sat on their porches like I did. They'd become desensitized to the redcaps' attacks and knew my guys could handle them.

If things started to get out of control, Daniel and Ryul would join the fight.

"Water?" Ryul asked and held out a cup.

I took it and guzzled it. "Thanks." I scooted a bit closer so I could lean my shoulder against his.

With the possibility of losing them so close, I was using every chance I had to touch them, spend time with them, and engage in whatever activities they wanted to. It resulted in several late nights where I ended up coated in sweat and smiling like a drunken fool, though no alcohol was present.

"Ready?" Myrin asked, smiling wide enough to show off his sharp canines. Black tendrils slid from his fingertips, down his sword, and coated the blade. The blade glowed with a black sheen, and I wondered what it would feel like to get cut with it.

He leapt forward and sliced off one of the redcap's arms.

Judging by the way the redcap screamed, the sword hurt a lot more than a regular one.

Venali stopped, inhaled deeply, and the muscular Seelie became even more muscular. I had never seen muscles expand before, and it was quite the display.

The guys had begun using new powers, ones I had never seen them use while warlords. They said that the continued exposure to Amara, though small, was helping to unlock their suppressed powers. They said they were also trying out some new powers, to try to prepare for our upcoming battle.

I hoped there wouldn't be a battle, but the likelihood of that was very small. Infinitesimal really.

Venali roared and began punching the redcap in front of him. He had to jump up to hit the redcap in the face, since it was twice his height.

The redcap swung his club and tried to punch Venali back, but Venali dodged out of the way and blocked the punches with his arm.

Durlan moved forward slowly, his walk slow and confident. The redcap tried to hit him, but Durlan sidestepped his wild swings like the redcap was moving at a slower pace. Once right in front of the redcap, Durlan stabbed his glowing sword into the redcap's chest. It screamed and then exploded into a piercing white light.

"That's definitely new," I whispered and squeezed my legs together at the sudden rush of wetness between them.

Amrynn, who usually fought with his sword, sheathed it and took a Venali approach, fighting the redcap hand to hand. He pummeled it to death with ease.

Something was happening to them that they weren't telling me. They were all a bit angrier than before and way more focused on powering up. It wasn't just the upcoming fight. There was a rage simmering amongst them that none of them would talk about.

"It would be nice if at least one of you was honest about why you are all so angry," I whispered.

"It would be nice if you told us everything going on in your head, too," Daniel said.

Touché.

Myrin finished cutting up the redcap and used his black flames to destroy the bodies of the rest of the monsters.

All four men returned to the house, walking past me.

Well, that was over too quickly. Not that I was complaining that the god of darkness was sending tests that were too easy. I preferred them to ones that left us injured.

"Coming?" Ryul asked. He stood beside me with his hand extended in an offer to help me stand.

I took his hand and let him pull me up. My head spun a moment, and I grabbed his arm to keep steady.

He scowled down at me. "You've been practicing magic when we're sleeping, haven't you?"

I smiled innocently. "Me?"

He snarled. "You're going to hurt yourself by burning the candle at both ends."

"Why can't I work to become stronger just like you guys are?" I asked, stepping away from him now that the dizzy spell was over.

"I didn't say you couldn't become stronger. Just that you shouldn't do it under certain conditions. One: don't do it when we aren't with you, and two: you shouldn't use magic when you've already spent the entire day training physically," he said.

I walked into the house and headed to the bedroom where Durlan waited for me. "I'll take your advice into consideration."

Durlan yanked me into the bedroom and slammed the door closed.

I hopped up onto him, wrapping my legs around his waist, my arms around his neck, and kissed him.

He tugged at my shirt, and I broke the kiss to remove it.

He tossed me on the bed and took his own shirt off. "Now, let's see what we can do about you being able to walk properly."

I smirked. "I like this challenge. Bring it on, mate."

He smiled and dropped his pants, showing me just how ready he was for the challenge.

CHAPTER 2
AMRYNN

We were planning a trip to the one place on the planet I did not want to go, a continent full of violent humans. If they caught us, they'd either kill us or do as Barry had, and use us for experimentation.

Okay, I didn't know that for certain, but it was highly likely.

Sitting in the middle of the living room, Myrin and Venali allowed me to experiment on them. I stood at their backs while they sat, focused on my magic, and tried to channel it into Myrin's aura, to make him invisible.

I'd made Venali invisible several times, but I wasn't certain it would work on Myrin.

My magic swirled within his aura, his body began to fade, and then the darkness of his Unseelie power shoved my magic out, knocking Venali and I away from him.

I released my magic and snorted as I laughed.

Venali sat back up and shook his head. "Well, that was different."

Myrin sighed and hung his head. "I'm sorry. I come preprogrammed to reject Seelie powers."

I patted his shoulder. "My feelings aren't hurt."

He looked around and scowled. "Where's Elara?"

"She's with Daniel," I said and fought against my urge to snarl at him.

Myrin and Elara were connected in a different way than the rest of us. I couldn't figure out how it was different or why, but it bothered me. It bothered Kydrus as well, but we hadn't spoken to the others to ask if they felt the same.

I knew she loved us all equally, but there was a difference when they were together, and it was obvious.

"Amrynn?" Myrin asked.

I looked up, realizing I had spaced out again. "Sorry."

Venali gave me a knowing look, while Myrin scowled.

Daniel and her were connected differently as well, but not in a way that bothered me. I couldn't explain it even to myself, so I kept my feelings inside.

I knew there was no reason for me to be jealous. Elara loved me and would never leave me. Yet, my possessive brain still tried to convince me every now and then to scoop her up and run far far away with her.

I wouldn't do it, but thinking about it did bring a smile to my face.

"Try it with Venali again, so I can watch," Myrin said.

I nodded and turned to Venali. "It doesn't last long, though."

Myrin shrugged. "The fact that it works at all is interesting to me."

"Don't I get a say in this?" Venali asked.

I arched a brow at him.

"It feels weird," he mumbled.

I rolled my eyes. "Just sit still."

CHAPTER 3
ELARA

No one was willing to take us to Zenlop and the ship we had come here on wasn't sturdy enough for the rest of our trek. So, I had to purchase a ship to use instead. Thankfully, my mates knew how to sail so we wouldn't have to hire a crew.

Myrin checked the ship over thoroughly before paying the owner. "Sold," Myrin said.

The man smiled and walked away, counting his money.

"When do we set sail?" Durlan asked with a scowl.

He hadn't been able to come up with a plan that satisfied him, but I was tired of waiting. We needed to go now, before *he* made a move.

"Tomorrow," I said. "We'll need to check the stores and be sure we have enough food for the trip there and back."

"On it," Ryul said and walked onto the ship.

"You're sure this is necessary?" Amrynn asked.

I spun to face him since he'd stood off to the side. He was the least happy that we were going to the humans' continent. "Yes."

He sighed, but nodded. "I'll do some supply shopping."

I watched him go until he disappeared among the crowds of the dock.

"Elara, I have a really bad feeling about this," Venali said.

I sighed and dropped my head. "I understand this is dangerous. I understand you hate the idea of taking me somewhere so dangerous. If there were another way, Amara and I would gladly take it. As it is, there are two options. One, give myself to *him*..."

Venali, Myrin, Kydrus, Daniel, and Durlan growled.

"Or, two, I get this container. So, you tell me which you would prefer."

No one spoke.

"I thought so," I said.

"Doesn't mean we have to like it," Durlan growled.

I wrapped my arms around him, and he immediately enveloped me in a hug. "I don't like it either," I whispered.

"Daniel," Ryul called. "Come help me with the purchases, please."

Daniel dropped a kiss atop my head as he passed.

"I've got some adjustments to make before we set sail," Myrin said. "Venali and Kydrus, I'll need your help."

"What am I supposed to do?" I asked.

"Go rest," Myrin said. "You look exhausted."

Arguing would do me no good, especially since he was right.

Durlan looped an arm around my waist and tugged me away. "Come on."

He teleported us to Daniel's house and led me to the bedroom.

I flopped onto the bed, face down.

Durlan climbed on beside me and stroked my hair.

For a bit, I just enjoyed being petted.

"I'm scared," I whispered.

"Of?" Durlan asked, still petting me.

"Losing you all."

"We're scared of losing you, too," he whispered.

He didn't understand that I meant losing him once Amara separated from me.

Was he afraid of losing me or Amara?

"I love you, Durlan," I whispered. "I want to do whatever I can to protect you." Even if it meant sacrificing myself or my happiness.

He turned me over and kissed away the few tears that had escaped. "You're hiding something from us. We all know it. We can all feel the difference in you since the day *he* came. I wish you would talk to us."

"It's not a secret," I said. "Just possibilities that I'm preparing for."

"Like us dying?" he asked.

I nodded. *Among others.*

"I can't promise that I won't die," he whispered. "But I can promise to try my hardest to live."

Except if his life could be traded for mine, he'd break that promise.

"Amara and I merged a bit more," I whispered. "It's becoming hard to know where Elara ends and Amara begins."

He stroked my face. "We love you both, so it doesn't bother us."

"She...we love you," I whispered.

"What aren't you telling us?" he asked softly.

"I...can't."

"Can't or won't?" he asked, his voice still gentle.

I didn't answer.

He sighed. "Go to sleep, Elara. You need the rest. Tomorrow is the start of a new adventure."

I snuggled up close to him and closed my eyes.

Instantly, I stood before a mirror with Amara glaring at me.

"What?" I asked and put my hands on my hips.

"You almost told him," she accused.

"I didn't, though," I snapped back.

"We're merging more," she whispered. "I hadn't anticipated this."

"What does that mean?" I asked.

"If we fully merge, I'm not sure I can separate us."

I gaped at her. "You said you're a goddess, so of course you could do it."

"That was before we merged more," she said and waved her hands frantically. "I thought I had stopped it, but clearly fate has other ideas."

"Maybe it's a good thing," I said softly.

She smirked. "So, we get our cake and eat it, too?"

I nodded.

"When you get to Zenlop, disguise yourself as a human. You'll have to break into the museum. Make—"

"Ryul use his magic on the guards so we can take the item right under their noses," I finished.

She nodded.

"I've got it," I said. "I just don't know how we'll get to the docks."

She smiled. "Leave that to me."

I didn't like that smile. That was our crazy idea smile.

CHAPTER 4
KYDRUS

"Do we even know how long the journey will take?" I asked Myrin as I held a wooden beam and he nailed it in.

"A few days was all I was told," Myrin said. He pounded the nail in and then added a second.

"Wonderful," I murmured.

Sweat beaded on my forehead as I continued to hold up the beam. It was hot below deck and incredibly stuffy.

Myrin finally finished securing the beam and grabbed another one.

"What are we building?" I asked.

"A room for Elara," he said. "I don't want her alone in the captain's quarters, or with just one of us."

I liked his plan.

"Good idea," I said.

Venali carried over more beams and some panels. "This should be it," he said and dusted off his hands.

Myrin nodded and placed the next beam. "Here."

Venali held it in place this time.

"What are we going to do about a bed?" I asked.

"I figured we could steal Daniel's since he's coming with us," Myrin said and smiled. "It holds on to her smell, even when she's not on it."

"I think we should leave Amrynn on the boat when we land," I whispered.

Myrin stopped his hammer, letting it fall to his side. "I was going to suggest it, but thought he would argue."

"He will," I said with a smirk. "He will also do as we tell him. We just have to be persuasive."

"I'll leave you to do it then," Myrin said with a wide smile and turned back to securing the beam.

I growled, but accepted my fate. "Jerk."

Myrin laughed, as did Venali.

"What do you want to bet that she's not sleeping but strategizing with Amara?" Myrin said.

Venali chuckled. "No one will take that bet because that's a given."

"You still think Amara will try to separate from Elara?" I asked Myrin.

Myrin's hammer hit the nail harder than usual and he growled. "Yes. I guarantee that is one of the options they are considering."

"That's why Elara is acting differently?" Venali asked.

Myrin growled again. "I'm not sure. They put up walls so thick I cannot break through. And Elara has been swinging back and forth so much that I can't get a read on her."

CHAPTER 5
ELARA

I WOKE with Durlan reading in bed with me, and the house silent.

"No one's back?" I asked as I sat up.

Durlan shook his head and closed the book he had been reading. "How do you feel?" he asked, smoothing down my hair.

Always the worrier of the group.

I smiled and leaned forward to kiss him. "I'm fine."

His eyes burned with hunger, and he rolled on top of me, sliding his hand up beneath my shirt to stroke my breast.

I gasped and arched into him, but there were blankets between us.

He growled and tossed the blankets off the bed and then pulled his erection free.

I was trapped beneath him, so I couldn't take my underwear off.

He tugged my underwear to one side and slid a finger inside of me, checking how wet I was. He moaned as it slid in easily. "You've been extra wet lately."

"I keep watching you kill redcaps," I said, my lower body coiled with anticipation.

He slid into me, both of us moaning at the same time. He reached up and gripped my hair, tugging firmly, but not painfully. "You like it when I'm rough?" he asked.

I gasped and breathed, "Yes."

He slammed into me hard, our skin slapping together. "You like when I'm in charge?"

"Yes," I moaned as he thrust in and out of me.

He flipped me over, grabbed my hair in his fist, and pulled me back so that I was sitting up on my knees, my throat bent to the side, while he was still inside me. Had he been shorter, this position wouldn't have worked.

Growling, he pressed his canines to my throat and licked. "You tell me if I go too far, okay?" he whispered.

I nodded.

His teeth pressed harder. "Use your words."

"Yes," I said, trying to rock my hips, but he dropped a hand to grab them.

Starting a fast rhythm, he brought me to climax again and again. Then, when I was sure I couldn't possibly have more, he bit my neck and groped my breasts.

A scream tore from my throat as the mother of all orgasms hit. I felt my own juices leak down the inside of my legs as my thighs quivered.

Durlan orgasmed a moment later and released my neck.

I fell onto my stomach, a contented mush pile.

Durlan disappeared and returned with a bandage. "I'm sorry," he whispered as he wiped my neck.

"Durlan, I'm fine," I said.

"You're bleeding," he whispered.

I was?

I grabbed his hand and made him look at me. "I enjoyed every second of that. Okay? Don't apologize for making me feel good."

He smiled and kissed me. "Okay."

After he bandaged my neck, I went to the bathroom to clean up.

That was a new side of Durlan I hadn't seen before.

I smiled at my reflection.

I could definitely get used to that side being around.

CHAPTER 6
RYUL

I STARED out at the ocean, water as far as I could see. Even knowing how to swim now, it scared me. I didn't like being scared.

"You'll be fine," Venali said from behind me.

I jumped. For such a large man, he moved silently.

"I don't like not being near land," I said, turning to face him.

He had a large sack on his shoulder, but stood loosely like it weighed nothing to him. "I don't like it either," he said. He shrugged, making the sack move. "But we have no choice."

Part of me wanted to ask to carry the sack to see if it was light, but I didn't want to be unable to lift it if it was heavy.

"What's in the bag?" I asked.

He glanced at the bag on his shoulders. "Potatoes."

Amrynn walked onto the ship with a bag over his shoulder. "How's it going?" he asked.

"We're almost done," Venali said.

I nodded my agreement.

Amrynn nodded and headed below deck.

Venali followed.

With nothing else to do, I followed as well.

They had transformed a huge portion of the area into a room, though no bed was there yet.

"You guys work fast." I smiled at their work.

Myrin beamed. "Thanks."

"We ready to head back?" I asked.

"I'm going to stay on the ship to guard it," Amrynn said.

Myrin nodded. "Great. We'll be back in just a few hours."

"Hours?" I asked.

"I want us to sleep on the ship tonight," Myrin said. "So we can get used to it before we set sail."

I guessed that made sense.

Kydrus sat against a wall of the new room. "I'll just stay here."

Amrynn chuckled. "Out of shape, old friend?"

"I'll still whip you in the ring." Kydrus snarled. Then he sighed. "But yes."

Daniel approached, having been in the storage area. "We done?"

"We're going to the house for a bit," Venali said. "We need to collect our mate."

Daniel looked at the room. "And steal my bed?"

Myrin smiled. "Is it stealing if you'll be using it, too?"

Daniel chuckled and pushed his way through, heading to the stairs. "Let's go. I don't want to leave her alone too long."

"She does attract trouble like a magnet," I said.

Kydrus smiled. "You don't know the half of it."

Sudden pain engulfed my mind.

Elara! She's in trouble.

Everyone crowded together, and Amrynn teleported us to Daniel's house.

Elara stood outside the house, Durlan on the ground beside her, not moving. Before her, three Cu Sith snarled and snapped their jaws. They were huge, black dogs with shadows flickering along their shaggy fur.

I had never seen Cu Sith before, but there were dozens of tales about them. They were supposedly harbingers of death, collectors of souls.

"Come closer, and I will kill you," Elara hissed through her teeth as she snarled at them. "You will not take my mate's soul."

The middle Cu Sith barked.

Elara cried out in pain and dropped to one knee. "No," she yelled. Her body began glowing, but she only raised one hand. The other had blood dripping down it.

Daniel shifted into his bear form and roared.

The rest of us drew our swords and charged forward, putting ourselves between Elara and the Cu Sith.

Amrynn stepped back and knelt by Durlan. "He's alive. Unconscious. Seriously wounded."

Elara's entire body trembled. "They were trying to take his soul," she whispered. "They were sent by *him*."

That much I had figured.

Myrin's darkness swirled around him, and he bared his teeth at the Cu Sith. "Leave now or we'll destroy you."

Daniel growled and stood on his hind legs, now over eight feet tall.

I would never admit it to him, but he was pretty intimidating.

The Cu Sith on the left growled.

Elara growled back. "You're not fully immortal. Even gods die, and so will you."

"You understand them?" I asked, keeping my eyes on the enemy.

"Yeah. Part of Amara's powers I think," she whispered.

The three Cu Sith leapt at Daniel, jaws snapping and claws bared.

Myrin kicked one in the side, sending it flying into a tree.

Daniel swatted another one away, his massive paw as powerful as our fists.

Venali grabbed the third by the throat and slammed it to the ground in front of Daniel.

The two that had been sent flying leapt up and charged back.

I sliced across the front leg of the one nearest to me, my sword cutting to the bone.

Turning, it tried to clamp its jaws on my arms, but I stepped left and tried to stab it in the chest.

The Cu Sith dropped to the ground, avoiding my strike.

Venali cut the head off the Cu Sith he was fighting, and then Myrin set it on fire with his black flames.

Spinning my magic, I used it on the Cu Sith facing me. He tensed and looked around with wide eyes.

With three swings, I decapitated it and pierced its heart.

"Myrin," I called.

He turned, raised his hand, and black flames covered the Cu Sith at my feet.

His flames were *really* useful.

The last Cu Sith snarled and backed up, looking like he was planning to flee.

Myrin rushed forward, grabbed it by the scruff, and flames engulfed it. "No one hurts my mate and lives," he growled and tossed the burning canine to the forest floor.

Daniel shifted back and tried to examine Elara's wounds, but she brushed his hands away.

Amrynn was still healing Durlan, a scowl on his face that made me uneasy.

Elara dropped to the ground by Durlan, tears streaking her cheeks, and then leaned forward to press her lips to his.

"Live," Amara's voice said from Elara's throat.

White energy floated from Elara to Durlan, sliding into his mouth.

When the last bit of energy left her mouth, Elara fell backwards on the forest floor, eyes closed.

Durlan sat up and looked around with wide eyes. He looked at Elara and reached over, resting his hand on her chest bone. A second later, he exhaled harshly. "Elara, you moron." He looked up at us. "What happened?"

"The Cu Sith are dead," Myrin said and indicated their burning corpses. "You tell us what you remember, and we'll fill you in."

Durlan picked up Elara's completely limp form. He noticed my worry and said, "She's alive. Though right now I want to kill her."

"How did she heal you?" Amrynn asked, standing with fists clenched at his sides.

Durlan turned and carried Elara into the house, ignoring the question.

We followed.

He set her on the couch, glaring at her.

Why was he mad at her? What had that white energy been?

"Durlan," Amrynn growled.

"I didn't ask her to do it," he snapped and bared his teeth at Amrynn. "I never would have asked that of her."

"Durlan," Myrin said softly.

He exhaled loudly and ran a hand through his hair. Or, attempted to, but there were tangles and debris that hindered his move. "She gave me part of her life force. Elara shortened her life to heal me."

"By how much?" I asked, my heart hammering in my chest.

"I don't know!" Durlan yelled. "This damn Seelie woman just doesn't listen. We're supposed to protect her, not the other way around. Why did Amara even agree?" He plopped down on the floor and put his face in his hands.

Daniel examined her wounds and scowled at her neck. "Why is there a bandage here?"

"That happened before the Cu Sith showed up," Durlan mumbled. "Don't ask."

Daniel tore her shirt open so he could clean her wounds. There were several cuts on her shoulder and chest, likely claw marks from the Cu Sith.

Amrynn said, "I'm going to the ship."

Kydrus set his hand on his shoulder. "Me, too."

No one missed the fierce expression on Amrynn's face. I just couldn't understand why he wore it. We were all shocked and upset, but it was hardly Durlan's fault.

"Let's finish packing and get back to the ship," Myrin said. "The sooner we leave, the better."

Durlan stood suddenly and loomed over Elara. "Amara," he growled. "Get out here, right now."

Elara's eyes opened, their color changing to Amara's. "Don't be angry," Amara said softly. "She wanted to save you and this was the only way."

"How could you let her do that?" Durlan snapped. "You know I wouldn't want that."

Amara smiled. "She loves you. She had other reasons, which she used to convince me."

"Like what?" Durlan asked and folded his arms across his chest.

"I won't reveal that. If she wishes to, she will, but I doubt it," Amara said.

"How much did she give me? How much of her life did she lose to heal me?" Durlan asked.

Everyone tensed, waiting for the answer.

"Do you really want to know?" she asked. "What will knowing benefit you or her?"

"I need to know," Durland said, his voice soft. "Please."

"Two hundred years," Amara said.

I fell onto the chair behind me. The others looked as stricken as I was.

Durlan stormed out of the house, not even shutting the door on his way out.

Venali left, too, I hoped he was going to follow after Durlan.

"She'll sleep for two days," Amara said. "Let her rest and don't be hard on her." She looked at Myrin. "She did what her heart felt was right. Don't punish her for that."

Myrin nodded. "Okay."

She smiled. "Don't fret, my loves. She and I have a plan."

"That you won't tell us," I guessed.

Her eyes stopped glowing and closed.

Amara had left.

"Anyone else convinced Elara is planning to sacrifice herself?" I asked, a lump in my throat at the thought of losing her.

No one answered me, but I knew the answer.

Now the question was, how to prevent it?

CHAPTER 7
ELARA

I REALLY HAD TO PEE, but I knew when I opened my eyes, I would have to face seven angry mates. One who was going to be *super* mad.

My bladder rebelled, and I was forced to sit up. I was on Daniel's bed, but we were not in his house.

I held still, let my senses adjust, and took everything in.

Wood creaked. The ground swayed gently. Water crashed nearby.

Ship. We were on the ship.

I slid out of bed and walked until I found what served as a restroom.

Once done, I headed for the stairs that led to the top of the ship where everyone likely was. Nervous, I froze at the bottom of the stairs.

What was I going to say to them? To him?

"Best to get it over with," Myrin said behind me.

I yelped and spun around.

He looked sad, which was not the reaction I had expected.

"I'm not sorry," I said. "I'd do it again...for any of you."

Myrin nodded. "We know."

I frowned. "You're not mad at me?"

He chuckled, but there was no mirth in it. "I'm furious, but yelling at you won't do either of us any good."

I wasn't sure I preferred this to yelling.

"Go on," Myrin urged. "You can't hide here forever."

I could try.

With a resigned sigh, I walked up the stairs and into the fading sunlight, shielding my eyes from it.

"You're awake," Daniel said. "How does your shoulder feel?"

I looked at my shapeshifter mate, his rounded ears peeking out of his hair and smiled. "Fine."

He didn't return my smile, just nodded and resumed carving a piece of wood.

At the front of the ship, Durlan stood, arms folded, looking out at the water.

Taking a breath for courage, I walked to him and stood at his side, looking out at the waves.

He dropped his arms to his sides, then dropped to the ground in a bow.

I turned, mouth agape. "Wh—"

"I failed you. I failed to protect you. By rights, you should cast me out. I deserve no less."

"You didn't fail me. You're not going anywhere. Amara needs you," I choked on a lump in my throat. "I need you."

He didn't move.

"Stand, please," I said.

He stood, but wouldn't look at me.

"Are you going to ignore me the rest of my life?" I asked. "If you want to yell at me, that's okay. I won't apologize, though."

"Why are you so carefree with your life?" he asked, looking up at me with a pained expression. "Why don't you value it?"

I rested my hand on his chest, over his fast beating heart. "I'm a Seelie girl. Raised a slave. Queen by blood. I have one goal, one reason for being important. That is as Amara's vessel. I am here to help defeat the dark god. Then..." Exhaling loudly, I continued. "Then, my usefulness to Amara is over. The Seelie need righting, but whether it is me or another who does it, is not important." I gripped his chest lightly. "Keeping you alive to help Amara, keeping you alive is what is important. I'll give up every year of my life to keep you alive to be with Amara."

He pulled me forward, crushing me against his body. "I want you to live. I want to see you smiling and laughing a thousand years from now. You are important. You are important to me...to them." He jerked his head over mine, and I turned, all of the others stood nearby. "You do not have to sacrifice yourself. We don't want you to sacrifice yourself. There must be another way. There *has* to be another way."

I pushed away from him, tears forming in my eyes. "You don't understand."

"Explain it, then," he yelled. "Why do you have to sacrifice yourself?"

"Because I'd rather die than live my life without you," I yelled back. I clapped a hand over my mouth, eyes wide.

Crap. I hadn't meant to say that out loud.

I ran to the captain's cabin and locked the door behind me.

Crap. Crap. Crap. What had I just done?

"You're going to have to face them," Amara whispered in my mind.

"I can stay in here until we get to our destination," I said.

"Just tell them," she said with a sigh.

The door to the cabin groaned and then was pulled completely off its hinges and tossed across the deck.

Daniel stood in the open doorway, dusting off his hands. "Much better."

I glared at him.

He stalked inside, grabbed me, and tossed me over his shoulder.

"Hey," I yelled and tried to get free.

A warm palm slapped my butt. "Quiet."

My eyes widened. He'd spanked me.

He carried me out to the deck where the others were, set me on a barrel, and folded his arms across his chest. "Explain yourself," he said.

"We're running out of options," I said. "Amara and I merged more, which wasn't supposed to happen. At the end of this, we'll have two choices: separate or merge. But it depends on how things go against the dark god. We may not have a choice."

Myrin's eyes hardened. "Amara is considering giving herself to him, isn't she?"

I nodded. "She'd separate from me if she does that. That's our last resort option."

"You have your own plan that involves sacrificing yourself," Amrynn said, his silver hair blowing in the wind.

I nodded again. "I do. It might be the only way to save you all and Amara."

All seven growled.

Folding my arms across my chest, I held their glares. "I'm preparing for worse case scenarios. I don't want to die, but I know it's possible."

"We won't let you," Amrynn growled. "I won't let you sacrifice yourself."

Shrugging, I hopped off the barrel. "You'll try, but I have plan for that, too."

"Why don't you share these plans with us?" Durlan asked.

"Because you'll try to come up with a plan to stop me," I said and rolled my eyes. "Let's focus on the current problem. Getting the container."

A creature ran across the deck.

"What?" I yelled.

A tiny goblin. It had something shiny in its hand.

My crown.

"It has my crown," I yelled and ran after it. Where did it think it was going to go?

The guys ran after it. Kydrus teleported in front of it, but the goblin veered left.

Myrin tried to grab it, but it suddenly disappeared.

My mouth hung open.

"Why would a goblin steal her crown?" Durlan asked.

"Where could it have gone?" Daniel asked, lifting his nose to try to find its scent.

I dropped to my butt on the deck. My crown, with Barry's universe, was gone.

"He took it," I whispered, numb.

Venali rested his hand on my head. "I'm sorry," he whispered.

Durlan had made the crown for me, the day we agreed to be mates.

I was fairly certain no one could do anything with the planets in it, but the fear of Barry being freed hit me a second.

Amrynn knelt in front of me. "It'll be okay. We know what type of technology they have and won't be caught off guard if he somehow happens to escape. I don't think he will, though."

Tears welled in my eyes. If I did live, I planned to cherish the crown for its sentimental value. It would remind me of them even when they were gone. Now, I had nothing from them.

"I can make you a new crown," Durlan said softly.

Why did everything always have to become so complicated? Couldn't the universe throw me a bone?

The ship was eerily quiet, all of our moods soured as we continued to sail. The moon rose as night set and the moon and stars shone above us, giving us light to see. The guys moved about robotically, taking care of the ship without uttering a single sound.

I thought I might go crazy with all the quiet, when Ryul began singing a song my mother had sung to me as a child. It was a story of a warrior sent to battle, his children and wife left behind. It ended happily, but was sad for most of it.

His voice carried on the wind, seeming to spread everywhere.

I joined in, my voice melding with his.

As the last lyric faded into the night, I closed my eyes and breathed in the salty ocean air.

Someone started singing a new song, their voice deep and melodic. I opened my eyes and barely stopped from gasping.

I'd had no idea Venali was such a beautiful singer.

Amrynn and Kydrus joined in on the song and then so did Durlan.

Theirs was a lively song, one that sounded like a marching song.

Venali pulled me to my feet and spun us around the deck in a fast dance while he continued to sing.

As soon as that song ended, they sang another. They took turns dancing with me, and by the time we all panted from the exertion, we were all smiling.

If they went with Amara and I lived, I would never find men who could replace them. They were perfect.

Leaning my elbows on the railing, I watched the water sliced through by the ship.

What lay beneath the waves? Were there creatures with as much sentience as us?

"Come to bed," Myrin called.

I turned around and then quickly spun back around as something shiny darted by the boat. I searched for sight of it again, but either I had imagined it, or it was gone.

"You see something?" Myrin asked from behind me.

"Not sure," I muttered.

He took my hand and tugged. "Venali's on watch. If there's something, he'll alert us."

Venali blew me a kiss from the ship's helm.

I pretended to catch it and put it in my pocket.

Myrin chuckled and tugged me below and to our bed.

Amrynn and Kydrus were already under the covers, snoring softly.

I sat on the bed and Myrin pulled my boots off for me.

Crawling slowly, I made my way to the pillows, trying not to disturb my sleeping mates.

I had just started to wiggle beneath the covers when Myrin flung them back.

"I was trying not to wake them," I whispered.

"They woke up as soon as you got on the bed," Myrin said.

Kydrus pulled me down and spooned himself around me. "He's right."

Nestled in his arms, I expected to fall asleep quickly, but sleep continued to evade me.

"You're fidgeting," Myrin said.

"Am not," I whispered.

"Are too," Kydrus said around a yawn.

"Sorry," I sighed.

CHAPTER 8
DANIEL

"She's so infuriating," Ryul growled as he paced across the deck.

Venali steered the ship and kept an eye out from the helm. We didn't need to be awake or out here, but we all felt it was better to have multiple people on watch, rather than just one of us. Plus, although the bed was large enough for us to share, it was nice when there were only two other males in it with Elara.

"She loves you guys. She doesn't want to live without you. I can understand that. I don't want to live without Amara," I said.

Ryul stopped pacing and looked at me, a fierce expression on his face. He took a breath and shook his head. "I keep forgetting that you haven't been around since we met Elara, so you don't know her as well."

That wasn't completely true. I did know her. I did care for her. I just wasn't in love with her like I was in love with Amara. I knew they were connected, but there was a bit of separation between them.

"Would you leave if Amara ceased to exist and it was only Elara?" Venali asked.

I sighed and dropped my head to look back at the carving in progress in my hand. "I don't know."

"She loves you," Venali said. "She can't separate her love for you from Amara."

I nodded. That much I knew.

"She'd be devastated if you left," Ryul said softly.

"I didn't say I would leave for sure," I grumbled.

"We just have to keep them from dying or separating," Venali said. "Easy peasy."

I let out a bark of laughter.

Ryul sighed and sat in front of me. "How are we going to accomplish that? How are we going to keep her from sacrificing herself? She already gave up two centuries of her life for Durlan."

"Don't look at me," I mumbled. "I can't even figure out how to get her to sleep when she's supposed to."

"I sleep when I'm tired," Elara said.

We all spun to look at her as she walked up onto the deck.

She was beautiful, but when the moonlight hit her, it highlighted her cheekbones and made her gorgeous.

Walking with her head raised, staring up at the moon, she made her way to us. Her arms were out a bit, her hands splayed, but I couldn't figure out why.

"If you looked where you were going, you wouldn't have to keep your hands out to avoid bumping into things," Ryul said.

She dropped her head, stuck her tongue out at him, and then raised her face to the moon again. "It's so bright tonight. Full and beautiful."

Venali darted down from the helm, picked her up, and carried her back to the helm where he hugged her against him. "You're beautiful."

Her cheeks reddened, and she smiled. "You're such a sweet talker. How did one of the most deadly males I know become so smooth with women?"

He averted his gaze, acting like he was checking the other direction. "Only sweet for you, my love."

She scoffed and pushed away from him. "Liar." Turning her back, she walked to the edge of the ship and leaned against the railing. "Do we know if there are any sentient creatures in the waters?"

"There are giant sea serpents who are quite intelligent," Venali said. "There are also some other beings who I have heard of, but have never seen."

"How large is a giant sea serpent?" she asked, a little quiver to her lower lip.

"Four times the length of the ship," he said.

Her mouth dropped open, and she spun to face him. "Are you serious? No, you have to be pulling my leg."

"I'm serious," he said. "You don't have to worry about them, Elara. We'll kill them before they hurt you."

"I'm worried about the ship," she said. "How would we get home if they destroyed the ship?"

"We'd have to repair the ship," Venali said.

She edged away from the railing with wide eyes. "What other creatures are out there that I haven't seen?"

"A lot," I said.

She glanced at me. "You've been awfully quiet the last few days. You okay?"

I nodded, resuming my carving.

"What are you carving?" she asked, coming to stand beside me.

"Not really sure yet," I said.

Ryul pulled her down into his lap and kissed her cheek. "Why aren't you sleeping?"

"I couldn't sleep, and I was keeping the others awake," she said.

"Fidgeting?" Ryul asked.

"I do *not* fidget," she grumbled.

"You totally fidget," Ryul said.

She stuck her tongue out at him, and he grasped it with his thumb and finger.

She yelped and tried to pull back, but he held on.

"I told you that I'd grab your tongue if you kept sticking it out at me," he whispered with a victorious smile.

"Let go," she said as he continued to hold it.

"Not until you say the magic words," he said.

"Ryul's a butt," she mumbled.

He tickled her side, making her squeal and thrash. "Say it."

"I'll never surrender," she said as she laughed and struggled against him.

He released her and kissed her cheek. "You're crazy."

"Crazy for seven crazy men," she said and looked up at me with a wide smile.

I wanted to return her smile, but couldn't.

Her smile slipped and she stood, pain etched in her features.

I'd done that. I had caused her pain.

"I'll try to go to sleep," she said in a soft voice, heading back towards the stairs.

Ryul looked at me, and I could feel Venali's eyes on me as well.

As much as I wanted to go to her, to end the pain I had caused, I just continued my carving.

"What was that about?" Ryul asked, standing with a scowl.

"That's between me and her," I said.

"She doesn't know what is going on between you two either, though," Venali said.

I looked up at him. "She said something to you?"

He shook his head. "No, but I can tell. She's hurt because she doesn't know why you're suddenly pushing her away."

There was a crash and then Elara yelled out in pain.

The three of us raced down the stairs.

Elara lay at the bottom of the stairs, body splayed out on the ground and her eyes closed.

"Elara," Ryul yelled and ran to her, checking her. "She's breathing."

The scent of her blood hit me, making me snarl. "She's bleeding."

Ryul looked her over and shook his head. "There are no wounds."

Crap. That was a bad sign.

I walked down to her and sniffed around her body, freezing and tensing when I found the scent in her head. "She's bleeding in her head."

"Wake up Durlan," Venali snapped.

Ryul dashed away.

I cradled her head in my lap and stroked her hair.

Was this my fault? Had she fallen because of the tears streaking her face?

Durlan dropped down beside her and looked at me.

"She's bleeding in her head," I said.

Durlan's eyes widened, and he reached out, pressing his hand to her forehead. Warm light glowed from his hand and covered her head.

A few tense moments later, which I wasn't certain whether I had breathed during, her eyelids fluttered open, and she looked up at Durlan.

"What happened?" she asked.

"You fell down the stairs," Ryul said.

She sat up, and I quickly backed away and stood.

She rubbed at her head. "Oh. I feel like an idiot."

"You need to be careful," Durlan said, giving me a side eye.

"You were bleeding in your head," I said from my new position away from her.

She glanced at me, but quickly averted her eyes. "Sorry to have bothered you," she said, her voice wavering. With slow movements, she stood and headed towards her room.

Durlan stood and arched a brow. "Want to talk about it?"

"He won't even talk to her about it," Ryul said.

I growled. "Mind your own business, boy."

"Boy? I'm over a thousand years older than you," he scoffed and his body tensed.

I hadn't fought against Ryul, but if he attacked me, I wouldn't hold back.

"What's going on?" Myrin asked, coming from the bedroom and stood between us.

I turned and headed back to the deck. "Nothing you need to concern yourself with," I said.

I took over at the helm, since Venali wasn't there.

"You know you can talk to me," Myrin said. "I'm in a similar situation as you."

"You're not sure about her either?" I asked.

He chuckled. "Oh, I'm sure of her, but I've been around her longer. Elara doesn't take long to worm her way into your heart."

"Why couldn't Amara just take her over, like we did with our bodies?" I asked. "It would have made things so much easier."

"Since when has Amara done anything to make things easy?" Myrin asked.

I laughed bitterly. Too right he was.

"Look, you may not be sure about her or any of this, but could you try to go easier on her? She loves you and she doesn't know what to do when you treat her like that. She's young and inexperienced, but her heart is big and she loves with all of it."

"It's not like I hate her or anything," I mumbled.

"She thinks you do," he said.

I spun and gaped at him. "What?"

"She thinks you hate her now. She said she doesn't know what she did wrong, but you are mad at her and hate her and she doesn't know how to fix it because whenever you look at her, she just feels awful and wants to cry," he said.

"She said that?" I asked, an eyebrow arched.

He nodded. "When she came to bed just now. She was in hysterics. Amrynn and Kydrus are calming her down."

I ran a hand through my hair and sighed. "I didn't mean to upset her that much. I don't hate her. I just don't love her like you guys do."

"She's extremely emotional. This entire plan has her on edge, and she's trying to forget that she plans to sacrifice herself and enjoy the little bit of time she has with us before she dies. You're making that hard for her when you're treating her like a stranger."

He held up his hand, stopping me from responding.

"I'm not saying to lie to her or just pretend everything is okay. Just talk to her. She'll understand," he said. He exhaled and asked, "Do you want me to take over so you can get some sleep? I don't think I'll be going to sleep anytime soon."

I shook my head at the thought of going down where she was. "No."

"You can't hide from her forever. You're on a ship together," he chuckled.

"I know," I growled.

He patted my shoulder. "Just think about what I said. She's a sweet girl and none of this is her fault. She didn't want any of this anymore than we did."

I nodded. "I got it. I understand what you're saying."

He nodded and walked away.

At first, I had thought she was fully Amara, just with memory loss or something. The more time I spent with her, the more I realized how different they were. Elara wasn't Amara and I loved Amara, had for centuries. It felt wrong to love another woman, even if she was the vessel. Even if the others loved her.

CHAPTER 9
KYDRUS

I HAD FINALLY GOTTEN her to fall asleep, her head on my chest.

Knowing that she'd had a bleed in her brain worried me and kept me from sleeping.

"Want a break?" Ryul asked as he climbed in bed.

I shook my head. "Just got her to sleep."

He nodded and lay down beside her. "I didn't even know she was hurt," he whispered. "If it weren't for Daniel..." He let his words trail off.

Durlan would have sensed it when he went to heal her, but it was worrisome that she had hurt herself so much.

Part of me wanted to punch Daniel in the face, but I did understand how he felt. I couldn't say I felt the same, because I had loved Elara since we had lived in Linta, but I could understand.

"Don't be hard on him," I whispered to Ryul.

Ryul scoffed and closed his eyes. "Whatever. If they separate, it just means one less man warming her bed with me."

My eyes widened. "So, you've chosen?"

"I had no choice. Elara has been my love for centuries. That's not going to change now. I love Amara, too, but Elara is my childhood friend and first love."

"Any ideas on what she might be planning?" I asked. Of us all, I hoped he might know something.

He sighed and shook his head. "No. I'm trying to think about what she could want or plan to do, but I can't."

"If you think of anything, let us know, okay?" I asked.

Elara stirred, nestling her head on my chest and sighing as her skin rubbed against mine. "Kydrus," she whispered in her sleep.

My heart swelled at the sweet sound of my name on her lips. The love she conveyed in that one word was beyond measure.

Ryul and I stopped talking and just watched her sleep.

"Someday, I'm going to kill that asshole who haunts her and we're going to live happily ever after," Ryul whispered.

I chuckled. "Let's hope so. First, we have to figure out how to deal with the humans we are headed towards."

He nodded. "I know. Apparently, Amara has a plan for us to get past their defenses and get on the island. Amara hasn't even told Elara the plan, though. That worries me more than anything else."

That worried me, too. What could Amara have planned that could get us past their defenses and to land without being seen or destroyed?

From what I had heard, no one made it to land. No one made it close without being blown up.

Would she cause a distraction somewhere else to draw attention away? Or would our crazy goddess do something else?

CHAPTER 10
ELARA

The day had been quiet, and then a cannonball landed near the ship, making the water spray up over me.

Two more feet and I would have been hit by it.

"Pirates," Venali yelled, excitement in his voice.

"Stay near the mast," Myrin ordered me.

I obeyed, running to stand against it.

Venali looked ready to jump ship and swim to fight the enemy.

The pirates yelled and raised their weapons as they drew closer.

Didn't they realize something was wrong when we weren't fleeing or cowering?

They fired another cannonball, and Venali caught it in his hands. The pirates and I gaped. He pivoted, leaned back on one leg, and then threw the cannonball back at their ship. It hit their hull and crashed through it.

The pirates still drew closer, their greed outweighing their survival instincts.

Ryul looked at Myrin.

Myrin shook his head. "Let Venali have some fun."

Venali smiled wide and then roared at the pirates.

Daniel came up to his side, shifted, and roared as well.

"They've got a shapeshifter," one of the pirates yelled.

"Try to keep it alive, they sell well," another pirate yelled back.

Daniel snarled.

The ship drew alongside ours and both Venali and Daniel leapt aboard their ship, tearing through them with ease.

A couple pirates made it onto our ship, but Myrin dispatched them with a bored expression on his face, most of his attention on Venali and Daniel.

"Elara," Kydrus yelled.

I turned and immediately had to duck a pirate's sword.

Amrynn grabbed the pirate, snapped his neck, and tossed him into a small boat that had come up on the opposite side of the ship.

It had snuck over while we had been distracted.

Amrynn jumped down, killed all of the humans in the small boat, and then punched a hole in the bottom of it. He leapt back up onto our ship.

The boat and bodies sank.

I reached my hand out, and Amrynn took it, threading our fingers together.

Kydrus came to my other side and kissed my cheek.

I smiled up at him. "Thanks for the warning."

"You're always getting into trouble," he said with a shake of his head.

I stuck my tongue out at him and then faced the pirate ship again.

The screams had tapered down and there wasn't as much movement.

"All clear," Venali called.

Durlan stumbled up the stairs, rubbing his eyes. "Everything handled?"

"Yes, go back to sleep," Kydrus said.

Durlan yawned and stretched his arms up over his head, his shirt riding up enough to give me a view of the v of muscles below his belly button. He caught me looking and winked.

"I'm going to go over," Kydrus said. "Keep an eye on her, she almost lost her head," he said to Durlan.

Durlan looked down at me with a scowl. "Explain."

"Pirates," I said with a shrug, like that answered everything.

Durlan looked at Amrynn, a brow arched.

"A pirate snuck onto the ship while Venali and Daniel were on the other ship. We were all distracted by that chaos. She almost lost her head," Amrynn summarized.

"I ducked," I whispered.

A long sigh came from Durlan, but no words.

Venali hopped back onto our ship, a huge smile on his face.

"Have fun?" I asked.

He pulled me from Amrynn and kissed me deeply, his tongue sweeping across mine twice before he pulled back. "I did."

Daniel leapt onto our ship, now in his human form. Unlike Venali, he wasn't smiling.

I wanted to ask him what was wrong, but the stab of pain in my chest had me turning away instead.

"Anything good on their ship?" Amrynn asked.

"Yeah. Kydrus and Myrin are figuring out what to grab," Daniel said.

"I'll go help," Amrynn said. He slid his hand along my lower back as he passed, the warmth radiating up my spine.

"I'm going to practice," I said, pulling away from Venali.

"You think that's wise?" Daniel asked.

"It will give you time with Amara," I snapped. "So, why are you complaining? Or do you not want to talk to her either?"

He growled and stalked closer to me, but stopped when I looked up at him with tears in my eyes.

Venali set his hand on my hip, but I refused to look at him.

Instead, I let Amara out.

This time was different, though.

Normally, she took over, but this time it was more of a merger. I was still in control, but she could move us or use her powers.

“We’ve merged more,” our combined voices said.

Venali and Durlan’s eyes widened.

“We’re going to have to stop this until I’m needed. If we merge much more, we won’t be able to separate.”

“Is that a bad thing?” Venali asked.

“It could be,” we said.

“Because your plans to sacrifice yourself won’t be possible?” Venali asked, his brows pinched.

“Yes.”

“We don’t want you sacrificing yourself,” Daniel said.

“You don’t get a choice,” I said.

Daniel growled. “Why not just separate now? Let Elara go back to her life and we will continue with our mission.”

Amara’s power flared, and I lost consciousness.

CHAPTER 11
VENALI

The changeover was obvious. When Amara took over, her body glowed, her eyes glowed, and her aura changed.

"Why have you suddenly decided you dislike her?" Amara asked. "You didn't seem to have an issue the first day, when you sealed your mate bond."

He flinched. "That was before I realized she wasn't my true mate. You are, but you aren't her all the time."

"She is your true mate. Even if I was gone, you two would be bonded," Amara said.

Daniel scowled at her. "What?"

"It's complicated, I know, but she would have been your mate even if I hadn't chosen her," she said.

I shook my head. "That can't be right. The only reason Myrin and Daniel became her mate was because of your connection to her."

Amara laughed. "You boys are so dense sometimes. No, she's been bound to you since birth. My joining with her was part of it, but even if I separated from her now, you'd be hers still."

"That can't be," Myrin said, having returned to the ship. "I've always had my memories and the only time I sensed her was when your powers were awoken."

"Is this why you two have been so standoffish to her? This is why you've been making her cry?" Amara asked, her brows creasing and power flaring.

Myrin's eyes widened. "Cry?"

"Listen to me," she snarled. "If you hadn't merged with your hosts, they would be her mates. You are my mates, but you are also hers."

"Our bodies may be hers," Daniel said. "However, our souls are yours."

"And since I can't separate you from your bodies, what does that mean?" she asked, hands on her hips and a brow arched.

"That we're hers, too," Myrin said.

"Separate from her so we can end this," Daniel said.

"Why are you so bent on not falling for her?" Amara asked. "What will you do if we merge?"

"If you merge, it won't be a problem," Daniel said. "Right now, she isn't you most of the time. Now, this body may want her, but my soul..." He hit his chest. "My soul wants you. How can you make us endure this?"

She growled and marched up to him, stopping when she stood before him and then her feet floated above the deck until she was eye level to Daniel. "Endure? What are you enduring? A girl loving you? A girl wanting to touch you and speak to you? You endure nothing, but your own stupidity and stubbornness. She is the one enduring. She is the one planning to kill herself so she won't live without you. She is the one practicing day and night to fight a battle I've forced her to have a part in. You know nothing of her pain and sorrow. All you do is feel sorry that your body enjoys her and are blinded to what the truth is. She would sacrifice everything for you and you are acting like a...a..."

"Moron?" I suggested.

"Yes! A moron. Pull your head out of your furry butt before she dies and all you have left are regrets."

"Help us stop her from killing herself," Amrynn pleaded.

"No," Amara snapped. "She and I have our plans. She and I will figure this out. I'm half tempted to send you all away so you won't be such a distraction."

"Don't," I pleaded. "Daniel may have his doubts, but I was Elara's mate before my memories came back. I can't lose her."

"You're the one who won't talk to us and let us help you," Daniel snapped.

She spun back to face him, fury etched across her features. "The next time I see you will be when we've reached the shores of Zenlop. Try not to upset your mate between now and then."

"You're our mate," Daniel growled.

Light burst from her, making all of us shield our eyes.

"So is she. The sooner you accept that, the better. I mean it, if you cause her undue stress, she and I will leave you behind."

With that, her light faded, and Elara's body settled on the deck, her eyes closed.

After several tense moments of staring at her, Daniel stalked off.

There wasn't much we could say to him at this point. Either he accepted what Amara had said, or we risked them fighting on their own.

I wouldn't let that happen.

Squatting down, I scooped Elara up in my arms and carried her to our room. Once she was tucked in, I returned to help transfer the items we'd found to our ship.

Myrin set the pirate ship on fire and Kydrus steered us clear of it.

No one spoke. All of us were absorbing Amara's words.

Whatever I had to do to keep Elara safe, I would do it. Even if it meant abandoning my brothers.

CHAPTER 12
ELARA

My body felt abnormally heavy, as did my soul. Instead of going up to the top deck, I stayed in bed, staring at the wooden beams overhead for several days.

I had no idea what Amara had told the guys, but they were more affectionate while seeming distant at the same time.

All of them, but Daniel.

He'd been missing for two days.

No, not missing...hiding.

I'd tried not to let it bother me, to be numb to the fact he suddenly didn't view me as a mate.

None of it worked.

Lying in bed, I tried again to numb myself.

It didn't matter because I likely wouldn't survive this battle anyway.

Footsteps approached.

I rolled over, facing away from the entryway.

"Are you going to lay in bed all day?" Amrynn asked.

"Yes," I replied.

He flopped onto the bed beside me, moving down so he could look into my eyes. "You need some sun. You're getting pale."

"I'm fine," I said. I used my power to draw on the sun, to fill my body with its warmth a moment and then released it. "There, I've had some sun."

He scowled. "Elara—"

"How close are we to our destination?" I asked.

"A day or two we think," he said.

I rolled over and closed my eyes. "Wake me then."

He left the room after placing a gentle kiss to my temple.

The day continued like that, with each guy stopping by trying to convince me to get up. Some brought me food, but none pushed me too hard.

At night, they took their shifts sharing the bed with me and on watch, but aside from soft words of love, they stopped trying to convince me.

The next two days, they didn't even try to ask me to leave. They'd sit with me a bit, bring me food and water, and that was it.

Finally, we reached Zenlop's shores.

I scarfed down a huge meal and then hurried to the figurehead.

There were long cannons atop walls lining the shores.

"I'll handle it," Amara said in my mind. "Tell the boys to shield their eyes."

"Shield your eyes," I yelled back to them.

Amara took control, but kept me conscious. She used my power of the moon to control the waves, creating larger and larger ones that had people running about. Then, a massive flare from the sun blinded everyone. She had the ship dock in the center of the docks and leapt into the middle of the people who were all covering their eyes.

Ryul placed a spell on the ship and then on us so we all appeared human.

Running, we moved as far into the town as we could before the humans could see again.

Amara's powers left, but I was still able to move with no issues. All of our practice had finally paid off.

Venali stayed at my side while the rest fanned out. We had decided a large group would draw too much attention.

The museum came into view, a small line waiting at the door, passing through machines that beeped.

"Metal detectors," I whispered.

Venali cursed. "I'll pass my sword to Myrin."

I nodded and continued forward, getting into line.

Once inside, I moved to the right to wait for Venali.

Ryul joined me instead. "He's checking the perimeter. Plus, I need to be in here to set my illusion."

We made our way around the exhibits, searching for the jar. I wasn't exactly certain what it looked like, but knew I would sense it.

When I was about to give up, I spotted it. The last item, near the exit.

Ryul and I stepped up to the glass box it sat in, both smiling.

"I never thought I would get this chance," Barry whispered in my ear.

Turning, I gaped at the gun now pressed to my side.

"When I was freed from the prison you put us in, I agreed to do whatever the man asked of me. Foiling your plot against him, getting a chance to kill you, those were bonuses."

Ryul growled, but I held up my hand.

"That man will destroy the universe. All he cares about is power," I whispered.

"He can destroy everything as long as you die," Barry hissed.

Ryul raised his hand, spinning his magic around the humans, and I spun away from Barry.

Barry smiled and shot me in the stomach. "Your illusions don't work on me."

I cried out and clutched at the pain and tried to stop the blood that flowed over my fingers.

Ryul kicked Barry's gun from his hand and then tossed him across the room.

Mustering my strength, pulling some from the sun, I shattered the glass box around the jar, grabbed it, and limped towards the exit.

Ryul picked me up and raced outside.

Alarms blared behind us and people in uniforms with weapons rushed after us.

Durlan, Myrin, Venali, and Kydrus teleported to us, and then teleported us to the ship.

I drew on my magic, pulled on the moon and had a huge wave of water pull us out into the sea.

The cannons exploded from the shores and cannonballs dropped around us.

Ryul set me down, and I cried out in pain.

"What happened?" Amrynn asked.

"Get us out," I snapped. "Now."

His eyes widened, and he rushed to the helm, steering us away.

Maniacal laughter floated on the wind. I knew it was Barry's.

Durlan tore my shirt open and started to heal me.

"There's a metal ball inside," I cried. I realized I was still holding the jar. "Myrin."

He stepped forward.

"Jar," I said, my lip trembling and body growing cold.

He took it and disappeared.

Daniel leaned down.

I wanted to swat him away, but had no strength.

"She's poisoned," he snarled.

Durlan pulled out a knife and pressed on my stomach, around my wound.

I screamed and felt like throwing up and passing out at the same time.

The cannonballs were still firing, but I couldn't tell how close. Sounds were distorted with some far away noises louder and close ones sounding far away.

"Ryul, charm her," Durlan said.

I whimpered.

Ryul set his hand on my head. "Dream happy dreams while Durlan fixes you up."

The ship disappeared, and I stood in the castle with Ryul. He tapped my arm and ran down the hallway.

"You're it," he yelled over his shoulder.

I laughed and ran after him.

CHAPTER 13
DANIEL

Regret tugged at my heart and made my inner animal angry.

I knew I should have gone with them.

Instead, I had stayed on the ship, hiding below deck like I had been for a week.

Now, she was dying and there was nothing I could do to stop it.

I stood in the entryway to the room Myrin had built for her and stared at the small woman lying in the center of the bed.

My mate.

It had taken me several days to accept Amara's explanation.

As I stood there, I could feel our bond, proving Amara's point.

The bond thrummed, but much weaker than before.

Whatever the poison was that the bastard had used, it wreaked havoc on her system.

Even Durlan's powers couldn't defeat it. He had done his best and the others took turns as well, but it seemed we had to let her body do the rest.

Elara whimpered in her sleep and sweat dotted her brow.

Without thought, I crossed the gap and sat beside her. Resting my hand against her head, I found it burning hot.

She stopped whimpering and pressed her face into my hand a bit.

Reaching over, I dipped the washcloth on the side table in water, and then draped it across her forehead.

She exhaled and her breathing evened out.

"I'm sorry," I whispered, spooning my body around hers. "Don't die on me, Elara. We need you. I need you."

She didn't respond.

"She'll pull through," Kydrus said from behind me.

I rolled over and stood. "How can you be so sure?"

He smiled as he looked at her, pure love glowing in his eyes. "Elara's always been a fighter. She's gone up against worse odds and pulled through."

"I wish I had known her before," I whispered. "You all have such a fondness for her it makes me wish I had known her longer."

"She's still very close to the same. Well, the same once she remembered a time before she was a slave," Kydrus said.

"You've known her the longest, right? Elara, I mean, not Amara."

He smirked. "I know who you meant. And, yes."

"Has she always been so..." I struggled for the right word.

"Frustrating? Endearing? Magnetic? Prone to danger? Yes," he said.

I chuckled.

"She wants to prove herself. She wants to save everyone. She rushes in without a plan. She does all this and it all comes from her heart. She's one of the most pure and honest beings I have ever met. She wears her heart on her sleeve and it often got her into trouble. She's tried to close her heart, but she loves fiercely, so it is impossible for her to be alone. She lived alone while in Linta, where I ruled, and I could see the toll it took on her. I tried to get close to her, but fear ruled her then."

"It seems to rule her still," I said.

He nodded. "Fear of being alone and losing us definitely make up most of her decisions."

"I didn't believe Amara," I whispered. "I did just like Elara did with you; I tried to push her away. But I can't. She's part of me."

Kydrus set his hand on my shoulder. "She'll live through this. You'll get your chance to apologize."

Would she accept it, though?

He squeezed my shoulder and left.

I hoped he was right. I needed a chance to apologize, to beg her for another chance. To worship her as I would Amara.

CHAPTER 14
AMRYNN

If I could, I would go right back to Zenlop, find Barry, and tear his head off.

That bastard had not only shot Elara, but had poisoned her as well.

My rage had no outlet, which only let it fester.

No matter how much we used our healing magic, we couldn't heal Elara.

Durlan sat beside me in the dining area, his shoulders slumped.

Perhaps I should have tried to console him, but no words came to mind.

Someone set a hand on my shoulder.

I grabbed their arm and jerked them forward, slamming their face against the table, my teeth bared and ready to tear out their throat.

Kydrus looked up at me with sad eyes. "Didn't mean to startle you," he said softly.

Quickly, I released him and sat back down.

"Any change?" Durlan asked.

Kydrus shook his head and sat beside me.

Durlan sighed, his eyes shadowed in darkness.

"Let's stop at the nearest port and see if we can find any medicines," Kydrus said.

Something I'd heard while captured on Barry's spaceship surfaced.

"What about a transfusion?" I asked Durlan.

He looked up at me. "Huh?"

"A blood transfusion. If we can cycle our blood into hers, maybe our magic will help her body fight the poison faster," I said.

Durlan's eyes widened, and he leapt to his feet. "Yes! Why hadn't I thought of that?"

"Do we have the items necessary for that procedure?" Kydrus asked.

"No, but if we can drop anchor, I can teleport to Emortalia, get the supplies, and teleport back," Durlan said.

It was difficult to teleport back to a ship, since it wasn't a stationary place.

"Are you sure?" I asked.

He smiled. "Worse that will happen is I teleport to the wrong place and have to swim a bit."

"We'll need to get near an island or somewhere with shallower water first," Kydrus said.

I stood and headed for the stairs. "I'll tell Myrin about our idea."

Finally, a chance to do something. A chance to help Elara.

The three of us raced to the helm, excited to tell Myrin.

We all came to a halt when a dark figure coalesced against the mast.

"I hear your pet is dying," a deep voice said from the figure.

"Leave," Myrin growled.

The figure looked at Myrin, his eyeless face still managing a glare somehow. “If it weren’t for you, she would have been mine thousands of years ago.”

Myrin smirked. “What can I say? I’m just more handsome than you.”

The figure, the dark god, sped towards Myrin, but stopped just before him. “I’m here to offer you assistance. You would be wise not to anger me.”

“We don’t want your help,” I snapped. “You helped enough by letting that maniac free.”

“Give me the jar, and I’ll give you the antidote. Your pet won’t have to die,” he said.

“No,” all seven of us said at the same time.

“You’re going to let her die?” he asked. “You’re going to sacrifice that poor, innocent girl? For what? A plan that won’t work?”

If it wouldn’t work, he wouldn’t try to get the jar from us. Plus, Elara almost died to get it. We couldn’t give it up and let her pain be for nothing.

“How do we know your antidote would even work?” Myrin asked. “You could be poisoning her more instead of giving us an antidote.”

“I may be ruthless at times, but I’m not heartless,” the dark god said. He sighed, seeing we weren’t swayed. With a flick of his wrist, he produced Elara’s crown. “A show of good faith.” He set it on the deck. “I’ll be back tomorrow. You’ll be a bit more willing to negotiate then, I’m sure.”

He disappeared, and I raced to Elara. His statement had fear coursing through my veins. No, she couldn’t get worse. Not when we had a plan.

Elara’s body was drenched in sweat, her cheeks red, and her breath came in pained gasps.

I tore the blankets from the bed, my eyes widening when I saw the blood staining the bandage over her gunshot wound.

“Durlan,” I yelled.

"Already here," he said, cutting open her bandage.

Hovering on the far side of the room, I waited for his prognosis.

Please let her be okay. Please.

With quick efficiency, he changed out the bandage and then dabbed the wet washcloth from the side table against her face and neck.

"The poison's spreading," he whispered.

I hurried out to Myrin, who was speaking to Kydrus.

Everyone looked at me. "Her wound was bleeding again. Durlan said the poison is spreading."

Myrin altered our course.

"Maybe we should give him the jar," Ryul whispered.

"No," Daniel said. "That's exactly what he wants."

Ryul stood and stepped into Daniel's face. "Just because you don't care about Elara, doesn't mean she should die. Some of us love her, Amara or not."

Daniel shoved Ryul back. "You have no idea what I think."

"Let's find out," Ryul yelled and waved his hand.

Daniel's body tensed.

"Ryul, stop," Myrin snapped.

Ryul kept his eyes glued to Daniel, working his illusion.

As wrong as it was, I wanted to know how he felt about Elara, too.

Daniel growled and tried to move, but Ryul's magic held him in place. Tears dripped down his face, and he fell to his knees. He dropped his head into his hands and his body shook with sobs.

Ryul stepped back and nodded. "Fine, you can live, but remember that I could do this to you a million different ways all day for thousands of years. You hurt her again and what you just saw will be a dream."

Daniel looked up at us and then around as if searching for something with wide eyes. "What?" he rasped.

Ryul went below deck, a smart move considering Daniel's fury.

"What was that?" Daniel demanded.

"Ryul can make you see whatever he wants you to," Venali said. "I'm guessing he showed you Elara die?"

"She's...she's not..." Daniel looked around.

"No, she's alive," Myrin said. "He wanted to see if you actually cared about her."

"What did you see?" I asked.

"Durlan carried her dead body to us," Daniel said. He stood and headed towards the stairs, no doubt going to check on her.

Once he was gone, I looked up at Myrin. "Well, now we know he cares for her."

Myrin shook his head. "Ryul's going to get his ass kicked one of these days."

"Most likely," I agreed.

"How far to the nearest island?" Kydrus asked.

"Half a day," Myrin said.

"That far?" I asked and looked back the way Daniel had gone.

Would she survive that long?

"We need to keep the jar safe," Kydrus said. "He's clearly threatened by it."

Myrin nodded. "Let's rotate someone staying in the room with both Elara and the jar."

"What are we going to do when he comes back tomorrow?" I asked. "He could sink the ship or send more creatures after us."

Myrin tied the wheel to keep it headed in the correct direction and then dropped to his back on the deck with a dramatic sigh. "I don't know. I don't have all the answers."

Kydrus walked over and sat next to him. "You mean you aren't perfect?"

Myrin laughed. "Hardly. Part of me wants to give him the jar just so we can be sure Elara is safe. But I know she and Amara would be pissed and if they risked themselves like this, it's vital to their plan."

"The plan to sacrifice themselves?" I asked.

Myrin scowled. "Why couldn't Amara have found a vessel less stubborn than Elara?"

"Wouldn't have been hard," I muttered.

All three of us laughed.

"Food," Venali called from below deck.

"I'll bring you a plate," Kydrus told Myrin. "You just keep stewing on the ground."

"Thanks," Myrin said.

I waited until Kydrus left to approach Myrin.

He arched a brow at me.

"Barry being lose provides many possible issues," I said. "Those humans were already more advanced than us if they had metal detectors. He could teach them how to make worse weapons and how to find Minloa."

He groaned. "Wonderful. We so needed a battle with the humans on top of everything else."

"A battle might help unite the Seelie and Unseelie," I said. "Especially if they see you fighting with us at Elara's side."

"Only if we survive this," he grumbled.

Only if Elara survived this.

"Any idea how to convince them to merge fully?" he asked me.

I laughed. "If I knew that, I would have done it already."

Myrin sighed. "Anxiety wasn't something I experienced before, but I find myself dealing with it daily now. How do we keep them both alive?"

"First, we get to an island so Durlan can get the items necessary for the transfusion," I said. "Then, we pray."

"It bothers me that Amara hasn't healed her. Is that a bad sign, or is it just not something she can do for her vessel?" Myrin asked.

"I've been wondering the same thing," I admitted.

CHAPTER 15
DANIEL

HER BODY BURNED with a fever that worried me more than the poison. High fevers in humans could cause brain damage. But she was Seelie, did that make a difference?

With gentle strokes, I dried the sweat from her body with a towel and then used the wet washcloth from the basin to try to cool her.

Ryul's powers had shown me her death, and it proved to me even more that I couldn't let her die. Seeing her dead body had shattered what was left of the wall I had built between us.

"You can fight this," I whispered in her ear. "You fought Cu Sith and redcaps. A poison should be child's play to you."

Carefully, I set her crown on her head, setting it so it rested on her hair.

The crown began to glow.

"Durlan," I yelled and stood from the bed, backing up in case some crazy magic started happening.

Durlan ran inside and his eyes widened. "What did you do?"

"I just set it on her," I whispered.

Elara's body began glowing and then she completely froze, no breathing and no heartbeat.

No. Had I just killed her?

We rushed forward, but Amara's voice whispered in our heads, "She's frozen herself. This will keep the poison from spreading and buy you some time. Leave her and hurry towards your healing solution."

My body shook as I stared at her seemingly lifeless body, but at least now I could sense the magic cocooning her.

"Stay with her," Durlan said. "Don't let the crown leave her head and keep the jar safe."

"Where are you going?" I asked and sat back on the bed.

"To see if we can make the ship move faster," he said. "I want to get the supplies as soon as possible so I can hear her heartbeat again."

We'd secured the jar by wrapping it in blankets and tied it to the wall so it couldn't fall and break. I double checked the blankets and then lay beside Elara.

"Hold on, beautiful. We'll save you soon," I whispered.

CHAPTER 16
KYDRUS

The dark god returned the next day, leaning against the mast in his shadowy black form again. "Your answer?" he asked.

"We will not give up the item we obtained. Be gone," Myrin growled.

The dark god sighed. "So be it."

He disappeared and then an ear-splitting roar made us all cover our ears.

The ship rocked and before the ship rose a sea serpent twice as big as any I had ever seen before.

"Wonderful," Venali said with a wide smile. "I've been itching to kill something." He cracked his knuckles and neck and walked towards the railing.

"Don't get reckless," Ryul called after him.

Venali rolled his eyes. "What are you, my mother?"

I snickered. "He'll be fine, Ryul. Let the big man have some fun and just sit back and enjoy the show."

Venali saluted me and faced the serpent. "Come on, you ugly, scaly, piece of carp!"

Apparently, the serpent understood our language because it screeched and tried to bite Venali.

Venali dodged its giant jaws, leapt up onto its head, and punched one of its eyes so hard that it exploded in a mess of goop and blood.

"Ouch," I whispered and cringed. I was all for killing the serpent, but that didn't mean I couldn't feel bad for it.

It thrashed and tried to dislodge Venali, but he held on to its now empty socket, laughing maniacally.

"He is definitely deranged," Ryul whispered.

Amrynn snorted.

Myrin threw a spear coated in his black flames into its throat. The flames spread quickly, but he kept them away from Venali.

Venali punched the serpent's head until the bone broke and then he fell into its skull.

"Uh..." I looked at Amrynn who was staring at the serpent and the spot Venali had fallen in with wide eyes as well.

Myrin extinguished his flames, likely unsure where Venali would come out and we all stood in silence as we waited to see what would happen.

"Should one of us—" Ryul's words were cut off by Venali roaring.

The serpent's head exploded, bits of it raining down on the boat and around us into the water.

Venali stood atop the ruined stump of the serpent, panting and snarling. Then, the serpent's body fell into the water with a loud splash and sent us careening backwards.

Venali teleported to us, flinging serpent goo off of him. "Well, that didn't go as planned."

I doubled over in laughter and everyone else joined in.

"Jump back in the ocean," Myrin ordered him. "You smell awful."

"Who wants sea snake steak for dinner?" Venali asked as he leapt overboard.

"Sounds great," I called down to him.

He scrubbed at his body in the sea water and then swam to the serpent and cut of some large chunks that he carried with him as he teleported back.

"You're all insane," Daniel said behind us.

We turned to find him standing at the steps, eyes wide and mouth agape.

We all just smiled at him, which earned us a headshake from him before he went back down to sit with Elara.

CHAPTER 17
ELARA

SOMETHING WARM WAS BEING PUMPED into my veins. It smelled like Venali.

Opening my eyes was a lot harder than it should have been.

What was going on?

Slowly, my eyes opened.

The room was dim, but I knew where we were instantly, the room in the ship.

"She's awake," Venali yelled.

I cringed. "Too loud."

"Sorry," he whispered and turned my head with his fingertips so he could look at me. He had tears in his eyes.

"Hi," I said softly.

Footsteps pounded on the wooden floor, and then all seven of my mates crowded into the room.

All were smiling.

"What's going on?" I asked.

Durlan rested his hand on my forehead and used his magic to check me over. "It's gone," he whispered. "The poison is all gone."

"Poison?" I gasped. "What are you talking about?" I looked at the tube in my arm and fear consumed me. Memories of Barry using similar tubes to steal my blood flashed before my eyes. I tried to rip them out with a cry, but several pairs of hands held me down.

Durlan removed the tube and bandaged my arm where it had been.

Amrynn kissed my brow. "It's okay. It was necessary to heal you."

Durlan removed a similar tube from Venali's arm.

"Barry shot you with a bullet covered in poison," Amrynn said. "You've been unconscious for a week."

"A week?" I screeched.

"We are about a day out from Eltare," Myrin said.

"The jar?" I asked.

They all pointed to a bundle of blankets on the wall.

"Safe and secure," Ryul said.

"A week," I repeated.

"*He* tried to barter an antidote for the jar, but we refused," Daniel said. "He's sent dozens of creatures, but we've defeated them all."

I looked around at my guys and realized what I should have noticed sooner.

They were all exhausted.

Most had dark bags beneath their eyes and their normally straight backs were slumped. It took a lot to do this to Seelie warriors.

"You've been killing yourselves," I chastised. "You're all tired."

"We'll rest when we get to Eltare," Myrin said. He pushed his way to me and kissed my forehead. "I need to return to the helm. I'm glad you're doing better."

The rest took turns kissing me and heading out until it was just Daniel and I.

He cleared his throat while looking at the floor and shifted nervously.

I patted the bed. "Sit with me."

He sat and then pulled me into his arms. "I'm so sorry, Elara. I'm a jerk and I know I don't deserve your forgiveness, but I really am sorry. I care for you and part of me was worried that I was being disloyal to Amara, but—"

I set my hand over his mouth. "I forgive you."

He rested his forehead against mine and closed his eyes. "I'm an idiot. You're amazing and almost losing you really showed me how stupid I was."

"I'm still very immature," I whispered. "The situation could have been handled better on my end."

"Are you hungry?" he asked.

"Actually, I really need to pee," I said and stood on slightly wobbly legs. Luckily, they held and I was able to walk without assistance.

After using the restroom and grabbing a bunch of food, we went to the main deck so I could get some sun.

"You'd think sleeping for a week would mean I wasn't tired," I whispered as I leaned against Daniel and ate some soup.

He pet my hair. "Your body was doing all it could to keep you alive."

"Sea king," Myrin yelled.

I leapt to my feet just as an enormous sea snake surfaced. It had spots on its body, teeth taller than me, and spikes along the side of its head.

Venali, Kydrus, and Amrynn were already on the move, racing forward across the deck with spears in their hands.

Daniel stepped in front of me. "Stay back, Elara. We've got this under control."

"You've fought one of these before?" I asked, still gaping at the huge creature.

"At least three," Daniel said.

"No wonder you all look so tired," I said softly. "You've been fighting a lot."

Daniel reached back and gripped my hand with his. "It's all worth it."

Two of the spears pierced the creature in its eyes, and the last went through its head.

It fell back into the water, causing a wave of water to push us away from it.

"That quickly?" I gasped.

"We've become efficient," Myrin said from the helm. "It helps save energy."

My mates, Amara's consorts, really were something special.

I had to do whatever I could to keep them alive.

Myrin tapped my forehead and bent to look into my eyes. "No."

"No, what?" I asked and rubbed my head even though it hadn't hurt.

"Whatever you're thinking. You've got your sad and serious face on. That usually means you're planning something stupid or dangerous. Or both," he said.

I leaned forward and kissed him. "I love you, Myrin."

He rested his hand on my cheek and rubbed his thumb across the bone. "I love you, too, Elara."

I pressed closer to him and slid my hands up his chest. "More than cookies?' I asked with a playful smirk.

He dropped his hand and stroked the side of my breast as he caressed my side, stopping at my hip. "More than cookies."

I tugged on his shirt. "Off."

He removed his shirt without question.

Taking my time, I memorized every inch of his exposed flesh. He was my Unseelie king.

With a jump, I wrapped my arms around his neck and my legs around his waist, and then kissed him.

He supported me easily, my weight meant nothing to him, and kissed me back.

Another set of hands slid around me from behind to cup my breasts.

I gasped into Myrin's mouth, but he just devoured the sound.

Myrin pried me off and set me on my feet.

Intending to object, I opened my mouth, but he pressed his hand over it.

Then, he tugged my shirt off and dropped to his knees to fondle and suck on each of my breasts.

Daniel, the one who had been behind me, spread my legs and rubbed me through my pants.

I arched my upper body forward into Myrin and my lower body backwards into Daniel.

Myrin stood, and I stuck my hand down his pants to grip his erection. He groaned and dropped his head back.

Daniel jerked my pants down, spread my legs even wider, and inserted himself into my wet core. He moved in and out slowly, letting my body adjust to him. Once fully inserted, he began pumping his hips.

I pumped my hand on Myrin at the same pace, watching his face to gauge his pleasure.

Daniel withdrew and spun me around.

Myrin slid into me, gripping my hips tightly.

I reached for Daniel, and as I slid my hand along his slick erection, he rubbed my aching nub.

The three of us developed a rhythm and it wasn't long before I screamed my first orgasm.

Myrin withdrew and spun me.

I expected to face Myrin, but faced Venali instead.

I reached up and traced my fingertips over his scar.

He dropped his pants, and I bent over, taking him in my mouth.

Hands gripped my butt and someone else entered me. I turned my head slightly.

Ryul.

He slammed into me hard and fast, making me orgasm three times before Venali finished in my mouth.

Someone grabbed my hair and pulled me into a standing position.

Durlan.

He took his time, building my orgasm, and then right when I was about to come, he pinched my nipple and pulled tighter on my hair.

The orgasm was the strongest yet. I screamed, and he didn't stop, pounding into me and squeezing my breasts.

He withdrew right before my next climax and before I could complain, Amrynn dropped to his knees and began licking and sucking my even more sensitive nub.

Kydrus slid into me while Amrynn continued licking me. Daniel and Myrin each took a breast and started sucking on them while rubbing themselves.

Kydrus withdrew and then inserted his fingers into me while he stroked himself. "Scream for us, beautiful."

My eyes rolled up into my head as all the stimulation caused an eruption from me. I cried out and so did the four guys with me.

When I opened my eyes, I found four spots of spilled seed on the deck.

My legs wobbled and Kydrus picked me up.

"Well, that was interesting," a deep voice said.

We turned, facing a dark shadowy figure.

The dark god.

"I see you survived," he said to me.

"I did. Thank you for returning my crown," I said with a smile.

His eyeless, smoky form smiled. "See, boys, this is how you're supposed to act."

"What do you want?" Myrin asked.

I realized none of them had bothered to get dressed, and they were all standing in their nude glory, staring at the dark god.

"Give me the jar," he said.

"You'll get it soon enough," I said, still smiling pleasantly at him.

"It won't work," he said.

I shrugged. "Only one way to find out."

"You test my patience," he snarled.

Amara took over, letting me stay again. "You test ours," we snapped. We flung our hand out, and his shadows exploded and then disappeared.

Amara left, and I slumped in Kydrus's arms.

"Stop doing that," Kydrus growled.

"Tell Amara, not me," I whispered and snuggled into him.

"Let's get dressed," Myrin said. "We're close to Eltare."

Eltare, the home of the Unseelie. It felt like a lifetime ago that we had been there.

By the time we'd gotten dressed and my hair was brushed, we were docked at Eltare.

I carried the jar in my arms, cradling it like a baby as we made our way to the castle.

Aerith met us out front and bowed to me. "Your Majesty," she said. "We are honored to have you back."

"Have preparations been made while I was away?" I asked and walked up the steps towards her.

She looked at Daniel with an arched brow, but wisely didn't comment on his presence. "Yes. Once you give the word, my people will be ready to go."

I nodded. "Good. We need two days to rest and then on the third day, we will leave at dawn. Let your people know."

Myrin opened the castle door for me, and we made our way to the room we'd used last time.

Venali checked the room and then opened the door for us all to enter.

Once inside with the door closed, the guys crawled onto the bed and promptly fell asleep.

I set the jar down, still wrapped in the blankets, and sat on the floor.

They were all exhausted, but I wasn't.

So, I took my first ever turn as lookout while they slept. My lookout turn was uneventful and boring.

When they all finally woke the next day, I'd created a mini universe with rocks that orbited each other like planets would.

They all stared at my tiny rocky universe in silent rapture.

I let the rocks fall to break their transfixion.

"I'm hungry," I said.

"How long did we sleep?" Durlan asked and ran a hand through his hair.

"A full day," I said and stood, groaning at my sore butt.

"Have you eaten?" Amrynn asked.

I shook my head. "I didn't open the door at all."

"You should have woken one of us," Daniel chastised me.

I shrugged. "You guys obviously needed the rest." Sticking my head out the door, I spotted a castle servant and waved him over.

He ran to me and bowed.

"Is it dinner time yet?" I asked.

"In an hour, Your Majesty," he said. "Would you like me to fetch you some food?"

"No, just let your queen know my mates and I will be coming for dinner," I instructed.

He bowed and ran off.

I waved down another castle servant, a female this time. "Can you escort us to the bathing area?"

She curtsied. "Certainly."

We followed her, and I admired her curly hair as it bounced about her shoulders.

I caught Kydrus watching her hair, too, and twirled my straight hair around my finger with a scowl.

Myrin looped an arm around my waist and squeezed. "Your hair is beautiful," he whispered in my ear. "No one has such unique coloring."

The bathing area was a huge cavern filled with dozens of pools of water, large enough for three people to fit in each one.

She handed each of us soap bars and pointed at a stack of towels. "I will ensure no one disturbs you while you bathe. Do you need your clothing washed?"

"Please," I said with a smile. I stripped from my clothes and handed them to her.

She took them with wide eyes and then quickly averted her gaze.

"Ours, too," Venali said.

All of the guys stripped and piled their clothes atop mine.

I wasn't sure her cheeks could get redder. She curtsied and hurried away, all but running.

The guys snickered and each climbed into separate pools, far apart from one another.

Scowling, I looked at them. Was I supposed to choose one? I didn't want to choose one.

Grumbling beneath my breath, I climbed into my own separate pool, close to the door. I moaned as the warm water slid around me like a comforting hug. Healing magic from the water seeped into me.

"Keep moaning like that and that girl will be even more embarrassed when she comes back and catches us in the act," Daniel said.

Floating in the pool, I closed my eyes and ignored him.

Something splashed in my pool, causing waves of water to splash over my face.

I spluttered as I sat up, then my jaw dropped.

Venali and Myrin held a male Unseelie by the arms, keeping him back as he tried to stab me.

The attacker growled at me and bared his teeth.

I stood, stepped into his face with my teeth bared, let a bit of power out, and growled back.

He stilled and then tried to back away, but Venali and Myrin held him too tightly.

"Who sent you?" I asked.

He shook his head and closed his eyes.

"Durlan," I called.

Durlan walked over and bowed to me. "Yes, my queen?"

"See if you can find anything from the knife," I said.

The attacker's eyes snapped open and he tried to thrash and escape, but he was no match for Venali.

Durlan touched the knife, and then growled loudly. "I know who sent him."

"Venali, knock him out. Dinner is about to get very interesting."

Venali's magic sparked and the man instantly slumped, eyes closed and breathing even.

They carried him out of my pool and tossed his body on the ground.

Durlan helped me out of my pool and into another one.

This time, I washed quickly instead of enjoying the water.

The girl returned with our clothes and gaped at the unconscious man. "How did he get in here?"

I waved at her dismissively. "Don't worry about it. Are our clothes clean?"

She nodded and sorted the piles.

I climbed out and she rushed me over a towel, keeping her eyes averted.

Except, the guys got out of their pools in her line of sight, so she had to avert her gaze to the ceiling, blushing again.

"It's okay," I whispered and took the towel.

"Would you like me to brush your hair?" she asked.

"No," Myrin said. "We'll take care of it. Just leave the brush."

She nodded, curtsied, and ran off, dropping the brush on a bench as she passed it.

"I wanted her help," I mumbled as I dried off.

Myrin dressed and picked up the brush. "I wanted to do it, though."

That was something I wouldn't say no to.

I sat and he sat behind me, taking my hair into his hands and began brushing the tangles out.

The others got dressed and then sat around me, watching.

It felt incredibly intimate, yet all that was happening was my hair being brushed.

When he finished brushing it, he helped me stand, and smiled. "Ready?"

I felt ready to take on the universe. "Yes," I said.

Venali picked up the unconscious man, and we exited the bathing area.

Clean and rested, we walked down the hallway with our heads held high.

Together, we could accomplish anything.

I just had to keep them together.

Guards gaped at Venali carrying an Unseelie, but opened the door to the dining hall without questions. Venali's glower likely had something to do with their silence.

The room was full of Unseelie, and as last time, Aerith sat at the head table.

Venali dropped the man on the table, splashing food

everywhere.

Aerith's eyes widened. "What's the meaning of this?" she asked, anger and confusion on her face.

Oh, she was an excellent actress.

"That's what I want to know," I said. "Are you such a coward that you couldn't even attempt to kill me yourself?"

She bristled and stood. "I am no coward and I didn't—"

I held up my finger, stopping her. "Be very careful with your next words. I do not tolerate liars."

Unlike Seelie, Unseelie could lie.

She folded her arms across her chest. "What proof do you have that I was involved?"

I waved at Durlan.

He stepped forward, touched the dagger, and the scene of her paying the man to kill me was projected above us.

"That's fake," she snapped and walked around the table. "You're just trying to steal my throne."

"Your throne holds no interest to me," I said.

"Why do you have a human among your consorts?" she asked. "What kind of *Empress* debases herself with a human?"

"Shift," I ordered Daniel without turning to look at him.

He came to stand behind me, his warmth pressing against my back, and shifted into his bear form, towering over me. He roared and it echoed in the room.

Unseelie gasped, and a couple of women screamed.

"These men are more than meets the eye," I said.

"Apologize and we'll forget it happened," Myrin said.

"I did nothing," she growled and bared her teeth.

"Ryul," I called.

He lifted his hand and she instantly began screaming and fell to her knees.

I let her scream for a full minute and then lifted my hand.

Ryul dropped his hand and Aerith panted on the floor.

"Admit to your people what you did," I said.

"I tried to kill her," she whispered.

"Louder," Myrin roared at her.

"I tried to kill her," she yelled and wiped at her face. "Unseelie and Seelie shouldn't mix. The Seelie are pompous and arrogant. They won't accept us."

"I have Seelie, Unseelie, and shapeshifter mates," I said loud enough to be heard throughout the room. "Clearly, they can coexist. You're as blinded by your hatred as the old Seelie."

The crowd murmured.

"Who is next in line?" I asked Myrin.

"Besides me?" he mumbled.

I rolled my eyes. "Obviously." Then, scowling I said, "Unless you want to be king."

"Larissa is next," he said.

I turned and searched the crowd. "Larissa?"

The girl who'd taken us to the bathing chamber stood.

My eyes widened, and Myrin gave me a small nod of affirmation.

"I hereby remove Aerith as queen and thus power goes to Larissa as next in line."

"You can't," Aerith yelled and drew power.

All of my mates tensed, but I stepped forward and stared into Aerith's eyes with no fear. "Try me."

Her eyes widened, and she tried to strike me with a bolt of electricity.

I absorbed the electricity with a smile, let the sun fill me, and burned her to a pile of dust. Her crown was all that survived. "I am Empress of the Galaxy. I am Goddess of the Universe," I said. I turned and smiled at the shocked Unseelie. "Our peoples will unite and those who oppose me may challenge me or my mates. Anyone care to challenge us?"

No one moved. I wasn't even sure they were breathing.

Releasing my powers, I smiled. "Good. Now, let's eat."

A few servants cleared the body of my attacker, dust of the old queen, and spilled food.

Larissa sat on the throne, smiling.

I picked up the crown, blew off bits of Aerith dust, tried to shine it with my shirt, and held it out to Larissa. "It needs washing, but this is yours."

She bowed. "I hope to be a better ruler than our previous monarch."

I winked. "You'll do great."

When Myrin sat beside me, I leaned over and asked, "Why didn't her guards intervene?"

He leaned close enough for our shoulders to touch. "Venali kept smiling at them. I don't think they breathed the entire time."

Venali leaned across the table and whispered, "I was inviting them to intervene. It's not my fault they're cowards."

"Also, there was a massive bear standing behind you," Kydrus whispered.

Daniel snickered.

Kydrus made a plate for me and then Daniel took it and smelled it.

I arched a brow, and he set it down. "I'm not taking chances," he said with no shame.

The guys chatted, telling Daniel what to expect when we reached Minloa.

Discreetly glancing around, I expected fear to still be present on the Unseelie in attendance, but most were smiling.

It appeared that Aerith had been disliked by several people.

A couple dozen people approached Larissa, giving their congratulations and support.

Good.

I saw my old self in her and hoped that meant she'd help those most in need now that she was ruler.

CHAPTER 18
ELARA

Larissa stood on the docks to see us off. A dozen Unseelie joined us for the trip, leaving behind their friends and families to become ambassadors in Minloa.

I waved and smiled to all of the Unseelie gathered on the docks.

"You look so queen-like," Venali whispered in my ear.

I chuckled and looked up at him. "Seems that I'm finally falling into my role, huh?"

He kissed my cheek. "You've always been a queen to me."

We set sail and I spent the time beating Ryul at dice.

The trip to Minloa was short, yet it felt like it took days. I had been gone for so long and I felt like a completely different person.

Myrin and Venali stayed with the Unseelie once we docked to help them get settled.

The rest of us teleported to the castle courtyard.

Guards rushed forward, but slowed when the recognized us.

One of the new warlords came forward and bowed. "Welcome back, Your Majesty."

I smiled. "Thank you." I would have added his name if I had remembered it.

"Any troubles while we were gone?" Durlan asked, stepping forward.

Amrynn stepped up next to me and whispered, "You don't remember his name, do you?"

"You guys picked and trained them," I mumbled. "How am I supposed to remember their names?"

"Your Majesty, are you aware there's a human with you?" one of the guards asked.

I sighed. "No, my consorts and I had no idea a giant human had hitched a ride."

The guard blushed.

"This is Daniel. He is one of my other consorts," I said. "Make sure all of the castle staff know."

"Yes, Your Majesty," he said and bowed.

"Oh, and you'll likely start seeing Unseelie around as well. Don't attack them or you'll pay," I added as I skipped into the castle.

I twirled around as I skipped down the hallway. Home. We were finally home.

CHAPTER 19
DANIEL

Knowing Elara was a queen and seeing her in her castle were two different things.

As soon as she stepped foot inside, her entire body relaxed and she started humming.

Watching her twirl about, a smile on her face...it stole my breath.

Mine.

My mate.

I would do whatever I could to keep her alive. Her plan to sacrifice herself would not come to fruition.

"Stunning, isn't she?" Kydrus whispered to me.

I nodded.

"When she's here, another side of her comes out. I like to think this is the true Elara, the one she would be if Amara hadn't chosen her."

Unsure how to respond to that, I just watched Elara.

She spun in a circle, but her feet tangled, and she fell onto the hallway's carpet runner. She laughed and Ryul helped her up.

"You always trip on that spot of carpet," Ryul said and shook his head.

She chuckled. "Maybe I should replace that patch."

He laughed. "You'd still trip."

She linked her hand with his and continued skipping down the hallway, forcing Ryul to lengthen his stride to keep up.

"Skip with me," she said to him.

"I'm not a child anymore," he said.

"Apparently you're an old, boring geezer," she said as she pulled her hand away.

Ryul growled, but it was obviously playful. "Take that back."

She walked backwards so she could face him. "Old. Boring. Geezer," she said, punctuating each word.

Ryul dashed forward, but Elara spun and took off down the hallway with a high-pitched, girly shriek.

"They were childhood friends?" I asked.

"Yes," Amrynn said from my right. "He saved her from the planned assassination of her family. He froze her in a crystal and then he waited a thousand years, alone, in this castle, for her to return."

My respect for Ryul increased dramatically. Even before his memories, he had been loyal to Elara.

Elara ran back towards us, pushing between Amrynn and I, and then hid behind my back, peeking her head around my side.

Ryul raced towards us, hands out, ready to grab her. "You can't run forever," he said, grinning wider than I had ever seen him before, even our prior life.

He darted around Kydrus, but Elara ran around Amrynn, in front of me. "Your joints will start hurting soon and you'll be ready for your nap, geezer."

"I'm older than he is," Amrynn said and folded his arms across his chest. "What's that make me?"

Elara's eyes sparkled. She backed away from us and yelled, "Ancient," before running away.

Kydrus and Amrynn exchanged a glance, and then both ran after her.

Ryul walked next to me as we followed, watching her dodge their half-hearted attempts to catch her.

"You okay?" Ryul asked.

I nodded, not taking my eyes off her. "Just wishing I'd been here sooner."

Ryul patted my shoulder. "Me too, brother. Me, too."

A tall Seelie man came out of a room with his head bowed over a book, stepping right into Elara's path.

She crashed into him, making him drop his book.

"We don't run in the hallways," he growled, bending to pick up the book.

Elara stood and folded her arms over her chest. "I'll do whatever I want."

He raised his eyes, power flaring, but the instant he saw her face, he dropped to a knee with his head bowed. "Forgive me, Your Majesty."

She patted his shoulder, her wide smile back in place. "No worries, I hate when I'm interrupted from reading, too."

Amrynn reached out to grab her and she started running again.

The man watched her go, eyes wide and mouth open.

"She's one of a kind," Ryul said to him as we passed.

"That she is," the man said softly.

When we finally caught up to her, Elara was sprawled on the carpet, panting.

"Food," she groaned. "So hungry."

Ryul picked her up and tossed her over his shoulder. "Come on, Your Majesty. I'll take you to get some food."

"And dessert?" she asked, raising her head.

"Only if you eat your vegetables," he said.

An ache formed in my chest. A combination of regret for the few days I had been a jerk to her, and remorse over not knowing her before she'd merged with Amara.

Everyone had pointed ears except for me and none could shift. Would I feel like an outsider while here?

Once in the kitchen, Elara sat on a counter and patted the spot next to her while smiling at me.

I hopped up beside her and watched as she kicked her legs back and forth.

So innocent and childlike, that was how she was acting.

"Durlan makes really good food," Elara said. "Venali is the best cook, but neither are here, so we will have to suffer through whatever those three can make."

"Elara," I whispered. My mouth closed, unsure what to say.

She looked up at me, smiling and so happy. "Yes?"

"I love you," I whispered.

She scooted closer until our hips and legs touched and said, "I love you, too, Daniel."

I draped my arm around her shoulders and hugged her against my side.

I would kill a thousand men, a universe of gods, or whatever I had to as long as it would keep that smile on her face.

CHAPTER 20
DURLAN

"You're certain it was him?" I asked Karlo, the new Warlord of Blustum.

He nodded. "I saw him myself. I used to live nearby, so I know what he looked like.

I snarled. We should have thought about the possibility of Feno returning once she opened Minloa to the Unseelie.

If he wanted to upset her and possibly further the discord between the Seelie and Unseelie, all he had to do was confront her in front of a crowd.

"Where and when did you see him?" I asked.

He pointed to Adlin, Menma's main city. "Here, near the river, four days ago."

Feno couldn't teleport, and Klinsot was a five day journey from Adlin by foot.

"Double patrols, but order them not to engage with Feno. You contact me immediately when you see him."

"Yes, sir," Karlo said.

The moment I saw Feno, I would tear his head off. He wouldn't lay a finger on Elara.

I followed the pull of our bond, winding my way through the castle to find her.

My searching lead me to the kitchen where I found Elara wrestling with Ryul, trying to grab a cookie he held out of her reach.

All of them were smiling and looked happy for the first time together.

Amrynn and Kydrus walked to me, their smiles gone.

"What's wrong?" Kydrus asked.

"Later," I said, my eyes back on Elara exaggeratedly pouting at Ryul who still had the cookie.

"Consort meeting tonight?" Amrynn asked.

I nodded and stepped around them. A smile lit up my face, and I snatched the cookie and held it out to Elara.

Her mouth opened as she smiled and took the offered cookie from my hand. Ryul stepped towards her and she shoved the whole cookie into her mouth, making her cheeks puff out.

We watched as she tried to chew it, but it was too large and she started choking.

Daniel handed her a glass of water, and I patted her back.

She sniffled, looking at the cookie pieces on the ground.

"If you'd eaten your vegetables, this wouldn't have happened," Ryul chided her.

"My cookie," she whispered. Raising her head, she had tears in her eyes. "That was the last one."

I wiped her eyes and smiled. Moments like this, moments when she could be carefree were my favorite. "I'll make you some more, okay?"

"Really?" she asked and wiped her nose.

What would her life have been like without Amara interfering?

I bent and kissed her. "Really, but you'll have to help."

She ran to the cupboards and started pulling out ingredients.

If necessary, I would hunt Feno down to keep Elara from having to deal with him and the painful memories he brought.

Ryul looked at me.

"Consort meeting tonight," I whispered.

His eyes widened and he nodded.

Rolling up my sleeves, I washed my hands and then smiled at Elara. "Let's make some cookies."

CHAPTER 21
VENALI

Durlan had called a consort meeting, and I'd had to use my magic to knock Elara out, so she wouldn't interrupt us.

I spun a pencil between my fingers, anxiety coursing through me. Durlan wouldn't have called the meeting unless it was something important.

Hopefully, it was something for me to kill.

Myrin sat beside me and sagged in his chair.

"Rough day?" I asked.

"I've had to answer five billion questions about what it's like being Unseelie. Why did your ancestors have to be such dicks?"

I chuckled. "It'll get better."

"It's about to get a lot worse," Durlan said as he slammed the door closed. Then, he put a seal on the door so no sound would escape.

I leaned forward, smiling. "I get to kill something?"

Durlan looked at me and the fire and anger I saw startled me. "He needs killing, and while I'd prefer to do it, I don't care which of us ultimately snuffs his life out, as long as he fucking dies."

All of us gaped at him. He never cursed.

"Who?" I asked, gripping my pencil.

"Feno," Durlan said.

I snapped my pencil in my hand and stood. "Where was he last seen?"

"Sit," Durlan snapped.

I growled, but complied. That bastard was still alive? Durlan was right, he needed to die. And soon. Before he got near Elara.

Glancing at Ryul, I realized he wasn't shocked. "You knew?" I asked.

"I assumed," Ryul said.

"There's more," Durlan said, getting our attention. "Fae creature attacks have tripled the past month."

"Too many for the Warlords to handle?" I asked.

Durlan nodded. "And they're seemingly random."

He set markers on several spots around Minloa. My eyes widened as he continued setting them, putting over a dozen down.

"This is just last week," he said.

"Where are they coming from?" Kydrus asked. "We never had that high of a population before."

"That's my question," Durlan said. "I think we need to search out where they're coming from."

"It would make sense that *he* is sending them," Ryul said. "Trying to separate us from her."

He had a point.

"I don't think separating is a good idea," Daniel said. "Leaving her without all of us would be the perfect time for *him* to attack."

"We can't just let our people die," Durlan growled.

"Easy," I said sternly to Durlan.

His head whipped towards me and he bared his teeth at me. Several tense moments later, he dropped his head and took a large breath which he exhaled audibly. "Sorry."

"Why don't we take Elara around the realms?" Amrynn asked. "She could see her people, greet them, and be seen to make the people accept her more. And, we could do some investigation at the same time."

"Two birds, one stone," I said, smiling.

Myrin nodded. "It's a good idea."

"And it will give the people time to see and get used to you two," Kydrus said and looked at Myrin and Daniel.

Durlan sat down and nodded. "I like it, but it does put her at more risk for attacks."

"We can't hide her in the castle," Ryul said. "The people will hate her if she doesn't walk among them."

"What about a ball?" I asked.

All eyes focused on me, most wide.

"You want to hold a ball?" Kydrus asked.

"A ball always makes the people happy," I added.

"Why not both? She could announce the ball to everyone she visits," Kydrus said.

"A personal invitation from the queen," Durlan said and smiled. "Yes, that's perfect."

"If we don't kill Feno before the ball, you know he will show up and try to kill her," I growled.

"It's too good an opportunity for her to solidify her place here. We should also invite the Unseelie, so they can mingle," Myrin said.

Elara burst into the room, shattering the door and breaking Durlan's spell. Her eyes glowed, not with Amara's power, but her own. "You spelled me," she snapped. "To have a secret meeting. What have you decided without me this time? What about my future have you planned for me?"

Her power made a wind swirl around her, and I realized her feet weren't even touching the ground.

"We're going to host a ball," I said. "So the Seelie and Unseelie can meet."

"And we thought it would be a nice gesture if you visited each

Realm and gave the invitation to your people yourself," Kydrus added.

In an instant, her power was gone, and she stood before us with disheveled hair and sleep rumpled clothes. "Oh." She looked at the markers and her brows furrowed. "What else?"

I started to stand, but she pointed at me, so I froze.

"You do not get to approach me right now. I'm still pissed you used that damn spell on me again," she said and growled at me.

I smiled at the most perfect and glorious woman in existence, and took my seat again.

She pointed. "Explain."

"The number of fae creature attacks have increased," Durlan said. "We're unsure where they're coming from."

She walked around the table, keeping as far from me as possible, and then froze and her face lost all color.

Daniel started to reach out for her, but she raised a shaking hand and pointed at the markers. "It's him," she whispered. "It's a message."

We all crowded to her side and looked at it. Knowing it was a word, or words, made seeing it easier.

Soon.

He'd orchestrated attacks so that the markers on the map would spell the word, soon.

Elara wrapped her arms around herself, but we could all see her shaking and sense her fear.

Myrin picked her up and whispered into her ear too low for me to hear.

She nodded, and he carried her out of the room.

We continued staring at the word and anger built within me until I was ready to burst.

I swiped the markers off the table. "I can't wait to kill that bastard."

CHAPTER 22
ELARA

For a full day, I lay in my room, staring at the jar.

He had done it to upset me. So, I shouldn't have let it upset me. However, that was much easier said than done.

"Elara," Daniel whispered as he sat beside me.

"When I die, who is going to take over ruling Minloa?" I asked. "I need to find and appoint an heir, since I won't have one of my own."

"Why won't you have one of your own? And you aren't going to die."

"Daniel, everyone dies," I said.

"Why won't you have one?" he asked again.

"I refuse to get pregnant. If I die during this battle, I don't want it to be while I'm carrying a child," I said.

"Let me guess," he said. "You and Amara worked out a deal?"

"Sort of," I said. "She made me infertile for the time being."

He growled.

"Growl all you want; I'm not changing it."

"Why are you so certain you're going to die?" he asked softly. "There has to be a way for us all to live."

"If we all live, that means you'll leave me to be with Amara," I whispered.

He tensed and said nothing.

"I don't want to live without you," I whispered back. "And I don't want to make you choose. You are Amara's mates first. You were separated for so long and you deserve to be together. I won't stand in the way of that."

"So, you're going to kill yourself?" he asked.

"No, I'm going to ensure you all survive," I said. "Hopefully, this jar will contain him. Then, Amara and I can decide what to do from there."

I wouldn't tell him our main plan because he and the others would try to stop us.

"You need to eat. Come on," he said and picked me up.

I snuggled against his chest and kissed the side of his neck. I would miss him so much if I had to live without him. It hurt thinking about it.

"Can't I wear pants?" I asked and tugged at the green dress I wore.

The guys had insisted I wear a dress and my crown to visit my people. Personally, I was certain they did it just to mess with me.

"You're a queen and queens shouldn't whine," Durlan said and brushed my hair over one shoulder.

"Do goddesses whine?" I asked.

Ryul snickered and then clamped his lips shut.

"Do you have the invitations?" Kydrus asked.

I held up the basket with a dozen rolled up invitations. "Here."

"Are we missing anything?" Amrynn asked.

Myrin phased through the wall next to me. "Me," he said.

I squealed and then smacked his arm. "You did that on purpose. The door is open."

His wide smile didn't falter.

"Okay, let's go," Durlan said.

"Where to first?" I asked.

"Crol," Amrynn said with a wide smile and set his hand on my shoulder.

We teleported right into the town square, atop a platform that had not been there last time I had visited.

Amrynn stepped back and I realized the courtyard was filled with Seelie, who looked at me expectantly, which meant they'd been warned of my arrival.

I cleared my throat and took one of the invitations from the basket and then gave the basket to Kydrus.

"People of Blustum, I've come today to extend an invitation," I said.

Several people whispered to each other.

"Amrynn," I called and then handed him the invitation to nail to the well in the middle of the courtyard.

As he did so, I continued, "I am hosting a ball, to celebrate my return and the unification of alliances I have made."

"Did you make the alliances by taking a man off their hands?" someone asked and snickered.

"Since when do queens associate with humans?" another asked.

I sighed. "Why are you all so ridiculous? Look." I waved at Daniel, who shifted into a bear. "He's not human. Secondly, it is none of your business who I take as a consort."

"Until she takes all the men, and we've got none left," a woman jeered.

"Jealousy is an ugly thing, Trinity," Amrynn said. "Since when do the people of Blustum lack respect and honor?"

"Who lacks honor?" a man shouted from the back of the crowd.

Amrynn waved his hand at everyone in the crowd. "All of you. Instead of insulting our queen and her consorts, why don't you challenge us to a duel?"

No one spoke.

"Lack of honor," Amrynn said and shook his head.

"I came here to invite you to a ball, to personally invite you. I only have one goal, to unite us. We've been segregated for too long. I hope you will come, but this is not mandatory. I would never try to force this. I realize you don't know me. I came to get to know you better, but if I am not wanted here, I will move on to another realm."

"Wait," a little girl cried out.

I squinted my eyes as I tried to find her, and finally spotted her trying to squeeze through the adults.

I jumped down from the platform, almost face planting because of the dress, and faced the Seelie before me. "Let her pass," I ordered them, but in a nice tone.

Many moved out of her way, but several still blocked her.

Kydrus jumped down next to me, raised his hands and acted like he was pushing something apart.

The people before me parted, creating a lane for the girl.

Most of the people Kydrus had moved gaped with open mouths.

I turned and kissed his cheek. "Thanks."

The little girl stopped before me, panting.

I knelt, not caring that my dress was getting dirty, and smiled at her. "What's your name?"

"Cassie," she said. She took a deep breath, her cheeks red, and said, "I'd like you to have this." She held out a beautiful purple flower.

I gently took it. "This is beautiful. I've never seen this type of flower before."

"I crossbred my favorite flowers to make it," she said.

Carefully, I tucked the flower above my ear. "Does it look okay?" I asked her.

She smiled wide and nodded quickly.

"Thank you, Cassie. I hope you'll come to my ball," I said.

"I'll try," she said and looked behind her, I presumed towards her parents.

I stood and she tugged on my dress to get my attention again.

I looked back down.

"Can...can I meet the other warlords, er, your consorts?" she asked in a whisper.

I reached back for Kydrus and pulled him forward. "Kydrus, I'd like you to meet my new friend, Cassie. Cassie, this is Kydrus," I introduced them.

Kydrus dropped to one knee, his fully charming smile on, lifted her little hand, and kissed her knuckles. "It's nice to meet you, Cassie."

She looked like she was going to explode with joy.

Kydrus stepped aside for Amrynn, then Ryul, then Venali, then Durlan.

When it was Daniel's turn, she tensed.

I squatted down and said, "He's just a big teddy bear. I bet he'd even shift for you."

Her eyes widened.

He knelt and kissed her knuckles. "Hello, Cassie. It's an honor to meet you."

"Daniel, sir, can I see your bear form?" she asked.

"Don't be frightened, okay?" he said.

She nodded.

He stepped behind me and shifted and then peeked his giant furry head around my legs.

Cassie gasped. Then, she reached out a shaky hand, and Daniel licked it, which made her laugh.

I squatted and waved her closer. I pointed to the side of his neck. "This is the softest spot." I buried my face in it and then leaned back.

Without hesitation, she stuck her face in his fur. "It's so soft," she gasped.

I grabbed Myrin and pulled him down. "This is Myrin," I told her.

He smiled. "Hello, Cassie."

She took a step closer to him and tilted her head to the side as she examined him. "Your teeth are sharp like mine."

"Oh?" he asked.

She opened her mouth, showing of her sharp canines.

"Those do look sharp," Myrin said. "And pretty."

Cassie blushed.

He reached out and took her hand, the tension in the air was palpable, then he gently and slowly brought it to his lips to kiss her knuckles. "I hope you'll save me a dance at the ball," he said.

She nodded vigorously and then threw her arms around my neck in a hug and ran back the way she had come. "Mama! I met the queen and her consorts. Can we go to the ball? I want to dance with Myrin."

People had gathered around and when I stood, many introduced themselves.

I needed to give Cassie a gift for breaking the tension.

When we finally left, I felt good about the day. I twirled my flower as we headed to our room, smiling.

"Elara made a friend," Kydrus said.

"Myrin got a date," I said with a chuckle. "I'll have to fight her to dance with him."

Myrin laughed.

"I hope tomorrow won't be as bad," I said and felt my smile slip.

"It'll work out," Durlan assured me.

I scowled at him. "You're only saying that because we're going to Adlin tomorrow."

He smiled. "Maybe."

"Could you stop making me shift on command?" Daniel asked softly. "I feel like entertainment."

I stopped and spun to face him. "I'm sorry. I didn't—"

He covered my mouth with his hand for a second. "I know. You are just showing them I'm not human."

"Did I overstep having Cassie touch you?" I asked, feeling like a total jerk.

"Had it been an adult, yes, but not for that little girl." Daniel kissed my cheek. "It's okay. I didn't mind today, but don't feel like doing that at each place."

The guilt didn't go away. "Okay. I'm sorry."

He linked our hands and tugged me into our bedroom. "Come on, we've been waiting all day to get you out of that dress."

"It needs to be washed," I said and twirled the skirts which were coated in dust.

"Yet another reason it needs to come off," Myrin said and began unlacing it.

Adlin and Vlink went extremely well. No one yelled rude things and everyone was excited to meet Myrin and Daniel.

As we prepared to go to Linta, my hands shook. The last time I had been there for more than a couple of hours was the night I had been pushed off the cliff.

Kydrus wrapped his arms around me. "It's okay. I'm going to be at your side the entire time."

"What if they won't accept me?" I asked in a whisper. "What if they—"

"I will handle them," Kydrus assured me, squeezing me tightly.

"Do you think my home...is there?" I asked.

He nodded. "Do you want to see it?"

I nodded.

"After you visit the people, we will go by, okay?" he said.

"Okay," I agreed.

We teleported into the field, just outside of the city.

I lifted my dress with trembling hands as we stepped onto the road.

"Why is she so nervous?" I heard Daniel ask.

"She was an outcast here and the others tended to pick on her," Kydrus said. "They challenged her to fight almost daily."

Not almost...every single day. He just didn't know about all of them.

I took a breath.

That girl wasn't me anymore. I was different now. Stronger. And I had consorts that never left me lonely.

As soon as I walked into Linta, people began whispering and saying my name. Some called out to Kydrus.

Once in the town square, I nailed the invitation to the board Kydrus had installed a few years after I had moved there.

A group stood behind me.

"This is your invitation to a ball I am hosting," I said and turned to face them. "I wanted to personally invite you."

Smiles were not expected and yet that was what I got.

"It's good to see you," Lansia said. She had given me work in her shop occasionally.

"We always knew Kydrus was going to snag you," Tara said from my right.

"Everyone saw how he pined for you, even when you were too afraid," Simon said.

Then, as if a dam broke, they came forward and hugged and congratulated me.

Halfway through, I was crying.

Four women rushed forward and enveloped me in hugs.

When I finally got my emotions under control, I talked with them and told them some of my journey.

They shook hands with all of my consorts, smiling even when meeting Myrin.

"I didn't expect this," I whispered to Kydrus.

He kissed my forehead. "I know, my love. Honestly, I didn't either."

"Aren't they the cutest couple?" Tara gushed.

Heat rushed to my cheeks.

Everyone laughed.

Just before sunset, we walked to my old house. I let my fingers trail along the tree trunks and closed my eyes.

The door was closed, but not locked. When I pushed it open, I found the inside untouched.

The guys looked in, scowling. There wasn't enough room for them all to fit.

"Whenever I lay in this bed," I whispered and ran my fingers along the dusty cover. "I wondered if I would be alone my entire life." I looked up at them and smiled. "I wish I had known how happy I would end up and how loved I would be."

Kydrus pulled me out of the house so they could all touch me. "You'll never be alone again," he whispered.

My chest hurt at his words because that may not be true. If Amara and I separated, she might take them.

How would I explain the disappearance of my consorts to Minloa?

I pulled free. "Don't make promises you can't keep," I whispered. Going back into my house, I looked around to see if there was anything I wanted to take.

There was very little and most items were just necessities for the room.

I walked out and headed to the falls.

Kydrus grabbed my hand and stopped me when I neared the edge. "I'd rather you didn't fall a second time."

"I didn't fall the first time. I was pushed," I said, but stayed where I was. Tilting my head back, I looked up at the stars. "I played with the stars often here."

"That explains why that constellation is different," Kydrus said.

I spun and glared. "I always returned them to their proper places."

He smirked, and I realized he had said that to rile me up on purpose.

"Let's go home," I said.

Would the castle feel like home without them?

I didn't think so.

CHAPTER 23
ELARA

"THE LAST GOD is the god of animals," I told Amara as I dreamed and looked at her in the mirror as we always did.

Her eyes widened. "Yes. Where has he gone?"

I shrugged. "Your guess is as good as mine, or better actually."

"Maybe he's been absorbed already," she whispered.

"Possible," I said.

"Well, let's assume that's a dead end," she grumbled.

"The ball will be interesting," I mumbled.

She smiled. "It will be good for Minloa."

"And it could be my last celebration with them," I whispered.

"I do not want you left alone," she said.

"They're yours first," I said.

"They love us both."

I nodded.

"With the container, we should be able to defeat him. However, I need you to practice with your own magic, not using mine."

"Okay," I said.

"It will likely take both of us at full power to seal him," she said. "Work on your stamina."

I huffed. "I hate running."

She chuckled. "A necessary evil, I'm afraid."

"Anything else?" I asked.

"That's all for now. Oh, wait. Remember to enjoy this time with the guys. Not just for yourself, but for them. If the worst happens, they'll likely be devastated after the battle and it will take them time to recover. They should have good memories from this time with you to draw on."

I nodded. "Understood."

Our dream ended, and I was thrust into another.

Darkness surrounded me.

"Hello?" I called out.

"You are not Amara," the dark god said.

I froze. "No, I'm not."

"You have a lot of magic. I could be even more powerful if I had you," he said.

"You already know my answer to that."

Heat exploded to my left.

"Your exposure to Amara has made you insolent and put barbs on your tongue. I should cut it out," he snapped.

"Why do you want Amara so badly?" I asked.

"She's mine. She belongs to me. We were supposed to become one, but those other meddling peons made those *boys*."

"Would you let me trade for her place?" I asked.

He was quiet a moment. "You want to trade places with her? Become mine in her place?"

"If you swore to leave her and her consorts alone for eternity, yes," I said.

"That is an offer I must think about," he said.

The dream dissolved, and I woke to seven growling mates.

"What?" I asked.

"You weren't speaking to Amara. We could sense the evil," Myrin said.

I nodded. "Once Amara ended our meeting, he grabbed me."

"What did he say?" Durlan asked.

I stood and stretched. "The usual. I want Amara. Those boys distracted her. Blah. Blah. Blah."

"You mumbled, 'for eternity.' What does that mean?" Daniel asked.

I tensed. I couldn't lie. What could I say? Silence was my only option.

Silence gained me growling.

I opened my wardrobe and debated what to wear and then remembered I had to start running. With a sigh, I changed into my training clothes.

"What are you doing?" Ryul asked.

I put my hair into a ponytail and smiled. "Going for a run. Who wants to join me?"

"Pass," Venali, Durlan, and Amrynn said at the same time.

I snickered. "You old men need your rest?"

"Yes," Venali said.

I skipped to him and kissed his cheek. "Okay. We'll be back soon. Running is not my favorite."

"I'll make breakfast for your return," Durlan said.

"Muffins?" I asked with wide, pleading eyes.

He smirked. "I can make you muffins."

I kissed him. "You're amazing."

"Let's go before it gets hot," Daniel said.

Ryul was still in bed. "I'm going to nap," he told me and waved. "Have fun."

Myrin and Daniel waited at the door.

Kydrus kissed me. "I've got some things to do. Have fun."

I rolled my eyes. "I'm sure this will be loads of fun."

I glanced back at the five staying behind. Why did I get the feeling they were up to something?

"Come on," Myrin said and gently pushed my back.

We used the back door and started a slow jog around the castle.

The three of us were quiet, but I didn't doubt they had a billion things going on in their heads.

Once I was warmed up, I pointed at a tree a ways down the street. "Race?"

Daniel and Myrin both smiled.

"Go," I yelled and ran as fast as I could.

They passed me in a blink, and ran neck and neck towards the tree.

Myrin raised his arms and circled the tree. "Winner," he yelled.

I finally caught up and leaned against the tree. "You guys are stupid fast," I said. I was embarrassed with how heavy my breathing was.

Myrin pinned me between his body and the tree. "I think I should get a prize," he said and kissed my cheek.

"Okay," I said.

"Tell us what you were discussing with him that involves eternity," he said.

I snarled at him and said nothing.

"You were trying to make a deal with him, weren't you?" Daniel asked.

I dropped my head.

"Elara," Myrin growled and his grip on my waist tightened.

"I did not make a deal," I said. That was true. I had offered and he had said he needed time, so a deal hadn't been made yet.

"Don't you dare try to make an offer with him," Daniel growled. "He won't keep his end. He'll just use it against us."

Myrin took my wrists and pulled them up above my head, successfully pinning me.

Daniel lifted my shirt, exposing my breasts.

"What are you two up to?" I asked, wiggling in Myrin's hold, but his vice-like grip gave me no room to move my arms.

Myrin slid his hand down, inside my pants, and slipped his fingers into me. He groaned and growled at the same time. "Always so wet."

Daniel bent and took a nipple into his mouth, sucking on it.

"If someone sees us," I whispered, my breath coming in pants as the pressure in my core built.

Myrin leaned forward, his mouth over mine, and said, "You should be quiet then."

Daniel lavished my breasts with attention while Myrin's fingers brought me to orgasm again and again. Each time I wanted to cry out, Myrin kissed me and swallowed my sounds.

My legs shook, and I wasn't sure I could walk back.

Myrin withdrew his hand and Daniel pulled my shirt down.

I arched a brow. "What about you two?"

"We'll handle that later," Daniel said.

I took a step and teetered.

Myrin picked me up with a chuckle.

"Don't be so smug," I mumbled.

We returned, grabbed clothes, and went to shower.

As soon as the water hit me, Daniel pinned me to the wall, his erection squished between us. "Here, you can scream as loud as you want," he whispered in my ear.

Myrin's gaze burned as he stepped into the water, eyes focused on mine.

I watched the water slide along his muscles. My dark mate.

Daniel lifted me and then slid inside, making me moan as he filled me.

Watching Myrin touch himself while Daniel pumped in and

out of me was a huge turn on, and I screamed my orgasm within minutes.

Daniel withdrew and set me on my feet, but kept his arm around my upper body, so my breasts stayed smooshed against his chest.

Myrin gripped my hips and slammed into me from behind, fully burying himself in one move.

As Myrin moved, Daniel reached down and rubbed me.

"What deal were you making with *him*?" he asked.

I growled.

He brought me right to the precipice of orgasm and then stopped. "What deal, Elara?"

Myrin didn't stop and I screamed that orgasm, but I wanted my other one.

"It doesn't matter," I panted. "He's probably not going to take it."

His fingers moved again.

So close.

So close.

They stopped.

"What was the deal?" Daniel asked.

Growling, reached to finish it myself, but Myrin took both of my hands and held them in one of his, behind my back.

Daniel started again, and I felt ready to pop. My head was spinning and my body ached for the release.

Myrin sped up, as did Daniel.

If I didn't answer, they would stop. I had to finish. I was so close.

"What deal?" Myrin asked.

They started to slow, and I yelled, "Me."

Finally, they let me finish and I swore it was the hardest orgasm I had ever had. It was so intense, I just opened my mouth and no sound came out.

Myrin and Daniel grunted and I realized Daniel had been touching himself the whole time.

Slumped against them, I let the aftershocks roll through me.

Neither spoke.

We washed, dressed, and headed to the kitchen in silence.

Coerced or not, I smiled and felt satisfied.

Inside the kitchen, the rest of my consorts whispered to each other while Durlan baked.

I hopped up onto a counter and watched.

"Muffins will be ready in five minutes," Durlan said, looking over and smiling at me.

"What else are you making?" I asked.

He looked at the dough he was kneading. "Bread."

Venali and Myrin whispered together, as did Daniel with Kydrus and Amrynn.

Then, they huddled around Durlan and Ryul.

"What are you all whispering about?" I asked.

Suddenly, Venali, Kydrus, Ryul, and Amrynn left the kitchen.

I looked at the door they exited. "Where are they going?"

"To work off some anger," Durlan growled and pounded on the dough much harder than he had been.

Ah, they must be mad about my offered deal. Myrin and Daniel must have told them.

"How are preparations for the ball going?" I asked.

"Fine," Durlan growled.

"If you want to yell, you can," I said.

He tilted his head back and roared, the sound so loud that it rattled the dishes in the cupboards.

"You can spank me later if you want," I said with a smile.

He glared at me. "Do not joke about this. I can't...I can't even..." He roared again and left the kitchen.

"You two haven't yelled at me yet," I said to Myrin and Daniel. "You didn't even growl when I told you."

"We had already guessed what the offer had been," Daniel said.

"We just wanted you to confirm it," Myrin said.

"So, what's on today's agenda?" I asked.

"You don't have anything today," Myrin said.

I smiled. "Awesome."

The timer dinged, and Daniel pulled out a tin of muffins from the oven.

I snatched one and wrapped it in a cloth so it wouldn't burn me. Then I skipped out of the kitchen and to my war room.

Sitting in my chair, I ate my muffin and looked at the map.

When the time came to fight, I would need all of my people to help. He would likely send too many creatures for my consorts and I to handle alone, plus fighting him.

With the powers of the other gods inside him, it was going to be a tough fight.

Even though we had the jar, we still needed to strategize fighting against him.

I walked to the arena and tried to talk to my consorts, but they ignored me, giving me the silent treatment.

With a sigh I said, "Fine. I need to find where Amara and you seven will live after the fight, anyway. I'll be back for dinner."

All seven turned, but I teleported to Pinolt before they could approach.

CHAPTER 24
AMRYNN

ELARA DISAPPEARED and I felt our bond stretched, not just on this planet, but to another. That made sense, since she couldn't teleport on the planet and only to different ones.

"She teleported to a different planet," I growled.

"What did she say before she left? I couldn't hear," Venali asked.

"She said she needed to find where Amara and the seven of us would live after the fight," Durlan growled. He threw his sword across the arena and it buried to the hilt in the stone wall.

I sat and put my head in my hands. I couldn't lose her.

"We need to figure out a way to make them fully merge," Daniel growled.

"You can't *make* them do anything," Kydrus said, and I could hear the frustration in his tone.

"There might be a way," Myrin whispered and paced along the fence line.

"How?" Ryul asked.

"It could kill us, though," Myrin said.

I watched him and realized he was so deep in thought, he hadn't heard Ryul.

"There could be other negative consequences," he said.

Ryul opened his mouth, and I waved at him to stay quiet.

He narrowed his eyes, but didn't speak.

"If we can get them separated...how, though? How do we convince them to separate?"

I had a feeling I knew where his line of thinking was headed.

"She may not forgive us if we die merging them," I said loudly.

Myrin growled and didn't stop his pacing. "I know."

"How do we keep her from making a deal with him?" Daniel asked.

"We can't," Kydrus said softly.

"I can," Ryul said softly.

We all looked at him, even Myrin stopped pacing to face him.

"How?" I asked.

"If I can control her dreams, he won't be able to invade them," Ryul said.

"You can control dreams?" Myrin asked.

Ryul nodded.

"You'll have to change your sleep schedule," I said. "She'll notice that."

He shrugged. "We should set up rotations in case he attacks anyway."

He wasn't wrong.

"I'll just volunteer for each night and the rest of you can rotate," he said.

"That's not a bad idea," Myrin whispered and resumed pacing.

"Have there been any sightings of Feno?" Kydrus asked.

"Not that I've heard of," Durlan said. "I think it is likely that he is lying low until the ball."

"Where he'll likely strike for maximum effect," I growled.

"There may be others who try to hurt her during the ball," Venali said.

I nodded. "Most likely."

Daniel spun, his nose lifted, and then growled. "We have company."

We grabbed our swords, Durlan having to yank his out of the wall, filed out of the arena, and walked past the courtyard and into the Dead Lands.

"Your nose is incredible," I whispered.

Daniel chuckled.

Twenty fae creatures of varying types and sizes stood together, growling and waiting for us.

Venali smiled. "This will be a much better way to work off my anger. I wish there were more."

Ten more appeared.

Durlan sighed. "Venali, stop talking."

Venali laughed and then ran forward with a mighty battle roar.

Daniel chuckled. "I never thought I'd meet someone who enjoyed fighting and killing as much as shapeshifters."

I patted his shoulder. "Welcome to the family."

He threw his head back and laughed and then shifted to his bear form.

Venali had killed a dozen already and he yelled, "More!"

Twenty more appeared.

For once, I wasn't upset at the enemies. For once, I took the gift before us and worked my frustrations out with killing. My frustration of Elara offering herself to him. My frustration of the humans taking me and then Elara prisoner. My frustration at having failed to protect my mate so many times.

When the year was over, I guaranteed there would be a lot more killing still.

"More," Kydrus yelled.

"More," Myrin yelled.

"More," Daniel roared.

The Dead Lands became a battlefield of our pain and frustration. Bodies, parts, entrails, and blood coated over two square miles before we stopped asking for more and sat together, panting.

Then, three giant creatures unlike anything we had seen before appeared.

We all stood.

"That's more like it," Venali said and as one, we charged the creatures.

CHAPTER 25
ELARA

Pinolt was as beautiful as I remembered. Lush green grass, flowers, and wildlife were abundant. It was utterly peaceful. Tranquil.

At least it was, until ten goblins appeared before me.

I sighed. "Really? He brought these beasts here? To my untouched planet?"

Standing, I drew my sword.

"Very well," I whispered. "I've got some anger to burn off anyway."

But I didn't want their blood ruining Pinolt.

I sheathed my sword, stepped forward, and let the goblins latch on to me.

Then, I teleported us to Anderelle, specifically the Dead Lands near Klinsot.

My teleportation skills sucked and I teleported into the sky above the Dead Lands.

Below me, I saw piles of dead bodies and my consorts fighting other creatures.

The goblins were biting and scratching me, fueling my anger.

I whistled and seven heads jerked up.

"A little help with my landing, please," I called down.

Drawing on the sun, I used it to burn the goblins, making them release me.

Free, I continued to fall towards the ground.

Myrin got a running start, and leapt up, snatching me out of the air, and then rolled with me tucked up against his body.

We stopped rolling and I stood, brushing myself off. "Thanks."

"What was that, Elara?" he growled.

I marched towards the goblins, who had survived the fall, somehow. The sun's power still coursed through me. "Teleporting isn't my specialty," I said and raised my hand. The sun's powers left my hand to incinerate the goblins before me.

Sweat dripped down my neck and back.

"I didn't realize the Dead Lands were so hot," I said and pulled my shirt away from my chest.

Myrin scowled. "It's not hot."

My hair stuck to my head, soaked. "It's boiling."

"Ryul," Myrin yelled.

He ran over and scowled at me. "You used the sun, didn't you?"

"I've used it several times before," I growled and fanned my face.

"You have to let the power go," Ryul snapped. "You're going to burn from the inside out."

"I'm trying," I snarled. And I was. It just wouldn't release its hold on me, or my hold on it.

"Would knocking her out help?" Myrin asked.

"No," Ryul said. "Elara, look up at the sky and shoot a flame as high as you can, like you're sending it back to the sun."

I did as he instructed.

Then, I watched as a giant creature was tossed through the flame, burning up instantly.

Two more creatures followed.

Calming down, I focused and closed my connection to the sun.

My body crumpled to the ground once the power left me.

"Elara?" Ryul called.

I lifted my hand. "Alive," I breathed.

The guys sat around me, their breathing heavy, too.

"What were you guys up to? There's like a hundred dead bodies."

"You first," Venali said.

"I went to Pinolt, like I said. While I was there, he sent those filthy goblins after me. I didn't want them tainting my clean world, so I teleported back here with them latched on to me."

"You *let* them bite and scratch you?" Kydrus asked.

I nodded. "It was the easiest way to get them all here. Your turn."

Silence greeted me.

I looked around and all seven had their heads in their hands.

Clearly, they needed a moment to absorb my genius.

One by one, they started laughing until all seven were clutching their stomachs, doubled over.

I waited patiently, closing my eyes to take a quick nap.

When they finally finished, Venali told me about the creatures showing up and how more came each time they asked.

It made me wish I had been here to watch them fighting.

Amrynn rubbed at his chest. "Could you not go to another planet without us next time? It was rather uncomfortable."

I stood without responding and brushed my pants off. "We should head back," I said and headed towards Klinsot, knowing they'd follow.

As I walked, I felt warmth, like a fire, behind me. Once at the road, I turned and saw all the bodies burning with black flames.

Myrin's flames.

The bites and scratches stung and when I resumed walking, I hissed a few times.

"Stop and let Durlan heal you," Daniel said.

I sighed and stopped.

Durlan stood before me, scowling, while he healed me.

"You're scowling," I whispered. "You're going to get wrinkles if you keep doing that."

"I'm surprised I don't have grey hair already," he grumbled. "Done."

I hopped up, kissed his cheek, and resumed walking to the castle.

"What were you doing on that other planet?" Myrin asked.

"I told you. Finding the best spot for a house," I said.

"Planning a vacation home?" Daniel asked.

They had heard me before I left. They knew what I had been doing there. Why were they asking?

"Something like that," I said.

"You should take us there," Ryul said.

I stopped and turned to look at them. "Why?"

"We want to see it," Daniel said.

"Now?" I asked.

"What else are we doing?" Kydrus asked.

Something fishy was going on.

"You seven are up to something," I growled and narrowed my eyes at them.

"Shouldn't we get to see the place we are going to live?" Ryul asked.

My heart clenched, but what would taking them there hurt?

"Fine. Everyone touch me," I said.

They all set a hand on me, and I teleported.

"Whoa," Ryul whispered.

"We were here during one of our jumps back to Anderelle, weren't we?" Amrynn asked.

I nodded.

All of their hands dropped from me.

"It's beautiful," Myrin whispered.

"It is my favorite in our solar system," I said and walked to trace my fingertips along a bright purple flower.

"So, where's our house going to be?" Daniel asked and looked around. "This is a pretty good spot."

Tears filled my eyes, but I avoided looking at them so they wouldn't see. "Yes, this was the spot I had picked for you," I whispered.

"We could put a fighting ring over there," Venali said and pointed to a flat, grassy area.

"A shop there," Durlan said and pointed in the opposite direction.

"Three story house?" Kydrus asked. "We'll need eight rooms and at least five offices."

My jaw clenched as they continued discussing where they would build everything, like they weren't talking about abandoning me.

"Elara?" Myrin called.

His voice sounded far away, faint, muffled.

Hands reached towards me.

"Don't touch me," I said and backed up.

Were they testing me? Were they toying with me? Or did they not care? No, they cared, so what was this?

Tears blinded me, the green grass an ocean of tears.

The pain spread, and I fell to my knees, then Amara took over without letting me stay conscious.

CHAPTER 26
AMARA

My seven consorts looked at me with varying expressions, but most were pained or sad.

"You are all assholes," I snapped at them.

"You don't—" Ryul started, but I hit him with a blast of power, knocking him to his knees.

"Amara," Myrin whispered.

"She's being ridiculous," Ryul gasped.

"Yes, she's being a tad childish, but she is also preparing for what she believes is going to happen. You want her to be more honest with you and yet when she is, you torture the poor girl. You are not the men I remember. The men I remember wouldn't torment a girl like this, even if she was being ridiculous."

"Help us keep—" Daniel started, but my fury would not be calmed.

I forced them all to their knees. "Do you remember what I told you?" I asked.

"No. Don't," Myrin gasped.

"You all need some time to think. Some time without Elara or I by your side. Spend some time alone and reflect on what you think is important," I ordered them, and then separated them around the planet. I teleported to a different place, so they couldn't teleport right back to find me, located a nice cave, and sealed Elara and I inside, so they could not use our bond to find us.

I used my powers to place another seal, this one to block the dark god from finding me. Elara needed sleep, the kind safe from *him*. Here, now, she could get that. And I would use the time to strengthen my powers.

CHAPTER 27
KYDRUS

Amara teleported us away.

She sent me to a mountain range covered in snow.

Immediately, I teleported back to the spot we had been, but she was gone.

"She sealed Elara and herself somewhere," Durlan said.

I turned and found him sitting in the grass.

"I can't feel them at all," I said and clutched at my chest.

He nodded, his eyes pinched.

This felt worse than when she'd gone to the other solar system.

"Why did we think that was a good idea?" I asked as I sat beside him.

He sighed. "Maybe we *are* just assholes."

"I can agree with that," Venali said and sat.

"How long do you think she is going to leave us here?" Amrynn asked and sat as well.

"No idea," Durlan growled.

"We should try to find Daniel and Myrin," I said. "They could be on the other side of the planet."

"Did we have a collective idiot moment, or what?" Ryul asked as he joined us.

"Yep," we all answered.

"How are we going to find Myrin and Daniel?" Ryul asked.

I said, "I can sense Myrin. Anyone sense Daniel?"

"I do," Venali said. "It is really faint, though."

"How do you guys sense them at all?" Ryul asked with a scowl.

"For someone who is extremely attuned to Elara, you're pretty blind to your brothers," I said.

He shrugged. "Is there a need to be connected? No offense, but Elara and Amara are my only concerns. You guys dying doesn't hurt them, aside from emotionally."

We all sighed.

"You really should have gotten out of that castle more often," Durlan said while shaking his head.

"You're such a socially dense person," Venali said and laughed.

Ryul shrugged, unconcerned.

"Let's split into two groups and leave one person here, in case they show up somehow," Durlan said and stood.

"I'll stay," Ryul said. "Since I can't sense the others anyway."

"Sounds like a plan," I said. "Amrynn, with me."

He stood and brushed himself off. "Yes, sir."

Amyrnn set his hand on my shoulder and I teleported us as close to Myrin as I could. Unfortunately, that put us over a waterfall.

"Shit," I gasped.

Amrynn sighed right before we fell into the water.

Surfacing, I wiped the water from my face and searched for shore.

Amrynn swam in front of me, headed to the left. "This was not how I foresaw today going."

We made it to shore and I took off my shirt to wring it out.

"While the water does look nice, I don't think this is time for a swim," Myrin yelled.

We looked up and found him smiling at us from above the waterfall.

"Never pass up opportunities. We can now say we are the first to ever swim on this planet," I called back, set my hand on Amrynn, and teleported both of us to Myrin.

"Well, I have a feeling we are going to be here awhile," Myrin said.

"Why?" Amrynn asked, pulled his boot off, and dumped water out of it.

"She's sealed herself away and closed our bonds. I believe she is amassing power to prepare for the battle," Myrin said.

"What are we suppose to do on this planet until she comes for us?" Amrynn asked.

Myrin smirked. "Build a house."

We blinked at him.

"I'm sorry, I must have water in my ears. Did you suggest we further piss off our mates?" I asked with an arched brow.

"Trust me, it won't piss them off," Myrin said.

I highly doubted that, but with nothing else to do...

"Okay," I said with a resigned sigh. "But I will totally out you if she gets mad."

He laughed and set his hand on my arm. "Deal."

CHAPTER 28
ELARA

"They're idiots," Amara said as she faced me.

For the first time, we stood facing each other instead of looking in a mirror.

"We agree on that," I said.

"We've been asleep for three days," she told me. "I've been storing magic and now, when he comes, I can separate from you."

"Three days," I gasped.

What were the guys doing?

"I'm going to wake you up now and release our bonds so the guys can find you, okay?"

I nodded.

"Try to ignore them and forget their asshole actions. Your ball is tomorrow and I want you eight to have fun. That's an order."

I wasn't so sure I could do that, but I nodded.

The dream world disappeared and my eyes opened.

Sitting up, I looked around the small cave I had been in. It appeared empty.

The cave entrance was suddenly illuminated, forcing me to cover my eyes.

"Elara," Ryul said and picked me up.

Before I could say anything, he teleported us back to the spot I had last seen the guys.

I rubbed the last of the stars from my eyes and then my jaw dropped.

In what used to be a field, a huge three-story house now stood.

They had built a house while I had been gone.

My other six consorts rushed to us, but I didn't look at any of them.

I just stared at the house they had built.

Tears filled my eyes.

"Elara, do you want to see inside?" Myrin asked.

I held out my arms. "If you want to go back to Anderelle, latch on now."

Once all seven were touching me, I teleported us to Minloa, over Klinsot. As usual, we were in the air, falling towards the ground.

Kydrus teleported us to the courtyard with a chuckle.

I walked away with my eyes focused ahead of me.

They had built a house.

A house for them to live in with Amara.

A house I would never see again.

A house so they could abandon me on Minloa.

I tried to shut my bedroom door, but Myrin blocked it with his foot.

"Elara," he whispered.

"I need to sleep. Tomorrow is the ball," I said, refusing to look at him.

"Weren't you asleep the past three days?" he asked.

Yes, while they had prepared for leaving me.

"You should rest, too," I said. "There are bound to be several attempts on my life tomorrow. It would ruin your plans if I died before the battle with the dark god."

"Are you going to look at me?" he asked.

I shook my head. "No, not today."

Using all my strength and the element of surprise, I shoved him in the chest, out of the doorway, and locked the door closed. Then, I put up a barrier so he couldn't phase through it.

"Elara," he yelled and pounded on the door.

I lay on the bed and fell into a deep sleep.

I TOOK MY BREAKFAST IN MY ROOM AND THEN LET A FEW handmaids help me into my dress and braid my hair.

Once ready, I shoved all of my feelings down into a box and left my room.

Castle staff ran about, making final preparations. I smiled at everyone I passed and went in the side door of the ballroom.

Gasping, I spun in a circle to take in the room. It was decorated in silver and purple and looked absolutely stunning.

Venali walked to me and dropped down to one knee. "Your Majesty." He wore a pair of black breeches and a light tunic.

"You clean up well, Venali," I said.

He stood and smiled down at me. "You look exquisite in that dress."

I stood on tiptoe and whispered in his ear, "Perhaps tonight, you can see how I look out of it as well."

He kissed my cheek. "Sounds like a plan."

I held out my hand, and he set his in it, linking our fingers together. "Escort me to our table?"

He dipped his head. "It would be my honor."

For the first part of the night, we would eat a meal, me and my consorts at the front of the room, and the rest spread out. Then, the tables would be removed and we would dance.

I sat in my throne, which had been moved to sit before the table, and watched the staff making final preparations.

"My queen," Myrin said as he stood on the other side of the table and bowed.

"Hello, handsome. Care to sit with me?"

He smiled. "I would love to." He walked around the table and sat beside me, dropping a kiss on my cheek as he sat. "You look beautiful as always."

"Thank you." I looked at him in a black outfit and asked, "Will you save a dance for me? I know your dance card will be full with your girlfriend showing up."

He chuckled. "I'm sure she will allow me to have at least one dance with you."

Kydrus walked in and scowled at me. "You're not supposed to be in here yet."

I rolled my eyes. "I don't need an introduction."

He sat and Myrin leaned over to whisper to him.

People began trickling in and Venali left to walk around the room. Ryul took his seat after kissing my cheek.

Some attendees noticed us and stood before our table to bow or curtsy and thank me for hosting the party.

A line formed, but I didn't want to rush anyone.

Then, a familiar child's voice yelled, "Elara."

"Make way for her," I said to Ryul.

He hopped over the table and directed the adults to the side so Cassie could run around the table to me.

I stood from my chair and then knelt so I could hug her. "You came," I said with a wide smile.

She nodded with a huge grin. Her hair was braided and she wore a beautiful pink dress. "My parents let me."

Myrin dropped to a knee beside her and bowed his head. "Lady Cassie."

She turned and then executed the most perfect curtsy I had

ever seen.

Myrin kissed her knuckles and she started talking to him.

"She worked all night last night on that curtsy," a woman said beside me.

I turned and smiled at a grownup version of the girl. "She's much better than I am. My tutors would have cried at such a perfect demonstration."

She bowed. "Your Majesty, it is an honor to be here."

"Thank you for coming and allowing Cassie to come," I said.

The man beside her bowed. "She's talked about you and your consorts nonstop since your visit."

I chuckled. "We've been looking forward to seeing her again." I pulled out the small box with her present knelt beside Myrin again. "Cassie, I have a gift for you."

Her eyes widened. "A gift?"

I nodded and held it out.

She looked at her parents.

"Go on," her mother urged.

Cassie took the box, untied the ribbon, and pulled out a gem on a necklace. I had put a shooting star inside.

"With it in the gem, the star will continually fly inside, never dying," I said.

She squealed and threw her arms around me. Thank you. Thank you."

"May I put it on?" Myrin asked.

She nodded and turned her back to him.

Gently, Myrin brushed her hair to the side and then tied the necklace on.

Cassie turned and asked, "How does it look?"

"Beautiful," Myrin and I said.

She hugged me again. "Thank you."

"I'll see you once the dances start," Myrin promised her.

She waved and showed her parents the present.

Hundreds more people came and then it was time to eat.

My cheeks were going to hurt from all of the smiling as I watched Seelie and Unseelie eating together.

Yes, things were in motion. Finally.

"Please head to the edges of the room," Durlan said loud enough for everyone to hear.

All of the guests did as he asked, lining the walls of the room.

As soon as it was clear, Kydrus stepped forward, clapped, and everything disappeared.

I spun, mouth agape. "When did you learn to do that?"

He winked and stepped back without answering me.

Several musicians entered and set up, and then began playing music.

Durlan bowed before me and held out his hand. "Will you honor me with a dance, Your Majesty?"

I set my hand in his and nodded.

He led me to the middle of the room, set one hand on my lower back and held my hand with the other. Then, we flowed into a dance.

No one else was dancing, though.

I opened my mouth to say something, and then saw Myrin pick up Cassie and start dancing with her.

"You look gorgeous, Elara," Durlan said.

I smiled. "You look handsome as usual."

A man started to walk onto the floor with a scowl and without a partner, but Venali intercepted him.

"Is that attempt number one?" I asked.

"Seven, actually," Durlan growled.

My eyes widened. Seven attempts on my life tonight.

The song ended and Durlan bowed to me.

Kydrus stepped up and bowed with his hand out.

I let him lead us into the next song.

He leaned closer and whispered, "There is a rumor that we

might be able to see you take that dress off tonight."

I laughed. "Is that so? I can't imagine where that rumor came from. Perhaps, it might not be a rumor, though."

"I would very much like to confirm this rumor," he said and then spun me beneath his hand.

"As would I," I said with a wink.

Kydrus laughed, and we didn't stop smiling the rest of the song.

Myrin and Cassie stopped by us when the song ended.

"Are you up for a trade?" I asked Cassie.

She was beaming, her entire body glowed. "Yes," she said.

Myrin passed Cassie to Kydrus and then took my hand and kissed my knuckles.

I stepped close to him. "I'm glad I had something to trade for a dance. Though, you seem to have downgraded."

He smiled, slid his hand up my cheek and around my neck, and then pulled me into a deep kiss. "I love you, Elara."

We began our dance and I rested my head on his chest. Love and pain swelled within me in equal amounts.

"I love you, too, Myrin."

The night turned into a blur of dances with my mates.

Then, women from Linta who I had known while living there asked for dances.

I accepted, and before long, I was dancing with everyone. Smiling like a fool.

As I was spun to dance with a new partner, I had to tilt my head back to look up at him. Our eyes locked and fear and fury filled me.

"Feno," I gasped.

He smiled. In all this time, he had not changed. He looked exactly like I remembered him as a child. "Hello, Elara. You look beautiful. You grew into an exquisite woman."

I didn't want to cause a scene, so I continued dancing with

him. "Why are you here?"

He arched a brow. "Did you not invite everyone in Minloa, Seelie and Unseelie?"

"Yes," I said.

When I was a child, I considered him an uncle. He would play with me while my parents were busy and snuck me treats.

"Why?" I asked.

His smile disappeared. "They were hiding the truth about the Unseelie. They and the monarchs before them knew the truth, but kept it hidden and I couldn't let it continue."

No, he had to be lying. My mother was an honest woman and wouldn't have done that.

"Answer me one thing," I said.

The dance ended, but we stayed locked in our dancing position.

"Would you have killed me that night?" I asked.

His eyes locked with mine and I forgot how to breathe. After several tenses moments, he said, "No, that was why I had the tip sent to Ryul and had him take you away. Though, things did not go as planned there."

"Are you here to kill me now?" I asked.

His gaze softened. "Pixie dust, I could never harm you."

Venali's arm shot forward, aimed at Feno's throat.

I pushed Feno back and spun around to face my scarred consort.

"Elara?" he asked, eyes wide.

The entire room had silenced, and my consorts began to converge.

"Stand at guard a moment, please," I said.

Venali straightened and focused his gaze on Feno.

I turned and met Feno's curious eyes. "An enemy unlike any we have seen before is coming. One that has the power to wipe us out."

Several people gasped.

"Will you fight at my side? Defend Minloa from this threat?" I asked Feno.

He dropped to one knee, drew his sword, held it out on his palms, and bowed his head. "I serve you, Queen Elara. My sword and my life are yours to command."

"Elara," Durlan growled.

I ignored him.

Amara tapped at my mind, so I let her join me, our minds and power combining.

She reached out and touched his sword, which began to glow. "Arise, Feno of Minloa, and become a guardian of Minloa."

The crowd dropped to their knees and bowed.

Feno stood and looked at me with wide eyes.

Amara left again, and I smiled at Feno.

He sheathed his sword.

A dark roiling mass appeared at the edges of my senses.

"Durlan," I snapped.

A woman screamed.

Venali ran out of the room with Myrin on his heels.

"Feno, protect the people," I said and headed after them. "Ryul, stay with him."

"Yes, my queen," Ryul said.

Amrynn and Daniel flanked me as we went out of the castle.

Outside of the castle, just beyond the walls, twenty of the large creatures stood together.

In front of them was an older Seelie man who worked on the kitchen staff. His eyes were pure black.

"Elara," the dark god said from the man's mouth.

I dipped my head. "Bellinor." It was the first time I had said or thought his name, and it stung a bit.

He smiled. "I have come to discuss your offer."

"There is no offer," Myrin growled and his body began to glow.

"You boys are so troublesome," the dark god sighed. "Children, entertain them a bit."

The creatures roared and stepped forward. They were over forty feet tall, had huge claws and fangs, and black matted fur covering their bodies. They had snouts and walked upright.

Venali and Daniel roared back at them.

In a single moment, my consorts and the creatures sprang into action.

The dark god walked calmly through the chaos, his creatures keeping my consorts from attacking him.

He stopped when he stood before me and smiled. "Now, where were we?"

"You came to bargain?" I asked.

I should have been afraid, but somehow, I knew he didn't plan to kill me tonight. Or, at least, not yet.

"Yes," he said and nodded.

The moon was close to full, so it provided us with enough light to see each other.

"I'm listening," I said.

"You willingly come to me, sever your mate bonds with those seven, and live the rest of your Seelie life as my consort," he said.

I arched a brow. "What do I get in exchange?"

"I leave Amara and her consorts alone, letting them live the rest of their lives never being tormented by me again."

"What of Anderelle?" I asked. "Will you stop spreading your darkness here?" I asked.

He scowled. "I allowed the light to reign. It is time for darkness to rule."

I shook my head. "I cannot let you drown my world in darkness."

He narrowed his eyes. "I am allowing the men you love to live out their existences with Amara. I will even agree not to touch Pinolt."

I glanced at the men. They were slaughtering the creatures quickly, and kept glancing at me.

A smile spread as tears filled my eyes a moment. I blinked them away and looked back at the dark god. "I want them to live, yes, but my first priority is to the people of Anderelle. If you cannot agree to cease spreading your darkness, we have no deal."

He glared at me and shook his head. "You are a stupid girl. So very much like Amara."

"It seems we are at an impasse," I said and bowed. "Have a good evening."

The dark god gave me a harsh glare and then his dark presence disappeared and the body of the Seelie man he had been possessing fell.

I caught the man before he hit the ground.

"Your Majesty?" he asked as he opened his eyes, and his body shook.

"It's alright. Just rest a moment," I told him and helped him lie down.

"Elara!" Venali yelled, fear coloring his tone.

I looked up and my eyes widened.

One of the creatures loomed over me, his arm raised, ready to slice me apart with his massive claws.

I had no sword and no time to protect myself.

A dark figure dashed between the creature and I, and blocked the strike with his glowing sword.

"Feno," I gasped.

Feno parried the creature's claws. "Are you hurt?" he asked.

"No," I said and stood. "I just don't have my sword."

The creature attacked and Feno blocked.

Quickly, I picked the Seelie man up and ran to the courtyard. "Go inside when you can," I ordered him. Then, I ran back out.

When I made it to Feno, all of the creatures were dead, including the one he had been fighting.

All six of the guys had blood splattered on them.

"Are you injured?" I asked Feno.

He shook his head.

I looked at the six men stalking forward. "Are any of you injured?"

Myrin grabbed my forearm and pulled me away from Feno and the bodies.

The six surrounded me.

"Don't you hurt him," I snapped.

Myrin's flames flared high on the bodies, and Feno leapt back from the one he had been standing beside.

I growled.

"Feno, return to the ballroom," Durlan said.

Feno nodded.

Before I could speak, someone teleported our group to the bathing chambers.

"What happened?" Durlan asked.

Myrin released me and stripped.

I watched the six of them pull off their clothes, transfixed.

"Elara?" Durlan asked.

I turned, trying really hard to keep my eyes on his face despite the fact that I knew he was naked. "Nothing. Feno told me my parents knew the Unseelie weren't evil, but planned to continue with the rouse. So, he killed them. He said he was the one who tipped Ryul off and that he never would have hurt me."

"What happened between you and the dark god?" Myrin asked.

"You couldn't hear?" I asked.

They all shook their heads.

"He didn't like my terms," I said and shrugged.

"You were negotiating?" Venali asked, walking closer to me.

"Trying," I said, "but he wouldn't budge."

"Let me get this straight. Even after we told you not to...you tried to sell yourself to him?" Myrin asked.

My eyes narrowed. "Did you just refer to me as a whore?"

"What did he offer you?" Durlan asked.

I sighed. "Don't you have blood to wash off?"

"Elara," they all growled.

Ryul walked in. "What did I miss?" he asked.

"Myrin called me a whore," I said.

Myrin groaned and walked into the nearest shower.

"I feel like that is taken out of context," Ryul said.

After everyone was done washing, we teleported to our room.

"Aren't I supposed to say goodbye to my guests?" I asked and hopped onto my bed.

"We explained you helped fight off an enemy and they were understanding," Ryul said.

"So, back to our question," Durlan said, dressed now.

"When I'm old, I think I'll move to the beach," I said.

"Elara!" seven voices shouted.

"He wouldn't agree to keeping his darkness from Anderelle," I said. "So, we couldn't reach a deal. My duty, first and foremost, is to the people of Anderelle."

"You're being really frustrating," Durlan sighed and pinched the bridge of his nose.

"How?" I asked and folded my arms across my chest.

"We want to know the full discussion," Daniel said.

I sighed and fell onto the bed. "He offered to leave Amara and you seven alone, letting you live on Pinolt for the rest of your lives. In exchange, I would sever our mate bonds and be his consort for the rest of my Seelie life. I want you to be safe, but I need Anderelle safe. He said it is darkness's turn to reign."

There was silence, not even breathing audible.

I sat up and all seven stared at me, eerily still.

"Don't ask questions you don't want answers to," I said, stood, and walked out to find a handmaid to help with my dress.

Rosalie, the one I used the most often, popped around the corner, her perfectly curled hair bouncing as she walked. "Need help getting out of the dress?" she asked.

I smiled. "Yes, please."

She followed me back to my room and into the attached restroom.

The guys hadn't moved, still staring at the bed and the spot I had been in.

I closed the door and whispered, "Just ignore them."

She chuckled and began unlacing my dress. "Are you adding that new Unseelie to your harem?"

"Feno? No. Ew." I pretended to gag.

"What? He's very handsome," she said.

"He's basically my uncle," I said and then exhaled in relief when she loosened my dress fully.

"Does that mean he's available?" she asked.

I chuckled. "I don't know, but feel free to find out."

After stepping out of the dress, she brushed out my hair and then gave me a nightgown for bed.

"Anything else?" she asked.

"Nope. Thank you for your help."

She curtsied. "I'll see you in the morning."

When I stepped out into the bedroom, the guys had moved to sitting, but still stared silently at nothing.

"I had fun tonight," I said as I climbed into bed. "It's definitely one of my favorite memories, and I will treasure it for the rest of my life."

None of them responded.

With a sigh, I lay down and went to sleep.

Hopefully, tomorrow would be a good day. First item was to meet with Feno. He and I had a lot to discuss.

CHAPTER 29
MYRIN

WE COULD HAVE LOST her yesterday.

Twice.

If the dark god had lied and said he would leave Anderelle alone, she would have severed our mate bonds to become his consort.

If Feno hadn't been there, she might have been killed by that creature.

My mind was made up, no matter the cost, we would get them to fully merge. I wouldn't lose them.

I wouldn't survive losing them...either of them.

Elara had been the light in the room last night. The sun that people had gravitated towards. She had smiled all night.

She'd said she would cherish last night as a favorite memory, and honestly, so would I.

I had wanted to confront her, to scold her when she woke, but as soon as her eyes opened, she smiled, and I didn't want to do anything to cause that beautiful smile to disappear.

It seemed my six brothers felt the same as we all chatted with her and mostly watched in enraptured silence while she went through her day with that smile in place.

After lunch, she summoned Feno and took him to her war room to talk. Since she hadn't said we couldn't come, my brothers and I followed and took up seats or standing positions around the room.

She sighed, but then smirked and sat in her chair.

With every confrontation and fight, she grew more confident in herself. Despite being so young and ignorant, she was fast becoming an amazing queen.

Had I not been her consort, I would have tried my hardest to win a place in her bed and then her heart. I would have bowed to her eagerly.

When we had first met, she'd worn mostly fighting attire with high necklines. Now, she wore lower cut shirts, giving us all glorious cleavage views, and dresses. The ones she wore with corsets were definitely my favorite.

"Feno, what do you know about the dark god?" Elara asked.

He sat across from her and treated us like we weren't even there.

Had I been him and receiving the glares Venali and Durlan were giving, I wouldn't have been so relaxed. Then again, he was like an uncle to Elara, so he probably felt safe. He might be safe from being killed by them, but there was still the chance that they'd fight him.

"Very little. I knew there was an increase in fae creatures, and weird creatures, around Minloa, but nothing else. I didn't know you were a vessel for a goddess either."

Elara tilted her head up, looking at the ceiling. "I won't be her vessel much longer."

My heart stilled and for a moment, I forgot how to breathe.

Venali, who had been standing, sat and stared at his fists.

Yes, I could sympathize. We were strong, powerful, and yet we could do nothing about this issue. Brute force couldn't solve this problem.

"Let's get you caught up on all that has happened, so you're and ready for the upcoming battle," Elara continued.

"Could you start with what happened after you woke up?" Feno asked.

She chuckled. "That feels like a lifetime ago. Like someone else's life."

"You are vastly different now," Kydrus said and smiled at her.

She returned his smile and then took a deep breath and began her retelling.

Ryul, Amrynn, and Durlan jumped in to add information she left out or forgot.

I watched Feno, waiting to gauge his reaction.

He didn't seem evil and last night I had seen love in his eyes when he looked at Elara. Still, better safe than sorry.

Feno's eyes grew darker and darker as he listened. Then, the room began to shake. He stood, the shelves rattling and books falling off, and left.

As soon as he left, the room stilled.

"He'll be back," Elara said and relaxed.

I walked to her and knelt on one knee beside her chair. "Do you want anything while you wait?"

She leaned over and kissed my lips, causing a fire that never seemed to die to burn brighter. "Just that," she whispered.

I would slay a thousand creatures to continue receiving those kisses.

I planned to slay a god to continue receiving them.

Feno walked back in, fully composed. He sat across from her again and said, "I have failed you many lifetimes over. There is no way I can repay you. I will stay with you and fight against this dark god."

She smiled. "Your sword will be a great asset for us."

"May I steal Durlan for a bit?" Feno asked.

Elara nodded. "Sure."

Durlan stood, and he and Feno left the room.

"Get him a position here," she said. "He is going to be a key player in our upcoming battle."

Her eyes glazed over a moment and she shook her head.

"Are you alright?" I asked softly.

She cleared her throat and nodded. "I'm fine."

Yet another lie.

"Elara," I growled.

She stood and smiled. "Let's go on a walk. We can scout out the best places to hold our battle."

"The Dead Lands will serve as a great place," Venali said.

"Well, we need to figure out where to set everything up. Come on," she urged. "Walk with me, boys."

We obeyed, but as we exited the room, we all made eye contact and I could see the shared concern there. Elara had a knack for making us worry.

"Fine?" Venali asked as he walked beside me.

I pinched the bridge of my nose. "Yeah."

"If we tickle her, you think she'll tell us?" he asked.

She did hate being tickled.

"Keep an eye on her," I whispered.

He scoffed. "That's all we do."

"And worry," I said.

CHAPTER 30
ELARA

"I WIN," Durlan said and set his final card down.

Everyone, myself included, growled.

That was the sixth game in a row he had won.

"Let's play a different game," I said.

Venali and Ryul nodded their agreement.

Durlan laughed.

I gathered the cards into a single pile for shuffling.

All seven of my mates raised their heads, looking towards the door. Then, Venali, Kydrus, and Daniel dashed out of the room. Amrynn, Myrin, Ryul, and Durlan surrounded me.

Durlan teleported us to my war room. As soon as we arrived, Ryul locked the door and drew his sword.

"Guys?" i asked.

"A large group of powerful people just showed up," Myrin said.

"I don't sense evil," I said with a scowl.

"It is better if we take you somewhere safe until we find out their intentions," Amrynn said.

Someone knocked on the door.

Myrin phased through it and then came back and nodded before pushing open the door for us to see the visitor.

I remembered the first time he had done that and scared me.

Outside stood Tamryn, Warlord of Blythe. He bowed to me. "Your Grace, there are visitors to see you."

I ran my fingers through my hair as I followed to my throne room through the side door. I should have changed clothes or freshened up a bit, but it seemed like they were in a rush so I didn't bother asking. Once seated, I nodded and the front doors opened.

Myrin and Amrynn stood at the foot of the stairs. Durlan stood behind me, ready to give me counsel if needed.

The others spread out around the room.

In through the doors walked ten men in silver fighting leathers with a flower crest on their chests. They had long, silver hair, and pointed ears like me.

They were not Seelie, though. They were long thought extinct.

I stood and skipped down the stairs to meet them on level ground.

The man in front walked with his head held high and a sword with a gemstone with a star in it. Their king.

We stopped a few feet apart. His face stoic. Mine smiling and excited.

The man to his right said, "Introducing, Elryd, King of-"

"The High Elves," I finished.

His stoic expression broke as he smiled. "You know of us?"

I bobbed my head. "I read a lot of old historical texts. We thought you were extinct."

Durlan cleared his throat.

I cringed and forced a stoic courtly face.

"I am Elara, Queen of Minloa, Empress of Anderelle, and vessel of the Goddess of the Universe, Amara."

His eyebrow twitched at my last title, but he made no

comment. He bowed, took my hand, and kissed the back of it. "It is an honor to meet you, Queen Elara."

I curtsied. "Likewise, King Elryd." I turned to Kydrus. "Table and chairs, please."

Kydrus snapped his fingers and the pews that had been in the room disappeared. Then, he replaced them with a huge rectangular table with heavy wooden chairs.

I waved at the end chair. "Please, have a seat." I stood next to the head seat and Durlan pulled it out for me.

As he pushed it in, he whispered, "Be wary. We don't know their motives yet."

I sat and smiled at Elryd. A few of his people sat around the table. Amrynn, Durlan, Kydrus, and Myrin sat with me. The rest of my mates took positions around the room in case things went south.

Elryd steepled his fingers. "There has been a rumor that you are fighting against the dark god, B-"

I held out my hand and he stopped. "We don't say his name."

He nodded.

"We have been and are fighting him. I predict a final battle soon."

"How have you been able to fight a god and his creatures?" the elf who had introduced Elryd asked.

"Your name?" I asked.

"Dyffros," he said.

I held out my hand and plucked the star from Elryd's sword and examined it. "Not without pain, but we are holding our own, Dyffros."

All of the elves leapt up.

Elryd smiled. "You're a Celestial Warrior."

I smirked. "I like how that sounds, but I am unsure it fits. I can manipulate the stars and planets, and harness the sun's energy."

He nodded and then snatched the star from me and bounced it

in his palm like a ball. "Yes, those are a Celestial Warrior's main abilities."

My mouth dropped open, and I looked at Ryul who had his eyebrows raised in surprise as well.

Elryd scowled. "You've not heard the term before?" He put the star back in the gemstone.

"Most records in regards to those with celestial powers are missing," Ryul said. "And Amara isn't one who cares much for titles."

"You said you are a vessel," Elryd said. "Can you prove it?"

"Why are you here?" Durlan asked.

Dyffros snarled. "Who are you to question a king?"

"He is my mate, consort of Amara, and a demigod," I said. "All of my mates are equal to me and are free to speak."

Dyffros scowled and quieted.

"Your mate and Amara's consort?" Elryd asked.

I huffed. "It's complicated."

He turned to Durlan. "We have come to help fight B-"

All of us yelled, interrupting him.

He sighed.

"Apologies, but we avoid drawing his attention as much as possible," I said.

He nodded. "We've come to help you fight him."

"Why now?" Venali asked from the back of the room.

"We've been watching and waiting," Elryd said. "We had to be sure you weren't going to fall to his charms or lies."

I chuckled mirthlessly. "No need to worry about that."

"Our fighters are excellent and with two Celestial Warriors, defeating him shouldn't be an issue," Elryd said.

"Test," Venali called.

I sighed. "Fine, Venali. Elryd, would you allow your strongest fighter to have a match against mine? So we might gauge your skills?"

He smiled. "Certainly."

I stood and all the men followed suit. "If you'll follow me, we can go to the training arena a—"

"Field," Venali said.

I scowled at him, but relented. "Fine, the field."

Myrin walked at my side, his hands clasped behind his back.

"So?" I asked without looking at him.

"Unsure," he said.

I nodded and we continued on in silence. Once in the open field between the Dead Lands and Klinsot, I stopped and turned to face Venali.

He dropped to one knee before me.

"No killing. No maiming. Test, only. Understood?"

He nodded. "Yes, my queen."

Elryd came to stand beside me. "You seem excited."

I smirked. "The fighting prowess of the High Elves has been in many fables and texts. I'm excited to see how it compares."

Dyffros stepped into the circle our groups had made and stood before Venali. While Venali was larger overall, I sensed a lot of power from Dyffros.

Venali bowed.

Dyffros bowed back.

"No killing. No maiming. Understood?" I yelled.

Both nodded.

"Begin," I snapped.

Dyffros dashed forward and Venali dodged his punch, spinning around his back, but Dyffros spun as well.

He was definitely fast, possibly as fast as Kydrus.

"Full power," I yelled at Venali.

He growled, backed away from Dyffros, and took a deep breath. When he released it, his body and eyes glowed a moment and then the glow disappeared, but I could feel his power now.

"Interesting," Elryd whispered as he watched.

Venali nodded once and then charged Dyffros.

They started off slow, exchanging blows and blocks, but a few hits later, both exploded into motion.

Each moved so fast, I could hardly keep track.

The sound of flesh hitting flesh made me cringe and worry for them, but I trusted Venali not to take it too far.

Minutes passed and then Venali stood over Dyffros's unconscious body.

The elves didn't even react.

Venali dusted himself off, walked to me, and nodded. "They'll do well in this battle."

Elryd smiled. "You're more than Seelie."

Venali smiled back. "We aren't at full power, but we are able to use some of our demigod abilities."

"I look forward to seeing you on the battlefield," Elryd said.

"Now that that's over, let's get back to business," I said.

"Why are you scowling?" Venali asked as we walked side by side.

"I'm pouting," I admitted. "I couldn't see most of your fight because you were moving so fast."

He hooked his arm around my waist and pulled me close. "I'm sure I could find another elf to knock out and go slower if you'd like."

Why did that actually excite me and sound like a fun idea?

"No," I said and shook my head. "No more knocking out elves."

"Disappointing," Venali said with a sigh. "I was hoping to challenge Elryd."

"No," I said and glared up at him.

He laughed and kissed my cheek. "Fine. Spoil sport."

I shook my head. These males would be the death of me.

CHAPTER 31
AMRYNN

THE HIGH ELVES were long thought dead. Now, they showed up on our doorstep claiming they wanted to help us fight the dark god.

I wasn't sure I could believe them. There was no malice or evil intent coming from them, but it was just so convenient.

"You don't trust them either, do you?" Daniel asked.

I glanced at him as we walked towards our bedroom. "No."

He nodded. "It is good to be wary. I'm really hoping they are here to help, though. We need it."

"He seems rather interested in Elara," I whispered.

Daniel chuckled. "Wouldn't you be? If I was him, I would be trying to find a way into her harem, too."

I sighed. "True, but that doesn't make me feel any better."

He shrugged. "Wasn't trying to make you feel better, just being honest."

"Think she will entertain the thought?" I asked softly.

Daniel stopped and turned to face me. "Why would she?"

"If she thinks we are going to abandon her, she would want someone to keep her company here. The King of the High Elves would be a suitable match for her," I said.

Daniel snarled. "We aren't abandoning her." His eye twitched, and I could sense the hesitancy in his words.

"The possibility is there," I whispered.

"She plans to kill herself, remember? We won't be able to abandon her because she will be dead," he growled and stormed off.

I caught up to him. "We won't let it happen. We will find a way to stop her. Myrin is fairly certain he has found a way to force them to merge."

"I hope he finds something. I don't want to lose her," Daniel whispered and glanced back at Elara who was walking between Myrin and Elryd.

She smiled and laughed at something Elryd said, and I watched several of his men focus on her.

Yes, when she laughed like that it drew you to her like a magnet.

"We can't lock her up just because other men fancy her," Daniel whispered to me.

I growled. "We could."

He chuckled and patted my back. "Glad I'm not the only one who has possessive issues when it comes to her."

I rubbed a hand down my face and turned back around. "They're going to ask to speak to Amara. We should be ready for their attack then."

His eyes widened. "You think they intend to hurt Amara?"

I shrugged. "I have no idea. I just want us to be prepared."

Once back in the throne room, as predicted, Elryd asked to speak to Amara.

Elara closed her eyes and when they opened, Amara looked out. Her body glowed, and I took an involuntary step towards her.

She smiled and Elryd and his elves dropped to one knee before her. "Elryd," she whispered. "You are alive."

He stood and nodded. "I hid a bit too well and lost my way, but I am here now."

"You know him?" I asked Amara.

She turned and smiled at me. "You do not need to worry, Elryd is a friend. He will not hurt me or Elara."

Elryd stood. "If anything, this strengthens my resolve to keep Elara safe. Why haven't you just merged with her?"

"A few reasons," Amara said and cleared her throat while looking away from him.

"Stubbornness," Myrin growled.

"You must be the first consort," Elryd said.

Myrin bowed. "I go by Myrin currently."

"How does Amara know him, but you don't?" I asked Myrin.

"She had gone off several times alone," Myrin said. "She told me about the elves, but since we didn't find them, I assumed they had been killed off as your texts said."

"Elryd and his elves saved me while I was walking the fields of Anderelle," Amara said. "I'd grown weak and he provided nourishment for me and healed me."

"You forgot to eat, didn't you?" Myrin asked.

Her face became stoic. "I don't know what you're talking about."

"She forgot to eat," Elryd confirmed with a smile.

Amara sighed. "Okay, fine. I admit it. I forgot that while on Andrelle I needed to consume the food here to stay nourished."

Myrin pinched the bridge of his nose a moment and then turned and bowed to Elryd. "Thank you for assisting my forgetful goddess."

"Where have you been hiding?" Amara asked.

"Deep underground," Elryd said. "We've been waiting for the right time to return."

"And you believe that's now?" I asked.

He turned to face me. "Your queen has united several continents and races who previously despised each other. She is about to face a battle that will affect the entire galaxy. So, yes, now is the time."

"They trust very few people," Amara whispered.

"Understandable," Elryd said.

"Elryd, Dyffros, and Talron will join you seven for battle strategy discussions," Amara said.

One of the elves in the middle of their group stepped forward. "Me?"

She smiled. "Yes. You are one of the best strategists in the world. You and Durlan should get along well."

He blushed and bowed. "I will do my best."

"I must leave. I cannot merge more with Elara. Protect her, Elryd. She will need your guidance."

Myrin growled, and Amara smacked his arm before she left.

Elara staggered forward a step, but held out her arms before anyone could reach out to her. "I'm fine."

"Did you hear everything?" Myrin asked.

She nodded, drew in a deep breath, and straightened.

"How many are you in your army?" Elara asked Elryd.

"One thousand," he said.

Her eyes widened as did my own. Where were they? They had not come here yet.

"They are waiting for my signal," Elryd said, answering our unspoken question.

"Venali," she called.

He came to her side.

She looked up at him. "Can you assist with accommodations?"

He nodded and immediately left.

Her face paled, and I teleported to her, wrapping my arm around her waist. "Elara?"

Her body was burning hot, and her breath came in short pants.

Myrin met my eyes and bobbed his head once.

I teleported Elara and I to her room.

She went limp in my arms, and her eyes rolled up in the back of her head.

I set her on the bed with a scowl.

She hadn't been having issues merging with Amara lately. So, why now?

Ryul teleported into the room and walked to her. He set his hand on her face and sighed. "She's fine. Just physically exhausted."

"From?" I asked.

"Apparently, secret sessions since none of us have seen her doing anything that would cause this level of exhaustion."

I sighed and sat in the chair beside the bed.

"Or, she's been doing something else," Myrin said as he walked in.

"Like what?" Ryul asked.

"That's what I plan to ask her when she wakes up," Myrin said and snarled.

"How could she sneak out without any of us knowing?" I asked. "With Ryul controlling her dreams?"

We slept in shifts so at least one of us was patrolling the grounds at all times.

"One of the guards said he had seen someone in the woods last night, but they disappeared before he could speak to them. He said it looked like Elara, but he wasn't positive." Myrin sat across from me. "Do you know what I found in the woods?"

"What?" I asked.

"Nothing," he said. "She's hiding something."

I scoffed. "She's always hiding something."

"Like you guys don't," she whispered as she sat up.

"What have you been doing at night in the woods?" Myrin asked.

She scowled. "I haven't been in the woods."

"Why are you so tired then?" I asked.

She shrugged. "Ask Amara. I've been sleeping with you all as far as I know."

Myrin's brows furrowed more. "Wonderful."

CHAPTER 32
ELARA

I FOLLOWED Amrynn to the area that had been provided for the elves between the Dead Lands and Klinsot.

Hundreds of tents were set up and over one thousand elves walked among them. It was a sight I had dreamed of as a child. A wish to see the elven army.

Elryd stepped out of the largest tent and walked to me. “Are you feeling better?”

I smiled. “Amara has been burning the candle at both ends it seems. She likes to keep her consorts on their toes.”

“Would you like to take a walk with me?” he requested.

“Sure. Amrynn, can you make sure there is water access?” Before Amrynn could respond to me, I quickly turned and hoped Elryd would follow.

He did. And, he waited until we were out of earshot of his men and Amrynn to speak.

“You seem at odds with them despite saying they are also your mates,” he whispered.

I sighed. “It’s complicated. We’re all trying to come to grips with the possible outcomes after this war.”

"Such as?" he asked and plucked a flower from the ground as we walked, twirling it between his fingers.

"Amara sacrificing herself. Me sacrificing myself. Amara and I merging. All of us dying."

He scowled. "Those are heavy outcomes."

I laughed. "Yeah."

"But those are outcomes in any battle. Something else is causing this." His eyes met mine and it was like he could see into my soul.

"Perhaps," I said and turned away, walking again. I headed into the Dead Lands and knelt, letting the sand slip through my fingers.

"If you and Amara separate, they'll have to choose, won't they?" he asked.

Without looking at him I grumbled, "You're rather intuitive."

He chuckled. "When you've been alive for thousands of years and dealt with gods, you pick up on things."

I continued playing with the sand. "I don't want them to have to choose. They were Amara's first. I will die long before her, her being immortal and all."

"Which is why sacrificing yourself sounds ideal." He sat in the sand beside me and drew unfamiliar symbols.

"I wouldn't say ideal."

"If they leave and you survive, will you take new consorts?" He drew a symbol of fire and the sun.

I had seen it somewhere before. Where?

"Potentially, but not for a while afterwards."

"Grieving time," he said and nodded.

He went to wipe the symbol away, but I snagged his wrist, halting him.

"What is that? I've seen it before." I looked up into his eyes, finding his bright with interest.

"It's a Celestial Warrior symbol." He drew another symbol, this one related to the moon.

"My mother had these powers," I whispered. "Perhaps I saw her draw them."

"You seem surprised to see me playing with the star earlier," he said.

I realized I still held his arm, so I released it. "If I let them go, they grow in size."

"Tonight, I will teach you," he said.

I smiled. "Really?"

He nodded. "But, in exchange, I want you to consider marriage to me, should you live and they leave. We could unite our people and my people could come out of hiding."

"Consider it only?" I asked.

He nodded again and smiled wide. "Yes."

Elryd was handsome, powerful, and a Celestial Warrior like me. He was also a king. Marriage to him would be politically brilliant. Could I do it if they left?

I nodded. "Very well."

He stood and dusted off his pants and then held out his hand for me. "We should return."

I let him pull me to my feet and brushed my pants off. "Have you spoken to Durlan yet?"

He shook his head, the silver strands sparkling in the sunlight. "I'll head there now."

Amrynn stood at Elryd's tent, arms folded and a scowl on his face.

Elryd bowed to me and then turned towards the castle.

Once gone, Amrynn stepped forward. "What did he want to talk about?"

I wrapped my arm around his, letting my hand slid along his upper arm and the muscular bicep. He'd bulked up a bit the past year. "He's going to teach me how to use my magic more." I leaned my head against his shoulder as we walked away from the elves.

"He propositioned you, didn't he?" he asked.

"He just asked for me to consider marriage to him, should I survive and you all leave with Amara."

Amrynn stopped and pulled me into a hug. "My love, I will not abandon you. I promised you wouldn't be alone ever again and I meant it."

Tears sprang to my eyes, and I gripped the front of his shirt. "You're hers first, plus, she will outlive me."

"My body and sword are yours. I wouldn't be able to live with myself knowing you were alone here."

"I wouldn't be alone if Elryd married me," I whispered.

Amrynn growled, the rumble vibrated against my face, pressed into his chest. "No. You're mine, Elara. You've been mine since the day I saw you pull a star from the sky." He lifted my chin and kissed me tenderly. "You can't get rid of me so easily. Our souls were destined to bond even without Amara's interference. You are mine and I am yours, end of story."

I rubbed my face against his shirt to wipe off the tears. "I love you, Amrynn."

He kissed the top of my head. "I love you, too. Always will."

CHAPTER 33
DURLAN

Elryd knocked on my open office door as he stepped inside. "Busy?"

He had his long, silver hair tied back, exposing his pointed ears and sharp features. Something about him screamed predator despite his non-threatening appearance.

"I'm always busy, but I've been expecting you." I waved at the chairs in front of my desk with a smile. "Have a seat."

He moved with a fluid grace that betrayed his age and fighter's training. Although we hadn't seen him fight, I had no doubt that he would hold his own against any of us.

"Elara told me she's considering sacrificing herself. How do you plan to stop her?" he asked.

My eyes widened and I stood dumbfounded for a moment. "She told you that?"

He set his hands in his lap and smirked. "Among other things."

I suppressed a growl. His attitude drew out my possessiveness. Why would she talk so openly with him? A stranger?

"How do you plan to stop her?" he asked again.

I set and met his gaze. "We want them to combine permanently."

"Amara seems against that idea," he said.

I nodded. "Both are."

"What if your plan fails?" he asked.

I let my shoulders sag. "I'm going to be honest with you."

He smiled. "Please."

"We have no idea. We all would sacrifice ourselves to keep Elara safe. Same with Amara. My plan is to keep at least two of us close to them during the battle. Amara hasn't separated from Elara and I'm not sure she can. If she can, that will be when Elara sacrifices herself."

He nodded. "Most likely."

Amrynn charged into the office, his eyes glowing with fury. Before I could stop him, he punched Elryd and tossed him across the room.

I got between them, pushing against Amrynn's chest to stop him from pouncing on Elryd.

Elryd stood and brushed himself off like nothing had happened.

"Amrynn," I snapped. "What are you—"

"Keep away from her," Amrynn growled, snarling to show off his canines. "King or not, I will tear your fucking head off if you mess with her mind anymore. She's mine."

I was totally in the dark about what happened, but grasped the basic situation.

"I'm not messing with her head. She told me of the possibility of you leaving. Only a fool would pass up the chance to ensure a potential courtship with her." Elryd shrugged. "If you were in my place, you would do the same."

"There is no possibility of me leaving," Amrynn snarled. "Elara is mine and I will stay at her side until she breathes her last breath."

Elryd eyed him skeptically. "You'll leave Amara for Elara?"

"Yes," Amrynn said with no hesitation.

My eyes widened. We had all been thinking about it, but Amrynn was the first I'd heard with such a decision.

"Same," Venali said from the doorway.

Elryd shrugged. "Then you have nothing to fear from me. If you don't abandon her, she won't need to consider me. Can we get back to discussing how to keep her alive?"

"Amrynn, leave," I whispered.

He stood snarling at Elryd still.

I looked at Venali for help, but he was glaring at Elryd, too.

Magic help me, how could I get them to leave?

Myrin pushed past Venali and looked around the room. "What's going on?"

"Amrynn and Venali were just leaving," I said and pushed against Amrynn's chest.

He growled, eyes locked on Elryd, but backed up.

Once Amrynn and Venali left, I shut and locked the door. "I'm sorry," I said to Elryd as I returned to my chair behind the desk.

Elryd righted his chair and sat. "No need to apologize. I expected at least one of you to threaten me at some point."

Myrin arched a brow as he sat next to Elryd.

"What happens to you seven if Elara dies?" Elryd asked.

"Our bonds are broken, which will momentarily stun us," I answered.

He tapped his finger on the arm of the chair. "So, we should have at least one of my men with you to protect you if she does sacrifice herself."

Myrin's eyes narrowed. "She won't be sacrificing herself."

Elryd looked at him. "You have a plan to stop her?"

"Merge," Myrin said.

I cocked my head as I looked at him. Something was off with Myrin.

"If that doesn't work?" Elryd asked.

"Will," Myrin said.

"Myrin," I whispered.

He looked at me and the rage in his eyes caught me off guard.

I sighed. "Even you?"

Myrin took a deep breath, closed his eyes as he did, and let it out. When he opened his eyes again, the rage was gone. "Apologies. You're the first true threat we've dealt with in a while."

Elryd smiled. "Thank you."

"Amara has been doing something without even Elara's knowledge. I think she's been separating from Elara, preparing for their plan to seal him."

"Which bodes well for your plan to force them to merge," Elryd said.

Myrin nodded.

"Amara asked me to protect Elara, which leads me to believe she plans to sacrifice herself." Elryd chuckled mirthlessly. "You boys have your work cut out for you. Not only do you have to fight a god and his monsters, you have to keep your mates from killing themselves."

"Sacrificing," I corrected.

He shrugged.

"Shall we move on to discussing the battle itself? I'll fetch the two Amara picked," Elryd said.

I spread the map out on my desk and pulled the wooden triangles we used as troop markers from my top drawer in preparation of our meeting.

Myrin sighed and dropped his head back. "She's making me crazy."

I chuckled. "Understatement of the century."

"Let's hope these elves can help us enough to save them," he whispered.

I nodded. "All we have is hope at this point."

CHAPTER 34
RYUL

THE FURY I sensed led me to the training arena where I found Amrynn and Venali sparring. Both were covered in sweat and snarling, though from the way they interacted it didn't appear the snarls were meant for each other.

I sat atop the fence. "What's up?" I asked loud enough for them to hear me.

They broke apart to turn towards me.

"Trying to quell our murderous desire," Venali said.

I arched a brow. "Towards?"

Amrynn growled. "Elryd."

Well, that was fast. He had not been here a full day yet and they already hated him. What had he done to anger them so much?

"He's trying to take Elara," Venali said.

Those words unleashed a torrent of emotions in me. With a deep breath, I squashed them.

"How?" I asked.

"You're overreacting," Elara said from behind me. She climbed up to sit beside me. "He only asked for consideration should you all leave."

"I'm not leaving," Venali said.

Pain flashed across her face so fast I almost missed it. She smiled warmly. "Then you have nothing to worry about."

"You don't believe them," I whispered.

"I believe that is how they feel currently. You all also built a house while we were separated."

"That's not—"

Amrynn cut me off. "Amara abandoned us for days. We were bored."

"I promised to be by your side," Venali said as he walked closer.

"That was before you had your memories," she said. She waved her hands. "This doesn't matter. It is all just possibilities of possibilities. Nothing will be decided until after the battle."

"I'm not going to let you sacrifice yourself," Venali said and set his hand on her leg.

She smiled, hopped off the fence, and turned away from us. "You'll try, my loves. You'll try."

We watched her go and the way she spoke, like it was a certain outcome, terrified me.

As a child, whenever she formed a plan, nothing got in her way. She accomplished it even against the greatest of odds. Would this be the same?

Daniel snapped his fingers in front of my face. "Hey."

I blinked and then scowled at all of my brothers now in the arena. When had the others arrived? "What?"

"Time for food," Daniel said.

"Where's Elara?" I asked and jumped down.

"Training," Durlan said.

Amrynn and Venali growled.

Durlan sighed. "Enough, you two."

"Where?" I asked.

Durlan pointed outside.

I walked that direction and felt the others follow.

It took two seconds to find her.

She stood in the black night, holding a star in her hands, a look of pure ecstasy on her face.

It made my heart skip a beat, and my dick twitch in my pants.

Gods, she was perfect.

Elryd clapped and after she returned the star to the sky, she hugged him.

Several growls sounded behind me.

"Easy," I muttered. "As much as we hate this, he is best suited to teach her."

"He could teach her without legs," Venali said.

My lips twitched up into a smile. The big man wasn't wrong.

"Maybe after the battle," I offered.

Elara's body began glowing, and my feet moved before my mind registered why. She was using the sun again.

I couldn't let her burn up. Last time had been scary enough.

As I neared, I realized she was much more in control, so I stopped.

"Think of it as a living thing. A pet. Treat it with respect and it won't burn you," Elryd said.

Elara cupped her hands as though holding a ball between them. A small sun burst into existence between them.

Elryd beamed. "Perfect. Now, throw it as far out into the Dead Lands as you can."

She turned and chucked it.

We all watched, our breaths held.

The light disappeared in the distance.

"What?" Elara asked, disappointment lacing the one word heavily.

Then, a huge explosion from the spot she had thrown it lit up the night. The shock wave knocked us all back. The night was dark again, save for the lights dancing in my vision.

Elryd created a source of light and tossed it up into the sky to show the destruction.

A huge crater at least two hundred feet wide with a smoking center was now in the place she'd thrown the sun ball.

"Well, that's going to hurt to get hit by," Myrin said.

I smirked. "Good thing she's on our side."

"Anyone else incredibly turned on?" Venali asked.

"Yep," all of us responded.

"Let's snag our mate and congratulate her on her new ability," Durlan said.

We snagged her and teleported to our room.

How did she keep getting sexier?

CHAPTER 35
ELARA

I WOKE SORE AND HAPPY.

Apparently, the way to turn my mates on was to destroy things. We had missed dinner, and my stomach was displeased to say the least.

Trying to get up proved impossible. Partly because of my sore body and partly because of the arms and legs piled on me.

"Food," I begged.

A few stirred, but none moved.

"Food," I begged louder.

"Yes, my queen," Venali said with a yawn and stood.

I watched his toned ass as he walked to the dresser and grabbed clothes.

One day, I would love to have a naked party, so I could spend all day admiring them.

He winked at me like he had heard my thoughts and then left.

Daniel pulled me into his arms and cocooned his body around mine.

I nestled into him, laying my head on his large bicep. Soon, I would need to leave for training, but we were all trying to take advantage of times like this. We had no idea when he would strike, and I wanted to have as many memories of them as I could.

"I love you," Daniel whispered.

"We love you, too," I whispered back.

He turned me over and stared into my eyes. "I was talking to you, Elara." He brushed my hair behind my ear and kissed the pointed tip of my ear. "When I first realized you weren't truly Amara, I wasn't sure what to make of you. I didn't think I would fall for you, but I fell so hard I'm surprised I remember how to breathe. I can't imagine my life without you in it. Your sarcastic comments, your beautiful face, your gorgeous smile, and that perky little ass. Everything about you is perfect, Elara. I wake up and my first thought is you. Life without you is impossible."

Tears slipped down my cheeks and I took a shuddering breath. Words weren't coming to me, so I kissed and hugged him.

"You're not supposed to make her cry before breakfast," Venali said as he came back in carrying a tray of food.

"It's a good cry," I whispered and wiped my face.

Daniel kissed my cheek and stood, getting dressed.

Myrin and Kydrus rolled over and tried to scoot closer to me to grab me.

I leapt up. "No, I need food."

"Cuddles," Kydrus said, his voice muffled in the pillow.

I jumped over them and pulled on one of their shirts from the day before. Inhaling, I realized it was Myrin's. "Cuddles are amazing, but if I don't eat, I'm going to die. If I die, then you can't have any more cuddles."

"Dramatic much?" Kydrus whispered.

I scowled as I looked at the bed. "Where's Ryul and Amrynn?" They'd been with us when we'd gone to sleep.

"Probably doing a perimeter check," Myrin said and sat up.

I'd started to turn towards Venali and the food, but seeing his bare chest and stomach caused me to pause.

Myrin smirked. "You won't die if you wait just an hour to eat."

I glared at him and turned away. "Evil. Temptress."

"Temptress? I'm not a woman," he said.

I shrugged and sat at the table next to Venali. "There's not a male version of temptress that I could think of." I grabbed a piece of meat and shoved the entire thing in my mouth.

"Chew your food. We can't have cuddles if you choke to death," Daniel said.

Myrin and Kydrus joined us at the table and we ate our breakfast in silence.

Just as I finished, someone knocked on the door.

Venali opened it and stepped back to let the person in. Elryd entered and stared at our food.

"What?" I asked.

"You eat meat?" he asked.

I nodded.

He looked disgusted. "I see. Anyway, it's time for your training. Are you ready?"

"You don't eat meat?" Venali asked.

"No, we don't eat meat," Elryd said. "We don't believe in killing things for food."

"I need to get dressed," I said and stood. "I'll be just a few minutes."

He nodded and stepped out of the room.

Quickly, I changed into my fighting leathers and slid my boots on.

The guys watched me silently.

"I'll see you guys later," I said to them.

They continued watching me, eating and staring.

Weird.

Elryd smiled at me, and we walked side by side down the hallways and out into the training arena.

"Create a sun," he said.

I focused on the sun while holding my hands towards each other, like I held an invisible ball between them. A small sun formed and gradually grew in size until it filled the space I'd made.

"Extinguish it," he ordered.

I scowled. I hadn't tried that before.

"How?" I asked.

"Imagine the power flowing back to the sun."

I did as he said and beamed when it worked.

Venali teleported to me right in the middle of my training with Elryd, grabbed my arm, and teleported me away.

I was preparing to berate him for stealing me for sex again, not that it would be a serious complaint, but froze instead.

Before us stood at least one hundred shapeshifters and humans.

The alpha I had met on Emortalia stepped forward and bowed to me. "Empress."

Venali turned his head to hide his smirk.

"I'm surprised you are here," I admitted.

She straightened. "Daniel sent us directions. I apologize for not being here sooner, but sailing took longer than expected."

"Venali, do we have more tents?" I asked.

He smiled. "I'll have some prepared."

"Thank you for coming," I said loud enough for all of them to hear. "We aren't sure when the battle will commence, so please stay alert."

Amrynn appeared beside me.

"Can you catch the alpha and her leaders up on the plan?" I asked him.

He dipped his head. "Yes, my queen."

"Empress," Venali whispered as he walked by us.

I rubbed my face to hide my smirk.

"Their teleportation is a rather annoying skill," Elryd said as he joined us.

I chuckled.

"Wait until you get teleported to another planet," Amrynn grumbled and then shuddered.

"Shall we return to training?" I asked Elryd.

A strange sound caught my attention.

I turned and Elryd's hand shot out, catching an arrow and stopping it an inch from my face.

My eyes widened.

He turned and threw it back in the direction it had come from.

Venali roared and teleported from behind me to a spot in the Dead Lands over a mile away.

Elryd grabbed my arm and tugged me towards the castle, but I dug my heels in and pulled free of his hold.

"Empress," a shifter yelled, "you should return-"

I walked through them, headed towards Venali who fought my attempted assassin in the distance.

Elryd walked at my side. "This could be a trap."

I nodded and lifted my hand, drawing a bit of the sun to form a shield around me.

He chuckled. "Not what I meant, but your control has definitely improved."

Amrynn teleported to Venali and they fought together against the enemy.

"Try manipulating the gravity," Elryd said.

"It could effect Venali and Amrynn," I countered. They seemed evenly matched with their opponent, otherwise I wouldn't have cared. I didn't want to be the reason they lost.

"I'll protect them," Elryd said.

I nodded, closed my eyes, and extended my senses.

This was the hardest to learn by far. One miscalculation or slip of concentration and I could kill the person. Or, empower them immensely.

The enemy cried out and then the fighting stopped.

I opened my eyes.

The enemy lay on the ground, struggling to rise.

"Perfect," Elryd praised.

We walked to them and I knelt by him...no, her.

She was a Seelie woman with beautiful lilac hair, but a fierce hatred burned in her eyes.

"Why did you try to kill me?" I asked softly.

"You're ruining Minloa," she snapped.

"Who sent you?" I asked.

"Your mom," she spat.

I punched her straight in the teeth. "Don't be rude. Who sent you? Who empowered you?"

"No one. I came on my own," she said. Blood dripped down her lip and onto the sand from her broken teeth and busted lip.

I stood and looked at Venali. "Kill her and burn her body."

He snarled. "With pleasure."

"You're going to kill me?" she asked, eyes wide.

I arched a brow. "You attempted to assassinate your queen. Should I hug you and let you go? You knew the consequences."

Amrynn set his hand on my shoulder, and I set my hand on Elryd's arm.

Releasing my spell let her jump up, but Venali plunged his sword through her chest before she could move more.

"Why was she able to keep up with you?" I asked.

"I don't know," Amrynn growled and teleported us to my war room.

"Her power was different," Elryd said. He sat in one of the chairs and scowled up at the ceiling.

I realized I still had a shield up, so I dismissed it, and sat in my chair.

Myrin walked in, and his brows furrowed when he saw us. "What happened?"

"Someone tried to shoot me in the face with an arrow," I said and yawned.

He pinched the bridge of his nose. "Could you take it a little more seriously?"

"Elryd caught it," I said and shrugged. "You should talk to Venali and Amrynn because she was really powerful."

He looked at Amrynn who was still snarling.

My right arm throbbed a moment and adrenaline spiked through me.

"Ryul," I gasped and stood.

Ryul teleported into the room in his chair. He groaned and clutched his left shoulder. "They're here."

Amrynn set his hand on Ryul's shoulder and began healing him.

"At the edge of the Dead Lands," Ryul said.

"Let's go." I set a hand on Myrin and Elryd when he came to me.

Ryul and Amrynn joined us, then we teleported to the elf encampment.

"Prepare," Elryd bellowed.

Ryul, Amrynn, and Myrin took turns kissing me before going in separate directions.

Venali teleported to me. "Ready?" he asked.

I nodded and kissed him. "Stay alive, please."

He smiled and kissed my forehead tenderly. "That's my line."

Elryd's army moved from their tents to the Dead Lands, forming ranks.

Elryd drew his sword and together we walked to the front of the elves.

The humans and shapeshifters lined up behind the elves. With them stood several Seelie and Unseelie warriors, men and women.

"They came yesterday saying they wanted to help fight according to Durlan," Elryd said.

As soon as everyone was in formation, we started the march to meet our enemies.

He wasn't here yet, which I had assumed would be the case.

I drew my sword, and holding the pommel calmed me. Our plan would work. If it didn't, my plan would.

Now was the time. This would decide the fate of not just Minloa or Anderelle, but our galaxy.

Myrin stood about a mile away from the enemy, his hands glowing black.

I had to resist the urge to run to him, keeping my pace with Elryd.

Our army halted a half mile from Myrin.

I continued on, head held high, only stopping when I was beside Myrin.

"Status?" I asked as I looked out over our enemy.

There were thousands of creatures. Most were fae creatures, but many were odd aberrations that oozed bloodlust and evil. Had he created them or twisted some of the fae creatures?

In the middle of their army were dozens of huge redcaps, easily three times the size of the ones we had fought before.

"Three thousand by my calculations, but I could be wrong," Myrin said. "They caught Ryul and Amrynn doing a patrol. Ryul had dropped his guard and got hit in the shoulder. Not serious, but it pissed him off. Amrynn sent him to gather everyone while he took care of his part. Aside from the sneak attack, they've just been standing there, waiting."

"Waiting for him? Or us to attack?" I asked.

He shrugged.

I sheathed my sword, turned to him, and tapped his shoulder.

He extinguished his flames as he faced me.

I stood on tiptoe and kissed him. "I love you."

He rested his forehead against mine. "I love you, too, Elara. Stay by my side, please."

I nodded and faced the enemy again. "Should we wait or attack?"

Durlan, Venali, Amrynn, Daniel, Ryul, and Kydrus teleported to us.

Those I hadn't received kisses from came to me, and then we formed a single line, facing the creatures.

"Wait," Durlan said. "Let's see what they do."

I shifted my feet in the sand, scowling. The guys had trained in the sand, as had I at their insistence, but most of the volunteers likely hadn't. It would impede them.

It would also impede the large enemies, which would help us a lot.

Venali had the most trouble in our group, so the plan was for him to get into the middle of the enemy so they came to him and he could limit his movements. Kydrus was going with him to watch his back, otherwise I wouldn't have been comfortable with that plan.

"Think there are any distance fighters among them?" I asked.

Durlan nodded. "There are a few who can throw fire among them. The goblins have bows and arrows, too."

"I love you all," I whispered. "No matter how this ends, thank you for loving me and giving me the most amazing life."

"We're all going to survive this," Myrin said confidently. "And we'll love you until the end of time."

"Always," Venali said.

"Forever and ever," Ryul said.

We stood in silence after that. As time past, I grew irritated. "Should I have brought chairs?"

Ryul snickered.

"You're our queen," Durlan said. "If you wish to attack, we will."

"It's been hours," I grumbled.

"I'm ready when you are," Venali said. I looked at him near the end of the line and saw his excited smile.

I looked back at the enemy and projected my voice, "Leave this land peacefully and no harm shall come to you. Continue this invasion and you will be annihilated."

A spriggan stepped forward, it was only child size, but once it was in front of the army, it grew to what looked like around six feet tall. It's mouth opened and it roared at us.

The rest of the enemy army roared as well. Their combined voices were a cacophony of terrifying sounds. Had I never seen or heard them before, I might have been intimidated. It did still make the hairs on the back of my neck stand.

I held my hands a foot apart before me, drew on the sun, and created a ball of sun power. "Ready?" I asked the men I loved more than life itself.

"Yes," they all answered and began glowing.

I threw the ball, directing it to go farther as Elryd had taught me, since my throws were so short, and smiled when it fell into the middle of their army, right next to one of the huge redcaps.

They looked at the glowing orb and then began laughing.

I smirked and snapped my fingers.

CHAPTER 36
DURLAN

Elara snapped her fingers and the miniature sun exploded. At least one thousand died, and many more were injured. A few ran around, their bodies on fire, screaming.

The enemy charged and our allies charged forward to meet them.

We surrounded Elara, giving her enough room to fight, but being close enough to step in if she needed help.

As much as it went against my alpha instincts, she could fight and I couldn't stop her. I wouldn't stop her.

This was as much her fight as it was ours, and she played a huge role in it.

My goal was to keep the enemy away from her, wait for the bastard god of darkness to show up, and then keep her and Amara alive. What happened after that was uncertain, but I couldn't think about that now.

Daniel and Myrin each grabbed one of Venali's arms and then used all their strength to throw him at the enemy.

Elara's mouth dropped open. "That was not the plan."

Daniel and Myrin threw Kydrus next and then we moved forward, keeping Elara between us.

"We're going to move through the enemy and meet them," I explained as I cut down a goblin.

She didn't respond, her eyes focused on Venali and Kydrus who fought back to back, slicing apart anyone who dared get close enough.

A huge redcap moved towards them, his movement encumbered by the sand.

Her lip lifted in a snarl, she raised her hand, and she shot a bolt of starlight into the redcap's shoulder.

The redcap jerked back and then turned and roared at us.

"Well, you pissed him off good," Daniel said.

Elara sighed. "Great."

I chuckled.

She shoved her blade into the belly of a spriggan who'd increased his size, and twisted.

Damn, she was so hot.

"Durlan," Myrin growled.

"Don't act like you weren't thinking the same," I said.

Myrin cut down several creatures and then set a group in the distance on fire with his black fire. "I didn't say that."

I chuckled.

"What are you talking about?" Elara asked, dodging the arrow of a goblin.

"They're aiming at her," I snapped and moved closer to her.

"I see that," Myrin growled. "I don't see them, though."

The redcap Elara had pissed off finally made it to us, knocking his own friendlies out of the way to reach us.

Elara smiled. "How's the shoulder, big guy?"

I groaned. "Don't taunt the enemy."

The redcap roared at her and my little, crazy mate roared right back at him.

"I never thought I'd say I got a hard on during a battle, but here we are," Daniel said.

I let out a bark of laughter as I sliced into several trolls. How were they out during the day time? The sunlight should have turned them to stone.

Myrin and Daniel fought the redcap alongside Elara. She darted around the giant creature, cutting into his tendons and keeping out of his range.

The familiar whizzing sound approached.

"Arrows!" I bellowed.

Ryul raised his hands and a translucent shield appeared over our allies and us.

"When did you learn that?" Elara asked as she dodged the redcap's attempt to backhand her.

He winked at her, dropped the shield once the arrows stopped, and returned to fighting enemies in front of us.

The redcap raised its left hand and then swung its right hand, catching Elara in the chest.

She flew backwards, but Elryd was there, and he caught her and steadied her.

Red filled my vision, and I roared at the redcap. Leaping up as high as I could, I stabbed my sword into its chest and then used it to propel myself upwards. Jerking my sword free as I flew up, I jammed it into the redcap's neck and roared right in his face.

It fell to his knees, blood bubbling out of his neck.

The red haze cleared, and I pulled my sword free. Several of the nearby enemies had stopped to stare, wide-eyed.

I stood atop the dead redcap's body and roared as loudly as I could.

A dozen or so turned and fled in the opposite direction.

"Think we could sneak off for ten minutes?" Elara whispered in my ear.

I growled at her. "You're awful."

She rolled her eyes at me and hopped down from the redcap.

With the fleeing enemies, we had a bit of space and breathing room. Elara wiped off her sword and looked around.

"No sign of him yet," she whispered.

We nodded and marched forward, regrouping and getting back into the fight.

"Show off," Kydrus called to me as we finally made it to him and Venali.

Venali was smiling as he killed. I hadn't seen him in a large battle like this in a very long time, and had forgotten how terrifying the brute was.

"Join the fun," Venali called to us.

"Your mates are strange," Elryd said.

"You don't know the half of it," Elara whispered back.

CHAPTER 37
RYUL

I'D NEVER BEEN in a battle like this before. I understood more about my brothers and their knowledge and skills.

Had I not been beside them, witnessing how calm they remained as they slaughtered hundreds of creatures, I might have freaked out a bit.

The most surprising was Elara, though. She got right into the thick of the battle and didn't back down.

Watching her roar at the redcap had been terrifying, and yet pride had swelled within me.

She had grown so much. As much as I wanted to take credit, it was all my brothers' doing. And Amara. Amara definitely had a huge impact on Elara. Partly due to their merging, but also her guidance.

A goblin charged me, sword raised.

I parried the strike and then punched him in the chest. He stumbled back, giving me the opening I needed to cut his head off.

Kydrus pushed my head down and stabbed a goblin behind me. "Saved your head," he said with a wide smile. "Don't leave your back open. This isn't a one on one fight."

"Thanks," I said, turning to fight a spriggan. The bastard kept changing size, which made it hard to hit him.

I growled my frustration, and he laughed at me.

Venali killed a redcap beside me, practically glowing with joy. "Overhead strikes," he said and brought his blade down, cutting the spriggan in half with one swing. "Doesn't matter if he changes size mid-swing, he'll still get chopped in half."

A goblin leapt at his back.

I opened my mouth, but Venali stabbed his sword backwards, making the goblin impale itself.

Venali jerked his blade free. "It's such a glorious day!"

I was so glad he was on our side.

Two redcaps marched forward, their feet sinking in the sand with every move.

Venali started to move towards them, but Myrin coated them in his black flames.

"Myrin!" Venali snapped.

Myrin rolled his eyes. "There are plenty more creatures for you to fight."

"Leave the big ones to me," Venali growled. He stabbed a weird tree nymph/goblin cross so hard in the chest that its upper body exploded.

My eyes widened.

"Fine," Myrin agreed.

Venali bobbed his head and killed a trio of spriggans racing for Elara.

The enemies' numbers were quickly decreasing while ours was diminishing at less than a quarter of the rate.

Elryd and his elves moved well even in the sand and were well-trained to work in pairs and quads.

Elryd used his celestial powers off and on, but it seemed to me that he was saving his magic.

With *him* not here yet, that made sense.

CHAPTER 38
VENALI

THERE WERE so many creatures to kill and yet not enough. My sword was coated in blood and gore. I tried to flick it off, but then it just got dirty again when I stabbed another creature.

The abominations he had created were disgusting and incredibly fun to kill. The tree nymph/goblin mixes screamed really nicely when I stabbed them.

A giant beast pushed his way through the enemies. He was covered in shaggy black fur, extremely muscular, and had at least six-inch-long claws from his fingertips and toes. He also had thick pointed teeth.

A goblin got in his way and he kicked it over our heads.

I took a breath and my muscles doubled in size, a handy power I'd discovered that helped boost my strength for a short duration of time.

"Mine!" I bellowed and ran towards it. "Mine. Mine. Mine."

"We heard you," Myrin said.

Energy coursed through me, aiding in my speed to reach him. The damn sand had always been a hindrance for me, due to my weight, but I didn't falter even as it shifted beneath my boots with each step.

The shaggy beast looked at me and snarled.

"Let's play," I said with a smile and spun my sword as I finally made it to him.

He swung a clawed hand with a roar.

I ducked, raised my sword, and let his own momentum slice his arm open on my blade. I used a bit of my special demigod magic to make the cut hurt even more than it should have.

He bellowed in pain and kicked at me.

Leaping up and over his leg and arm, I cut across his chest, landed, and rolled away before he could hit me.

Laughter bubbled out of me as I danced with the beast.

CHAPTER 39
MYRIN

My brothers were insane. I knew that, but watching Venali laugh while he cut apart a huge beast was eerie, even for the big guy.

Kydrus, Durlan, and Amrynn weren't much better. They might not have been laughing, but they kept smiling while they killed creature after creature.

Daniel and Ryul were quiet as they fought. Both focused and brutal in their efficiencies.

Even Elara was enjoying it.

I had wanted to scold her for roaring at the redcap and standing on the other one's body with Amrynn, but realized there was no point.

With the exception of Venali, we kept our formation tight enough that any one of us could race to Elara's aid if she needed us.

The feisty queen hardly needed our help, though, it turned out. Bodies piled up around her, blood splattered her face and clothes, and she fought on with a snarl curling one of her beautiful lips.

"You should rest," I called to her. "Save your energy for the main fight."

She growled at me in response.

I sighed and stabbed the troll in front of me.

"She'll calm down in a little bit," Kydrus said with a wide smile, hacking off the troll's head.

A tall, thin creature with brown mottled skin, sunken black eyes, and red tipped claws walked towards me calmly. It's gaze was locked on mine and all of the other enemies moved out of its way. As it neared, the evil it emanated was so intense, even I cringed. "You must die," it said in a guttural voice.

"What are you?" I asked.

It smiled, revealing long, serrated teeth. "A creation with a sole design and purpose of killing you."

Bowing, I said, "How kind of him to admit I'm such a worthy adversary."

"Just another stubborn weed to be pulled," it said with a graceful shrug of its shoulders. Reaching back, it drew two curved swords. "It is time for you to die."

With a flick of my hand, I covered it in my black flames. I didn't have time to waste on this thing.

Unfortunately, the screaming that usually followed that move did not happen.

Instead, the creature smiled and the flames disappeared.

"Well, that's new," Amrynn muttered behind me.

I narrowed my eyes.

Immunity to my flames should not have been possible.

The creature dashed forward with incredible speed, reaching me in no time.

I ducked the first blade and blocked the second with my sword.

We danced, exchanging blows and parrying each other in

equal measures. I lost count of the number of strikes once I reached one hundred.

After a strike that vibrated up my arms, we leapt apart.

"I can see why he views you as a threat," the creature said and wiped blood off its cheek. "It's time to get serious."

It leapt forward again, but Elara stepped between us, pressed her hand to the creature's chest, and it exploded in a burst of sunlight.

"Elara," I growled.

She looked back at me, her eyes glowing orbs, and said, "He is here."

A cloud of black smoke swirled down from the sky to the ground in front of us, and he stepped out.

I pulled Elara back so she stood beside me.

He glared at Elara. "You destroyed my creature."

She smiled, her eyes back to normal. "I've destroyed a lot of your creatures."

"Give yourself to me, and I will spare your men," he said.

Elara raised her chin. "Submit to me or perish."

Darkness gathered around him, and he yelled, "I am darkness. I am—"

Elara gathered sunlight around her and yelled, "I am light. You do not frighten me!"

Hot damn, she was sexy.

"You will bow to me," he growled.

"We bow to no one," Elara said, her voice a combination of hers and Amara's.

Ah, my goddess had joined the fight.

He drew up and magic built around him.

Amara took over, her magic built in an instant, and she hit the dark god in the center of his chest with a blast of light.

He staggered, his eyes widening, but sent a blast of fire at her.

I threw up a wall of black fire that absorbed his.

He growled and snapped his fingers.

Dozens of creatures that appeared to be made of darkness popped into existence between him and us.

"Group!" I bellowed.

My brothers finished killing what was in front of them and tightened our circle around Amara.

Elryd dashed into our circle, standing at Amara's side. He weaved his hands around his body in a strange motion. Then, tiny orbs of light popped up around him. He aimed each at a dark creature and it burned holes through their bodies, crippling some and killing a few.

Venali stood beside Kydrus. "Ready?"

Kydrus offered an evil grin. "Yes."

What did those two have planned?

Kydrus clapped his hands and a pile of spears appeared at his feet.

Ryul, Daniel, and Venali each picked one up and then threw them at the dark god.

He dodged a few, knocked one away, and one cut his cheek as it sailed by his face.

I joined them, grabbing spears and chucking them as fast as we could.

Amara laughed and threw bolts of light shaped like spears at him, too.

CHAPTER 40
AMARA

The spears wouldn't kill him, but that wasn't the point. The point was to make him deplete his magic and stamina to make it easier to seal him.

My consorts hadn't told me this part of the plan, but I totally approved.

Elryd adapted to our tactics easily, and I even saw the king smile.

The dark god roared his rage and flung his magic in a wall.

I threw up a barrier as did Ryul.

The magic shattered Ryul's barrier and almost broke mine.

If we didn't act soon, we would run out of steam and magic ourselves.

"Ready?" I asked Elara.

"Yes."

CHAPTER 41
ELARA

Amara reached into a spacial pocket, and pulled out the jar. Then, she gave me control.

I held the jar and took slow, deep breaths. This would work. It had to.

I took another deep breath and cringed as Amara separated from me.

The pain was intense, making me drop to one knee to catch my breath.

Amara helped me stand and smiled at me. She was gorgeous and despite seeing her in my dreams, seeing her in real life was incredibly different.

"Begin," I said with a nod.

She returned my nod, and we faced the dark god.

His eyes focused on the jar, and he clapped his hands, brining more creatures to fight.

How many did he freaking have?

Amara and I held out our hands, created a rope of light, and secured it around him.

She tapped the jar, activating its magic, and a vacuum began to suck him towards it.

He struggled, digging his heels in, and fighting our constraints. “You are not strong enough. You’re weak just like the other gods I absorbed. You cannot seal me,” he yelled, but I could see the doubt in his eyes.

Amara and I pulled with all our might. Inch by inch, he drew closer.

The guys fought the creatures, keeping Amara and I free and safe to do this.

Amara’s teeth ground together, sweat beaded on her forehead, and her light flickered a bit.

She wasn’t as strong in her own body. If she faltered, he would get free.

I looked at the fight around us.

Our allies, my people, and my mates fought against the darkness, but there seemed to be no end to them.

My mates had deep gashes on each of them from the new wave of enemies that pressed down upon them.

Being unable to move about restricted their fighting abilities, and caused them to get hurt.

If this didn’t end soon, our side would lose. Minloa would fall to the darkness, and then it would spread across Anderelle and the rest of the galaxy.

No, I couldn’t let that happen.

I had to save them. I couldn’t let my mates die. I wouldn’t survive that.

I had to activate my plan. I had to save my galaxy.

Myrin met my eyes from where he fought creatures and I smiled at him. “I love you.”

CHAPTER 42
MYRIN

AMARA AND ELARA HAD SEPARATED, which caused us a dilemma. Who did we protect?

Ryul, Kydrus, and Amrynn moved closer to Elara, protecting her back from the creatures. Daniel and I were closest to Amara, so we protected her.

Venali stood in the middle, smiling and killing.

"Now!" Amara shouted.

Amara and Elara raised their hands and the dark god cried out as a wind swirled around him and dragged him towards the container.

"No," he yelled and clawed at the dirt and any nearby creature, trying to stop his progression.

Amara grunted, her forehead beaded with sweat, and her face red from exertion.

They weren't going to make it.

Elara's eyebrows pinched, her jaw set with determination. She looked around at everyone fighting, at Elryd and his elves fighting, and at Amara, and then her eyebrows and jaw relaxed. She met my eyes, smiled, and said, "I love you."

"No," I screamed. I cut down the creatures before me, but I was too slow.

Elara grabbed the dark god, wrapped her body around his, and they both disappeared into the jar.

"No," I roared and fell to my knees. She was gone. She'd sealed herself into the jar with him, to save Amara, and to save us.

"No," Venali, Ryul, and Kydrus roared.

All seven of us knelt on the ground, our tears uncontrollable as our mate vanished, our bond severed, and our hearts froze.

Elryd and his elves surrounded us, protecting us against the enemies while we were weak.

Amara looked at me, her own cheeks soaked with tears. "I didn't know her plan. She hid it. I'm sorry. I'm so sorry."

There was no way to set Elara free without setting the dark god free, too. Could he hurt her in the container? Would he hurt her?

"Please," Amrynn begged. "There has to be something you can do." He looked up at Amara, clutching his chest.

"Please," Venali begged.

"No, this can't be," Daniel whispered. "She can't be gone."

Amara looked at each of us, the sorrow and pain evident as we all clutched at our now cold chests.

She knelt beside me and kissed me softly. "I love you, Myrin. She cannot be left in there. I can save her, but—"

"You will die," I guessed.

She nodded and sniffled. "I cannot bear to see my mates so distraught. I will bring her back. Will you help me?"

"We don't want to lose you either," I snapped. "Why must we lose one of you?"

"That is that only way," she whispered.

I hugged her tightly. "I don't want to spend another lifetime without you. I love you, Amara. Don't do this. There must be a way for you both to live."

"We cannot merge now. If we both live, the god will be freed and you seven will die," she whispered. "Neither Elara or I want that."

"Don't leave me again," I begged, a fresh wave of tears slipping down my face.

"A bit of me will always remain with Elara. Cherish her and help her. She deserves happiness."

"Amara, no," Daniel begged.

She turned and kissed him. "She will need you to be at your strongest. Our separation will greatly weaken her," Amara whispered.

"Don't," Kydrus choked. "She wouldn't want this. She sacrificed herself for a reason."

"Be strong, my loves," Amara said. She backed up, glowed brightly, and then disappeared.

"Plan M," I snapped and saw the others nod once.

We looked around unsure what had happened to Amara, and then time rewound itself. We watched Elara and the dark god come out, the creatures still held at bay despite the seven of us being at Elara's feet now.

I would not let them do this.

As soon as time began to move again, I stood and yelled, "Together."

The moment Elara made her decision, her eyes meeting mine, the seven of us grasped hands with each other and our two mates, chaining Elara and Amara together.

Their magic channeled through us, using us as a bridge, and with a burst of light and surge of power, the two women became one.

CHAPTER 43
ELARA / AMARA

All seven of my consorts fell to the ground, their magic drained to fully merge us.

The dark god bellowed and a bolt of dark energy slammed into Daniel's chest.

With a sweep of my hand, we finished sealing the dark god, and sent his container to a distant star where no life existed.

"You fools," I snapped as I dropped to the ground beside Daniel. "What have you done?" Daniel hadn't moved since the dark god hit him. He looked peaceful and even had a small smile on his face. Tears streamed down mine.

"Saved you," Myrin gasped. "Elara sacrificed herself. Amara reversed time to trade places."

"We couldn't lose either of you," Ryul said, tears on his face.

"Daniel?" I whispered and rested my hand on his cheek.

Our link was dark. Our connection severed.

"No!" I set my hands on his chest. He wasn't breathing and his body was growing cold. "Daniel," I cried and pressed my hands to each side of his face. Tears streamed down my cheeks as I looked at my shapeshifter mate.

CHAPTER 44
MYRIN

DANIEL WAS the least powerful of us all. He had very little magic in comparison to the rest of us. I should have thought about that before we used our powers to merge them.

He was dead. His life snuffed out to save Elara and Amara.

She pressed her hands to his chest and a bright white glow surrounded him as she tried to use her magic on him.

It wouldn't work. She couldn't bring him back to life like she had Durlan because she couldn't give up years of her life now that they were merged.

"Me," Feno said and knelt beside Daniel's body. "Take part of my life."

She shook her head, tears dripping from her jaw. "I can't—"

Feno took her face in his hands and said, "Take as many years as you need. I have been on this planet long enough and I will not sit by while you are mourning if I can change it. I took your parents from you. I will not sit idly by and let your mate be taken from you either."

She stared at him for several moments before placing one hand on Feno's chest and one hand on Daniel's chest. Her eyes glowed bright white and then a white smoke passed from Feno into Daniel.

Daniel's eyes snapped open and he gasped in a breath.

Feno fell to the side, his eyes closed. I watched his chest to be sure he breathed before looking back at Daniel.

He looked at me and asked, "What did I miss?"

I chuckled. "I'll tell you everything later. We still have a battle to fight."

CHAPTER 45

ELARA / AMARA

I LET OUT A LONG SIGH, kissed Daniel, and then stood. I looked out over the Seelie and Unseelie still fighting the dark god's creatures despite him being gone.

It was time for this to end. It was time for us to enter a reign of peace.

"Enough," I snapped loud enough for everyone on the battlefield to hear.

Every being froze.

"This battle is over. He has been defeated. Unless you wish to be exterminated, leave now. As Goddess of the Universe, I command you."

Immediately, all of the dark creatures fled, hightailing it before they were obliterated.

The Seelie and Unseelie cheered and some hugged each other. Some even hugged the elves who were stiff, but did not rebuke the affection.

Feno stood with help from Elryd, both smiling.

"What shall we call you now?" Myrin asked and knelt before me.

Smiling, I said, "I've decided to keep the name Elara, due to her sacrifice. And, as promised to us, the goddess powers will be accessible though not always present, and we will live out the next hundred years as Elara. After Elara's one hundred year rule, we will return to the stars."

"And us?" Amrynn asked, standing and moving closer to me.

I smiled. "You go where I go. You seven are stuck with me for eternity."

Taking a breath, I released my goddess powers and stood before my mates once again as Elara, though we were fully merged now, so I was still us, but a bit more myself.

Wobbling slightly, I stepped closer to my mates.

All seven leapt to their feet and reached out to steady me.

Smiling wide, I asked, "Who wants a bath? We're all covered in blood and muck."

Daniel picked me up and kissed me deeply, his tongue dancing with mine. He pulled away, leaving my heart fluttering. "We'll do whatever you wish, my goddess."

A huge thundering overhead drew everyone's attention.

The fading sunlight reflected off the side of a large flying ship. At the helm stood Barry, a smug smile on his face as he flew down towards us.

Most of those gathered stared warily at the ship, unsure what it was or what to think of it.

"Shall we destroy him before he lands?" Myrin asked.

I smiled. "No, let's see what he does. Ryul, a shield, please?" I rested my hand on his shoulder to give him a bit of extra magic, since he'd used up so much of his during the battle.

Ryul lifted his hands and a translucent shield spread out to cover all of our people.

"Surrender the woman to me and I will leave the rest of you unharmed," Barry called through a loud speaker.

"Pass," I said and smiled warmly up at him.

Barry scowled and said something I couldn't hear to the human beside him. Four cannons on the bottom of the ship swiveled around until they were pointed at us and then shot over a dozen metal projectiles at us.

They exploded when they hit Ryul's shield, but did no damage to us.

I waved at Barry with a wide smile.

His scowl turned into a glare and he barked orders at his crew.

More shots hit Ryul's shield.

"May I?" Amrynn asked.

I knew he wanted revenge on Barry far more than I. So, I nodded and kissed his cheek. "Be safe," I whispered.

He smiled and kissed my cheek back. "Yes, my goddess."

He squatted down and then leapt up into the air.

He was nowhere near the ship, so I wasn't sure what he planned to do.

Venali was thrown into the air by Kydrus and Durlan, and then Venali grabbed Amrynn and threw Amrynn with a mighty bellow.

Amrynn tucked his arms against his body and flew right at the main deck's viewing window where Barry stood.

Barry looked at Amrynn with an arched brow, the confusion obvious.

Amrynn drew his sword and with two quick swings, shattered the glass.

The crew inside screamed and Barry ducked down, covering his head to protect himself from the glass falling around him

I thought he would torment Barry. Or grab him and say something. Draw out Barry's death a little bit.

Amrynn did none of that. He swung his sword once more and decapitated Barry.

"Well, he is definitely dead," Ryul whispered.

Amrynn stabbed his sword into Barry's chest, tilted his head back, and roared.

"Toss me," I ordered Myrin.

He grumbled, but threw me up to the ship.

I used a bit of my power to make my landing smooth and stood before the humans who cowered around the control panels. "I am the goddess of this universe. This is my consort. We had a score to settle with this man." I indicated Barry's dead body. "You are free to return to Zenlop. Or, if you wish to continue this fight, we can slaughter you here and now."

"We will return to Zenlop," a willowy man in the back said.

I nodded. "Good choice."

CHAPTER 46
ELARA

I THREW a feast for the entirety of Anderelle, inviting everyone from Minloa, Emortalia, and Eltare to celebrate our victory.

Using my magic, I reshaped the Dead Lands and returned it to a rich and thriving grassland as it once had been. I offered the lands to Elryd and the shapeshifters, giving them a place to live on Minloa, should they wish it. The shapeshifters opted to return to Emortalia, while Elryd and his elves accepted my offer and moved into the Dead Lands, now renamed Amlantia.

For a full day, I danced with my seven mates, ate, drank, and played with my people.

Watching shapeshifters, humans, elves, Seelie, and Unseelie laugh and dance together brought tears of joy to my eyes.

I had done it. I had united everyone. Well, minus Zenlop, but they were an issue for another decade. No, my mates had done it. While I had sacrificed myself initially, their love was the reason Amara rewound time to rescue me.

Daniel shifted into his bear form and became a play structure for a group of toddlers.

I covered my mouth with my hand to keep from laughing.

"You look happy," Venali said as he came to stand beside me.

I jumped up to kiss the scars below his eye. "I am."

He pulled me against his side, squeezing me. "Good."

"Any suggestions on who my heir should be?" I asked, looking out over the crowd.

He turned me so we were facing each other, a smirk making his eyes bright. "I thought we could try making one."

My eyes widened. "Making one?"

He nodded. "The world would benefit by having your blood heir here, when we return to the stars."

"We've been talking," Kydrus said behind me. "And we all think you'd make a great mother."

I stepped back from Venali and folded my arms across my chest. "More consort meetings behind my back?"

He smiled. "Maybe."

Arms wrapped around me from behind. I inhaled.

Myrin.

"If you don't get pregnant, we thought you'd at least enjoy our attempts," Myrin whispered and pressed his lower body against mine to make it clear what he meant.

"I suppose I could be persuaded to try," I said breathlessly.

"There's no time like the present," Daniel said and tossed me over his shoulder.

I laughed. I hadn't even heard him approach.

He carried me into the castle, my other mates following behind, and all I could do was smile.

These seven were perfect and while life wasn't always perfect, I would enjoy every moment with them.

I wasn't just a former slave. I wasn't just a queen.

I was Elara, Goddess of the Universe, mate to seven glorious demigods, and I wouldn't have it any other way.

EPILOGUE

10 YEARS LATER
MYRIN

Elara stood in front of our daughter, Nyura, both of their hands out before them, palms up. "Ready?" Elara asked.

We had no idea who the father was, since it felt like we could all see aspects of ourselves in Nyura, but none of us cared. She was Elara's daughter, a damn near replica of her, and we had been wrapped around her finger with the first cry she'd released.

While she was only ten years old, Nyura already had great skill with her celestial powers.

"Deep breath," Elara whispered.

Nyura took a deep breath, as deep as her little body could make.

"Envision a sun ball in your hand. Warm, but not hot. Just like the sun on your face on a warm spring day," Elara said.

Nyura bobbed her head once, her black hair with white streaks bouncing, pressed her lips together, and then a ball of sunlight appeared, hovering over her palms. The ball rotated slowly, like a planet.

Elara rested her hands on Nyura's shoulders. "Turn slowly, look towards your target, and then throw it."

My mouth dropped open, my arms fell to my sides, and I took three steps before Venali grabbed my arm and stopped me.

"Stay," he whispered without taking his eyes from the two girls we loved more than life itself.

"Ven—"

"Shush," he ordered me, his tone harsh, while the love in his eyes as he continued to stare at the girls did not waver.

I sighed and folded my arms across my chest. "I'm not cleaning shit up."

He smiled wide.

"Throw it as hard as you can and then if it doesn't go far enough, use your connection to it to push it even farther," Elara said.

Nyura nodded, turned slowly, keeping her eyes on the swirling ball, and then she lobbed it away from us and out into the ocean. With narrowed and focused eyes, she sent the ball out to a small rock formation and then released it.

The sun ball fell onto the rocks and then the light disappeared.

Nyura's lower lip trembled and she said, "I told you I couldn't—"

The rocks exploded and the shockwave knocked all of the water away from the rocks.

Ryul threw up a translucent shield, protecting us from the flying debris.

Nyura squealed and jumped up and down, pumping her arms as she did, and then did a little dance.

Elara hugged her and kissed the top of her head. "That's my girl."

"Momma, how much longer do you have?" Nyura asked, her face pressed to Elara's chest.

Elara looked over at us, tears welling in her eyes.

The seven of us hurried over, dropped to one knee in a circle around the girls, and looked at our demigoddess daughter.

"I have ninety years, baby. Plenty of time left with you," Elara whispered, tears brimming.

"Ninety years is so little in our lifetime," Nyura whispered. "Why can't I have more time with you and my fathers?"

I took Nyura's hand and rubbed the back of it. "I'm sorry, beautiful, but that is what must happen. We will return to the stars and you will rule over Minloa as queen."

She turned her little head and sniffled as she held back tears. "I'm going to miss you, though."

I pulled her into my arms and hugged her tightly. "We have a lot of time to spend together before that happens. When you're one hundred, you'll probably be tired of us and beg us to leave."

She shook her head. "No, I won't. I never want you to leave."

Elara covered her mouth with her hands and tears dripped down her face as she looked at us.

I was having a tough time keeping from tearing up myself. I hoped this child stayed as sweet as she was now.

"Hey, what about us?" Venali asked, pulled Nyura from my arms, and picked her up, cradling her against his chest. "Won't you miss me?"

She threw her arms around his neck and squeezed. "Yes."

"Even me?" Daniel asked.

Nyura leaned back, wiped her face, and looked at each of her fathers. "Every single one of you."

Daniel took Nyura and hugged her. "You're going to be the greatest queen in history."

"Hey," Elara protested.

Ryul tweaked the tip of Nyura's nose. "Even better than your momma."

"I'm standing right here," Elara said, but her smile was evidence that she was playing along.

"It wouldn't be hard," Nyura teased, looking at her mother with a wide smile.

Elara's mouth dropped open and she tickled Nyura while Daniel held her.

Nyura laughed and squealed as she was tickled.

She broke free of Daniel, only to be snatched up by Kydrus. "There is no escape for you, little princess." He tickled her more, making her laugh harder.

Then, Amrynn grabbed her and ran towards the castle. "I'll save you, my princess."

Nyura slid around Amrynn as he ran, wrapping her legs around his stomach and her arms around his neck. "Hurry, Father! They're gaining on us."

Venali teleported to them, trying to grab her from Amrynn's back, but he spun away, making Nyura shriek with laughter.

Ryul tried to grab her next, but Amrynn grabbed her arms and tossed her high up into the air, knocked Ryul's legs out from under him, and then caught her the moment she fell back down to his reach.

Elara gasped, but I wrapped my arms around her waist and held her captive. "Even after ten years you don't trust us?" I asked.

She relaxed in my arms, her body melting against mine. "She's my baby."

"As she is ours. Stop fretting." I nipped her ear and she hissed through her teeth.

"That's never going to happen," she grumbled, but leaned her head back against my shoulder and stayed with me while the others continued to run around with Nyura.

"She's going to be okay when we leave, right?" Elara asked.

"My goddess, she is going to be more than alright. I bet by the time we are preparing to leave she will have her own harem of consorts and will be begging us to leave her alone. You have no need to worry about her. She's better with her magic than you were two decades ago."

"Rude," Elara muttered, but did not try to deny it.

A group of people marched across the lands towards the castle. The person at the head of the group ran forward, closing the distance to Nyura quickly.

Elara pulled away, preparing to run for Nyura, but the newcomers beat her. With lightning quick movements, he stole Nyura from Amrynn's arms and then tossed her up into the air within a translucent bubble that held her there.

Elara let out a breath and sagged her shoulders. "I wish he wouldn't do that."

Elryd walked towards us, Nyura and the bubble hovering over his head and moving as he did.

"There you are," he said as he got to us.

The bubble popped and I caught a laughing Nyura in my arms.

"I hate that you do that," Elara grumbled, but stepped forward and hugged Elryd, a smile slipping out.

He patted her back and smiled at me. "Your little one loves it, though."

Nyura wrapped her arms around my neck and cuddled against my chest with a yawn.

She was getting to the age where she didn't want to be cuddled often, so I treasured every moment she gave me.

"Would you like to join us for dinner?" Elara asked Elryd.

He smiled and nodded. "My troops came to do some more cross training with your people. I'm sure they know the way by now."

"I'll take them," Venali called and waved at us.

"Why am I so sleepy?" Nyura asked softly.

"You expended a lot of energy to blow up those rocks," I said. "It makes you sleepy and hungry."

"Blow up rocks?" Elryd asked and looked at Elara. "She can already make the sun ball?"

Elara beamed and nodded; her pride obvious. "She can."

"I thought it had fizzled out at first," Nyura said and yawned. "Then it exploded and it was awesome."

"Come, let's get her some food so she can take a nap after her belly is full," I said and headed to the castle.

"I'm not a baby," Nyura mumbled, her eyes half-closed.

"You'll always be my baby," I whispered and kissed her cheek.

"Even when I'm one hundred?" she asked.

"Even when you're one thousand," I replied.

"How long do you live?" Kydrus asked Elryd.

I barely managed to stop myself from jumping since I hadn't heard or felt him teleport to us.

"I likely have a few hundred more years left," Elryd said. He looked from Kydrus to Elara and then to me. "Why?"

"Kydrus, will you take Nyura?" I asked.

"You're going to talk about me, aren't you?" Nyura asked as Kydrus took her.

I smiled. "Why would you think that?"

She rolled her eyes. "You're a terrible liar, father."

Kydrus teleported away with Nyura, and I turned to face Elryd. "There's something we haven't told you," I said.

He stopped walking and faced Elara and I with folded arms. "Out with it."

"I'm only here for another ninety years," Elara said. "Then my consorts and I return to the stars, becoming gods and goddesses once more."

His eyes widened and his mouth dropped open. "You're serious?"

We nodded.

Elara bent over at the waist, bowing to Elryd. "Would you please continue watching over my daughter once she becomes queen? I can watch her, but won't be able to meddle. She'll be an adult, but I would rest much easier knowing you were going to look out for her and assist her should she need it."

Elryd gripped her shoulders and straightened her. "You do not need to humble yourself to me, my friend. I would have done it without being asked. I will, of course, watch over our little Nyura. She's like a niece to me."

Elara threw her arms around Elryd and hugged him tightly. "Thank you."

He patted her back and said, "You're welcome."

Elara turned to me and smiled, her posture and smile more relaxed than I had seen her in a decade. "Let's get some food."

Elara skipped ahead and I walked beside Elryd. "Thank you," I said and looked at him.

He shook his head while smiling. "You don't need to thank me. Seriously, I would have done it no matter what. Even if you'd told me to mind my own business, I likely would have sent a spy or two to ensure she stayed safe."

I laughed and draped my arm around his shoulders, giving him a quick squeeze. "I would expect nothing less from you."

"So, when you disappear in ninety years, does that mean I get first dibs to Venali's weapons?" Elryd asked.

I laughed and said, "You'll have to take that up with the brute."

"I'm not a brute," Venali grumbled from in front of us.

I looked up and smiled. "You are, too."

He sighed. "I'm just a misunderstood teddy bear."

"I resent that statement," Daniel yelled from within the dining hall.

Elryd and I laughed and we entered the dining hall to find it full of his men and ours.

Elara and Nyura sat in the front, surrounded by some of my brothers and some of Elryd's men. The girls smiled nonstop throughout dinner and I found myself doing the same.

This was what I had always wanted. This was perfection.

As long as I could keep my girls safe and happy, I would be happy as well.

A young boy peeked out from behind one of Elryd's men, his eyes glued to Nyura.

I looked at Elryd who whistled as he looked away from me.

"Already scheming, aren't you?" I asked.

He laughed and took a bite out of a bread roll, chewed it up, and then said, "I have no idea what you're talking about."

I pointed my bread roll at him. "Just remember that we are all still here for the next ninety years, so we won't let your schemes be accomplished so easily."

He winked as he took another bite of bread.

A second boy around Nyura's age entered the room with one of Elryd's men and walked right up to her.

I looked at Elryd who shrugged with a smirk.

The boy bowed to Nyura and then held out a flower to her.

Nyura's cheeks turned bright red as she took the flower and smelled it.

I growled and heard six other growls resound around the room.

Elara rolled her eyes, whispered something in Nyura's ear, and then smirked at me.

I arched a brow, but she just continued smirking.

Nyura grabbed her plate and she and the two boys went to the far side of the room to an empty table and began talking as they ate together.

"Check. Mate," Elryd said and brushed invisible dust off his shoulders.

"Scheming elf," I grumbled, but there was no heat to it. As long as these boys were good to her, I didn't care. Nyura deserved someone to make her happy. I just doubted they would meet our standards.

"Aren't they adorable?" Elara asked from behind me.

I hadn't seen her move, but kept from jumping as I turned to her. "You're okay with this?"

She shrugged. "They're children. She'll likely find many males to flirt with between now and when she chooses a mate."

"Or mates," Elryd said.

Elara nodded. "Yes."

"So, does that mean we can start trading for the summer?" Elryd asked.

Elara arched a brow. "Trading?"

He smiled. "I give you my boys for the summer, to learn from you and your consorts. Then the next summer you let Nyura come stay with me for the summer to learn from us."

Elara scowled a moment and then sighed. "That's likely a really good idea. It will let her experience other cultures and learn from you. And, I wouldn't mind having some more kids running around the castle."

I pulled Elara down into my lap and whispered into her ear, "There are other ways to have more kids running around the castle."

She chuckled and slid her hands down my chest. "Oh? Perhaps you should show me these ways."

"Excellent idea," Venali said, grabbed Elara, and teleported away.

"Asshole!" I yelled and stood.

"You seven are a riot," Elryd said and laughed.

"Keep an eye on Nyura?" I asked.

Elryd saluted me with his bread roll. "Yes, sir."

Kydrus set a hand on my shoulder and smiled. "Let's catch our mate and try for heir number two."

I smiled and nodded. "Let's."

We teleported to our bedroom and found Elara standing over a hogtied Venali.

"What?" I asked as I held in my laughter.

"He wasn't going to wait for you," she said and shrugged. "So, I tied him up."

I looked down at him. "Why aren't you breaking out of the ropes?"

He shrugged his shoulders. "She enjoyed having tied me up. I didn't want to break free and ruin her enjoyment."

Elara narrowed her eyes. "You can break free?"

Venali flexed and every rope broke and fell off. He stood and dusted off his body. "Yes."

She groaned. "Of course you can."

Venali tried to grab Elara, but she squealed and darted around us to the other side of the room.

"Let's make this a game," Elara said.

"A game?" Ryul asked as he and the rest of my brothers entered the room.

"Whoever is the last man standing gets first try at making heir number two," she said, smiling wickedly.

"Last man standing?" Ryul asked.

Amrynn wasted no time, knocking Ryul's legs out from under him.

Ryul landed on his side and groaned.

"Ryul's out," Elara announced.

The five of us that remained, turned and faced each other with wide smiles.

"Let the games begin!" Elara announced.

No matter what happened, these were the times I would cherish and remember the fondest. The times when everyone was smiling and laughing.

I couldn't wait to see what the next ninety years had in store for us.

ABOUT THE AUTHOR

Catherine Banks is a USA Today bestselling fantasy author who writes in several fantasy subgenres and has multiple pseudonyms. She began writing fiction at only four years old and finished her first full-length novel at the age of fifteen. She is married to her soulmate and best friend, Avery, who she has two amazing children with. After her full-time job, she reads books, plays video games, and watches anime shows and movies with her family to relax. Although she has lived in Northern California her entire life, she dreams of traveling around the world. Catherine is also C.E.O. of Turbo Kitten Industries™, a company with many hats including being a book publisher and Etsy store full of nerdy fun.

facebook.com/catherinebanksauthor
twitter.com/catherineebanks
amazon.com/author/catherinebanks
bookbub.com/authors/catherine-banks

MORE FROM CATHERINE BANKS

YOUNG ADULT PARANORMAL & FANTASY ROMANCE SERIES

Artemis Lupine Series

Song of the Moon
Kiss of a Star
Healed by the Fire
Battles of the Night
Artemis Lupine, The Complete Series

Little Death Bringer Duology

Mercenary
Protector
Little Death Bringer, The Official Coloring Book

Pirate Princess Series

Pirate Princess
Princess Triumvirate

ADULT PARANORMAL & FANTASY ROMANCE SERIES

Zodiac Shifters Paranormal Romance Series

Centaur's Prize
Tiger Tears
Lion About

Ciara Steele Novella Series

True Faces
Barbaric Tendencies

ADULT REVERSE HAREM PARANORMAL & FANTASY ROMANCE SERIES

Her Royal Harem Series

Royally Entangled
Royally Exposed
Royally Elected
Royally Enraged
Her Royal Harem, The Complete Series
The Demon's Fair
Her Royal Harem, The Coloring Book

Wings of Vengeance Series

Of Dragons and Cruelty
Of Minotaurs and Sacrifice
Wings of Vengeance, The Complete Series

Their Fae Goddess Trilogy

Queen of the Stars
Empress of the Galaxy
Goddess of the Universe
Their Fae Goddess, Complete Trilogy

Bonds of Madness Series

Sealing the Deal

Her Super Harem Series

Lucky Strike

VELLA ADULT PARANORMAL REVERSE HAREM ROMANCE

Shark (Season One)

The Golden Alicorns (Season One)

MORE FROM CATHERINE BANKS

STANDALONE YOUNG ADULT PARANORMAL & FANTASY ROMANCE BOOKS

Monster Academy
Daughter of Lions
Lady Serra and the Draconian
Of Sky and Sea
The Last Werewolf
Sybil Deceived
An Outcast Among Wolves

STANDALONE YOUNG ADULT PARANORMAL & FANTASY REVERSE HAREM ROMANCE BOOKS

Moon Academy
Claws & Wings

STANDALONE ADULT PARANORMAL & FANTASY ROMANCE BOOKS

Dragon's Blood
Last Ama Princess
Transforming Rose
Alys of Asgard
Phoenix Possessed
Stone Heart

STANDALONE URBAN FANTASY BOOKS

The Pawn

CHILDREN'S BOOKS

Calvin's Alien Adventure

MORE FROM DAISY EMORY

The Boyfriend Deal

Their Purple Girl

ACCIDENTAL MOBSTER SERIES

Accidental Mobster
Unintentional Pirate
Suddenly Baroness
Unexpected Assassins*

LIPSTICK & LEATHER SERIES

Trinity
Alicia*

*Coming Soon

www.ingramcontent.com/pod-product-compliance
Lightning Source LLC
Chambersburg PA
CBHW020615310726
48979CB00008B/1500/J
9781946301703